WHISKEY JACK

J.F. TRAINOR

ZEBRA BOOKS
KENSINGTON PUBLISHING CORP.

ZEBRA BOOKS are published by

Kensington Publishing Corp.
475 Park Avenue South
New York, NY 10016

First Printing: January, 1994

Printed in the United States of America

For Karl, Mary Lou, Megan and Kathleen

"What kills a skunk is the publicity it gives itself."
—Abraham Lincoln

Chapter One

"I'm *not* taking her back!"

The speaker's name was Chang. Nelson Chang. My boss. He's a stoop-shouldered fellow, perhaps two or three inches taller than my petite five-foot-four, with high Oriental cheekbones, a small nose and a wide, downturned mouth.

I'd spent the past four months looking at his dyspeptic expression, hustling dinner trays around Chang's Corral, one of the more unusual eateries in Pierre, South Dakota. The *Capitol Journal* called it "the world's one-and-only country western Thai restaurant."

And I'll second that. Where else can you get an eggroll that doubles as a hockey puck?

Chang and I were glaring at each other across a gleaming oakwood conference table at the Department of Corrections office. I shot a resentful glance to my left. Sitting at the head of the table was our chief mediator—my parole officer—Paul Holbrook. The man primarily responsible for my waitress career.

Paul isn't bad-looking. He's tall, well over the six-foot mark, with curly, wheat-colored hair, low, thick eyebrows and a pair of warm, friendly, chestnut-colored eyes. He has a long face with a good strong jawline—the kind I love to nuzzle just before the kiss.

Of course, I've never kissed Paul Holbrook. Darn it! Not

that I haven't been tempted. It's just that Paul's a real straight arrow, a former marine sergeant turned Department of Corrections counselor. He has this silly hangup about parole officers fraternizing with the clientele.

One of these days I've got to cure him of that.

Anyway, there sat Paul, reasonably well dressed in his light brown herringbone sport coat, button-down white Oxford cloth shirt and olive green tie. And there was Chang, looking as if he'd just raided the closet of Johnny Cash. Black western frock coat and Stetson to match. Pale lavender shirt and silver-tipped string tie. And of course, yours truly ... Angela Biwaban, Anishinabe princess, recently sprung ex-convict, and a most reluctant waitress in Paul's Work Experience program. Stunningly attired, as always, in a single-breasted blazer in houndstooth check, a pleated gray skirt and a pristine white turtleneck blouse.

Glancing at us both, Paul let out a weary sigh. "I'm still not quite clear about this particular conflict."

"Angela came to work out of uniform." Sitting back in his chair, Chang resembled a Japanese Buddha. "She refuses to follow orders—"

"Bullshit!" I snapped. "I wore the silly thing, didn't I?"

Chang made an angry gargling sound. "You were out of uniform!"

"No ..." I raised a contradictory forefinger. "I wore it with white slacks. There is a difference."

"That's not how it is supposed to be worn!"

Showing Paul a humble smile, I added, "Actually, it goes quite well with white slacks."

"Whoa!" Paul said. "Wait a minute. What's all this about a uniform?"

"Oh, it's just Chang's latest brainstorm," I explained, making a steeple of my fingertips. "The take's down on Fridays and Saturdays, so he's making a pitch for the singles crowd. Especially the single guys. He's put us all in uniform. And it's really tacky, Paul. A cheap knockoff of the Dallas

Cowboy Cheerleaders. And that *dress* . . . well, here, let me show you."

Rising from the swivel chair, I zipped open my brushed-leather bag. Chang's mouth tensed in silent fury. Blithely ignoring him, I withdrew a bundle of rolled-up satin, put the high mandarin collar against my throat, and let the shimmery dress spill down the length of my body.

Paul blinked in surprise. The hem didn't quite reach the bottom of my blazer. He tried awfully hard not to smile. "It's, uh, a little short."

"Not only that, it rides up in the back." Deftly I refolded the satin minidress. "You should see what happens whenever I bend over to clear a table."

Features tensing in anxiety, Chang rushed to his own defense. "It's a very nice dress. My cousin in Bangkok got them for me—"

"Correction, Chang! It's a very nice *blouse*. It needs another five inches to qualify as a dress." Tucking the offending garment in my shoulder bag, I added, "Anyway, that's the master plan. Our legs are supposed to lure the cowpokes."

Glaring at me, Chang blurted, "No one else has a problem with it. She's the only one who ever complains."

"That's because the others don't dare," I said, resuming my seat. "A lot of them are divorcees, Paul. Single mothers with little kids. They can't afford to lose the job, so they swallow their pride and keep quiet."

"You must understand, Mr. Holbrook." Chang struggled to build an amiable smile. "It's all part of the restaurant's ambience. The sight of all those lovely young women is most pleasing to my customers."

"It sort of makes up for the lousy cuisine," I teased.

My Thai boss had no sense of humor. A pudgy forefinger stabbed at my nose. "You're fired, Angela!"

I showed Paul an expression of saintly endurance. "You know, he's been saying that all morning."

"And I'm going to say it again. You're fired!" he hollered, leaning over the tabletop. "You're a troublemaker, Biwaban. I never want to see your face again."

"Pardon me, Chang, but I don't think you've ever seen my face!" I shouted, rising from the chair. "You've spent the last four months staring at my behind!"

With that, Nelson Chang lost control, along with his immediate command of the English language. Shaking his fist, he cursed me in singsong Thai. Me, I gave it right back to him in my people's language—Anishinabemowin. Much lively commentary on Chang's immediate ancestry, toilet training and amatory prowess. Or lack thereof.

I felt Paul's broad hands on my shoulders. Drawing me back, he said, "All right, all right. Time out, you two. We're not accomplishing anything here."

"Ookwe!" I spat. Then brushing strands of raven black hair away from my forehead, I gave my nose a spoiled adolescent upturn.

Disapproval colored Paul's firm tone. "Angie . . ."

"Holbrook, if you really think I'm going to prance around that greasy chopstick in a minisarong, you're out of your bureaucratic mind!"

"No one's suggesting that, Angela. You don't have to wear it if you don't want to."

I brightened at once. "Why, thank you, Mr. Holbrook."

"Don't I have anything to say about this?" Chang interjected. "It's my restaurant!"

"And Angela is my client." Paul's hands came to rest once more on my shoulders. "Technically speaking, she's *my* employee outstationed at your business. If she feels the uniform is personally degrading, then she doesn't have to wear it."

"I don't accept your resolution, Mr. Holbrook," Chang replied, his hateful gaze on me. "The rest of my girls are all in uniform."

"Angela is not a regular employee. She's a Work Experience participant." Paul was using his counselor's tone. Level, low-pitched and nonthreatening. "Look, there has to be room for compromise here. Suppose Angela wore it with slacks—"

"I've got no problem with that," I interrupted. "Hey, I could even wear it with black stirrup pants."

"Unfortunately, I do have a problem with that," Chang said, reaching for his Stetson. "My employees wear what I tell them to wear. And they wear it when I tell them to wear it. Or they are no longer my employees." He placed the Stetson on his small bald head. "I really don't know why I'm even discussing it with you, Biwaban. You're no longer my employee. You're fired!"

"He's at it again," I told Paul.

"Mr. Chang," my parole officer added. "Under the terms of the worksite agreement, only the department can remove Angela from the worksite."

"Then you had better remove her, Holbrook." Again with the quaking fist. "Or the department's going to be hearing from my lawyer!"

Out he went, muttering in Thai. Paul followed close behind, pleading for another round of negotiations. Shaking my head ruefully, I tugged at my blazer cuffs and walked over to the window. Smiled at the sight of all those russet leaves and that bright October sunshine. Just across the avenue loomed the Capitol building, that monumental Greek citadel of whitish Marquette sandstone and Bedford limestone, with its Ionic pillars and awesome grayish green dome made of solid copper. The Capitol was perched high on the hillside, on an old glacial terrace overlooking downtown Pierre and the Missouri River.

I'd been living in Pierre (pronounced *Peer*) since the end of June. You see, Paul had given me an emergency furlough, and I had overstayed it a couple of weeks. And this was the penalty I had to pay. One year in Pierre. One year's residence at the Dunning House, the department's halfway house for female parolees.

11

If that sounds rough, believe me, it isn't. I've lived in worse places than Pierre, South Dakota. Notably, the State Correctional Facility for Women at Springfield.

And how did I wind up in there? Well, a few years ago, my mother suffered a recurrence of cancer, and I desperately needed money to pay for her operation. So I embezzled it from the small South Dakota town for which I worked. To make a long story short, I eventually got caught, and the judge sentenced me to hard labor at Springfield.

It was a first offense, and had I played my cards right, I might have been out of the slammer in twenty months. But I was young and headstrong and did not meekly submit to the discipline of the correctional officers. As a result, the charge sheets piled up, and your Angie spent just over three years sorting clothes in the prison's sweatshop laundry.

A month before my twenty-eighth birthday, the parole board turned me loose, assigning me to the hefty caseload of counselor Paul Holbrook. I was ordered to "participate willingly and with diligence" in Paul's Work Experience program and to avoid anything that might lead to a return engagement at the Big Dollhouse.

Masculine footsteps sounded behind me. Folding my arms, I shot a quick glance over my shoulder. "Well, that's the end of that job."

"Don't be too sure about that, princess."

Slouching against the windowsill, I flashed my parole officer a small, inquisitive smile. "Don't tell me Chang's taking me back?"

Rubbing the back of his neck, Paul replied, "Give me a little time to work on him."

"*Hol*-brook! I have a much better idea. Why don't I just find myself another job? Say . . . in Rapid City?"

"You know the answer to that one."

"Come on! It's bad enough I have to spend a whole year in Pierre. Do I really have to spend all three hundred and sixty-five days waiting on tables, too!?"

Straightening his tie, Paul showed me a stern smile. "You know what Baretta used to say. 'If you can't do the time, don't do the crime.' " He buttoned his sportcoat. "Besides, if you must wait tables, Chang's Corral is a lot more pleasant than the Springfield dining room. Right?"

Absolutely! But I wasn't telling Paul that. Instead, I showed him an expression my prison mom, Becky Reardon, had dubbed a *fussbudget face*. Eyes narrowed in irritation. Two vertical ridges just above the bridge of my nose. And a pair of tightly compressed lips.

My grimace bothered him not at all. Gesturing at the conference room doorway, he said, "Walk you home?"

So we took our discussion into the Foss Building's glass-walled stairway. My tall heels raised a clatter during our descent.

"You're not going to be on parole forever," Paul lectured. "Some day you're going to have to compete for a real private-sector job. When that day comes, it'll help a great deal if you can show your prospective employer a solid work history. It'll look good if he sees that you came out of prison and stuck with a job for a whole year."

"Oh, Paul, I *hate* being a waitress. It's so damned hectic. They only let you sit down once all night."

Cracking a grin, he pushed open the glass door for me. "It builds character—at least that's what my sister Gina says."

"Builds bunions is more like it! I go limping home at the end of each shift. All I want to do is fill the basin with hot water and soak my feet."

Emitting a wry chuckle, Paul said, "There was nothing wrong with your feet the last time we went jogging."

Puckering my lips, I took hold of Paul's right arm—the one he'd injured in combat. One of Noriega's soldiers had dropped a live grenade on Paul's squad in Panama. Sergeant Holbrook had been the first to spot and grab it. His quick reaction time had earned him a Silver Star. But the close-up blast had peppered his right side with shrapnel, ending his

Marine career and sending him to civilian life with a fifty percent disability.

Snuggling against his arm, I asked, "Speaking of jogging, are we still on for tomorrow?"

"Afraid not, Angie," he replied, crestfallen. "I've got some packing to do. I'm flying out the first thing Sunday morning."

"What!? And missing this lovely Columbus Day weekend?"

"Can't be helped. Fact is, I'll be gone all week."

"Where are you going?"

"Washington, D.C." Paul shepherded me along Capitol Avenue, through the chilly shade of the elms. "The Bureau of Prisons is holding a week-long symposium on positive alternatives to incarceration. I'm representing South Dakota."

"No more incarceration, eh? Hey, I approve."

He grinned. "You would! Tell me, as a parolee, can you recommend any positive alternatives?"

"Not off the top of my head," I replied, enjoying his closeness. "Tell you one thing, though. Waitressing *isn't* one of them!"

Hugging his arm, I sent my gaze downslope, past the Victorian housetops and the railroad trestle and the smart shops of lower Highland Avenue, to the flame-tinted trees on La Framboise Island. I thought of all the times Paul and I had gone jogging down there. And the memory kindled a sudden keen twinge of disappointment.

Paul seemed to sense my dismay. "What is it, Angie?"

I wasn't quite ready to admit how much I enjoyed those Saturday afternoons together, so I gave a blithe shrug and replied, "Oh, just wondering what I'm supposed to do while you're in the District of Columbia."

"I'm glad you brought that up, Miss Biwaban." Turning right at the corner of Highland, Paul escorted me uphill. "Mrs. Sadowski's thinking of having you ladies do some fall

14

cleaning. The whole house, top to bottom. So you're going to do your roommates a little favor, Angie."

"You want me to clean that big old house!? *Me?* All by myself!?"

Paul nodded. "Working eight hours per day, you could have that place shipshape in . . . oh, eight or nine days."

I had a sudden mental image of myself in rumpled old clothes, my hair bound up in a kerchief, sponging a grimy attic window. Wail of dismay. "Paaauuulllll!"

His grin widened. "You've been complaining about your feet. Now you can let your shoulders and elbows do all the work."

Frosty retort. "Oh, thank you so much!"

"Besides, you owe it to your roommates," he added. "Mrs. Sadowski tells me you tend to disappear whenever a floor needs mopping."

"Hey, is it my fault if I'm first to answer the phone?"

Comforting pat on the shoulder. "Make me proud, princess."

Fussbudget face. "You're really going to make me do it, aren't you?"

"You bet! You're not sitting around the parlor all week, watching soap operas. You're going to work."

"You know, Paul, I might be more willing if I had the proper incentive."

"What kind of incentive?"

Hopeful Angie smile. "Weekend furlough, maybe?"

"Not another furlough!" Paul halted at the corner of Highland and Euclid. Curiosity gradually softened his stern expression. "Okay, I'll bite. What for?"

"Well, if you're not going to be around, there's really no need for me to stay in Pierre." I folded my arms casually. "And . . . well, I've got this invitation from Jill Stormcloud. She's living with her mother on the Pine Ridge reservation. They're having a powwow this weekend. An

15

Honor the Earth powwow. Sort of an antidote to Columbus Day. If you don't mind, I'd really like to go."

"Antidote to Columbus Day?" he echoed.

"Sure! That media bullshit is enough to turn my stomach. Columbus the heroic navigator. Give me a break! Old Chris was a pirate and a butcher." My indignant gaze found the Dunning House, one block ahead on Prospect Avenue. "New World . . . right! I mean, my family had only been living on Michimackinakong for the past ten thousand years."

"Mishi-what?" Paul blinked in confusion.

"Michimackinakong. Island of the Great Turtle. That's this country's real name, Paul. And it was called that long before Columbus set out for the gray Azores. You want to start an argument? Just parrot any of that Columbus crap in front of any indigenous person."

"I never realized you felt so strongly about it."

"Why shouldn't I? It was our neighbors he killed." Somber frown. "He washed ashore in the Bahamas practically shipwrecked. The Taino people took him in. And how did he repay their hospitality? By making them his slaves!"

Escorting me across the street, Paul said, "I don't think it was quite like that."

"Wasn't it?" I flared, shaking free of his hand. "That Italian killed three million Tainos, Paul. Somehow that fact never gets mentioned in the history books."

"Angie—"

"Columbus Day!" Sniff of disapproval. "Why don't you give Adolf Hitler his own day, too?"

"Hold on there, Angela!" Paul stopped in his tracks. "Okay, I admit it—Christopher Columbus was no saint. But he never went around tossing people in gas chambers."

"No, he just sicced the dogs on them." Quick angry breath. "I'm afraid I don't see the difference. Perhaps you'd like to explain it to me."

Paul's expression turned troubled. He was silent for a few

16

moments; then he took my hands in his. "This powwow means a lot to you, I guess."

My gaze softened. "Sorta. It's an intertribal gathering. We're all going to be there. Lakota, Anishinabe, Hidatsa. We're honoring our mother the Earth, and we're mourning what was lost. And we're telling the world that we're still here—that we're here to stay."

"Well, I'd say you've got yourself a furlough, princess." Paul's warm country-boy smile did disturbing things to my heartbeat. "I'll tell Mrs. Sadowski to expect you back Monday afternoon."

"Monday night?" I dickered.

"Monday afternoon," he repeated firmly.

"Paul, it's an awfully long drive from Pine Ridge."

"Then you'd better leave the first thing Monday morning."

"Holbrook, you are the biggest turd—"

"In South Dakota," he finished for me. "And the only turd who can sign your weekend furlough." One hand on my spine, he ushered me up the front walk. "Come on. Let's get you signed in."

These days, it's officially known as the South Dakota Department of Corrections Residence Hall for Women. But, in its day, the old Dunning place on Prospect Avenue was one of the grandest homes in Pierre. It was built in 1907, a three-story Queen Anne home with a steep, protruding gabled roof, a spacious, glass-enclosed veranda, and a mammoth Victorian fireplace. The huge brick chimney snaked its way up the front of the house like a narrow nose. For which we can thank Wallace L. Dow, the celebrated Prairie Architect. Wally designed the house for a prosperous cattleman named Caleb Dunning. One of the Sioux Falls Dunnings. Here in South Dakota, that was roughly akin to having an ancestor in the Knights of the Round Table.

A spinster daughter named Caroline inherited the family manse, living there in seclusion until her death in 1978. If

17

not for the recession of the early Eighties, the Dunning house probably would have been razed and its lot transformed into a corner minimall. Instead, the state purchased it from old Miss Caroline's estate, renovated and refurbished it as a work project for South Dakota convicts, and then turned it into a halfway house for female parolees.

I'm not complaining, though. I had a room of my very own on the third floor, complete with an old-fashioned walnut bedroom set consisting of an eight-foot armoire, four-foot chest of drawers, and a queen-sized bed. Twin full-length mirrors on the armoire. Bright butternut wallpaper and an aging Turkish rug. Wonder of wonders, I even controlled the lock on my door. Quite a change from my previous situation in Springfield!

Following a brief meeting with Paul and Blanche Sadowski, the Dunning housemother, I scurried up to my room, doffed my blazer and spike-heeled pumps, wiggled my nyloned feet into a pair of comfy doeskin moccasins and then, kneeling on the rug, wrestled my big Samsonite suitcase out from under the bed.

Just then, Emma Cowdell's shrill voice rocketed up the central stairway. *"Annnnngieeeeee!* Telephone!"

Descending the winding oak stairway, I spotted Emma in the front hall, hefting the receiver in an impatient hand. She was a short, broad-faced woman of African descent, my age or thereabouts, and a recent arrival at our haven for naughty girls. Chestnut eyes radiated a gleam of amusement.

"It's a man." Grinning, she handed me the receiver. "Whitey know about him?"

Waving her away, I said, "Hello?"

"You are livin' dangerously, gal." The possibility of romantic intrigue delighted Emma beyond measure. "Boy Scout got you that furlough, and now you're runnin' off with this here slick for the weekend."

Because of Emma's cheery braying, I missed the caller's

18

first faint words. Cupping my free ear with my left hand, I repeated, "Hello? Who is this?"

"Angie?" The tenor voice stirred sudden recognition. "Angie Biwaban?"

"Mick!" I yielded to a burst of pleasantly surprised laughter. "Mickey Grantz! Hey, it's great to hear from you. What's up?"

Mick's voice was oddly strained. "I-I've been trying to get in touch with an old friend of yours. I thought maybe you'd heard from her."

Confused blink. "Her?"

"I'm talking about *Sara!*" His tone became more urgent than ever. "Have you heard from Sara lately?"

Instantly I was on my guard. I had an awful hunch as to where this conversation was headed. Resisting the surge of panic, I licked dry lips, then murmured, "Sara who?"

"Sara Little Star."

A frosty tremor glided up my spine. The receiver trembled in my grasp. Thank you, Mick, for not using the actual name. Sara Little Star was the English translation of a euphonious Ute name—*Sara Soyazhe.* A name I had ample reason to remember. I'd used it as an alias recently while engaged in some highly questionable activities in northern Utah.

Michael Reuben Grantz, fondly known as the Mick, crusading attorney and dedicated environmental activist, knew full well that I'd adopted the Sara identity to hunt down the murderer of my cousin Bill. If not for the Mick, right now I'd be slinging laundry at the Utah version of the Big Dollhouse. Thanks to his surreptitious help, I'd gotten out of the Beehive State one step ahead of the sheriff.

"Listen, Angie, I really have to talk to her." Desperation put a shrill edge on Mick's tenor. "As soon as possible, understand? Face-to-face. Got that? Will you please pass on the message?"

"Sure, Mick!" Anxiety tightened my own lovely contralto

19

voice. "But you know Sara. She comes and goes. Uhm . . . is it important?"

"Angela, you have no idea how important this is!"

My face tensed in puzzlement. "What is it, Mick? What's going on down there in Salt Lake?"

"I'm not in Salt Lake." His voice was on the verge of breaking. "I'm in Washington. I'm in trouble, Angie. Big trouble! I-I have to speak to Sara. You've got to get her here—*fast!*"

"Where are you?"

It took him five or six seconds to spit it out. "I . . . I'm in jail."

"Jail!?" I blurted.

"I've been arrested." A strange tone of panicky indignation. "I-I didn't do it. They've got the wrong man. You—*Sara* has got to help me." Suddenly, it all gushed out in a torrent of shame and fear. "I got picked up yesterday morning. The police have been at me for hours. They want me to sign some kind of statement. They keep saying I did it. *I didn't!* Angie, listen . . . I'm in the Cedar Creek Correctional Center, okay? I'm being held for trial. The center's in Littlerock—Route 121—midway between Olympia and Chehalis. Write it down the minute I hang up. *And tell Sara!*"

"I don't understand, Mick. You're a lawyer, for heaven's sake. Can't you make bail?"

His voice cracked. "Not possible. The judge refused my request."

"Why?"

"Because of the charge, Angie. It's first-degree murder."

Chapter Two

Sunday morning, October eleventh, found me a goodly distance west of the Pine Ridge reservation. Instead of dressing for the Lakota powwow, I was speeding down Interstate 5 in the maroon Camry the nice folks at Avis had given me.

A green sign passed over the windshield, alerting me to the interchange just ahead. Slowing the Camry, I hit the blinker and eased into the right lane. I got off the freeway, stopped at a gas station in Tenino for directions, and then picked up Route 121 just north of town, heading for Littlerock.

In no time at all, I was tooling down Washington 121 beneath a sky of broken clouds, flanked on either side by mima prairie, listening to American Country Countdown on a Tacoma station. *Kay-Jay-Uou-Nhn . . . Country Gold Ray-dee-oh!*

Any other time, I would have been singing right along with Paulette Carlson. But not today. I really didn't feel like singing. Not even with my favorite Minnesota vocalist. I couldn't stop thinking about Mick.

Murder One. Ohhhh, Mickey, what have you gotten yourself into?

My spirits sank even lower as I caught my first glimpse of the prison. It was a sprawling one-story cinderblock complex, half-hidden by the numerous grassy mima mounds. Three layers of high fence, topped with barbed wire, encircled the complex. Guard towers and TV monitors and shotgun-toting sentries. All in all, the place bore an uncomfortable resemblance to the Disciplinary Unit in Billsburg, South Dakota. The place where I'd languished for sixteen months of my life. The ladies had a number of amusing names for Billsburg. *The Heartbreak Hotel. Petticoat Junction. Little Outhouse on the Prairie.* And my personal favorite, *Miss Carlotta's School for Girls.*

I experienced a sudden, uncontrollable urge to wheel the car around and hightail it back to the interstate. Taking a deep breath, I steeled myself to resist the impulse. Mick was a friend. And perhaps more than a friend. If not for him, I'd be sitting in a Utah prison just like this one. He was my friend, and he was in really big trouble. And I had already put my own parole at risk flying all the way out here.

So I pulled into the prison's parking lot, put on my best four-hundred-watt smile and told the guard that I was there for Sunday visiting hours. He asked for identification. My mouth dry, I handed him my phony South Dakota license in the name of Joanne Larue. Then sat nervously as he gave it a thorough scan.

I'd picked up the license the previous day in Rapid City, along with a SunWest credit card in the same name. My friend and one-time cellmate, Jill Stormcloud, had guided me to the vendor—a disreputable trucker bar on lower Saint Cloud Street. The deal set me back four hundred in cash, but it couldn't be helped. The name Angela Biwaban could not appear on any plane reservations or car rental agreements. For obvious reasons.

Once inside, I stopped in the ladies room and gave myself the once-over. I touched up my lipstick, smoothed the dark eyebrows with my pinky finger, and ran a small plastic brush through my windblown raven hair. The lengthy wall mirror showed me a grimly smiling Anishinabe princess, smartly turned out in a white chambray long-sleeved blouse, a sleeveless denim jerkin with white piping, and a matching denim slim skirt with the hem two inches above the knee.

Nervous? You betcha! The last place I wanted to get caught bearing false I.D. was inside a prison. No doubt the warden would be showing me accommodations of my very own, with the full approval of the South Dakota Department of Corrections. But this was the only way I could have that face-to-face chat with Mick. So . . .

The visitor's room was a long, beige-walled chamber, its ceiling studded with recessed fluorescent lights. A pock-marked table ran the length of the room. A Plexiglas divider bisected the table into longitudinal halves. I seated myself in one of the visitor's chairs, folded my hands primly, and waited for the prisoners to arrive.

They brought Mickey in ten minutes later. My heart froze. Gone was the dapper and somewhat casual attorney, with his curly black hair, hawkish nose and well-trimmed Van Dyke. His beard was growing wild. Greasy hair spilled across his pale forehead. He came shuffling toward me in a wrinkled white coverall that was two or three sizes too big for him. Dark shadows highlighted his blinking, apprehensive blue eyes. Eyes that shone with the fearful awareness of the small animal that knows it is prey.

He rushed forward the instant he saw me. His underlip quivered, and I knew he was going to shout my name. So I hugged him over the divider, whispering, "Joanne, Mick . . . call me Joanne."

"Miss!" the guard thundered. Two hundred pounds of former hockey player stuffed into a khaki uniform. His beefy hand tapped the wall-mounted sign. "Read the rules. No physical contact with the prisoner."

"Sorry." Showing him a tepid Angie smile, I resumed my seat. "How are you doing, Mick?"

"How can you even *ask*—?" Taut as a coiled spring, he sat upright in the straight-backed chair. Beseeching dark blue

23

eyes found mine. "You've got to get me out of here . . . *Joanne*. Please! They keep saying I killed Mona. I-I didn't!"

"Mona?" I echoed, keeping my voice low.

"My wife." Mick's expression shifted from apprehension to a strange blend of sorrow and embarrassment. "Ex-wife, I mean. We-we divorced a little over four years ago."

I wanted to reach out and squeeze his trembling hand, to assure him that everything was going to be all right. Conscious of the guard's wary gaze, however, I kept a distance. "Whoa. Let's start at the beginning, Mick. Where did it happen?"

"The San Juans. Late Wednesday night." He ran a hand through his touseled, unwashed hair. "I got picked up when I stepped off the ferry in Anacortes the next morning." Haunted expression. "You've got to get me out of here! If I get convicted, I'll be coming back—*to stay!* They'll put me in the Max Unit. It's fucking bedlam in there. I can't live like that. I can't!"

"Mickeeeeee." Tears tickled my eyelashes. Swallowing hard, I murmured, "What happened?"

"S-Someone killed Mona. Beat her to death on a beach." He sobbed aloud. Running his fingers down his face, he looked about in bewilderment, not quite certain where to begin. "I-I came home for Rosh Hashanah, you see. Home to Tacoma. There's four of us kids. All married . . . or used to be. Dad passed away last winter. We decided we didn't want Mom spending the high holy days alone. So we all came home. Mom isn't like me, you know. She's never really liked the Northwest. I guess she still misses New Jersey." Pausing, he took a steadying breath. "Anyway . . . Mona called the house. Four hours before Kol Nidre. She said she needed help—legal help—and she asked me to come to Port Wyoochee."

"Port Wyoochee?"

Brisk nod. "It's a little town on the strait. Yennis County. Just north of Olympic National Park."

24

The name sounded vaguely familiar. I'd spent a summer in Washington during my coed rangerette days. "West of Port Angeles, right?"

"That's right. Mona grew up there."

"And moved back after the divorce?"

Mickey didn't like to talk about that. "She went into business for herself. Owned a small store on Dollar Avenue. Heritage Antiques."

From the look on Mick's face, it was obvious that he wasn't willing to discuss their split in any way, shape or form. So I opened another line of inquiry.

"How did Mona know you'd be in Tacoma?"

"She didn't." Sigh of undisguised grief. "It was just pure dumb luck. Or maybe I should say *bad luck*. Mona called the house hoping to get my phone number from Mom. I just happened to pick up the phone. She had no idea I was living in Salt Lake. We-We had no contact after the divorce. That was *her* idea. I always mailed the alimony to a bank in Seattle. I was really surprised to hear from her. She was in trouble, and she needed my advice."

"What kind of trouble?"

"Politics!" Anger tensed Mickey's vulpine features. "You've got to understand something. Mona and I . . . well, we were always activists. But we disagreed as to the right approach. Mona had a tendency to rush right in. She was a bulldozer. Take no prisoners. That was her philosophy."

"So she stepped on some sensitive toes?"

"Stomped all over them is more like it." Touching the divider, Mickey leaned forward in his chair. "She rejoined the local environmental group. The Gemini River Greenway Committee. Until Mona came along, it had been more a debating society than anything else. Overnight, she turned it into Nader's Raiders. The Geminis lit a dozen fires under the EPA. Mona went after the local paper mill. She called it the biggest polluter in town. Trouble is, it's also the biggest employer in town." Wry expression. "We environmentalists were never the most popular people in the Northwest. But it's gotten a lot worse since that spotted owl controversy. Half of Washington blames us for the recession. And there was Mona threatening to put eighteen hundred people out of work." He shook his head remorsefully. "Dammit, why didn't she get in touch with me sooner? I could have—"

"Don't," I murmured, touching his wrist. "Don't do this to yourself, Mick. It won't bring her back. It'll just ruin—"

"Miss!" the guard snapped.

Frowning, I withdrew my hand. "Why did Mona want your help?"

"Some of those rightwing yahoos vandalized her store. Spray-painted the walls. They wrote some pretty ugly things. Anti-Semitic crap!" He grimaced at the rancid memories. "Somebody even printed up a flyer, accusing Mona of being an agent of the Mossad. She found it stuck under her windshield wiper. She showed it to me."

"What did she want you to do?"

"She wanted me to file a civil suit against that asshole Thurber. A libel suit. I told her to forget it. We'd have a hell of a time proving it was him."

"Who's this guy Thurber?"

"An A1 asshole! Hitler's Number One cheerleader in the Northwest."

"What is he? Some kind of underground publisher?"

"Among other things. He's pastor of the First Church of Jesus Christ-Adamite. It's one of those Aryan Nations groups." Mick's bleak gaze found the windows. There wasn't much of a view. Just the bars and the gunmetal gray sky and the tiled roof of a watchtower. "Mona wanted to sue Thurber's ass for defamation. And she wanted me to take the case. We spent a few days together in Port Wyoochee. I gave her a few pointers on how to handle Kulshan Paper. As for Thurber, I advised her to let the Anti-Defamation League handle it."

Chin in hand, I flashed Mick a quizzical look. "Did Mona go to the police?"

"Uh-huh. Cops staked out Mona's store and the local synagogue, B'nai Emunath. But the vandals didn't show. Thurber may be a lunatic, but he isn't stupid. He knows better than to stage a repeat assault right away."

I noticed that he was steering the conversation away from Mona. Mr. Thurber seemed to be a safer and more preferable topic. We needed to get back on track.

"Did you take her to the San Juans?" I asked.

"No. Mona went over on her own. Her dad owned a fishing camp on Orcas Island. He gave it to us as a wedding present. She-She used to fly over there once a week."

"From Port Wyoochee? That's quite a haul."

"There's an air charter company in town. One-man operation. His name's Jon Waterman. The San Juans are a popular weekend destination."

Again I could feel him slip-sliding away from the topic of his ex-wife. And I thought I understood why.

Sympathetic Angie smile. "It was pretty rough, wasn't it? Seeing Mona again."

A tic twitched at the corner of his mouth. He shifted uneasily in his chair. "A bit."

"If you don't mind a personal question . . ." I phrased it as delicately as I could. "Was the divorce Mona's idea?"

Tense seconds passed. For a moment, I feared Mickey wouldn't answer. And then, drawing a ragged breath, he muttered, "All right! If you must know . . . yes, it was. And did I take it well? No, I didn't." Painful memories narrowed his dark blue eyes. "What's a man supposed to do, eh, when his wife comes up to him after four years of marriage and says, 'Look, we've made a big mistake—let's get a divorce'? Especially when I don't think it was such a fucking mistake at all!" His voice rose sharply. "Does that mean I killed her? No, it doesn't! Does it mean they're going to pin the murder

27

on me? Yes, it does! Now then, is there anything else you'd like to know?"

"Just this." I gave him a level businesslike stare. "What were you doing on Orcas that day?"

Closing his eyes, Mickey uttered a dismal sigh. "Okay . . . so I followed her over there. I-I was on my way back to Tacoma and . . . I don't know! Seeing Mona again . . . being with her . . . it did something to me, I guess. I-I just couldn't walk away. I couldn't leave Washington without seeing her one more time. So I didn't go to Mom's. I drove up to Anacortes . . . rode over on the ferry."

"Mona was at the cabin?"

Slumping against the backrest, he nodded wearily. "Thursday was her day off. Usually, she flew over with Waterman. But she had some business in Port Angeles Wednesday morning, so she took the ferry from there."

"Was she surprised to see you?"

"Somewhat." He rubbed the back of his neck. Bitter smile. "I don't know what I expected. Maybe I was hoping we could try again. I asked her to dinner. She surprised me and said yes. We had dinner at the Chulananuk in Eastsound. Just like old times." Sudden dry chuckle. "Maybe too much like old times. We had a spat. Mona said something about the king salmon count being down all along the strait. I said, 'Don't you mean the steelhead?' And she got all huffy and told me it was no picnic being married to Mr. Know-It-All. Once we were on the topic of each other's faults, we had at it for a while. She raised her voice, and I raised mine." Forlorn sighed. "Just like old times."

"Did anybody see you two scrapping?"

"Oh, just about everyone in the restaurant," he said morosely. "Mona had no scruples about quarrelling in public. If there was an audience handy, she always put on a show. She threw a breadstick at me. I caught up with her while she was making her grand exit. After I paid the check, we took our battle out on the dock."

"Did you escort her home?" I asked.

Mickey shook his head. "Mona left in a cab."

"How far away was the cabin?"

"Six miles south of town. Just past Olga. They call it Obstruction Pass."

"What did you do?"

"What *could* I do?" he challenged. "Nothing had worked out the way I'd hoped. Mona wasn't even speaking to me. I'd screwed up everything good and proper." His expression saddened. "I was staying at the Crestwood Inn. But I didn't want to spend the rest of the night staring at all four walls. So I went for a walk."

"Alone?"

Ironic smile. "That's why I'm here in jail."

"Where did you go?"

"South. All the way down to Rosario."

"Anybody see you?"

He shook his head slowly.

"What time did you get back to The Crestwood?"

"Late. I'm not sure. Maybe after two. I didn't see anybody in the front lobby when I came in."

Pronounced fussbudget face. "That's one hell of an alibi, Mick."

His palm slammed the table. "You think I don't know that?"

Casting an anxious glance at the burly guard, I whispered, "Take it easy, Mick."

"Take it *easy?*" he echoed, stiffening all over. "I'm locked up in here, accused of a murder I didn't commit. The woman I loved is dead, and everybody's blaming me—!"

Scowling, the guard stepped forward. Flashing a scintillating Angie smile, I motioned for Mick to sit still.

"I'm not blaming you," I murmured. "I'm on your side. Come on. Settle down, Mick."

He cupped his curly head in both hands, letting out a deep, desperate exhalation.

"Tell me what happened to Mona."

Mickey's features showed the incredible strain he was under. Hands trembling, he rasped, "All I know is what I've been able to piece together from the Q & A session. S-Some woman found Mona early Thursday morning on Shaw Island. She had been pretty near beaten to death. The San Juans police think it happened on Orcas. Somehow Mona got away from her assailant and waded into the sea. She washed up on that beach more dead than alive. The woman called the Coast Guard . . ." His eyelids shut tightly. "But it was too late. Mona died before they could arrive."

Disbelief altered my tone. "Mona swam across the strait?"

"I-I'm not sure. It's possible. Mona was a terrific swimmer. When she was in college, she worked summers as a lifeguard on Whidbey Island. I think she was only trying to get across the East Sound. It's just about two hundred yards. The minus tide must have caught her . . . swept her over to Shaw."

"So where were you early Thursday?"

"Sound asleep at the inn," he replied. I detected a twinge of shame in his voice. He seemed to believe that he could have prevented Mona's death. That notion was going to haunt him for a very long time. "I got up around seven-thirty. Checked out a little over an hour later."

"Who did you talk to?"

"The desk clerk. Her name was Kelly, I think. I asked her what time the next ferry left for Anacortes."

I remembered what Mickey had told me over the phone. "The police picked you up when you got to the Anacortes dock."

"It's a frame, Angie! Dolan's behind it! I'm sure of that!"

Ohhhhhh, I sure hope the guard didn't overhear that. Quick reassuring smile. "What do you mean, Mick?"

"That bastard Dolan! He stole my sweater and planted it at the scene."

"On the beach?"

30

"No, no! At Mona's cabin." Inching forward, Mickey lowered his voice to a conspiratorial whisper. "The police got a quick I.D. on Mona. That's no surprise. She's pretty well known in the islands. They searched her cabin, and they found a sweater. Cable-knit black cardigan sweater. *My* sweater! That's why they came after me." Anxiety gave his bearded face a sickly pallor. "That's why I know it's a frame. Listen. When I was packing to leave, I couldn't find that sweater anywhere. I was pretty certain I'd brought it to the islands—"

"Pretty certain?" I interrupted.

"Okay, okay . . ." He spread his hands haplessly. "When I left Port Wyoochee, I wasn't concentrating on packing. I was thinking about Mona. I don't know what I had in those suitcases. I just sort of had the feeling I'd brought it along. When that detective showed it to me, I knew it was a frame. Somebody sneaked into my hotel room. It had to be Dolan. Just had to be!"

"Who's Dolan?"

"John A. Dolan. He's a big shot in Port Wyoochee. He holds controlling interest in Kulshan Paper. That's how Mona and I came into contact with him."

"Mick, why would he want to frame you? You live in Salt Lake. You haven't been home to Washington in years."

"Dolan had it in for both of us," Mickey explained, his face haggard. "It goes back five or six years or so. There was a bad spill at the Kulshan plant." Seeing my puzzled expression, he made a frame of his hands. "Let me explain, okay? You know how a mill makes paper. Right?"

"Sure! It's a big industry back home in the Northland."

"Well, after the wood gets mashed, they dump it into a *digester*. This reduces the wood to millions of fibers. The fibers get poured into bleaching vats. Those vats use a lot of water. Kulshan draws an average of twenty million gallons per day out of the Gemini River. The effluent that comes out of the vats—that's called *white liquor*. It's very toxic. Chock-full of ti-

31

tanium, magnesium and zinc. Kulshan pumps it into large concrete settling tanks called *clarifiers*. There it sits until all the sulfides have precipitated out. Only then can the wastewater be safely returned to the river."

All at once, I understood. Sickish expression. "How bad was the spill?"

"Very bad." His hands curled into tight fists. "That bastard Dolan never spent a dime on upkeep and maintenance. A valve on the containment tank rusted out. Two hundred thousand gallons of effluent poured right into the river. They saw salmon leaping out of the water—trout trying to climb the riverbank. There were fish floating belly up from Port Angeles to Clallam Bay."

"So you and Mona took the case."

"That's right. We had our own activist group in Seattle. I filed an *amicus curiae* on behalf of some Port Wyoochee fishermen. Mona and our student volunteers did the legwork." Small grin of triumph. "We nailed them to the wall. The EPA slapped a big fine on Kulshan Paper and ordered them to upgrade their containment system. Dolan was livid. He swore he'd get me and Mona if it was the last thing he ever did." Quick desperate glance at the guard. "That's why I need your help, Angie. Dolan must have had Mona under surveillance. When he saw me and Mona together again, he knew it was his big chance. Kill Mona and pin it on me. He's the one who framed me. I'm positive!"

"Mickey . . ."

Reaching across the divider, he seized my hands. "You've got to help me. I know what you did in Utah. I want you to do the same thing for me. Go to Port Wyoochee and pull a *Sara* on that murdering bastard. Find proof that he killed Mona!"

"Awright! That's it, dolly. Visit's over. On your feet, Grantz." Showing a menacing glare, the guard slipped the riot baton off his belt. "You know the rules. No physical contact. Let's go!"

Mickey looked up indignantly. "Look, I still have ten minutes—"

Horrified, I watched the guard's free hand snake out and snare my friend's shirt collar. The baton rose swiftly. I jumped to me feet. "No! Don't argue with the man, Mick."

"That's good advice, homeboy. Better take it." Seizing Mick with both hands, he hauled him away from the table. "The visit ends the second you break the rules. Remember that!"

He stumbled toward the open doorway, propelled by the guard's merciless two-handed shove. A final wild-eyed glance of desperation leaped over Mick's shoulder. "Help me."

Poor Mick. He was making all the mistakes of a new fish. He still didn't realize where he was yet. He still thought he was a respected attorney-at-law. The guards would teach him different in the hours and days to come. He'd learn a lot of hard lessons out there in the yard.

My tears blurred his departing image. Wiping my cheeks, I promised, "Mick . . . I'll do whatever I can."

The door clanged shut with an utter finality.

On Columbus Day morning, I steered my rental Camry north on Interstate 5, heading for the hills and homes and office buildings of downtown Tacoma. The day was a true rarity for the Pacific Northwest, sunny and warm, a sapphire sky without a hint of clouds. Perfect shirtsleeve weather, and your Angie was dressed for it. Snug-fitting, single-breasted khaki blazer with a sweetheart neckline trimmed with appliqued white lace and four imitation pearl buttons. Smart khaki miniskirt to match. Black pantyhose and matching Aigner dress pumps with three-inch heels. My costume for today's scam.

I picked up the Schuster parkway near South Thirty-second, rode it north to the bay, and then got off in Old Town. And . . . sure enough, that little costume shop was still on Yakima Street. Exactly where I remembered it. I purchased a pair of aviator-style theatrical glasses, with windowpane instead of prescription lens, and a stylish black Afro wig.

I told the nice lady I was getting an early start on Halloween.

Then I cruised down Division until I found a walk-in print shop open on the holiday. Walked inside, plunked down the cash, and requested a quickie order of fifty business cards.

My next stop was a Payless drugstore. There I visited the cosmetics counter and purchased a dark foundation makeup. Camouflage for today's scout.

In no time at all, I was in the first-floor ladies room at the *News-Tribune,* carefully staining my face and hands. Recapping the foundation jar, I carefully scrutinized my mirror image. Hmmmmm . . . not bad. The foundation had turned my copper-brown hide a rich shade of chocolate. The khaki suit would make my face and hands seem even darker. Smiling impishly, I pinned my raven hair back and tucked it beneath the Afro wig. Clipped on the golden clamshell earrings. Slipped on the glasses. Excellent! The frames tended to mute my high cheekbones.

Perhaps I was being overly cautious, but, when I strolled into that newsroom, I wanted the staff to remember Joanne Larue as a stylish black woman of medium height and not as petite Angie. On those rare occasions when they're sober, reporters tend to be keen observers of the people with whom they come into contact.

Just past nine-forty-five, I stepped out of the elevator and into the newsroom. The room was surprisingly quiet. Hasty footsteps of the copy boy. Beep-and-squeal of the video display terminals. Rat-a-tat-tat of the AP teletype. I told the counter girl why I was there, and she referred me to a dark-haired, hefty, middle-aged reporter pecking away at a desktop keyboard.

He looked up as I approached, a broad, appreciative smile

34

on his simian face. I pegged his age at over fifty. The face was a flat oval with pronounced forehead wrinkles and pudgy cheekbones. A stubby Celtic nose and shrewd gray-green eyes. He was built like a World Federation wrestler gone to seed. Meaty shoulders, massive chest and a belly like a medicine ball. His short-sleeved blue shirt lay open at the neck, exposing a tuft of sweaty black hair. A rumpled pack of cigarettes peeked out of the frayed shirt pocket. My friend was a Marlboro man. Also a leg man. He seemed extremely interested in the way my hem rode my thighs.

I flashed my prettiest Angie smile. "It'd go a whole lot faster if you used all ten fingers."

Snort of baritone laughter. "Spoken like a true secretary."

"Not quite." Halting beside his desk, I handed him one of my newly printed business cards.

Joanne Larue
Case Officer
Human Rights Commission

"What is this?" Ugly features tensed in disbelief. "Some kind of crock?"

Panic time! He's not buying it, princess.

I snatched the incriminating card away. "It's no crock, Mister—?"

"Hanlon. Bob Hanlon." Leaning back, he put both hands behind his neck and gave me a skeptical look. "Congratulations, Miss Larue."

Wary glance. "What do you mean?"

"You're the first state employee I've ever seen out pounding the pavement on a holiday."

I gave myself a swift mental kick. Think fast, Angie.

Sudden inspiration! I struck a dignified pose. "Believe it or not, Mr. Hanlon, we don't all sit around eating watermelon."

That threw him! Hanlon may have cracked a few jokes

35

about black people at the corner bar. In the office, though, he tried to be sincere and polite with all minorities. Fearful that he might have offended me, he offered a conciliatory smile. "Listen, I didn't mean it like that. I've covered the state house from Albany to Olympia, and I have yet to see a state employee working a holiday."

"You're seeing one now." Angie the streetwise social worker. "The case file landed on my desk five minutes before quitting time Friday. I've got to be in Littlerock first thing tomorrow for the site investigation. And libraries are closed on holiday weekends." Planting my fanny on his desk, I snapped, "What can you tell me about the Mona Grantz murder?"

"Mona Hanauer, you mean." Hanlon drew his wrinkled cigarette pack, shook one out, and wrapped his lips around its filter tip. "The lady in question went by her maiden name."

"The girl at the counter tells me you covered it for the paper."

"Sure did." He rummaged around the cluttered desk top, then grabbed a two-toned Bic lighter. "Beat the high-and-mighty Seattle crowd over to Orcas, too." The lighter's flame cast a fleeting glow over those anthropoid features. "Let's make it a two-way conversation, eh? You've tweaked my curiosity. Why is the Human Rights Commission taking an interest?"

"The victim was Jewish."

"So's the suspect. Her ex-husband."

"Ms. Hanauer's antique store was vandalized by an anti-Semitic group. We think there's a connection."

Bluish smoke spiralled away from his mouth. He stifled a wisecracking grin. "Afraid you're barking up the wrong tree, hon."

My Angie smile turned frigid. "Mr. Hanlon, it's *Joanne* or *Ms. Larue*, got it? When—and if—we ever start dating, you can call me *hon*."

36

Hanlon shot me an anxious look. I think he was afraid I was going to file a grievance with the home office. When he spoke again, his voice was quite respectful. "You can forget about the bigotry angle, Ms. Larue. The husband did it."

"Sure about that?"

"The San Juans D.A. is." The cigarette dangled from Hanlon's lower lip. Somehow he managed to talk around it. "Ellen Durkin over at the *Post-Intelligencer* had the same idea. She thought it was one of those Aryan loonies in Port Wyoochee. But Lemuel Thurber had a pretty tight alibi."

"What makes you so sure it was the ex?"

"Cops found Hubby's sweater in her cabin. Black cable-knit sweater. Aran sweaters, I think they call 'em." His simian face wrinkled in thought. "A blue named Pisaturo found it. Draped over the sofa's armrest. They took hairs from the sweater and matched them against hairs taken from the suspect. No question about it. Perfect match."

"Ever heard of planted evidence, Mr. Hanlon?"

"Nobody planted those two eyewitnesses."

My eyes widened in alarm. "Eyewitnesses!?"

He slid open his center desk drawer, then withdrew a ragged cluster of newspaper clippings. "Lemme refresh my memory a sec." Cagey grin. "Yeah, here we go. Two witnesses saw a dark-haired man approaching the cabin just after midnight. Couple of teenagers. They were in a parked car down the road. Wade Baxter and Jessica Nash. The girl spotted him first."

"Don't tell me Jessie had the house under surveillance!"

"Not quite." The reporter's grin turned lascivious. "Jessie and the boyfriend were just getting all cuddled up. She heard somebody thrashing around in the woods. Then she looked up and saw the man headed for the cabin."

"Sounds pretty thin to me, Mr. Hanlon."

"I saved the best for last, Ms. Larue." Taking the smoldering cigarette from his mouth, he flicked the ashes into a Styrofoam coffee cup. "The D.A.'s got a sworn statement from the woman who found Mona Hanauer on Shaw Island. Mona lived just long enough to name the killer. Her last words were *Mickey Grantz.*"

I froze. Talk about damning evidence. A verbal accusation from the dying murder victim. No wonder the judge had ordered Mick remanded without bail.

"Who found Mona Hanauer?" I asked.

"A nun."

"A *what?*"

"Hey, would I shit you?" Hanlon leaned back in his swivel chair again, his ugly face filling with good humor. "I kid you not. A Roman Catholic nun. Sister Mary Katherine. She was out taking her morning walk when she came across the Hanauer woman."

"What was a nun doing on Shaw Island?"

"The Franciscans run a little trading post over there. That's where the sister works."

"And she heard Mona Hanauer say 'Mickey Grantz'?"

"Heard it plain as day." Lifting the sheaf of clippings, he added, "If you want, I'll make you a photocopy for your—"

His desk telephone jangled. Moving with surprising speed, he snatched the receiver from its cradle. "Hanlon!" Then he listened carefully. "Obit? Yeah, I'll take it." Pinning the receiver between his left ear and shoulder, he swivelled to face the video display terminal. "Gowan, shoot!"

While Hanlon took the obituary, I let my gaze wander through the mounds of desk clutter. Rueful smile. If ever my Aunt Della saw that desk top, she'd be handing Bob Hanlon a whisk broom and a Hefty bag. What a mess! Stacks of pink telephone messages. Neatly printed news releases from Puget Sound firms. Old glossies from the sports desk.

And then an open folder drew my gaze, the FBI emblem on the cover piquing my interest. Casually I scanned the blocks of newsprint. And then a familiar name jumped out at me.

Sara Soyazhe!

My blood congealed instantly. Heart hammering, I tossed my gaze at the bottom of the page. Experienced a dreadful shiver as I spied the black-and-white illustration there.

It was a disturbingly accurate artist's sketch of my favorite Anishinabe princess, featuring the same long, glossy, raven black hair, bright obsidian eyes, aquiline nose and breathtakingly lovely smile I see every time I glance in my compact mirror. The sketch was nowhere near as revealing as an actual photograph, but it was close enough to send me reeling into the ladies room, clutching a queasy stomach.

Somehow I resisted that mindless urge to flee. I was still perched on the desk, glaring at that incriminating sketch, when Hanlon hung up the phone.

"Hey, Larue!"

Feeble Angie smile. "Ah, I was just looking over this package you got from the FBI." I was mightily glad to be wearing that foundation makeup. To say nothing of the wig and glasses. Swiftly I closed the folder. "Where did you get it?"

Taking the folder, he replied, "This? Ahhhh, I picked it up in Seattle last week. Governor's putting together some interagency crime task force. He's got to look good for the election, you know. The Bureau was handing these out to all the reporters."

"Who's the girl?"

"Pocahontas." Hanlon let out a hearty chuckle. "That's her code name. The FBI's out looking for her. An Indian, I guess."

"Native American," I corrected.

"Whatever." He handed me the advisory folder. "Bureau's been looking for her since June. She robbed some bank in upper Michigan. There's a federal warrant out. She was last seen in Utah a couple of months ago. Feds think she's headed our way."

"Really?" I wondered if Hanlon could hear the terrified beating of my heart.

"Well, the net's out in California. That's what Special

Agent Williamson said. The FBI figures she'll surface in L.A. Grifters usually do. Every office on the coast got a copy of that FBI advisory."

Plucking the sketch out of the folder, I gave it a neat fold. "Mind if I hold on to this?"

"On one condition," he replied. "If you dig up anything on the Hanauer case, I get the exclusive. Deal?"

"You have my word, Mr. Hanlon."

And then, spike heels tapping, I made a hasty retreat, ignoring Bob Hanlon's admiring glance. I had other things to worry about. The FBI advisory trembled in my grasp.

The whole West Coast! I thought, striding around the counter. They'll be watching the bus stations . . . Sea-Tac airport!

My index finger quivered as it pressed the elevator button.

How was I supposed to help Mick with the FBI breathing down my neck?

Ohhhh shit! I watched the elevator doors slide open. What am I going to do *now?*

Chapter Three

With a final revving of the engines, my commuter Bonanza rolled to a stop beside the Rapid City terminal. I fired
a hasty glance out the window, and ... sure enough, there
it was, the familiar dark green 1969 Mercury Montego
parked in the short-term lot. Poor Clunky. Among all those
Japanese compacts, he looked like a fourth grader con-
demned to spend the afternoon in kindergarten.

A friendly Dakota voice drawled out of the intercom.
"Thank you for flyin' Monument Aviation. The captain 'n'
me'd surely appreciate it if you'd all stay in your seats till we
come to a complete stop."

Mindful of the copilot's advice, I surreptitiously undid my
safety belt. When the flight attendant stepped forward to
pop the hatch, I abandoned my cramped seat, snatched my
carryon out of the overhead bin, and became the first passenger down the steps.

It had been a hectic Columbus Day. Following my unnerving interview at the *News-Tribune,* I had headed straight
for the ladies room at Sea-Tac airport. There I shed the
khaki suit, the specs and the Afro wig. Cold cream and hot
water restored my complexion to its original shade. Adios to
Joanne the diligent social worker. Say hello to Schoolgirl
Angie, looking all of fifteen years old, ready to fly home after
the holiday weekend. Comfy casual clothes added to the il-

lusion of youth. Long-sleeved white cotton shirt with a placket embroidered in a thunderbird motif. Multicolored belt with a huge, stylish concho buckle. Form-fitting jeans and a Hillary headband in a delightful shade of teal. Camouflage designed to allay the suspicions of any passing FBI agents.

Strolling toward the Rapid City terminal, I watched the setting sun vanish behind a rampart of graying cumulonimbus. A stiff breeze raised gooseflesh on my arms. I wished I hadn't packed my jacket away. *Paha Sapa* in October is a good deal chillier than Seattle.

As I sauntered into the crowded lobby, a gravelly voice rang out.

"Noozis!"

I turned at once, unable to believe my ears, but there he was—all five feet, eight inches of him. My grandfather, Charlie Blackbear. Grizzled Anishinabe senior citizen in a sheepskin jacket and workaday jeans. Broad, square head, with its lush white hair combed meticulously back. Small, flat ears. Deep-set obsidian eyes bracketed by wrinkles. He bore a slight resemblance to old Chief Rain-in-the-Face. Which was the reason I gave him such a teasing nickname.

"Chief!" Rushing forward, I slipped into his welcoming embrace. "What are you doing out here?"

"Well, I had my choice of powwows, Angie," he said, giving me an Anishinabe bear hug. "It was either the Mdewakanton powwow down in Prior Lake or the Oglala get-together out here. Figured to surprise you." Curious sidelong glance. "The surprise was on me, though. I had them announce your name from the stand. But instead of my daughter's daughter, up comes this Lakota girl I never saw before."

"Jill," I guessed aloud. "You talked to Jill Stormcloud."

"You bet." Chief's broad head nodded quickly. "Met her mother, too. Nice lady. Jill told me about your urgent business out of state."

My gaze zigzagged through the lobby crowd. "Where is she?"

"Back at Pine Ridge. She let me drive that old green bomber of yours." Holding my arm, Chief steered me toward the baggage claim. "Matter of fact, I insisted on it. You 'n' me have some talkin' to do, missy."

Worried smile. "I couldn't agree more."

"What's going on?" he asked, lowering his voice. "How come you're putting your parole at risk? Damn it, Angie, you know you're not supposed to leave South Dakota."

"It's a long story," I replied, quickening my stride. "Let's grab my luggage, okay? I'll fill you in on the way back to Pierre."

Sundown caught up with us as we were speeding through Kadoka, heading east on Interstate 90. Clunky's 351-cubic-inch engine thrummed harmoniously beneath the pitted hood. My grandfather had the wheel. He listened without comment to my narrative, then leaned forward and flicked on Clunky's low beams. Me, I was curled lazily in the passenger seat, poking through my shoulder bag. The broad windshield showed two parallel bands of asphalt highway—both nearly empty—streaming east across the undulating prairie.

". . . and about the only thing I got out of the damned trip was *this!*" I concluded, pulling out the FBI advisory.

Chief kept his eyes on the road. "What is it?"

"Souvenir of Tacoma!" Depressed frown. "Boy, I'm really in the shit now. The FBI would dearly love to get its hands on your granddaughter, alias Andrea Porter, alias Sara Soyazhe. Here, take a look for yourself."

I put the crisp sheet in his outstretched hand. He gave it a fleeting but thorough scan. Elderly features tensed in a warpath scowl.

"When your Uncle Sam catches up with you, it's going to be a mighty busy woodshed."

"You think I don't know that!?" I snapped irritably. "If I get nailed for that Michigan bank job, I'll be spending the next eight years sorting laundry in Alderson, West Virginia!"

Disapproving grunt. "Should have thought of that *before* you knocked over that U.P. bank."

"Look, it was the only way to get Mary Beth's money back."

"True enough." Sudden inquiring glance. "So what do you plan to do about Mick?"

"What can I do?" Mammoth fussbudget face. "They've got enough on him to send *three* lawyers to the gallows." I counted them off on my fingers. "No alibi for the time of the murder. Eyewitnesses placing him at Mona's cabin that night. His sweater found on the premises." Sighing in dismay, I leaned against the backrest. "There's nothing I can do, Chief. I don't dare go back out there. The FBI's tearing up the West Coast in search of Pocahontas—"

"Who?" interrupted Chief.

"Me! Pocahontas is my FBI code name. At least until the U.S. Attorney hands down the indictment. Shit! If I get caught . . ." A brisk shudder rippled through me. "Mickey and I will be waving to each other from opposite sides of the prison yard."

My grandfather began to chuckle.

Glare of indignation. "What are you laughing at?"

"Della sure had you pegged. Sarah Bernhardt!" Relaxing behind the wheel, he added, "What did you do, Angie? Write that dialogue on the flight home?"

My mouth fell open.

"You know damned well you're going to help him. You made up your mind last Friday when he called." He flashed me a sidelong smile. "The performance is supposed to show me how much you've agonized over .this decision. Don't waste your time, girl. I know you a whole lot better than that."

"You think I'm going to help him, eh?"

"You are." He nodded decisively. "And here's why. Because you think he's innocent. Because you feel you owe him. And, most of all, because he helped us to avenge Billy."

Briefly I considered protest. But then I showed him a crooked Angie grin. "I never could pull anything over on you." Hushed sigh. "You're right. If not for the Mick, I'd be scrubbing floors in a Utah prison right this very minute. And there's no *think* about it, Chief. I know he's innocent."

"What makes you so sure?"

"Mick's a lawyer, Chief. Pretty good one, too. He knows the rules of evidence. No alibi puts him in the top tier of suspects. If he was going to kill Mona, then he would have made damned sure he had some kind of plausible backup story."

My grandfather's profile resembled a granite cliffside. "That means somebody set him up. Dolan?"

"Could be. Or maybe somebody else. Somebody with a grudge against Mona. Maybe one of those neo-Nazis." I scratched my denimed knee. "I'm betting it was the cabin's nighttime visitor."

"The fella those teenagers saw."

I nodded. "He and Mona must have left the cabin together sometime after the teenagers split. Sometime after two, perhaps. They walked down the beach together. Our mystery man beat her to a pulp. I'm not sure what happened after that. Either Mona got away from him and tried to swim for it. Or else he left her for dead, and somehow she crawled into the sea."

"How do you explain the sweater?" he asked.

"The killer draped it over the arm of the sofa."

"When?" he challenged. "Those two kids didn't see him with a sweater."

"He could have been wearing it, Chief."

45

Just then, a huge eighteen-wheeler roared by us on the left, its twin diesel horns blaring. Tightening his grip on the steering wheel, Chief remarked, "Whoever framed Mick knew plenty about his past relationship with his ex-wife. It ain't likely Mick's friends in Salt Lake knew the intimate details of his divorce. That makes it somebody on Mona's side of the family, so to speak."

Pert Angie nod. "Somebody in Port Wyoochee."

"So that's where we start."

Showing him a bemused glance, I echoed, *"We?"*

"Someone has to watch your back while you're out there."

"Don't you have to close up at Tettegouche?"

My grandfather shrugged. "Plenty of time yet. We don't get our first snow till the end of the month. Besides, if you're going *nandobani* out there, you'll need all the help you can get."

Dimples enhanced my Angie smile. *Nandobani* is an old, old word among our Anishinabe people. Father Baraga said it meant to go on the warpath. Its true meaning, however, is far more complex. *Nandobani* implies a shift in spiritual outlook. It means to give up your normal life—to become a hunter of men. To steal through the forest in search of the hidden foe. To lay him low with one well-aimed arrow.

"And we're going to play it straight this time, too," Chief added, giving me a stern look. "I don't care how dirty the bad guys are. No more Robin Hood! We're going out there to learn how they framed Mick. Once we've got that information, we drop it on some honest officers of the law. That understood, missy?"

"Hey! One thing at a time, Chief," I replied, flashing a rueful grimace. "First I've got to find a way to sneak out of South Dakota!"

Actually, I really had an idea or two along those lines. To make them work, however, I had to reach Paul's office in the Foss Building before ten A.M. on Tuesday morning.

46

I almost didn't make it. And for that I can thank my overly suspicious housemother, Mrs. Sadowski. She gave me the fish eye when I asked for a pass to go to K-Mart. And she was still reluctant to open her pass book—even after I showed her the empty bottle of Prevail All-Purpose Cleaner.

So I guess it was a good thing she wasn't up and around at five A.M., when I poured the lime-colored cleaning fluid into the toilet.

Stern Polish look. "Straight there and straight back, Angie!"

"Yes, ma'am."

And so, armed with a pass from Blanche Sadowski and a list of household necessities to be purchased at K-Mart, I bustled down the front walk of the Dunning House just after nine-forty that morning. Cheerful Anishinabe princess in her hot pink jewel-neck sweater and snug white stirrup pants. Angie the homemaker.

Clean the whole house, eh? I thought, halting at the corner. Holbrook, if you honestly think I'm going to spend the week going scrub-a-dub-dub while Mick's in trouble, you'd better get some counseling of your very own—the psychiatric kind!

The Department of Corrections occupied a pair of suites on the second floor of the Foss Building, looking out onto the southern end of Capitol Avenue. The esteemed director, Randolph T. Langston (*R.T.* to his colleagues, *Mr. Langston* to us parolees), rated his own private office, natch. Paul and the rest of the parole officers had their desks sandwiched into a long, rectangular office with three tall, sunlit windows and walls painted in a pastel shade known as *blue mist.*

Thanks to numerous visits to Paul's office, I was pretty familiar with department routine. By nine-thirty, the parole officers are all out on the road, making their daily site visits and leaving the bullpen, as it's called, in the capable hands of three youthful secretaries. Until ten o'clock, that is. That's

47

when the Typing Trio departs on their customary thirty-minute coffee break.

Meaning I had to be inside that office before Langston's secretary, Stephanie Poulsen, locked the door.

Slipping through the open doorway, I spied Stephanie busily hammering her computer keyboard. Stephanie was thirty, a harried-looking divorcee with a diamond-shaped face, sultry brown eyes, and a taut mouth adorned with Passion Red lipstick. Her hair was a metallic strawberry blond, dark at the roots and rigidly coiffed in a Veronica Lake style, the ends curling upward like dahlia petals.

"Hi, Steff!"

"Morning, Angie." She had a noticeable East River accent, befitting a farmer's daughter from Avon. Her long, skinny fingers never missed a stroke. "If it's Paul you're looking for, he's in Washington all this week."

"I know." Catching her sudden interrogatory glance, I presented my grocery list. "Actually, I'm looking for old man Langston. Mrs. Sadowski's running low on purchase orders. She told me to stop over here and pick some up."

"He ain't here, Angie." I couldn't quite tell if Stephanie was annoyed or relieved by the boss's absence. "He's got a meeting. Probably blowing smoke up the governor's ass . . . as usual."

"You don't mind if I wait here for him, do you?"

"Hell, no. He'll be back in another hour. Got himself another meeting at eleven." Stephanie's glance darted impatiently to the white-faced wall clock. Lipsticked lips puckered in anticipation. "You can stick around and wait if you want."

"Sure! I don't mind waiting," I said, plopping onto a vinyl settee. No sooner had I touched down on the cushion, than a joyous soprano voice rang out.

"Coffee break, ladies!"

Within seconds, Stephanie's two compatriots were at her desk, pestering her to hurry up. As she fumbled through her purse for the keys, Stephanie explained that she would have to lock me in. Office security, you understand. I was graciousness personified. I told her I understood perfectly, plucked a copy of *Glamour* from the magazine rack, and wished them all a very pleasant break. Out the door they went, grinning and chatting, leather purses brushing slender hips, smelling faintly of lilacs.

The lock snapped shut. I waited thirty seconds, and then, tossing the magazine aside, I rose swiftly from the settee and sidled up to the door. Hasty peek out the chickenwired window. No sign of anyone in the corridor. Good!

Rounding the corner of Stephanie's desk, I slid open her side drawer, ruffled through the standup olive green folders, and located the one containing the Department of Corrections stationery. I helped myself to a handful of blank sheets. Then, after easing the drawer shut, I beelined it to Paul's vacant desk.

Good old Holbrook. He stubbornly refused to make the transition to the twenty-first century. Instead of a computer outstation, like the one on Stephanie's desk, I found myself facing a durable sand-colored IBM Selectric II typewriter.

And bless you, Geraldine Blackbear Biwaban, for putting your dainty foot down all those years ago. If not for you, Mother dear, I never would have signed up for that Business Typing course at Central High School.

Roll the department's bond paper into the carriage. Set the margins, tabs and center. And now, in the approved Katie Gibbs fashion, concoct the literary fraud that's going to get me out of South Dakota.

Dear Mr. Langston:

As you know, parolee Angela Biwaban has been notified that her services are no longer required at Chang's Corral. However, on her own initiative, Miss Biwaban has found an alternative Work Experience site. A Pacific Lumber warehouse just opened in Belle Fourche, and a clerk-typist position is available in their front office. The store's management is amenable to a year-long Work Experience contract.

I would like to send Miss Biwaban to Belle Fourche for a week to interview for this position and for any others that may become available. I would greatly appreciate it if you would authorize Miss Biwaban's job development leave, effective Tuesday, October 13.

Thanks again for your time and cooperation. I'll talk to you as soon as I get back from Washington.

Grinning, I yanked the letter out of the typewriter. Then, letting it rest on the blotter, I slid open Paul's center drawer and poked through the neat array of office supplies. Pencils, black pens, bottles of whiteout . . . ahh, here we go—Paul's signature stamp. It was standard department issue for mass mailings. Turning it over, I gave the rubber a hasty glance. The ink had long since faded to a dull gray.

Take a deep breath, princess. You can't afford a pair of shaky hands. If you smudge the signature, you're going to have to type this letter all over again. Open the stamp pad. Rest the carved signature very lightly on the bond paper. Give it a second to soak, then . . . up, up and away!

Hmmmmm, not bad at all! If I didn't know better, I'd swear Paul had signed it himself.

Rising from Paul's chair, I scanned the letter again. Mild scowl of dissatisfaction. I had the gut feeling it just wasn't enough. Langston was such a suspicious old bastard. He might not go for it. Or worse, he might phone Paul in Washington and ask for confirmation.

If only I could add a little personal note in the upper corner—a testimonial in Paul's own handwriting. . . .

Then my gaze zeroed in on the row of upright manila folders rimming the edge of Paul's desk. Sly Angie smile. I peeked through each folder, searching for his tickler file. Luck was with me. Within seconds, I found Paul's urgent correspondence folder. Each letter was marked with a yellow adhesive note containing instructions for Steff and the other girls.

I found just what I was looking for. A yellow scrap with a message reading *R.T.—Please expedite this matter at once. Talk to you when I get back. Holbrook.*

I peeled that sticker off the original letter, closed the folder, tucked it back in the row, and then planted the note firmly on the upper left corner of my bogus letter.

And then it was pitter-pat to Mr. Langston's office door. Plastic mail trays stood sentry on a table to its immediate right. Whistling to myself, I slipped the letter into Langston's in-box, making certain it was right on top. Then I returned to the settee and my magazine. Ahhhhh, bureaucracy!

Don't dawdle at that meeting, R.T. I've got a Seattle-bound flight to catch!

Wednesday morning. Fourteenth day of October. I was back in the Pacific Northwest for the second time in as many days. My week-long pass from Mr. Langston occupied a cherished niche in my leather shoulder bag. I was standing on the observation deck of the *M/V Nisqually,* huddled in my cranberry-colored stadium jacket, idly watching the fir forests and low cliffs of Lopez Island fall away astern.

I felt as if I'd been away a month. What a change in the weather! Monday had been a textbook summer's day in Tacoma. Not today, though. I glanced at the ponderous gray overcast, then shivered as *Keewadin,* the north wind, came howling down Rosario Strait.

Leaning against the ship's railing, I had the strangest feeling of déjà vu. My intellect told me that the gunmetal sea beneath *Nisqually*'s keel was Puget Sound, that the wooded isles all around were the San Juans. Still, I had the strangest feeling I was on Lake Superior, cruising through the Apostle Islands. I almost expected to see the *Island Queen* chugging around the forested point up ahead.

Of course, the *Nisqually* is a whole lot bigger than the *Island Queen*. Ten times bigger, to be exact. She's a blunt, bulky, formidable car ferry, with a pilothouse, cavern-sized openings at both ends, and a streamlined smokestack amidships emblazoned with a stylized T. I pretty much had the deck to myself. My fellow passengers—elderly couples, most of them—sat on white park-style benches in the enclosed section up forward.

A raucous squawk sounded overhead. Lifting my chin, I spied a quartet of white gulls, their wings arched and rigid, gliding in a wobbly formation just off the starboard rail. The wind bothered them not at all. I was very thankful, however, that I'd had the good sense to dress in layers that morning. Cotton-knit mock turtleneck in porcelain blue. Soft, white, pleated corduroy pants. Heavy gauge woolen sweater with knitted cuffs and crewneck collar. Maritime Angie.

This was my first trip to the San Juans in eight years. Last time around, I'd ridden the ferry to Friday Harbor with a passel of collegiate companions from the Student Conservation Association. I'd spent that whole summer as a coed rangerette for the SCA. They gave us one week's intensive training at Rainier, and then it was off to the North Cascades. Since I was from Minnesota, and presumably used to Arctic weather, I got sent to the Paysayten Wilderness. I'll never forget the day I arrived at the Granite Creek ranger station. The district supervisor said, "There's two things you'll need in this park, young lady—your tampons and your crampons!"

The *Nisqually*'s diesel horns let out a titanic bellow in B flat. Leaving the rail, I rejoined the other passengers beneath the steel overhead. Through the huge storm portholes, I could see two heavily wooded islands dead ahead with just a sliver of placid water between them.

I turned to the elderly, sharp-nosed lady at my side. "Which one is Shaw?"

"That one." Her bony finger picked out the one on the left. "Ferry landing's on the other side of the point."

Thanking her, I made my way to the fantail. Far astern of the ferry, a verdant, hilly peninsula reached into the sound, straining to touch Blakely Island. I spotted a tiny fishing village nestled against a steep, forested slope. That would be Olga, I realized, remembering the wall map I'd studied in the *Nisqually*'s dining room. Mona's cabin was located on the peninsula's stony tip.

That was my next stop. *After* I finished my chat with Sister Mary Katherine.

Shaw Island was a real shock. I don't think I've ever seen a marina that small. It made the one in Cornucopia, Wisconsin, look like the Twin Ports.

The dockmaster was an even bigger surprise. A squat and sturdy woman in her middle fifties with short gray hair, a weatherworn Irish face, and the crinkly, determined expression of a veteran skipper. Clad in an oversized yellow storm slicker and rubber hipboots, she struggled to wrestle a stiff fuel hose back on the dock. If not for the brown Franciscan veil streaming away from her headband, I never would have guessed she was a nun.

As gracious as a Vatican diplomat, Sister Dockmaster pointed out the general store uphill and told me I could find my quarry at the cheese counter. Giving her my thanks, I shouldered my heavy-duty leather bag and started up the trail.

I found Sister Mary Katherine slicing cheddar on a circular board. *Ka-chunk, ka-chunk.* Slender woman about five-foot-seven, hardly any hips at all. Brown veil and matching brown jumper. A white chef's apron shielded most of the jumper. Her hem brushed a pair of very shapely calves. If ever she tired of the convent, Sister Mary Katherine could probably make a pretty good living modelling pantyhose.

Letting go of the chopper, she stood upright, then placed the back of her hand against her moist forehead. And noticed your Angie. She turned at once, radiating a truly welcoming smile. She had a rather long and narrow face, but her large, soulful brown eyes and spacious mouth seemed to balance it, creating an impression of youthful prettiness. Thick brownish blond sheepdog bangs covered her high forehead.

"Hello." She had a fine vibrant alto voice. "May I help you?"

Show time, Angela!

"Hi, Sister!" I went into my act. Schoolgirl Angie. Opening my shoulder bag, I chattered, "My name's Anne Marie Nahkeeta, and I'm a student at the University of Puget Sound, and I'm hoping you'll talk to me so I can do this story for *Around the Sound* magazine—"

"Take it easy, Anne Marie." She giggled, stepping away from the cheese counter. "Slow down. I'm not going to bite you." Reaching behind her, she undid her apron strings. "You're a reporter?"

"Well . . . not exactly." Flustered Angie smile. "I'm a journalism major. I've got to do this term project. It's half the grade for the course." I withdrew my copy of the magazine, the one I'd picked up at the newstand in Anacortes. Letting the sister thumb through it. I added, "Professor Hanlon said he'd give me full credit if I could sell a story to *Around the Sound*. You know, a story with my byline. So I came over on the *Nisqually* to ask you a few questions."

"Really, Anne Marie, if you're interested in the store, you'd be much better off talking to Mother Superior."

"Oh, it's not about the store." Angie the wide-eyed journalism major. "I wanted to ask you about that woman you found."

Sister Mary Katherine coughed into her closed fist. "Ah, Anne Marie, I'm really not sure I ought to talk about that.

The district attorney advised me to say nothing until after the trial."

"Oh, please, Sister! I could really use an A on this project."

"Well, I don't know . . ."

"Just a few questions, Sister, please? You don't have to go into deep detail or anything. Just tell me whatever you told those reporters from Seattle."

The nun shot me a leery gaze.

"Please? Look, I'll even let you read my rough draft before I turn it in. And if you tell me not to submit it, I won't."

Brown eyes brightened once more. "Fair enough!" She gestured at an empty table beside the store's front window. "We can talk over there." Pleasant smile. "Can I get you a Pepsi or anything?"

Minutes later, the sister and I were seated at the corner table, sipping Diet Pepsis and swapping personal background tales. I turned *Anne Marie* into a rancher's daughter from Winthrop. Sister Mary Katherine hailed from Chehalis, the youngest of seven sisters, and had just returned from a tour of missionary duty in Bolivia.

I flipped open my school notebook. "How did you happen to be on that beach, anyway?"

"It was the Lord's doing, Anne Marie." She seemed utterly sincere in that belief. "We have a half-hour to ourselves after morning prayers. I usually go for a walk. A gust of wind came along just as I was passing that stretch of South Beach. It blew the fog back out to sea." Ladylike sip. "The poor woman was lying facedown on the stones. Her feet were in the water. At first I thought she was a dead seal. Then I looked again and realized it was a woman. She was wearing a dark gray jacket. That's why I mistook her for a seal." Thin features tensed in recollection. "I ran down the beach, grabbed her wrists, and pulled her out of the water. I knelt beside her and turned her over . . ."

"And then?" I prodded.

The nun shivered. Her expression betrayed the horror she had witnessed that morning. "H-Her face . . . that poor woman! Th-There were these ghastly bruises. Blood trickled from her mouth."

The ugly memory sent her thin shoulders into a spasm. Swallowing hard, she steeled herself to go on. "I-I'll be all right." Haunted brown eyes sought mine. "It's just . . . when I found her, Anne Marie, she . . . I thought she was dead!"

"What did the Hanauer woman look like?"

"Well . . . her skin was like wax. Cold to the touch."

Good description of advanced hypothermia, I reflected.

"I thought she was dead, but she wasn't. H-Her hands began to move. She was trying to speak. I knew I had to get her warmed up. I learned that at the hospital in La Paz. You have to raise the temperature of the body core. So I peeled off my jacket and wrapped it around her."

"Was she in shock?"

"Very much so." The nun nodded vigorously. "I'd seen it before, working with trauma victims in Bolivia. My coat warmed her a little. It got her shivering again. That was a good sign. But . . ." Tears of regret made her brown eyes glisten. "I-I'd gotten there too late. She was pretty far gone."

I squeezed her hand tenderly. "Listen, you did everything you possibly could."

"I know. That's what Monsignor Beauboin told me when the two of us talked about it. Still . . ."

"Did she ever regain consciousness?" I asked.

Sister Mary Katherine pursed her lips thoughtfully. "I-I can't really say. I'm not exactly sure. While I was holding her, Ms. Hanauer opened her eyes. She seemed quite delirious."

And now, the million-dollar question. "Did she speak to you?"

"Well, not exactly *to* me. She did say something. She cried out quite suddenly." Puzzlement filled the nun's slender face.

"I'll never forget it, Anne Marie. All at once, she cried out, 'Whiskey Jack!' "

Whiskey Jack?

I blinked, sitting there in astonishment, watching the sister consume the last remnants of her Diet Pepsi. Whiskey Jack! That was a far cry from *Mickey Grantz*. So much for Bob Hanlon's insider tip. He had probably picked up a bit of squadroom gossip.

Scribbling in my notebook, I asked, "Are you sure Mona Hanauer didn't say her ex-husband's name?"

"Absolutely, dear." Expression of mild shock. "Where did you hear that?"

"Seattle." I tilted my thumb toward the mainland. "The cops say you heard Ms. Hanauer mention her ex-husband's name."

"I most certainly did not!" Sister Mary Katherine sat upright in indignation. "I'd like to know how these idiotic rumors get started."

"Well, you know. Cops chewing the fat around the squadroom—"

"I heard it as plain as day," she added, mildly annoyed. "She didn't mumble, either. She said it right out loud, as if she were some kind of radio announcer. 'Whiskey Jack!' "

Closing my notebook, I showed the nun a pronounced fussbudget face.

Whiskey Jack?

For some strange and unknown reason, that name had a familiar ring. For the life of me, though, I couldn't quite recall where I'd heard it before. Or under what circumstances.

Whiskey Jack ...

Whatever could it mean?

Chapter Four

After leaving the general store, I rode the ferry over to Orcas and dropped in at Beluga Bikes. I dickered with the owner, plunked some cash money on the counter, and then pedaled away on a brand-new pastel green Fox River twenty-six-inch mountain bike. Knobby tires, white pedals and sprockets, thumb shifters for the fifteen gears, and a comfy padded seat anatomically suited to women. The owner even threw in a water bottle, a plastic rain poncho, and a foldout road map.

After six miles of pumping my way across mountainous Orcas, I decided that I could give my daily jog a skip today. I ground to the grateful halt in Eastsound village, enjoyed a leisurely lunch at the Chulananuk Restaurant, had a peek at the scene of the Mick-and-Mona quarrel, and declined an invitation from a group of Seattle yuppies to join them on a bike tour of Turtleback Mountain.

It's just as well. Riding alone down that rollercoaster roadway gave me the chance to do some thinking. *Whiskey Jack*. That nutty phrase refused to stop bouncing around inside my head. I just knew I'd heard it somewhere before.

And then, veering left to pick up the Obstruction Pass road, I suddenly remembered where.

It's a common expression back home in the Northland, the colloquial name for a feathered member of the *Corvidae* family. *Perisoreus canadensis,* also known as the camp robber or the Canada jay.

Among my people, he's known as *Wisskachon,* meaning Meat Bird. And, like the rest of our words, the new people managed to garble it into something else, namely, Whiskey John. Since that was a little too formal for the average Northland logger, the name became Whiskey Jack.

Wisskachon is a voracious little guy, about the same size as his cousin, the blue jay, but with the look of a fat chickadee. Gray body, white throat and forehead, and a black stripe through the eyes.

If Sister Mary Katherine was correct, and I had no reason to doubt her testimony, then Mona Hanauer had shouted a bird's name as she lay dying.

Skeptical fussbudget face. Oh, come on! Only in those goofy British mysteries on "Masterpiece Theatre" does the victim die with a cryptic message on her lips.

Why don't things like this ever happen to Miss Marple? I mean, think about it. It's truly absurd. Suppose you were dying, and all you had left was one last breath to name your killer. What are you going to shout? "Oh, look! An oriole!"

Give me a break.

Whiskey Jack . . . dammit, that phrase has to mean something.

Thoughtful pause. Of course, perhaps the killer's name really is Whiskey Jack. Or perhaps that's how Mona knew him. It could be some sort of coy nickname.

Perhaps it was Whiskey Jack who planted Mick's sweater on the premises.

The narrow road ended at a cluster of vacation cabins overshadowed by the moist fir and red cedar forest. I spotted a mailbox marked *Hanauer.* Mounting up once more, I pedalled fifty yards back up the road. After wheeling my rental bike into the dank undergrowth, I concealed it behind a moss-covered boulder. Then, with my trusty rain poncho under my arm, I headed for the shore.

Emerging from the woods, I found myself on a pebbly beach. Ahead of me was a placid semicircular cove, opening into Obstruction Pass. Blakely's green mound dominated the watery horizon. To the right lay its twin, Cypress Island.

I left the beach quickly. Clattering pebbles make too much noise. In our time-honored Anishinabe style, I made my way through vacant backyards, crouching behind picnic tables, sidling up to hemlock trees. They were very easy to lean against. Decades of Puget Sound storms had given them all a noticeable inland tilt.

At last I came to the Hanauer cabin. It was one of those Swiss chalets that had been so popular about thirty years ago. Steep, A-lined, shingled roof with bright blue gingerbread trim. Bevelled cedar log walls and ceiling-high bay windows. A rusting steel chimney poked out of the left side of the roof.

Approaching the rear deck, I spotted tattered yellow ribbons dangling from the screen door and the wooden railing. *Police Line—Do Not Cross.* Storm winds had really done them damage. Apparently, the San Juans sheriff hadn't bothered to take them down following the on-site investigation.

I figured Mona probably had an emergency key stashed near the back door, so I gave the rear deck a thorough toss. No luck! For a moment there, I wondered if the sheriff had taken it with him. And then my flustered gaze noticed something odd.

Thirty years of Hanauer family footsteps had cleared a noticeable trail to the beach. Sitting on the back steps, I watched the path shoot straight downslope from the house, meander between a pair of half-buried boulders, and then roll toward a stand of stately Sitka spruces.

Before the path reached the trees, however, there was a balding patch of grass on the outside edge. As if somebody had scuffed the vegetation with his heels.

Deciding to have a closer look, I knelt beside the sparse patch. The grass dampened the corduroy at my kneecap. I touched the stubbly grass with my fingertips. The blades were shredded, as if they'd been stepped on frequently.

Taking care to stay on the dry path, I flattened out on the ground and peered between the roughened stalks. Yeah, someone's been leaving the path at this point, all right. Craning my neck slightly, I spotted the faint outline of a human trail flowing away from this spot, beelining it to a thicket of prickly salal bushes.

What's over there? I wondered.

Nimble as a fawn, I rose from the ground and bustled across the lawn. Fingering the thorny leaves aside, I gingerly followed the faint trail through the salals, down through the exposed roots of a shoreside hemlock, and out onto a tiny scrap of sand beach flanked by large boulders.

Crouching on the wet sand, I had a look around. Hmmmmm—quite the little hideyhole we have here. All I could see was the sound and the sharply peaked cabin rooftop. The cutaway bank concealed me from the road, and those boulders kept me safe from the prying eyes of other beachgoers.

Just as I began wondering if Mona had ever donned a swimsuit here, I spied a yellow glimmer behind the hemlock's exposed roots. Reaching through the stiff tangle, I got my hand around it. Smooth nylon met my grip. Surprised Angie blink. It was a small rope, the kind pleasure craft use for Danforth anchors.

Rocking back on my heels, I gave it a tug. All at once, a jagged fissure magically appeared in the sand. Another hard tug. More nylon line appeared. The crumbly fissure rocketed toward the water.

I was starting to feel like that British colonel in the movie *The Bridge On The River Kwai*.

After shedding my stadium jacket, I rolled up my sweater sleeves and trouser legs and headed for the water. Damp sand tried to swallow my Reeboks. I beat a hasty retreat to drier sand, removed my sneakers and slouch socks, and then tried it again. You can always dry your feet afterward, Miss Biwaban. And you really don't want to pedal those twelve miles back to the Orcas dock in wet footgear, now do you?

Ten minutes later, I salvaged the pot of gold at the end of the rainbow. Or, in this case, the olive-green canister at the end of the nylon boat line. I wrestled the weighty container up the beach, set it on dry sand, and pulled on my jacket.

Fortunately, the canister wasn't locked. As I peeled back the lid, it rose with a soft sucking sound. A thick rubber gasket ran all around the rim's interior, ensuring that the container remained waterproof despite its immersion.

One by one, I removed the contents and put them on the sand. The largest item was a Ziploc bag containing four kilos of dried marijuana. I also found a set of brass house keys, a penlight, a roll of twenty-dollar bills, a very funny X-rated cartoon featuring a former president and his matronly first lady, and just over two dozen home-rolled joints.

Well, now I understood why Mona had deep-sixed that container.

And how did I know that the contents belonged to Mickey's ex? Very simple, Doctor Watson. The trail leads directly to this spot from the Hanauer cabin. Judging from the wear and tear on the lawn, the lady is a frequent visitor. Most importantly, though, one of those joints sports traces of ruby red lipstick at one end.

I pocketed the keys, left the cash where it was, and popped the grass back into the canister. Forced down the lid, making certain it had a nice tight seal. I marvelled at the lady's ingenuity. Not many women would think of hiding their dope stash in the sea. And the few that did might not know enough to compensate for the twice-daily tides running out of the sound.

You thought of just about everything, Mona. The steel canister goes straight to the bottom. The nylon line prevents it from drifting out with the tide. Beach sand conceals the nylon tether. Smart girl!

Retracing my steps to the cabin, I yielded to a mild fussbudget face. No question about it, I had an awful lot to learn about the former Mrs. Grantz. The picture Mickey had painted did not quite mesh with the reality of the clandestine doper. Was Mick aware of his ex-wife's indulgence? If so, then why hadn't he told me about it?

Perhaps there was a whole lot Mickey didn't know about her personal life. What had Mona been up to during the past four years? Had she taken lovers? Was there another man in her life? Questions, questions.

There were four keys on the ring, so naturally I went through all four before I found the one that opened the cabin's back door. Keening squeak of hinges. I slipped inside, letting my fingertips catch the steel mesh, hoping to avoid a banging slam.

The gray, overcast sky offered no indoor illumination. From the doorway, the furniture resembled a jumble of bulky silhouettes. Reaching into my jacket pocket, I retrieved Mona's penlight.

Ahhhhh, much better! A pale circle of light drifted across the deep-shadowed room. A kitchenette occupied a rear corner. Plush secondhand easy chairs, an old-fashioned floral sofa and lacy curtains cast the illusion of a comfortable parlor. The walls were knotty pine, smelling faintly of sap. Stained walnut molding ran along the ceiling and floor. I spotted a handful of framed photographs. Pictures of Mount Baker and seaside towns unfamiliar to me.

Soundlessly I glided through the gloom. My sneaker soles encountered a hooked throw rug. The penlight's illuminated circle tagged two bedrooms—one large, one small and vacant. A canopied double bed occupied the larger one, attended by a chest of drawers, fraying drapery, a littered vanity table, and a portable TV. Quick stop at the vanity table. Uncap Mona's lipstick. Well, well—the same shade as the stain on that joint. It's so nice to have your hunches confirmed.

One look at the bedroom closet told me I'd gotten there too late. Empty wire hangers dangled from the crossbeam. Someone had already cleaned out the place. The sheriff, most likely.

Just then, something solid nudged my foot. Whirling, I swivelled the penlight beam in that direction. A bear's face appeared in the spotlight, its ferocious jaws agape. I grinned. Say hello to your clan totem, princess. *Ursus americanus,* also known as the black bear. My beam ran the length of her flat ruffled skin. A sow, at one time tipping the scales at three hundred and fifty pounds. She had been four years old when her luck had run out and she'd wandered into some hunter's gunsights. I wondered what had happened to her cubs.

Nearing the sofa, my nostrils detected the subtle odor of talc. Putting my nose to the upholstery, I took a whiff. The sudden stinging sensation brought tears to my eyes. Fingerprint powder! The cops had given this place a thorough dusting.

Kneeling beside the sofa, I trained my penlight on the armrest. I was looking for stray hairs, loose threads, dandruff—anything that would have hinted at the presence of someone other than Mickey Grantz. No such luck.

Arrrrrgh! This just isn't your day, Angela.

All at once, a flat thump shattered the silence. Reacting instantly, I huddled behind the armrest, masking the penlight's glow with my left palm. The tumult continued. Hefty footfalls ascending the front porch stairs.

Oh, terrific! I thought, switching off the penlight. The sheriff picked a fine day to inspect the premises. *Now* what do I do?

Obeying my first instinct, I stayed down. But I had to know exactly what I was dealing with. So, taking a speedy breath, I risked a peek over the armrest.

The front window displayed a tall, heavyset man in his early twenties, wearing a brown leather jacket and wrinkled Levis. My brain took a snapshot of his face; then I dropped to my hands and knees again. The afterimage burned its way into my memory. Brownish blond hair shorn in the regulation crewcut of a Marine D.I. High forehead, stark eyebrows, noticeable bridge at the top of his nose. Thick neck and lantern jaw. Hard, glittering aquamarine eyes and a small, churlish mouth vaguely reminiscent of a spoiled little boy.

The heavy footfalls ceased. I heard the front doorknob rattle impatiently. A muttered obscenity followed. Silence.

Stay where you are, Angie. Don't you dare stick your head above that armrest.

The silence became infuriating.

Okay . . . one quick peek. But you do it in the way Daddy and Chief taught you. Get down on the floor, cheekbone to the rug. Slide your head past the sofa's leg. Peer up at the window. See? Just like scouting the elusive whitetail.

There was Mister Crewcut, his large frame filling most of the glass. Black silhouette against the gunmetal gray sky. He had both elbows outflung, so I guessed he was trying to peer through the dusty glass.

Good luck, pal. With you blocking the only source of illumination, you won't be able to see much.

Mister Crewcut came to the same realization. Or maybe he was just reacting to the distant sound of an automobile engine. Whatever the cause, he swiftly stepped away from the window.

Rising silently to my feet, I caught a fleeting glimpse of his broad back descending the porch stairs. Turning abruptly to the right, he crossed the narrow road and passed out of my field of view.

Who are you, friend? I asked myself. And what were you doing, poking around Mona Hanauer's cabin?

Those questions could wait, I decided. Settling down in an easy chair, I gave Mister Crewcut plenty of time to leave the area. Two hours, to be exact.

Only then did I depart the Hanauer cabin, retrieve my

rental bike, and begin the long ride back to the Orcas ferry dock.

"You're from Port Wyoochee?" The man's wrinkled face beamed with interest. He was well over seventy, and that blunt clam-digger's face had spent many a blustery morning working the Strait of Juan de Fuca. He had pebbly chocolate-colored eyes, a short, scraggly beard, and a nose mashed flat by some long-forgotten maritime accident. "What's your name, lass?"

"Anne Marie Nahkeeta," I replied, offering my hand.

Those work-roughened hands looked fearsome, indeed, but his grip was as light as a dowager's.

"Klallam." He nodded sagely. "You have people in Sequim, do you?"

He gave it the shore pronunciation—*Skwimmm*. I figured my best bet was to pose as a local Indian, and this side of the strait was the original Klallam homeland.

Polite Angie smile. "My grandmother lives there."

He gestured at the high Victorian window. The view offered a glimpse of mansard rooftops sweeping downhill to meet the sapphire blue of Luckutchee Bay.

Offering a sagacious smile, he added, "You'll find your old hometown's changed quite a bit, Anne Marie."

"Actually, I don't remember all that much about the shore. My parents moved to Spokane when I was two. I grew up in the Inland Empire."

"So you've come to have a look at your roots, eh?"

"That's about it, Mister . . . ?"

"Meeker. Bill Meeker. Tell me, where are you staying?"

"A bed-and-breakfast on Fourth Street." It took me a second to remember the name. "The Parmenter House."

"Right in the heart of Silk Stocking Row!" he cried. Then, tugging at my blazer sleeve, he led me across the arched,

66

high-ceilinged lobby. "You'll want to see the general's library, of course. This way, lass."

Now, I'd thought the Parmenter House was the ultimate in Victorian foofaraw. But that was before Bill Meeker whisked me through this fine old lumber baron's mansion. They called it Bayview, and it was definitely *La Bon-Bon Grande* of the entire south shore. Carved oak panelling and Florentine alabaster light globes. Damascene drapery spun from the hair of Angora goats. Monumental Jacobean fireplace. Quarter-sawed oak flooring. The original owners, the Alworth family, had long since died out, leaving their prize possession in the loving hands of Bill Meeker and the rest of the Port Wyoochee Historical Society.

I hadn't had much luck locating Mona's surviving relatives. There were eleven Hanauers in the Port Wyoochee phone book. Rather than telephone at random, I tried the local high school, hoping to dig Mona's girlhood address out of an old yearbook. The lady at the front desk coolly informed me that yearbooks were School Department property and School Department property was out-of-bounds to out-of-towners. I told her I would keep that in mind the next time a School Department salary increase came up at the town meeting.

Which brought me to Bayview, reportedly the repository for all Port Wyoochee historical records. Down the hallway we strolled. Angie, lovely as always, in her smart wool flannel blazer, fuschia with black piping, and matching slim skirt. And Bill Meeker, retired clam digger and local history fanatic, casually clad in a houndstooth jacket, white shirt and dark slacks.

". . . first whites who settled here were the McGrath brothers. They were wreckers. The Revenue Service run 'em out of Florida, so they set up shop in San Francisco. They made their pile in the Gold Rush, putting lanterns on mules and luring ships hard aground. Then a crimp told Joe McGrath his name was on the vigilantes' list. He and his brother, Frank—they loaded their schooner and sailed up north." Halting at the library's imposing door, Meeker reached for the huge iron ring. "They built the first dock down in Chickamin Cove. Called it McGrath's Landing. Name never caught on, though."

"Who named it Port Wyoochee?"

"That was old Mrs. Cook. Her husband built the sawmill." He swung the large door open. "We put together the general's library the same way it was at the Parmenter House. The society's owned all these books since 1940."

The library was a cozy room trimmed with bright cherrywood. Tall walnut stacks held old books smelling vaguely of damp leather. Meeker explained that the collection was well over a century old. General Parmenter had shipped it north from Vancouver Barracks in 1904, the year he retired from the army.

Taking an oxhide album from the shelf, Meeker opened it and showed me an old photograph of the general, his formidable wife Jane, and President Theodore Roosevelt. There was no mistaking Teddy. Rumpled slouch hat, Coke-bottle glasses, Nietzschean moustache—and a dead grizzly bear at his feet.

The year that photograph was taken, there were well over a thousand grizzlies roaming the Black Hills of South Dakota. Today Teddy's face adorns a mountainside in *Paha Sapa*, and there are less then ten of the great bears left.

I'm sorry. That's not what I call an improvement.

"Friends of the Roosevelts?" I inquired.

"Teddy Roosevelt," he corrected. "Old Miss Jane despised Franklin and Eleanor."

"Republicans?"

"The general was a Republican, but he voted for Grover Cleveland all three times. Miss Jane was a Democrat. Well, at least until FDR came along. She wasn't like the others. You know, the Alworths, the Cooks and the Denhams. She didn't come from money. She grew up in mining towns."

Fond smile of remembrance. "She was a character, though. When I was a kid, back in the thirties, she used to come to the Fourth of July picnic, and us kids—we'd pester her to do some shooting. Finally, Sheriff Holland would loan her his Colt forty-five, and she'd pick those empty bottles right off the fence." He pantomimed a western gunfighter fanning a six-shooter. "Blam-blam-blam! White-haired old lady blasting away like John Wesley Hardin! Funniest damn thing you ever saw!"

"Where'd she learn to shoot like that?"

"Well, she told me the Sundance Kid was her boyfriend before she met the general, but I think she was just pulling my leg." Another fond smile as he turned the page. "There ought to be a picnic photo in here ... wait! There's Miss Jane."

My gaze followed Meeker's forefinger to the photo. It was a Depression era shot, showing the seventyish Miss Jane with a striking white-haired man. He resembled a badly aging gigolo with his flowing hair, furry eyebrows, well-chiselled features and pencil-thin moustache. A Bogartian trenchcoat hung from his narrow shoulders. His operatic stance gave him the look of a storybook prince.

I burst into laughter. *"Who* is that!?"

"William Dudley Pelley." Seeing my blank look, the guide added, "You wouldn't know him, of course. He was way before your time, Anne Marie."

"Who is he?"

Embarrassment flooded the tour guide's face. I could sense his sudden reluctance to discuss the man. "He, uh, founded a group called the Silver Shirts. Called himself the American fuehrer."

My obsidian eyes widened. "A Nazi!?"

"Well, in a way ... sort of. It's a long story." Apparently, Bill Meeker was in no mood to tell it. "Miss Jane became interested in the Silver Shirt movement at the end of her life. Like I said, she despised FDR. She invited Pelley to speak

69

before her group back in 1938. That's how he and Tessie became such good friends."

"Tessie?" I echoed.

"Theresa Noelle Thurber." Grim smile. "Your old hometown has sure had its share of characters, Anne Marie."

"Any relation to Lemuel Thurber?"

Surprised look. "You've heard of Lem?"

Showing him a cool smile, I replied, "News travels fast in the minority community, Mr. Meeker."

He looked as if he wished he'd stayed home that morning. Flipping a few more pages, he mumbled, "I guess that Lem has sure been stirrin' up a peck of trouble. I'm almost tempted to say it runs in the family. 'Ceptin' I knew Tess. She was a few years ahead of me in school. She wasn't always like that, you know. Against the Jews and all. Depression's what turned her sour. Same way that Vietnam mess changed her boy." His index finger stabbed another black-and-white photo. "That's her . . . Tess the Terrible. Ol' T.N.T. herself."

I looked. Tessie Thurber resembled a Disney chipmunk. Snub nose, pointed chin, and a smile showing a good deal of overbite. Dark hair carelessly styled in the Jean Harlow fashion. Rimless Trotsky eyeglasses made her bright eyes seem even larger than they were. Never was there a more unlikely firebrand!

Yielding to curiosity, I said, "Tell me about her."

"Well, there really ain't that much to tell. Tessie was sort of born with the town. General Parmenter—he came from old money, you know. Philadelphia Main Line. He got together with old man Alworth and Jake Denham, and they founded the Kulshan Paper Company. That was back in 1905, same year the town incorporated. The company commenced to cutting in the Olympics, and loggers came streaming over here from Seattle. In no time at all, there were shacks strung out along Shore Avenue. *Sawdust Flats*— they called it. Tessie was born there. Her daddy worked as an edgerman at the Cook sawmill. Then one day—I guess Tessie was about nine—they were running a big red cedar down the carriage, and the bandsaw broke. That saw jumped right back at the men on the short side. Pretty near cut Dan Thurber in half! He didn't live more'n a week after that. His wife Grace started takin' in laundry. No such thing as insurance for a mill worker. Not back then."

"How did Tessie become involved with the Parmenters?"

"That was Miss Jane's doing." Meeker smiled in recollection. "See, Tessie was awful smart. Always did well in school. Grace Thurber became upset because she was afraid Tess wouldn't finish. Tessie thought she ought to be working full time. Well, you know neighbors and back fences. Pretty soon word got back to Miss Jane, and she made up her mind to help them. She knew Grace Thurber would never accept outright charity, so she pulled a few strings and got her a job keeping house for old Mrs. Cook. Then she put Tessie to work after school, organizing the general's personal papers." His smile broadened. "Tessie graduated in 1933. Valedictorian. And to hear Miss Jane clapping, you'd have thought it was her daughter up there on the stage. She got Tessie a scholarship to some Bible Baptist college in Kentucky. Said she'd be damned if Tessie was going to run off to Hollywood like Frances Farmer."

"Miss Jane wasn't a fan of the silver screen, I take it."

"Definitely not!" Meeker closed the album. "In fact, that's why Miss Jane started the Women's Mayflower Society. The group was open to all Port Wyoochee women of Anglo-Saxon ancestry. Miss Jane said they were going to 'combat vice, liquor, incivility, Sabbath-breaking and the lasciviousness of Hollywood.' They had a lot of guest speakers. Pelley was one of 'em. He'd been a Hollywood screenwriter in the Twenties, before he got into Spiritualism, and he entertained the ladies with true stories of Sin City. Miss Jane was a little leery of him. She'd grown up in the Old West, and she knew a smooth-talkin' four-flusher when she saw one. Tessie, though . . . well, she was different. She didn't have much experience with men. Pelley wined and dined her. By the time he left town, there was no more ardent Silver Shirt in the whole Northwest than Theresa Noelle Thurber. Tess attended their Christian Nationalist conventions in Boise and Oklahoma City. After Miss Jane died, she quit her librarian's job, took over the Mayflower Society, and started up her own newspaper, *The Explosion*. She wrote all the articles herself, signin' 'em with her initials—T.N.T."

"Thunder on the right, eh?"

"That's for damned sure! Why, Tessie sometimes made old man Pelley sound like a flaming liberal. There was no story too crazy for *The Explosion*. FDR's homosexual affair with Harry Hopkins. Eleanor Roosevelt dressed up as a rabbi. You name it."

"What happened to her?"

"Well, Tess got her ass in a crack with Uncle Sam. She claimed Roosevelt paid the Japanese to attack Pearl Harbor. A federal grand jury indicted her for sedition, and the FBI picked her up. She sat out the rest of the war in Bremerton."

There was one unanswered question left, so I asked it, "Why does Lem have his mother's last name?"

Turning his back abruptly, Meeker replaced the album on the shelf. "Guess I've done enough talkin' for one day." Suspicious glance. "Just why is it you came here, Anne Marie?"

Hopeful Angie smile. "I'm trying to find some of the kids I used to play with."

"You remember that far back?"

"Very vague memories, Mr. Meeker. Memories of the sandbox at Klallam Park. There were a couple of little girls. They were two or three years older than me. I can't remember their names."

My tale had him hooked. "Really? Then, how do you expect to find them?"

"I wanted to look through some old school yearbooks. I thought maybe I could match a face with a name."

Brightening at once, he replied, "Well, I think I can arrange that. We've got yearbooks goin' back to the twenties. Denham High, Pike Junior High and both elementary schools." He pointed out an empty chair at the reading table. "You'd be best off lookin' at the elementary schools, Anne Marie. What year were you in the first grade?"

So I told him. And noted the aisle he went down. A few minutes later, he returned with a stack of thin volumes. Bright cartoon covers. Winnie the Pooh and Tigger, too. I thanked him, opened one, and frowned, studying it intently. Meeker told me he'd be down in the lobby if I needed anything.

The moment his footsteps receded into silence, I slipped out of my chair, darted down the proper aisle, and located the stack laden with yearbooks. Ran my finger along the row. Found the Jacob Denham High School *Schooner* from fifteen years ago. Plucked it from the shelf, ambled back to my seat, and then idly thumbed through its glossy pages.

Hello there, Miss Mona Irene Hanauer, nickname *Mo*, daughter of Mrs. Ruth Hanauer of 105 Sanwetlah Drive, Port Wyoochee. A very impressive list of activities, my dear. President of the Debate Club. Vice president of the French Club. Two seasons on the Girls' Golf team. Honor Roll all four years.

Mona's yearbook photo was one of those artsy-fartsy shots. Pretty face emerging from a shadowy background. She had a little too much chestnut hair, and she wore it in the teased swirl favored by too many teenaged girls. Still, she was quite a stunner. I couldn't help feeling a tad jealous of her strikingly lovely facial planes and dark, expressive eyes and lush, sultry lips. Our girl was casting a smoky glance at the photographer—a look that somehow managed to be both a challenge and an invitation at the same time.

Hmmmmm, I wonder how *your mother* reacted to that photo, dear.

That was one very worldly and sophisticated eighteen-

73

year-old, I thought. A girl with those looks and that attitude must have left a string of broken hearts scattered around Denham High. There just might be a couple of men in Port Wyoochee deeply resentful of her marriage to the brash Jewish attorney from Tacoma. Perhaps a couple of likely suspects for the San Juans slaying.

Time for a heart-to-heart with Mom.

Ruth Hanauer lived in the Alder Beach section of town. Formerly known as Barnacle Point. The peninsula had been stripped of its lumber during the boom years. After World War II, an enterprising developer had purchased the acreage, pulled the stumps, levelled the hills and tossed up several dozen cottage-style homes.

The Hanauer house was a raised cottage on Sanwetlah, which, if memory serves, is Chinook for *speaker*. Just as my own alias, Nahkeeta, is Klallam for *princess*. Rangerette Angie picked up a smattering of the Salishan languages while leading all those backpacking tourists through the Paysayten Wilderness.

The cottage had a broad, sloping roof that covered the front porch, tall twin chimneys, sky windows and a pair of cozy, copper-roofed dormers. The American Dream still lives in Port Wyoochee, folks. I parked beside a shady black cottonwood, locked the car, and then sauntered up the Hanauer front walk, mentally rehearsing my speech.

A slim, unassuming matron answered the door. She was the same height as your Angie, with superbly coiffed gray hair, noticeable wrinkles, a high forehead, tapered eyebrows and an aquiline nose. Her lipstick was a dull rose color, cracking a bit on her underlip. She wore a pair of crisp twill heather slacks, a white raime cardigan and a bronze-colored blouse.

"Uhm . . . Mrs. Hanauer?"

Bright blue eyes flashed me an inquisitive glance. "Yes?"

74

"I-I'm sorry to bother you this way." Sad-eyed expression of sympathy. "My name is Anne Marie Nahkeeta. I went to school with Mona."

Sudden wariness tightened Ruth's mellow contralto voice. "You knew my daughter?"

"Well, just to say hi to." Timid Angie smile. "We were in Mrs. Schmidt's geometry class at Denham." Remembrance flickered in those blue eyes, and Ruth's wariness dissipated. "You see, I just moved back to Port Wyoochee, and I got talking to Susan Cabrillo, and she told me what happened to poor Mona. I-I couldn't believe it! I . . . I . . . well, I thought I ought to come right over and pay my respects."

"How very thoughtful of you, dear." Ruth opened the front door a little wider. "Please come in."

Mona's mother ushered me into a spacious living room with a high ceiling and a wagon-wheel chandelier. Sand-colored walls, a white brick fireplace, a plush tapestry sofa and matching chairs. Large oval-shaped cherrywood coffee table in mid-room, supported by some sturdy Queen Anne legs. A well-thumbed novel by Jayne Ann Krentz occupied a corner of the table. Standing at the opposite end was a tall, willowy brunette wearing aviator-style glasses and a floral dress in dark blue silk jacquard, with puffy half-sleeves and a full skirt. Squirming on the brunette's hip was a lively baby boy. I pegged his age at just over six months. Dark curls, white baby shoes, a denim Oshkosh B'Gosh playsuit, and a pudgy, well-scrubbed face.

"I'd like you to meet someone," Ruth said, touching my sleeve. "Lisa, this is Anne Marie Nahkeeta. She went to school with Mona. Anne, this is Lisa Rotenberg, the rabbi's wife."

"And this is Davey!" Showing a proud smile, Lisa boosted her offspring with both hands. "Welcome to Port Wyoochee. Shore person?"

"A long time back." I waited until Davey was safely back aboard her hip, then shook Lisa's hand.

"Port Townsend?" Lisa's face brightened in sudden recognition. "I went to school with Karen Nahkeeta."

"My cousin." I took advantage of Lisa's reminiscence to strengthen my alternate identity. "Karen's from the Sequim side of the family."

Davey began to fuss. And so, in the time-honored fashion of young mothers everywhere, Lisa made him the center of attention. Lifting him once more, she cooed, "Say hello, punkin."

Poor Davey. Bright brown eyes blossomed in alarm. Who is this Anishinabe woman, anyway? Baby features tensed suddenly, and I decided to make friends before he burst into tears.

Extending my pinky finger, I waggled the lacquered nail very slowly. Infant curiosity banished those feelings of apprehension. He caught my finger in a warm, moist and surprisingly firm little grip. David Rotenberg, future quarterback for the Denham High Mariners.

I let Davey shake it to his heart's content. As he let go, I gave him a cheerful Angie smile, tickling him just beneath the chin. High-pitched squeal of babyish delight.

"He likes you!" Lisa announced. And then she recited a list of her son's accomplishments during his first eight months of life. Never in the history of the world had there even been a baby boy as smart or as hyperactive or, God help us, so prone to infections of the upper respiratory tract.

I soon learned that Mona's mother and Lisa Rotenberg were close friends and key figures at the Luckutchee Bay Hebrew Center. Ruth taught the aleph class at the *yeshiva*. Which was the reason why Lisa was at the Hanauer house this morning. They were working on plans for the parents' dinner in November.

"I told myself I wasn't going to get into this," Lisa said, shifting her baby to the other hip. "But the only thing that interests our current chairperson is socializing, and I didn't want the dinner to fall flat on its face."

"That's the committee's problem, not yours. You try to do too much, dear," Ruth chided. Then she gave Davey's cheek a loving pat. "You have enough to do right here."

"Don't I know it!" Lisa's expression radiated a cheerful weariness. "A rabbi's wife can't win, Anne Marie. If you stand back and let others manage it, they say you're stuck up. But if you get involved, they accuse you of trying to run everything!"

Just then, the kitchen telephone rang. Ruth moved in that direction, but Lisa put out a restraining hand. "I'll get it. It's probably the caterer. Besides, you want to talk to Anne Marie."

And off she went, loose skirt swirling about her long legs, holding the cooing infant in the crook of her slender arm.

I found a comfy corner of the sofa, watching as Ruth seated herself in the tapestry chair. She asked me many questions about my earlier life in Port Wyoochee. Thanks to the information I'd gleaned from the yearbooks, I was able to craft some believable anecdotes. Gradually I shifted the topic of conversation to Mona.

"You know, I think I drove right by Heritage Antiques on my way over here," I said, crossing my legs very casually. "How long had Mona been back in town?"

"Four years."

"Last I heard, she was married and living in Seattle."

"That's right." Ruth's voice turned a shade cooler. "She returned to Port Wyoochee right after her divorce from ... *him.*"

Uh-oh. In-law trouble. Ruth couldn't even bring herself to say Mick's name.

Remembering the yearbook gossip, I asked, "Did Mona ever get back together with Luke Kavalnov?"

"I wouldn't know, dear." Ruth sat erect, trying without success to conceal the expression of maternal hurt. "I didn't see that much of Mona after she moved back."

"No?"

"No." Sad shake of the head. "I invited Mona to live here, and she declined. She took an apartment on Dungeness Circle. She wanted to be free to . . . how do you young people say it? . . . live her own life."

I sensed that Ruth wanted to talk about it, to release the tensions she'd held in check for so long. In a way, she was still trying to cope with the finality of her daughter's death.

I kept my tone sympathetic. "A divorced woman feels strange about coming home to Mother. Maybe she'd felt that she'd failed. Maybe she didn't want you to see that."

"That wasn't it." Ruth made an impatient gesture. "Mona knew I'd understand about the divorce. I-I went through the same thing myself. With Mona's father." Anguished eyes sought mine. "She knew I wouldn't approve of her lifestyle. That's why she stayed away."

"Uhm . . . you two had words, I take it."

Slow nod. "On many occasions. She was so much like her father. She wouldn't listen to me. I-I told her . . . Mona, you just can't live with the man. Not here! Not in a small town like Port Wyoochee. People are going to talk." The words came gushing out, as if an emotional dam had broken deep inside. "She wouldn't listen. Even when she was a little girl, she used to tune me right out." Emotion clotted her voice box. Sniffling, she dabbed at a tear trail with her fingertips. "I-I'm sorry. I don't know what got into me. I'm telling you things . . ."

"Don't worry about it," I added softly. "We Klallam princesses come equipped with a pair of friendly ears. And a mouth that stays shut."

So Mona had taken a lover after returning to her hometown. My first instinct was to leave Ruth alone, to steer the conversation back into a series of pleasantries and then take my leave. But I couldn't do that. I had to learn the identity of Mona's boyfriend.

Feeling my way back into the subject, I flashed a sympathetic look and murmured, "I gather she was pretty serious about him."

"As a matter of fact, she was." Ruth blew her nose with a delicate paper tissue. "I'm afraid I never understood the attraction. He was such a change from ... *her husband.* He wasn't much of an intellectual at all. Flying was his entire life."

"Flying?" I echoed.

"Yes. Jonathon owns a floatplane. He runs a little air taxi service." Ruth's lips crinkled in disapproval. "I told her, what are you going to do? Support that man for the rest of your life? He's incapable of holding down a job. Why, he thinks he's Indiana Jones." Exasperation overwhelmed her sorrowful expression. "Mona is—*was*—my daughter. I'll never stop loving her. But, for the life of me, I will never understand her taste in men. She-She was always attracted to the wrong kind."

Naturally, I was dumbfounded by her cavalier dismissal of Mick. Instantly I leaped to my friend's defense. "I understand she married a very successful attorney—"

"Who threw away a lucrative practice with one of Seattle's most prestigious law firms to defend animal-loving ... *hippies!*" Ruth interrupted. "I knew there was something wrong with Michael. I could tell. He had that restless gleam in his eye. That's the key. That restless gleam. That's the man you have to watch out for. You'll never be happy if you're married to him." She shook her head sadly. "Mona could have gone to Brandeis if she'd wanted. I don't think I'll ever understand it. The men she chose ... first Michael, then Jonathon." Deep sigh. "Although I suppose I'm hardly the one to talk, considering my experience with Leon."

That had to be Mona's father, I guessed. The intervening years hadn't quite washed away the animosity.

Polite Angie smile. "I'm afraid I don't understand."

"And I'm afraid I'm not going to explain, Anne Marie. There are some things a woman does not discuss. Let's just say I had ample reason to seek a divorce."

"I didn't mean to offend you, Mrs. Hanauer."

"That's quite all right, dear." Seeking to make amends for her frosty outburst, Ruth stood and gestured at the kitchen doorway. "Let's have some tea. I know Lisa could certainly use a cup."

Rising from the sofa, I asked, "What's going to happen now?"

Ruth flashed a hasty glance of inquiry.

"With your son-in-law, I mean."

"Former son-in-law!"

Chastened, I added, "I hear he's been charged."

"That's correct." Her gaze drifted to the tall window. I watched the sorrowful shadows steal across her face. "I suppose the jury will find him guilty. Then they'll lock him away for the rest of his miserable life."

"You sound as if he's guilty."

"He *is* guilty!" The depth of her antipathy stunned me. I didn't think this little woman capable of such passion. "He murdered my daughter. Just like he said he would!"

Now *that* threw me for a loop. *"What?"*

"He beat Mona to death. Then he threw Mona in the sea, hoping the police would think it an accident. He hated my daughter—!"

"You sound so sure—" I cut in.

"I *am* sure!" Blue eyes blazed at me. "Michael threatened my daughter when she asked him for a divorce. Mona told me all about it. She said he flew into a rage. Shouting at her. Pushing over furniture. My daughter was terrified."

I said nothing. But I was remembering my chat with Mick at Cedar Creek. Remembering his reluctance to discuss the divorce. Wondering what else he might have hidden from me.

"There's no doubt whatsoever in my mind." Ruth's chin lifted angrily. "Michael Grantz murdered my daughter. And I hope he spends the rest of his miserable life in the state penitentiary!"

Chapter Five

I spent the remainder of Thursday morning on Dollar Avenue, scouting out Mona's old store. Heritage Antiques occupied the first floor of the Campbell Building. Like its neighbors on both sides of the avenue, it dated from the Age of Teddy. Red brick structure, three stories high, with white Italianate brackets and tall paired windows.

Sometime in the Thirties, someone had done extensive renovation on the first floor, replacing the front door with one of those recessed entryways. Wall-sized windows converged at the steel cage protecting the front door, offering the casual shopper a luxurious array of antique merchandise. Telltale dust streaks frosted the arms of the oak dinner chairs. Down in the corner stood a large sign reading *For Lease - Tatoosh Realty - Call (206) 555-2647.*

Rounding the building's corner, I stepped into a narrow asphalt alleyway and surveyed the brick wall. The anti-Semitic graffiti had been completely erased, leaving only bright red spots on an otherwise dull brick surface.

Seeing nothing that could help me in my quest, I decided to break for lunch. Exchanging nods and neighborly smiles with the midday crowd, I strolled into a seafood cafe called the Drift Net. The cafe offered a wide selection of clams, steamed or fried. Indeed, just about every species in the

Strait of Juan de Fuca. Razor, bent-nose, horseneck and littleneck.

Sorry, but I'm not a devotee of Washington shellfish. I tried the geoduck, pronounced *gooey-duck*, during my first trip to the San Juans, and it was just like chewing an eraser.

So I stuck with familiar finny friends. One item intrigued me. *Flattie $4.95*. This turned out to be a rather large halibut, as round as a coffee table but skinny enough to slither through the slats of a venetian blind. The kind they take photos of on the docks of Skagway.

Following a tasty lunch consisting of flattie filet, French fries, coleslaw and cranberry sauce, I paid the check and hit the streets once more. Strong winds had splintered the Port Wyoochee overcast, offering unimpeded views of the mountains the Klallam call the Hohadhun. Better known as the Olympics to you recent arrivals to our continent. Sunlight gleamed off the snowy peaks. I halted at the corner of Dollar Avenue and Fourth Street, marvelling at the panoramic view of the waterfront.

Like my hometown of Duluth, Port Wyoochee is situated on a steep hillside leading down to the water—in this case, an inlet known as Luckutchee Bay. The town's main avenues run along a series of ancient Pleistocene beaches. There are four such terraces, with their corresponding avenues— Ahtalah, Hiaqua, Dollar and Crosshaul—before you reach the ridge and Summit Avenue. The streets begin at Summit and run straight down the hillside into Sawdust Flats.

From my vantage point on Dollar, I could see the ferry dock and the seaside restaurants, the placid sapphire bay, distant sandy Sahale Point, and the whitecaps of the strait. The sea breeze ruffled my long raven hair and wool flannel blazer, carrying with it the pungent odors of fresh-caught fish and moldering seaweed.

All at once, a familiar gravelly voice rumbled behind me. *"Machiya, Noozis! Ginoondaam ina ezhiwebak noongom?"*

I turned, and there was my grandfather, his rugged fea-

83

tures split in a welcoming grin. He wore a quilted Northwest Territory flannel shirt and a pair of tan Wrangler jeans. His lank white hair flickered in the breeze.

"No, Chief," I replied, answering his question. "I haven't heard what's happening today. What's up?"

Aged expression of impatience. *"Ikigo anishinabemowin, Noozis."* His wary gaze took in the white passersby. *"Endaniibowa gitchimookomaanag jiigi."* His gnarled brown hand waggled in invitation. *"Wewiib! Ambe!"*

So, to avoid being overheard by people of European ancestry, I made the switch to our people's language. In Anishinabemowin, we're no longer Chief and Angie. We become *Nimishoo* and *Noozis*. Grandfather and Granddaughter.

Falling into step beside him, I inquired, *"Aandi gaa-izhaayan noomaya?"*

"Been up in Tacoma, *Noozis*, getting that false identification you wanted." Shaking his head ruefully, Chief reached into his pants pocket. "It didn't come cheap. That printer you recommended got a little nervous about the license."

"What's his problem? It's a South Dakota license. There's no law against making a facsimile of an out-of-state license."

"Still, he wanted three hundred for it. Cash. Tens and twenties. Fortunately, I was prepared." He handed me a folded envelope.

Peeling it open, I asked, "Any problem getting the credit card?"

Chief shook his head. "Your phone-in application went through, just like you said. They called me at the motel. I gave Anne Marie Nahkeeta a glowing recommendation."

As we strolled along, I examined my grandfather's booty. There was my South Dakota license in Anne Marie's name, my SunWest credit card, a phone bill from Pacific Northwest Bell, and a handful of newly printed business cards. Not what you would call an ironclad cover, but it would serve me well during my sojourn in Port Wyoochee.

"What have you learned thus far, *Noozis?*"

So I brought Chief up to date, describing my interview of Sister Mary Katherine, my discovery of Mona's marijuana stash, and my chat with Ruth Hanauer. Finishing up, I remarked, "*Nimishoo*, didn't you stop at Bremerton during the war?"

Quick glance at me. "Did I tell you about that?"

"Years ago. When I had that seventh grade history paper, remember? You were recuperating at a hospital in Hawaii, and they let you go home early."

"That's because I had the points." A strange faraway look altered Chief's obsidian eyes. He always gets that way whenever he talks about the great war of the 1940s. "Combat rifleman. Participation in three amphibious assaults. Wounded in action on Okinawa. I had points out the kazoo. Fleet HQ was set to ship me to San Francisco. But there was this gunny sergeant, and he owed me one. So I shipped out aboard a destroyer headed for Bremerton. Bummed a jeep ride into Seattle, bought my ticket to Duluth, and travelled home in style on the Northern Pacific."

"Did you ever hear about Americans being interned on the base?"

He gave me a strange look. "Americans?"

"Rightwingers, *Nimishoo*. American Nazis."

His aged Anishinabe mouth tensed thoughtfully. "You know, child, come to think of it . . . I do remember something about that. There was a handful of those home-grown goosesteppers sweating it out in the brig."

"Including a woman named Thurber?"

Chief shrugged. "Only thing I remember is the scuttlebutt. They had some seig-heilers under psychiatric observation. A Navy commander had custody of 'em."

Okay, so I was reaching. I was wondering if Lemuel Thurber had some sort of long-standing grudge against the Hanauers. Wondering if perhaps he blamed them for his mother's imprisonment.

Noting my sour expression, Chief remarked, "What's wrong, *Noozis?*"

"Everything," I complained. "Mick wasn't entirely honest with me. There was a lot he held back. Those teenaged eye-witnesses on Orcas Island. The fact that he threatened Mona before their divorce."

"All you have is her mother's word on that."

"You didn't talk to him, *Nimishoo*. I did. Mick didn't want to discuss the divorce at all. Even after four years, it was still eating away at him."

"Are you wondering if maybe he's guilty?"

Forlorn sigh. "I don't know what to think. Why wasn't he open and up-front with me?"

"Maybe he *is* the one who did it."

Flustered Angie glance. "I don't think so, *Nimishoo*. If Mick killed her, then what has he got to gain by dragging me into it?"

"A desperate man isn't always logical, *Noozis*."

"*Nimishoo*, if Mickey Grantz wanted to roll me over, all he had to do was call the guard. There was no need to send me charging off to Port Wyoochee." Troubled frown. "He really thinks I can save him. Me, I'm not so sure. There's an awful lot of circumstantial evidence."

"What about jealousy as a motive for Mick?" Chief asked. "You said yourself Mona was living with a man until recently."

"Jon Waterman." Skeptical frown. "I don't think so, *Nimishoo*. I don't think Mick was aware of her affair with Waterman. For one thing, he mentioned Waterman's name in passing. Told me Waterman used to fly Mona over to the San Juans. There was no emotion in his voice at all. He talked about Waterman as if he were just another guy on the street."

"You could be right. Judging from the way he felt about Mona, there's no way he could've been so blase about it. If he'd known Mona had been sleeping with Waterman, you'd have seen some reaction."

Turning to my grandfather again, I changed the subject. "A little earlier, you said something's going on today. What?"

"Remember that environmental group Mona Hanauer belonged to?"

"Sure! The Gemini River Greenway Committee. What about it?"

"They're having a meeting this afternoon at the library. It was on the radio. That woman you mentioned . . ."

"Which one?"

"Georgianna Waterman. The current chairwoman. Think she's any relation to the floatplane pilot?"

My obsidian eyes gleamed with sudden interest. "I don't know, *Nimishoo.*" Smile of gratitude. "Thanks, anyway. That's my next stop."

"Anything you want me to do while you're busy rubbing elbows with the avant garde?"

"Well, you could make the rounds of the taverns," I suggested. "There has to be one or two in town catering to the millworkers."

"What am I looking for?"

"Idle conversation, *Nimishoo.* I want you to drop Dolan's name a lot. Let's see what kind of reaction you get. Let's find out how well Kulshan Paper has weathered the recession."

"Do you think Mona Hanauer was a threat to the company?"

"Mickey seems to think so." My smile turned grim. "Let's find out if he's right."

The public library occupied the corner lot at Hiaqua and Second, one block uphill from City Hall. Back in 1910, Andrew Carnegie had made it his gift to the town. Nestled against the steep hillside, it was a two-story yellow brick building with cement keystones, oversized arched windows and a decorative balustrade.

Shortly before four o'clock, I strolled through the oak-trimmed lobby. A pair of enthusiastic college coeds promptly buttonholed me and shoved a slew of flyers into my hands. They seemed delighted to learn that I had come for the meeting.

The auditorium resembled an old-time British music hall with its small velvet-curtained stage and polished oakwood floor. Three dozen foldout chairs formed a crude semicircle around the stage. Standing by the doorway, I gave the top flyer a hasty read. It was a photocopied clipping from the *Port Angeles News*.

KULSHAN TO APPEAL EPA RULING

Port Wyoochee, Wash. (AP) - The Kulshan Paper Company has filed an appeal in U.S. Circuit Court to lift the citation and fine imposed three months ago by the Environmental Protection Agency.

The EPA cited Kulshan Paper for failure to remove the decades-old sludge bed from the west shore of Sahale Point. Local environmentalists have complained that the accumulated wastes are a "biological hazard."

Rolf Lauridsen, Kulshan Paper's general manager, said the waste accumulation was the fault of the mill's previous owner. "A corporate entity," he added, "that no longer exists.

"Our firm acquired the Kulshan mill twenty years ago," Lauridsen said. "Our waste management has always fallen within acceptable state and federal parameters."

Lauridsen claimed that "EPA bureaucrats and la-la-la environmentalists" were "seriously affecting the profitability" of the company, which is Port Wyoochee's largest employer.

Then an elderly lady graciously invited me to sample the committee's refreshments. Flashing a grateful smile, I made my way over to the long table, poured myself a cup of sugarless java, and then joined the nearest committee quartet, introducing myself as Anne Marie and voicing my support for the cleanup.

Two of the chatters drifted away, leaving me engaged in lively conversation with Carol Shea and Marcella Caputo. Carol was a student at Yennis County Junior College, a tall young woman verging on anorexia, with fine brown hair and a beauty pageant smile. She wore a lengthy green lambswool sweater and skintight black slacks. Several women of my acquaintance would kill to look that good in stirrup pants. Marcella was a few years older, a secretary at Pacific Northwest Bell, and dressed for the part in a navy blue blazer, a white crépe de Chine blouse and a light gray dirndl skirt. She had curly jet black hair that caressed her shoulders, a Sicilian nose, sultry mahogany-colored eyes, and a smile that hinted at some experience in juggling boyfriends.

Carol refilled her yellow-and-white paper cup. No Styrofoam here. This group was committed to biodegradable throwaways. "How'd you hear about us, Anne Marie?"

"You Geminis are making a real name for yourselves," I replied, trying to remember everything Mick had told me. "Our group in Spokane heard about how you got the EPA after Kulshan."

"That was Mona's doing," Marcella remarked.

"Mona?" Angie the Echo.

"Mona Hanauer. She was Mona Grantz back then. She took up her maiden name when she came home after the divorce," Marcella explained.

Carol made a wry face. "That was way before my time. I was still in high school."

I tossed out another lure. "I hear Mona was a real go-getter."

"The best!" Grinning, Marcella brushed a wing of black hair away from her face. "She blew the whistle on those Kulshan bastards the first time. They've been on the EPA's shit list ever since."

Frowning, Carol took a sip. "Georgianna's no slouch, either."

Condescending smile from Marcella. "Darling, there is absolutely no comparison. Mona knew how to lead. She motivated people to get the job done. All Georgie ever does is scream into microphones."

"She's doing the best she can." The younger woman turned defensive all at once. "It's a lot harder for groups like ours today."

"Really? Do you know how many times Mona and her ex got busted for trespassing on Kulshan property?"

"I know, I know. I've heard all the old war stories." Carol did a ladylike about-face, crushed her paper cup in a most unladylike manner, and dropped it in the trash bin. "If you two will excuse me . . ."

I watched Carol slip into another cluster of Gemini activists, then glanced at my brunette companion. "Georgie has her defenders, it seems."

Apologetic grimace. "You'll have to forgive Carol. She wasn't around in the bad old days."

"You have a problem with Ms. Waterman's leadership style?"

"Sort of. Georgianna's a control freak. She spends too much time trying to convince you she's the boss." Marcella's dark eyes surveyed the crowd. "You know, two weeks ago, we had twice as many members. The list gets shorter with every meeting."

"How did Georgianna become chairperson?"

Shrug and sigh. "Power vacuum, I guess. A couple of people tried it after the founder, Mrs. Leighton, died. Then Georgie got the top spot. She was one of the founding members. She's a librarian. Works right here in the building. Good thing, too. We Geminis aren't exactly welcome elsewhere in town." Lush lips twisted in an uncertain frown. "It's not a personal thing, Anne Marie. It's just that Georgie puts too much emphasis on the wrong things. We ought to be out there recruiting new members. Georgie would rather stage media events. She sends out weekly news releases."

Slowly the facts sank in. "Georgianna ran the committee before Mona returned home."

"Yeah. Little over a year, I guess. After Mona joined, our group really caught fire. I actually began to look forward to meetings. There was so much energy you could feel it crackling." Her hands fluttered delicately. "It was like Mona was a little generator, and she charged up everybody." Rueful smile. "Georgie got voted out at the next annual meeting. She wasn't too pleased about that. And then there was that mess with Jon-boy."

Surprised Angie look. "She's related to Jon Waterman?"

"They used to be married." Marcella showed an arch smile. "That's something else that changed when Mona moved back home."

"Mona met Waterman here?"

"You bet!" She nodded briskly. "Georgie dragged him to one of our meetings. That was the biggest mistake she ever made. You'd never know it to look at him—he's so *goony!* But Jon is quite the ladies' man."

Teasing tone from Angie. "And how would you know?"

"Personal experience!" Marcella offered a sly wink. "I was sunbathing on Sahale Point a few years back. I swear, that man spent at least an hour giving me the eye. Then he comes over and asks if I need any help smoothing on the Coppertone. 'No thanks,' I told him. Then—I swear to

91

God!—he stands there real macho and says, 'Tell me, babe. What's your sign?' So I said, 'Do Not Disturb!' "

I laughed out loud. Displaying a puckish grin, Marcella added, "He got all red in the face, gave me a really nasty look, and stomped away. That is one fragile male ego there."

"Weren't you worried, Marce?"

"Not much," she replied, putting down her coffee cup. "My friend Bethany was right nearby. And I've got three brothers. They're big, Sicilian and deckhands aboard my Uncle Louie's boat. Any guy comes on too strong with me— he's going to be flipping through the Yellow Pages, looking for the section under *Plastic Surgeons*."

I finished my coffee. Jon Waterman sounded like a bit of a ladies' man, an incorrigible skirt chaser. A bit like Mick. It seemed strange that such a strong-minded woman as Mona Hanauer should be drawn to that type. Well, there's no accounting for taste.

"Why did Georgianna bring her husband to the meetings?" I asked.

"Guess she wanted to keep an eye on him," Marcella replied. "That Jon—he sure had the hots for Mona."

"Was it that obvious?"

"Gosh, no! Thinking back on it, though, maybe we should've guessed. I mean, Jon had never shown any interest in the Greenway committee before." Her voice became a gossipy whisper. "First I heard about it was the meeting when Georgie got up and began screaming at Mona. She called Mona a tramp and a husband-stealer. That Georgie has a mouth on her. Her language pretty near took the varnish right off the stage."

"And then?"

"Georgie quit the committee for a time. Then she began coming around again. That was about the time things cooled off between Jon and Mona."

"Did Mona break it off?"

"Don't ask me!" Grinning, Marcella leaned against the refreshments table. "I wasn't Mona's social secretary. That lady kept her love life pretty private. All I know is, Waterman moved out of her place ... oh, about four months ago."

I'd taken that line of inquiry as far as I could. Any further prods were certain to stir suspicion. Marcella might start wondering if I'd come to the Geminis' meeting for the juicy gossip.

Just then, a shrill alto voice cried out. "Ladies! You can discuss the man situation *after* the meeting. Some of us would like to get started."

Marcella's resentful gaze streaked toward the stage. Mine followed, and I caught a glimpse of the speaker, a stern-featured woman in her middle thirties. She had an oval face which tended to thicken along the jawline. High forehead, vulnerable gray-green eyes set somewhat apart, faint eyebrows, and the rigid nose of a British nanny, a stalwart proboscis turning upward at the tip. I'd say her mouth was her best feature. Perfectly proportioned lips that were firm and full. Her hair was sleek, glossy and brownish blond, done up in a no-nonsense French braid.

A few people in the audience tittered. Showing everyone an apologetic smile, I took a seat in the back row. The lady at the podium shot me an irritated look. How dare you gossip, Angie, when I'm about to speak. My smile vanished. I decided that her oversized diamond-pattern sweater did absolutely nothing for her figure.

"I hope you've all seen today's *News!*" That clarion alto carried into the far crannies of the auditorium. "Kulshan Paper wants the EPA to let them off the hook. The company's in trouble, they say, and it's all the fault of those 'la-la-la environmentalists.' You know who that is, don't you? He's talking about us, my friends. He's talking about you and me!"

Her white-knuckled fist shook the group's flyer. "The neofascist news media is taking Kulshan's side in this. There isn't even a mention of what Kulshan's done to our river.

93

The bloody company treats it like their own personal property! The shit that comes back down their spillway doesn't even qualify as water! A glass of it would kill a full-grown man. So you can imagine what it's doing to the salmon!"

Stage lights heightened the perspiration gleam on Georgianna's face. Teeth gritted, she plunged on. "Mr. Hefeneider! You remember, don't you? You remember what the salmon runs were like when you were a kid."

"Damned right!" bellowed a white-haired old man. "There used to be hundreds along the riverbank after the spawn."

"Right!" Georgianna cried, her voice shriller than ever. "Hundreds! Thousands! You had to walk over them to get to the river. Tell me, people, when's the last time you saw a salmon in the Gemini?"

She had the crowd at fever pitch. I sneaked a glance at Marcella. The brunette sat there with her arms folded, plainly unimpressed with the speaker's histrionics. On the other hand, the coeds could barely contain their enthusiasm. One raised a clenched fist. "Tell 'em, Georgie!"

Looking as sincere as Phil Donahue, Georgianna removed the microphone from its mount. Then she took her harangue to the edge of the stage. "Bee . . . oh . . . dee! We all know what that is, don't we? Biological oxygen demand!" The bulky floral skirt swirled about her muscular calves. "It's how we determine the harmful effects of toxic effluents on the water."

A young red-haired woman, intent on getting into the act, stood up suddenly, hugging her textbooks to her small bosom. "According to the EPA study, Kulshan wastewater has a B.O.D. of fifteen!"

"That's right!" Georgianna's face betrayed a measure of irritation. She didn't appreciate the interruption. Hers was definitely a solo act. "Kulshan waste requires a minimum of fifteen pounds of dissolved oxygen to decompose. In other words, that waste is using up the dissolved oxygen the fish and crustaceans need to survive." She paced the edge of the stage. "The salmon is a cold-water fish. It needs a habitat with an oxygen level of five parts per million. My distinguished predecessor"—judging from the acid in her tone, that had to be Mona—"commissioned a water quality survey of the river. They found that the water at the mouth of the Gemini had a dissolved-oxygen level of two point four parts per million. Upstream, the water just beneath the dam was one point three parts per million. And that's why you don't see any salmon in the Gemini, ladies and gentlemen. There's no oxygen for them to breathe!"

Sensing the crowd's receptiveness, Georgianna went for the kill. "For ninety years, the Kulshan Paper Company has been dumping their shit in our river. And where did it all end up? Out there!" A dramatic forefinger swivelled toward stage left. "Out there on Sahale Point! You've got tons and tons of contaminants sitting on the bottom out there. Ninety years of contaminants! And do you know how big that Kulshan sludge pile is? Eight hundred feet wide and twenty feet high! Twenty feet—that's a bloody two-story house!"

Waving the flyer like a war flag, she shouted, "Mr. Rolf Lauridsen doesn't seem to understand B.O.D. So we're going to educate him!"

"Fucking straight!" hollered a college student.

Georgianna's gray-green eyes sparkled. Oh, she was truly in her element now. Shrill alto cry. "What are we going to do, people?"

Just then, the elderly woman who had offered me refreshments raised a timid hand. "Maybe if we all wrote to Congress . . ."

A fearsome rumbling undertone drowned her out. Sitting down again, she aimed a timid apologetic smile at the fuming collegians.

The former Mrs. Waterman wanted no part of any such reasonable solutions. Face reddening, she screeched, "Stop Kulshan! Shut it down!"

The college crowd took up the cry, adding embellishments of their own. "Stop pollution! *Shut it down!* Fuck Lauridsen! *Shut it down!*"

"We're going to shut down Kulshan Paper!" Georgianna roared. "And it's going to stay shut until the fucking capitalist patriarchy agrees to remove their sludge pile from Sahale Point. There is going to be an end to the earth-raping, antihumanist, masculine imperative, and it's going to start right here—right here in Port Wyoochee!"

Cries of jubilation. Basking in the flood of admiration and approval, Georgianna concluded, "I move that we demonstrate at the mill gates tomorrow afternoon at three o'clock. All in favor say aye!"

A tremendous whoop exploded from the college crowd. Most of them voted with both hands. Grinning youthful faces, earsplitting chaos and impromptu clog-dancing. I counted the hands, divided by two, and realized that Georgianna only had the support of forty percent of the people present. Looking toward the door, I saw the senior citizens and the families with children already making an unobtrusive exit.

"Fuck Lauridsen! Shut it down!"

Tuning out their megadecibel chant, I stepped into the center aisle, sidestepped departing guests, and weaved a crooked path toward the stage. Georgianna had left the podium. She was on the main floor, her slender back to the throng, gathering stray flyers as she prepared to leave.

Feigning a smile of admiration, I made my approach. "Ms. Waterman?"

She reacted like a startled elk, turning abruptly. Gray-green eyes narrowed in suspicion. Tiny frown of disapproval as she surveyed my wool flannel suit. Evidently her rancor wasn't limited to white males from the private sector. It extended to anyone with an income beyond the librarian's tax bracket.

"Yes?" The speech had definitely strained her vocal cords.

"My name is Anne Marie Nahkeeta. I want to commend you on the wonderful job you're doing."

"Thank you."

"A fine speech. Tell me, are you really going through with that demonstration?"

Curiosity twinkled in those hostile eyes. "Are you a reporter?"

"Not quite." Bright Angie smile. "I'm an investments advisor. I just moved back to Port Wyoochee."

Learning that I wasn't a media representative, she lost all interest in me. "How marvelous for you." I found myself facing her shoulder blades. "And now, if you'll excuse me . . ."

"Well, I was hoping we could chat for a moment."

"I'm afraid that's just not possible, Ms. Nahkeeta." Stacking her extra flyers atop a ring-bound notebook, she shot me a glance of curt dismissal. "I'm quite busy. Sorry."

Brushing right past me, Georgianna headed for the doorway. I stayed glued to her heels. Relentless Angie.

"I'd like very much to join the committee," I said, trying to slow her headlong rush. "Perhaps we could meet and—"

"You'd better talk to Alma Lagerquist. She's our membership secretary." The librarian left an invisible contrail of frost in her wake. "Good *day*, Ms. Nahkeeta!"

Friday morning, October sixteenth, found Port Wyoochee huddled beneath another impenetrable overcast. I did a lot of early-morning dashing about, hoping to finish some vital chores before the rain arrived. First and foremost was a trip to the local offices of the Washington Department of Licensing. There I turned in my bogus South Dakota driver's license, submitted my telephone bill as proof of residence, took the written exam, posed for a face-front photo, and received a legitimate State of Washington license in the name of *Anne Marie Nahkeeta*.

Once armed with a legit license, I dropped in at the Avis

office on Ahtalah Avenue, gave my SunWest credit card a workout, and drove away in a brand-new powder blue Mercury Topaz.

Well, thus far I hadn't had much luck scaling the legs of the Mona triangle. Georgianna had been a complete washout. But there was still her ex-husband—Mona Hanauer's erstwhile live-in—the floatplane pilot.

I steered the Topaz west on Ahtalah, all the way out to the end, and came upon the town's small but thriving industrial park. Turning right, I tooled up Sahale Point Road, heading for the village and marina the locals called Charterboat Row.

The peninsula reminded me vaguely of Orcas with its narrow road, shadowy forests and curbside salal. Here and there I spied a weathered cabin tucked away in the greenery. Windbent hemlock and red cedar gradually petered out, giving way to rolling sand dunes and sere brown eelgrass. I drove by a huge cement emplacement—bunkers for the old U.S. Coast Artillery. Then the road veered toward the bay side, offering misty glimpses of Port Wyoochee's fabled waterfront two miles due south.

I parked beside the white clapboard general store. The wharves were vacant. That was to be expected, of course. Uncle Louie, Marcella's brawny brothers and the rest of the fishing fleet had put to sea a good five hours ago. Several feet beyond the store stood an aging airplane hangar. Out in front of it, a barnacled dock stretched over water. Out at the end, bobbing at the end of her tether, was a white Kenmore Super Turbine Beaver sporting some very sharp bronze and gold livery.

Into the general store walked your Angie, carefully cradling the Minolta camera she'd purchased at Jungert's Photo Supplies earlier that morning. I was in an Emma Peel mood, dressed for damp weather and fashionably turned out in a soft black leather anorak, snug black stirrup pants, and black Ipanema riding boots. I went straight to the counter, asked the heavyset female cashier for a roll of 35 millimeter film, and inquired about the plane outside.

The cashier lady referred me to a man sitting alone in one of the store's luncheon booths. Georgianna's ex was a little over thirty. A lean and sturdy six-foot-one, unless I missed my eagle-eyed Anishinabe guess, with a vulpine face and a sharp aquiline nose and wearing a pair of steel-rimmed glasses. Prominent cheekbones, narrow chin, bristly eyebrows and dry reddish auburn hair parted on the right. His part was perfectly straight—his glasses, as clean as the windows at Bloomingdale's. Unfortunately, a tuft of rebellious hair sprouted at the peak of his head, defeating the effort at diligent grooming. A diehard cowlick that defied all attempts at restraint. Very fit, this guy. His shoulders added bulk to his brown bomber jacket, and his belly was as flat as a prizefighter's. Beneath the jacket, he wore a striped broadcloth shirt and a pair of navy Dockers.

All at once, my gaze was captured by the porcelain mug in his big-knuckled hand. The mug bore the logo of the Algoma Central Railway. Surprised Angie blink. I hadn't expected to see one of those way out here.

Waterman smiled as I approached his booth. He had a nice smile, too. Very wide and friendly, with just a hint of impending naughtiness.

"Hello." His appreciative glance started with my riding boots and travelled upward, lingering on the power curves. Ladykiller Jon. "And what can I do for you, Miss . . . ?"

"Nahkeeta. Anne Marie Nahkeeta." I kept my tone cool and businesslike, ignoring the frank stare. "Are you Mr. Waterman?"

"That's right." Letting go of the Algoma Central mug, he gestured at the empty seat across from him. "Sit down, please. And there's no need for such formality. *Jon* will do just fine."

"I understand you run an air taxi service, Jon."

Nodding, he added, "Where would you like to go?"

"Nowhere in particular. Just a quick spin around the bay area."

His keen emerald-eyed gaze focused on my camera. "If you're doing some photo-mapping, you may have to wait a few days. There's a storm system coming down the Slot."

"This is strictly low-altitude stuff." Pleasant Angie smile. "Survey of potential real estate."

"When are you thinking of going?"

Careless shrug. "We can go right now, if you're ready."

"All right." He picked up his mug. "Let me file a flight plan with the county tower and top off at the gas dock. And we'll be off."

Twenty minutes later, there was your Angie, following Georgianna's ex down the barnacled dock to the floatplane. Waterman hopped nimbly onto the Edo float, took hold of the nylon line, and pulled the plane closer to the dock. I ducked as the aluminum wing passed overhead. Glancing upward, I noted the dipping aileron and the large black identification number—N5973WJ.

In no time at all, the Beaver was freely afloat on Luckutchee Bay. Nestled securely in the passenger seat, I buckled my safety harness, loaded my camera with film, and then grimaced as my knees clouted the underside of the dash. Waterman ran through his pre-flight checklist, switched on the radio, primed the engine, and then turned the key. Solenoids clicked. The starter sputtered to life. White smoke spurted from the turbo exhaust pipes on either side of the cowling. The broad-bladed propellor began to whirl.

"Have you ever flown before, Anne Marie?"

I nodded. I'd put in some floatplane time with my good friend Bob Stonepipe back home in northern Minnesota. But I wasn't about to discuss that with a possible suspect. Casual shrug. "Once or twice."

The engine din smoothed itself into a vibrant *thrummmm*. The Beaver fishtailed across the choppy surface, her nose turning to meet the wind.

"It'll be a bit bumpy at first," Jon said, putting both hands on the yoke. "No need to worry, though."

An accurate prognosticator, Jon Waterman. The Beaver began porpoising as we picked up speed. Again and again my spine thumped the padded seat. Waterman's grin betrayed his enjoyment. Leaning toward the dash, he switched on the wipers, then punched the throttle knob forward. "She'll smooth out. The trick is getting her up on the step."

"The step?" I echoed.

Sidelong grin at me. "Getting her trimmed good and proper so she shoots along like a speedboat." He gave the throttle another firm push. I glanced at the RPM indicator. Bright red numerics read 1800. As unperturbed as a moose, Waterman slowly eased the yoke backward.

"The second trick, Anne Marie, is getting unstuck from the water."

Waterman turned the yoke slightly, then stepped down hard on the left pedal. "First we lift this float out of the water. Like soooo." I felt the cockpit tilt toward the right. He repeated the same maneuver with his other foot. "Now the other one."

The right float came free with a muted splash. The Beaver rose suddenly like a castaway kite.

"See?" The ladykiller grin widened. "No problem at all."

As with most floatplanes, the Beaver underwent a long and gradual climbout. Those floats tend to add to the wind resistance. Rarely do pilots win speed races in floatplanes.

Our flight path took us along the strait's southern shore, from Murdock Creek to Pillar Point. Removing the lens cap, I looked out the windshield and saw Mount Muller poking its snow-clad peak through the boiling gray overcast. Beyond my side window, Sahale Point, looking like a gigantic letter

C, slid underneath the wing. Taking aim with the Minolta, I began shooting.

Thoroughly at ease in the pilot's seat, Waterman asked, "Why are you taking those pictures?"

"I'm interested in site development." Effortlessly I slipped into my famous Angie, Girl Realtor, persona. "There's a big market for shoreside condominiums these days."

Just then, an abandoned factory complex passed beneath the propellor arc. Lowering my camera, I inquired, "What's that?"

Craning his neck for a quick look, Waterman smiled. "Torpedo Junction." His smile became rueful. "The plant used to build torpedoes for the U.S. Navy. I'm afraid there wasn't much call for them during Desert Storm. The Navy cancelled the contract two years ago, and the company went belly-up."

"How many people worked there?"

"Pretty close to nine hundred. The closing was quite a blow to the local economy." I could feel the weight of his curious gaze. "Tell me, Anne Marie, are you here on holidays?"

"Nope! I'm a recent returnee. And here to stay." Impish Angie smile. "How about you, Jon? What part of Ontario are you from?"

Waterman did a sudden doubletake. "How did you know I was from Ontario?"

"You said *holidays* instead of *vacation*. That made you a Canadian." I pointed at the railway mug in the plastic coffee caddy. "The Algoma country is in Ontario. East side of Lake Superior. You're a long way from home, Jon."

He mirrored my grin. "Very observant of you."

"So where are you from?"

"Geraldton."

"Ahhhh, a Nipigon boy."

All at once, he gave me a long, searching look. "You've been there?"

Watch it, princess! Anne Marie grew up in Spokane, remember? She shouldn't be so familiar with the Lake Superior region.

Quick save. "I went to Toronto right after graduation. Figured to try life above the border. I went on a lot of job interviews, but no luck, though. Passed through Geraldton on the way to Winnipeg."

He seemed satisfied with my explanation. "I know what you mean. Jobs aren't all that easy to find." Another curious look. "Are you truly serious about those condos?"

"Well, if I can get the financial backing, I just might be able to pull it off. There's a lot of that going on back East. Taking old factory buildings and converting them into condos. It's rare to come upon an abandoned property right on the water, though."

Waterman put the Beaver into a long, looping turn. A dolorous drone emanated from the engine. Keeping a close watch on the turn-and-bank indicator, he said, "Perhaps you'd best speak to Mr. Dolan."

Waterman's casual use of the name took me by surprise. Fortunately, I managed to keep my expression unruffled. "Who?"

"John A. Dolan. He's president of Luckutchee Real Estate," Waterman explained. "You'll want to talk to him if you're truly serious about developing the junction."

"Know where I can reach him?"

He gave my question a few seconds' thought. "Try Bert Reisbeck at the chamber of commerce."

"Does Dolan hold the title to that property?" I asked.

"No." Shaking his head, Waterman glanced at the compass. "He's merely marketing the property for the Alworth Trust."

"Is Dolan a friend of yours?"

"Not really. Just a steady customer."

"Does he do a lot of flying?"

"He's involved in a number of enterprises all around the sound. Usually I fly him to Seattle."

I was sorely tempted to ask Mr. Waterman if his good friend Dolan was a frequent flyer to the San Juan Islands. But I decided against it. And against any questions about Mona. Better that I kept this a casual encounter.

Showing him a mildly flirtatious Angie smile, I switched topics and asked him if there were any good watering holes in town. Preferably one that doubled as a dance club. He recommended a place called Millicent's Pub and hinted that he might show me around personally. I let the suggestion sail harmlessly past, and we spent the remainder of the flight in idle chitchat.

Coming in on final approach, I noticed that Port Wyoochee was no longer visible. A wall of mist veiled the mainland from our cockpit. Raindrops spattered the windshield. Seemingly oblivious to the worsening weather, Waterman lowered the Beaver's flaps, eased us down to wavetop height, and cut the throttle. The floats touched down with a jarring splash.

It took us ten minutes to taxi back to the dock. While Waterman lashed the plane's tether to a stanchion, I grabbed my camera and shoulder bag and made a fleet-footed dash to the store.

Once inside, I paid the pilot for the flight, complimented him on his expertise, then watched as he scribbled our arrival time in the countertop flight log. After bidding me goodbye, he carried his empty coffee mug into the back room.

Lingering at the counter, I deliberately made myself conspicuous. Dinah, the hefty cashier lady, came waddling over. She had a blunt Slavic face, a sullen lipsticked mouth, and ash blond hair curling at the neck. Rumpled Basque sweater and corduroy slacks.

"Lookin' for sumpin?" she muttered, no doubt eager to get back to cleaning the grill.

"I hear you make the best coffee on the strait, Dinah."

The lady positively simpered. "Who says that?"

"Mr. Waterman." Tilting my head toward the back room, I artfully planted my bag on the counter. Judging from the rosy color flooding her cheeks, I could see that Waterman had made at least one conquest out here on the point. "So I thought I'd find out for myself. One with cream, no sugar, please. Uh, and how about a slice of that Danish?"

Dinah beamed. Any friend of Mr. Waterman's was welcome at her lunch counter. "You'll like that, miss. I made it fresh this morning."

"Looks yummy!"

Soon Dinah was at the coffeemaker, showing me her ample backside. Sidestepping to the left, I opened the flight log and ran my finger down the page. Nope! Wrong week. Backflip a page. Nope! Another page. Ahhhhh, here we are. Wednesday, October seventh. The night Mickey and Mona were on Orcas Island. I wonder where Jon Waterman was.

A scribbled notation caught my gaze.

Departure Time	1600 hours
Destination	Nitinat, B.C.
Arrival Time	1830 hours

Weather: Sunshine, then evening fog. Winds out of the northwest. Strong gusts.

My gaze zipped to the very next entry. Thursday, October eighth.

Departure Time	0800 hours
Destination	Nanaimo, B.C.
Arrival Time	1015 hours

Interesting, I thought. At roughly the same time Sister Mary Katherine was making her discovery on that Shaw Island beach, Mona's one-time lover, Jon Waterman, was doing his pre-flight check prior to taking off from Nitinat, B.C. Wherever *that* was!

Think a minute, princess. B.C.—that's British Columbia. But where the hell is Nitinat? Oh, well, call for Rand-McNally.

So Waterman was up north, eh? Nowhere near the San Juan Islands.

Just then, I caught a flicker of motion on my visual periphery. Dinah was reaching for the cream bottle. Keeping close watch on her, I quietly closed the logbook, then took my wallet out of my shoulder bag.

I left the general store a few moments later, sipping hot coffee from a Styrofoam cup and nibbling Dinah's chock-full-of-nuts-and-calories Danish. I did a lot of thinking about Georgianna's ex-husband. I was mightily intrigued by Mr. Waterman's associations.

How do you do it, Jonathon? Juggling your membership on the Greenway committee with your job as John A. Dolan's aerial chauffeur?

For a man once married to one of Dolan's arch-enemies and gleefully bedding another, you are uncommonly friendly with Mr. Dolan.

And wasn't it kind of risky, romancing the lady Mona while she was serving on the committee with your wife?

Which leads to the next intriguing question. I tossed out a realtor's term—*hold the title*—and you didn't even blink an eye. Then you started talking about the Alworth Trust. Why does a floatplane pilot take such a keen interest in Port Wyoochee real estate?

So, Mr. Waterman, no questions about Mona for you. Not for the moment. And not until I find out exactly where you stand with Mr. John A. Dolan. I don't want you carrying tales about Angie back to the big man.

Not until I've had a crack at him first!

Chapter Six

Eleven A.M. found me at the Chamber of Commerce. If John A. Dolan was as powerful as Mickey implied, then there was no way I could get to him on my own. I needed someone to clear the path for me. So I decided to pay my respects to Bert Reisbeck, Dolan's boy at the chamber.

First, however, I made a quick change at the Parmenter House. Emma Peel wouldn't have gotten the time of day from a small-town chamber honcho like Mr. Reisbeck. So I turned the task over to Corporate Angie. Off with the black leather anorak and stirrup pants, and on with the white mock turtleneck, the short braid-trimmed V-neck jacket in brushed gray suede, and the narrow skirt with its knee-grazing hem. The hard part, of course, was trading in those comfortable boots for a pair of ouch shoes. Pointed-toe patent leather Lifestride pumps with three-inch heels.

Well, I really didn't plan on doing any long-distance hiking.

The chamber office was on Crosshaul Avenue, in a modern one-story building colored a stunning clamshell gray. Venerable Italianate bon-bons flanked it on either side. Displaying a truly radiant smile, I tock-tocked into that spacious outer office, hailed the efficient thirtyish brunette behind the walnut reception desk, presented an Anne Marie business card, and asked if I could please speak with Mr. Reisbeck.

107

The dark-haired receptionist warmed at once. She seemed quite impressed with my card. Particularly the phrase *Investments Advisor*. Pointing out a stout leather sofa, she informed me that Mr. Reisbeck would be back shortly.

While waiting for Bert, I thumbed through the chamber's promotional magazine. *Port Wyoochee—Your Home in the Scenic Northwest*. Award-winning schools. Ultra-low utility costs. Tax abatements for new industry. The usual chamber bullshit.

I was still reading when Bert Reisbeck came in. He was a short, lanky man in his early forties, nattily attired in a navy blue pinstripe Geoffrey Beene suit. A very quick and alert fellow, with a stride like a preening pintail. Poor Bert. Testosterone had not been kind to him. He must have worn out a lot of towels wiping all that face. It started at the peak of his head, swept over the faintly freckled crown, and dropped down the front side, ending in a narrow dimpled chin. Broad Scandinavian nose, heavily lidded pale blue eyes, and a taut, curving smile that showed only the upper teeth.

We shook hands. Then, taking my arm, Bert escorted me into his private office. There was a large brass nameplate on the door. *G. Bertram Reisbeck—Chamber President*.

Bert's private office was neat and well-kept, furnished in vinyl and polished cherrywood. The tiled floor looked as if it had been designed by Boris Spassky—an Art Deco checkerboard in black and white. I spotted many large framed photographs of Bert with uniformed players from the Denham High School Mariners.

I made the mistake of asking Bert about them, and he explained that he was a weekend volunteer coach for the team. He thoroughly dissected the strengths and weaknesses of each youthful player in the starting lineup and gave me a season's pass to all of their home games.

And then he started in on the Seattle Sea Hawks!

Forty minutes later, Bert suddenly remembered my presence there. I was seated in a low-backed guest chair, legs demurely crossed, ears ringing of football. Aiming a sharp glance my way, he remarked, "So you're an investments advisor, eh?"

"That's right." Polite Angie smile. "I'd like to join the chamber."

"Hey, glad to have you." Bert relaxed, leaning back in his plush swivel chair. "Got your stockbroker's ticket yet?"

"I'm taking the exam in Olympia next week. Right now, though, I'm looking around for some office space."

"Striking out on your own, eh? Good for you, Anne Marie. We need some fresh blood around here. We haven't had a stockbroker in town since old man Brunton retired back in '87. You don't mind if we talk, do you? See, I got into this CD deal last year, and it hasn't gotten out of the cellar . . ."

Within five minutes, I knew more about the Reisbeck family finances than Bert's wife. But I didn't mind. Bert had handed me the perfect opportunity to strengthen my cover.

". . . so, like I said before, Anne Marie, I'm getting screwed. The short-term CDs are paying peanuts. If I want better than five percent, I have to commit for five years or more."

"Bert, you'd probably be better off in a couple of good mutual funds," I said helpfully. I always knew that Master's in accounting from Montana State University would come in handy some day. "Even if the economy stays in the dumpster another year, you're looking at twenty percent earnings' growth in mutuals."

"You're kidding!" Bert blinked in disbelief. "Twenty percent!?"

"Well, that's the average in the funds handling small and medium growth stocks."

"What about the cash position?"

"Seven and eight percent, average."

"That good?"

"Bert, stocks have been lagging for the past five years. Upward movement in the next year could boost earnings by forty percent."

"You're shitting me!"

"Not at all." Tugging at my hem, I showed him an amiable smile. "The lower the interest rates, the better the mutual funds handling small and medium stocks will do. So long as the Fed holds down the interest rates, those funds will be doing all right."

Bert's face tensed in a leery expression. "Yeah, but what about taxes? I don't want to get clipped."

"The trick is knowing when to get in and out, Bert. The funds pay out on gains and dividends at the end of each year. Share payments are taxable income. Your best bet is to call the fund and find out their date of distribution, then invest *after* that date."

Bert was busily digesting my investment advice, doing a little math in his head. "Sounds good, sounds good." One arm on the blotter, he leaned my way. "Listen, Anne Marie, if you could put together a presentation, I'd love to have you speak at the next chamber dinner. You know, it's a great way to meet clients."

"Thanks, Bert, but maybe I ought to keep a low profile for a while."

Scandinavian features registered surprise. "Whatever for?"

Time to ease into the delicate question of Mona's murder.

"Wellllll . . . I'm a minority, a Klallam Indian." My voice had more than a trace of cool dignity. "I hear that minorities aren't exactly welcome in Port Wyoochee."

His eyes closed. Whispered groan. Stroking that broad expanse of brow with his fingertips, he muttered, "Jesus!" Frown of sympathy. "Please, Anne Marie, don't judge us by that asshole Thurber."

"Well, my mother told me a Jewish woman was killed—"

"*That* didn't happen in Port Wyoochee!" Bert interrupted, horrified by my assertion. "Your mother's got it all wrong, Anne Marie. That was no hate crime. Mona Hanauer was killed in the San Juans. I knew Mona. She was a member of the chamber. Hell, I knew the whole family. My wife's been

110

going to Doc Hanauer for her glasses for years." He shook his head sadly. "Poor Doc! Mona was his only child, you know. He was crazy about that kid."

I suppressed an arch smile. Kid, indeed! When Mona was in diapers, Bert Reisbeck was an eleven-year-old halfback in Pop Warner football.

"Did you know them well?" I asked.

"Doc and his wife, yes." Wincing, Bert corrected himself. "Ah, *ex-wife,* I mean. Doc was always pretty active in community affairs. Mona's mom kind of stayed in the background. She was mostly into Hadassah. As for Mona herself . . . well, I've only been here twelve years. Mona was gone for much of that time. I only got to know her after she opened her store."

"What sort of community affairs was he involved in?"

"Just about everything, Anne Marie. He was on the chamber board for years. United Way, Kiwanis, Lions Club, Rotary—you name it. On the board at the hospital, too."

"Is he still in practice?"

Bert nodded. "He's partners with Joe Bailey and Pam Welbes in Bay Vision Associates. They give all the school kids their eye exams."

"He likes partnerships?"

Wry chuckle. "Oh, yeah! Doc Hanauer made a good deal of money in this town, and he was always looking for way to reinvest. Did pretty well, too. The only time he ever got stung was when Kulshan took a slide in the last recession."

My ears tingled at that. "Doc was involved in Kulshan?"

"You bet! He bought in right after he cleaned up on that Alder Beach development. He built one of the first homes in there." Bert's thin fingers drummed on the blotter. "Kulshan really got hurt, though. That's why they sold controlling interest to Evergreen Industries. There was a big shuffle at Kulshan after that, and Doc lost his seat on the board." His blunt face softened in sympathy. "Poor fella. I don't think he'll ever get over Mona's death. I don't mean the way it

111

happened, either. I mean . . . Jesus! Losing your kid—I don't even like to think about it. I keep wondering what I'd do if anything ever happened to Tracey or Lynn."

I said nothing. At that second, my thoughts were in Utah. I was wondering how Aunt Della was coping with Billy's death. I made up my mind to phone her just as soon as I returned to Pierre.

Lifting his bony wrist, Bert glanced at his gold Rolex. "Listen, Anne Marie, it's just past noon. Rotary's meeting at the Halibut at one o'clock. Why don't you come along as my guest?"

"I don't want to impose on you, Bert."

"Nonsense! No trouble at all. It'll give me the chance to introduce you around. What do you say?"

I yielded to a glorious Angie smile. This was working out even better than I had hoped.

"Why, thank you, Mr. Reisbeck. I'd enjoy that very much."

The Rotary Club met every other Friday at Just For The Halibut, a four-star seafood restaurant on Shore Avenue, just east of the state ferry dock. The glass-walled ballroom stood on barnacle-encrusted pilings extending sixty feet out into the bay. Very classy interior. Spacious and roomy, with a low ceiling, thick, hand-hewn cedar beams, a polished oak floor, and a mammoth fieldstone fireplace. Bas-relief panelling framed the fireplace, giving the entire wall the appearance of a Quillayute longhouse. Totem faces and stylized killer whales. The tables seated four and were covered with spotless white linen hemmed with a broad aquamarine stripe. Walnut captain's chairs. Wooden ship models on the windowsill. Drift nets tacked to the overhead beams. The bar occupied the center of the room, flanked by a gleaming brass Chadburne.

Four years ago, when I was a lowly clerk at the tax assess-

or's office in Cameron, South Dakota, I'd always wanted to represent the town at a meeting of our local Rotary Club. My boss, however, refused to let me attend. Now I understood the reason why.

Before coming to Port Wyoochee, I had always thought of Rotary as the place where the town bigshots get together and, with quiet dignity and sober deliberation, determine the course of community affairs. And it's just not like that, people. No, it's not!

I've seen less silliness at a junior high sleepover.

I'll never forget the sergeant at arms. Or whatever he's called. Apparently, he had begun his homage to Dionysus a little earlier. The big guy stumbled from table to table, belting out *Tipperary* in A flat and periodically whapping a fellow Rotarian on the skull with a miniature fish billy. Each wallop was punctuated with a hearty shout of "Fine!" And then the wounded one had to reach into his wallet for a five-dollar bill.

Thankfully, I wasn't the only woman at the meeting. Also in attendance was Phyllis De Lancie, who chaired the local school board. The two of us shared a table with a pair of retired Rotarians, Fred Dantzler and Gene Price.

I am pleased to report that the two were perfect gentlemen. No raunchy jokes. No clandestine squeeze of Angie knees. And, fortunately, no alcoholic renditions of *Tipperary*.

I enjoyed the *salmon en papillotte*, washed it down with a glassful of Riesling, and, joining their conversation, mentioned the planned environmentalist protest at the paper mill.

"No," Phyllis responded. She was a sharp-eyed woman, aged forty-five or thereabouts, with a gaunt face and short frosted hair. "Only a handful of the kids at the high school are involved. Too many of them have parents working at Kulshan. They're afraid their parents may be laid off."

Gene Price scowled. He was a retired plumber—short, florid, bald, with merry blue eyes and a Kitchener moustache. "Maybe Georgie Waterman will hire them. She's the one with the answers to every damn thing."

"They ought to run that rabble-rouser out of town," Fred Dantzler said. At first glance, I thought he was a retired college professor. Widow's peak, aristocratic bearing, and a Mephistophelian goatee. Turned out he was the owner of Bayside Bowl-O-Rama. "Before she does some *real* damage. Sam Mooney might as well take that sign down at the industrial park. He won't be getting any more queries."

Phyllis was in dissent. "Now, Fred, it isn't that bad."

"It isn't!" His fork clattered onto the plate. "You read the Seattle paper lately? Who in their right mind is going to invest in Port Wyoochee, knowing that Waterman and her tree-huggers are gonna lay siege to their business?" Frowning, he picked up the fork. "I don't understand these liberals. I just don't understand 'em. How are people supposed to support themselves without jobs? Maybe if that Waterman broad had to work for a living—like the rest of us—she wouldn't worry so much about how many damned salmon are in the damned river!"

Phyllis's nose tilted in distaste. "Georgianna may know a lot about salmon, but she doesn't know the first thing about men." Sagacious smile. "If you handle them right, they aren't likely to stray."

Meeeeeowww, Phyllis! Boy, I'm glad I don't work in your office.

"I don't know about that, Phyll," said Gene thoughtfully. "It was kind of hard to resist that Hanauer girl."

Teasing Angie smile. "Personal experience, Mr. Price?"

Shaking his head, he added, "Naaahhhhh, second-hand. My boy Tommy had a fling with Mona in high school. She really got to him. Poor kid didn't know which pants leg to put his foot in first. What a mess that was."

"What do you mean?" I prodded.

"Well . . . Tommy was really serious about her." Embarrassment flitted across Gene's pudgy features. "Then Mona

114

tossed him over for another guy. And . . . well, Tommy just couldn't let it go. He started calling her up at all hours. I used to be good friends with Doc Hanauer. But that ended it. He called me up—furious—screaming that Tommy was harassing his daughter." Look of regret. "Oh, we talk to each other these days, Doc and I, but it ain't like it was."

Fred let out a grunt. "Well, we all know who Mona took after."

Putting down her fork, Phyllis shot him an annoyed glance. "And they say women like to gossip. Fred . . . really!"

"Come on, Phyll," he replied, reaching for a napkin. "Face facts. Like father, like daughter. It's heredity every time."

Taking that as my cue, I steered the conversation onto another tangent. "Sort of like Lem Thurber and his mother?"

"Hey! Now you're talking, Anne Marie." Fred's face tensed in an acerbic scowl. "There's another bazoonie this town could do without—Lem Thurber! Sooner or later, he's going to wind up in Steilacoom. Just like dear old Mom! What the hell are they waiting for? Why don't they just drop the butterfly net and be done with it?"

Gene grimaced in reproof. "Come on, Fred. That ain't fair."

"Don't tell me about Tessie Thurber. I grew up in Sawdust Flats." Riesling seemed to bring out the belligerency in the bowladrome owner. "Did she or did she not wind up in the state looney bin?"

Phyllis's lips tightened. "Frederick, people have been known to become ill."

"Yeah, and we know what made her ill, too." Undaunted, he wiped his mouth with the napkin. "She was up to a fifth a day when they hauled her in."

"Considering the trouble that poor woman had, her drinking problem was really no surprise." Turning to me, Phyllis added, "Theresa N. Thurber was the very first woman to run for Congress in this district. People seem to have forgotten that."

"She ran for *Congress?*" I replied, taken aback.

Curt nod from Phyllis. "She ran in 1940 on the Liberty Now ticket."

"Tessie did okay, too." You just couldn't keep Fred Dantzler out of a conversation. "She got four thousand votes. Half were invalidated, though."

"How come?" I asked.

"Very simple, Anne Marie." Fred's cynical eyes twinkled. "She ran against Thorvald Nilsson, the incumbent. Nilsson was Ned Alworth's boy in Washington. The old man put a big bundle into Nilsson's reelection campaign."

"Why?"

He looked at me as if I were learning-disabled. "Honey, if a congressman's in long enough, he gets seniority. If he has seniority, he gets the chair of a subcommittee. And then he really brings home the bacon!"

"In this case," I added, "lucrative logging contracts up in the Olympics?"

"You got it!" He let out a burst of baritone laughter. "Old man Alworth dropped a cool million on the Potomac to get Thorvald made chairman of the Forestry Subcommittee. He made it all back in one winter logging on the Tokloshe."

"So Tessie was a threat to the local establishment," I observed.

"Only briefly." Knowledgeable chuckle from Phyllis. "Fortunately for Mr. Alworth, his nephew, Roger Alworth Lindsey, just happened to be chairman of the state election commission." She shook her head wryly. "That congressional seat was one of Mr. Alworth's most valuable assets. No way was he going to hand it over to Tessie Thurber."

My apologies, fellow diners. How stupid of me. I keep forgetting what planet we're on. The one where money does all the talking.

Deciding to end our lunchtime conversation on a cheerful

note, I turned to Gene Price. "Your son . . . what's he doing these days?"

"Tommy's down in Texas. Chief accountant for a natural gas firm." Gene displayed a grin of paternal pride. "That's where he met Raquel. She's the one who took his mind off Mona. They've been married . . . oh, ten years now. Living in Beaumont. Three kids."

While Phyllis inquired about the Price grandchildren, I sneaked a glimpse at the head table. Earlier, my companions had mentioned that John A. Dolan was Rotary vice president, and I wanted a look at him before Bert Reisbeck introduced us.

No trouble at all finding Dolan. He sat at the corner of the table, a tanned, fit, iron-haired man in his early fifties. You could tell he was the point man in Port Wyoochee. Rotarians were constantly coming around, shaking hands with him, laughing at his jokes, leaning over to whisper requests for favors. Dolan did a lot of listening. And his movements, like his judgments, had an air of finality. Slow nod of agreement. Frown of disapproval. Casual wave of dismissal. He reminded me of those old-time gladiator movies. Caesar turning thumbs down in the arena.

A few minutes later, Bert brought me over, and I got a closer look at Mickey's nemesis. Immediately I knocked ten years off Dolan's age. He was in his middle forties, but his close-cropped, prematurely gray hair and wrinkled brow gave him the appearance of an older man. He had a chiselled, angular Celtic face with arched eyebrows, a narrow, tip-tilted nose, and high, rosy cheekbones. Crow's feet accentuated his porcelain blue eyes. His smile was rigid, artificial, as if it had been set in concrete. He looked as if he could snap a salmon's spine with a single bite.

Like me, Dolan was in corporate uniform. His linen suit had a distinctive tailored look. Heather gray sportscoat and trousers to match. Dark brown club tie and wingtipped shoes. His hands fascinated me. They were constantly in mo-

117

tion, nudging the empty dinner plate, tap-tapping the napkin, fondling the long-stemmed glass. Thick-knuckled, stubby-thumbed hands, with skin as tough as a sea otter's. He hadn't always been a CEO. From the look of those hands, John A. Dolan had started on the docks. Or perhaps in the fishing fleet.

"Anne Marie Nahkeeta . . ." He had a pleasant, low-pitched voice. "Bert tells me you're from Port Wyoochee."

"Long time back, Mr. Dolan."

"So what brings you back home?" He made a pyramid of his work-roughened fingers.

"There's a surplus of brokers out there in the Empire." I noticed that he hadn't asked me to sit. "And I always wanted to try life on the shore."

"Bert tells me you know your business." Shrewd, quizzical eyes gave me a lengthy scan. "If you're looking to get rich, though, this is hardly the place."

"You seem to have done all right, Mr. Dolan."

His clenched smile widened. "Why are you really here, Nahkeeta?"

Casual shrug. "Make a few bucks."

"Giving stock market advice to a bunch of senior citizens?"

"I wasn't planning on confining myself to investments, Mr. Dolan."

"What were you planning on branching into?"

"Development."

A wary gleam appeared in Dolan's blue eyes. "What were you planning to develop?"

I had a strong hunch Dolan had already had a cozy chat with Jon Waterman, so I fell back on the exact same cover story. With luck, I might even be able to use it to move in on him.

Conspiratorial Angie smile. "Torpedo Junction."

Dolan let out a deep-throated chuckle. "Let's you and me cut to the chase, okay? I don't have to say, 'I'm marketing that site.' And you don't have to bat those pretty dark eyes and say, 'Why, Mr. Dolan, I had no idea!' Let's get to the bottom line. What do you have in mind?"

"Luxury condos, Mr. Dolan. Shoreside condominium units."

"What kind?"

"Single family. One- and two-bedroom units."

"Why are you interested in Torpedo Junction?"

"The walls are already up," I said, shifting my weight to my left heel. "It's a lot easier—and cheaper—to rehab an existing structure than to build from the cement up."

"Not that cheap." Skepticism flavored Dolan's smile. "You've got an awful lot of space to fill, Anne Marie."

"How much industrial space are we talking about, Mr. Dolan?"

He did some quick mental math. "Three hundred and sixty thousand square feet."

I performed some hasty calculations of my very own. "Okay. You're talking about four hundred condo units in all, evenly split between the one- and two-bedroom styles. The property is right on the water. And, best of all, there's plenty of acreage for future expansion."

Dolan began to show an interest. "Give me a rough cut of your specifications."

Leaning forward slightly, I placed both hands on the backrest of an empty chair. "I'd say we're looking at an initial capitalization of four-point-eight million for renovation of the main assembly building. After that, we market the finished units at seventy K for singles and one hundred K for two-bedroom units."

"*We?*" he echoed, his fine gray eyebrows arching.

Wry Angie smile. "I can hardly swing it alone, Mr. Dolan."

"So what are you bringing into the deal?"

Dolan's reptilian gaze surveyed me with all the passion of an Alaskan glacier. Blunt and right to the point.

119

Oh, John, you romantic devil, you!

"Money, Mr. Dolan. Lots of it. I can deliver the initial financing."

"Got a few investors already lined up, eh?"

"You could say that. Fact is, there's *one* who's very, very anxious about the outcome of my work here."

And I wondered how the Mick was adjusting to institutional life down there in Cedar Creek.

Dolan's expression turned thoughtful. "Who are you representing in Seattle?"

"I'm not with that crowd."

"All right, then. Who's your prime backer in Spokane?"

I stood erect suddenly. "Not so fast, Mr. Dolan. Thus far, we've only discussed Torpedo Junction's assets. There are liabilities."

"Such as?"

I took my cues from Fred Dantzler. Cool Angie smile. "We could have trouble interesting a contractor. Port Wyoochee's getting a bad name in the industry."

Dolan's expression soured. He knew what I was driving at but feigned ignorance. "I'm not sure I understand."

"It's kind of hard to build condos with people milling around, screaming into bullhorns."

Those blue eyes became chips of Antarctic ice. A furious tic pulsed at the corner of his mouth. "Don't worry about it." The chill in his tone would have frozen Puget Sound. "The problem will be taken care of."

Hmmmmm . . . and what do you mean by that, *Mr. D?*

I was eager to learn more but knew I had to approach the issue in a roundabout fashion.

"Mr. Dolan, that's a very aggressive environmental group. They're young. They're articulate. They're not afraid to file lawsuits—"

"They're assholes!" he interrupted. "And they're wearing out their welcome fast. Damned fast! Especially that Canadian bitch."

"Georgianna Waterman?"

"That's the one." Flicker of an admiring smile. "You did your homework, kid."

"I have some very demanding clients, Mr. Dolan. They want a good return on their investment. They don't want controversy. Or trouble. Or their names bandied about in the newspaper. Lawsuits give them tummyaches. If things get too rowdy in Port Wyoochee, they're liable to pull out and go elsewhere."

"No problem. I'll take care of the Greenway bunch."

"Are you sure? Georgianna Waterman inherited a formidable organization. They're on record as being opposed to any further development in the Gemini River area."

"You're jumping at shadows, Anne Marie." Sudden expression of contempt. "Georgianna Waterman is a flake. Chicken Little in skirts. She runs around in a permanent state of hysteria." He cocked his middle finger and then let fly, lashing out at an imaginary insect. "All it'll take is one good whack. They'll be carting her off to Steilacoom in a straitjacket. Guarantee it."

"You know all about her, eh?"

Feral grin. "Everything, kid. Right down to what size batteries she pops into her vibrator."

"What about the group itself? I hear Mona Hanauer trained them well."

"True enough. But Hanauer's dead, isn't she?" The thought cheered him immensely. "No more trouble from that corner."

"You sound all broken up about it, Mr. Dolan."

"Hey, don't get me wrong! I knew the girl. Met her dad when I first took over Kulshan." His expression was unreadable. "Mona was a little more down to earth, and that made her dangerous. She had her problems, though. She took after her old man." Genuine lighthearted chuckle. "You know, Leon Hanauer must be the only Jew in this world who can't

121

hold on to money. He and his partners drove Kulshan right into the ground. I'm the one who had to clean up the mess."

"You're awfully quick to pass judgment, Mr. Dolan."

"You never saw the size of that deficit, Anne Marie." He leaned forward in his chair, welcoming the opportunity to debate. "And where's Doc Hanauer now, eh? Working in a clinic with a pair of optometrists young enough to be his kids."

"Maybe he just doesn't want to retire."

"Don't kid yourself. Doc would like nothing better than to be down there in Miami Beach, feasting his eyes on all those string bikinis." Laughter melted the frost in his voice. "He can't go yet, though. He's still got a few creditors to pay off."

Finally I had Dolan in an expansive mood. I was content to let him talk, and he didn't disappoint me.

"Two of a kind. Him and Mona. Romantic adventurers." He let out a snort of contemptuous laughter. "She actually looked up to him. A Daddy's girl if ever I saw one!"

Entering his impromptu game of amateur psychiatrist, I remarked, "Maybe that's why she had so many boyfriends."

"Absolutely! She was waving a big red flag at Daddy. When he didn't respond, she began looking elsewhere for a father figure." Dolan scratched his nose. "You know what Mona needed? A good, swift kick in the ass! Sure would've gotten one if she'd been mine!" Grimace of disapproval. "The way she drifted from man to man . . . she never stuck too long with any of 'em. Not that I'm blaming her, you understand. She had a knack for picking the real losers."

"Like Jon Waterman?"

"You said it. I didn't."

"I understand Mona was married for a few years."

"Yeah! To the biggest loser of them all." Dolan displayed a chilly half-smile. "That's why she's dead. Son of a bitch killed her." Meaningful glower. "Do me a favor, Anne Marie. Don't ever mention that asshole to me again. Okay?"

"If you say so." I had time enough for one last impertinence. "But I understand he's the one who helped Mona go after Kulshan."

Dolan's scowl looked as if it had been chiselled from basalt. "That's right." His baritone voice held a dangerous edge. "We had a little industrial accident at the mill a few years back. Grantz jumped right on it. We got hit with a quarter-million-dollar fine. I mean, I really needed that. And right in the middle of the financial reorganization, too. Because of that little prick, Kulshan's bond rating went right through the floor. Nearly put me out of business, that sneaky little . . . *shyster!*"

Careful, Mr. Dolan. You almost said the J-word.

"I take it Grantz isn't one of your favorite people."

"Not by a long shot!" I watched those massive hands curl into angry fists. "Those ecology nuts are bad enough. But these fucking lawyers—these goddamned ambulance chasers getting rich off harassment suits! They're the ones who frost me!"

I feigned a look of curiosity. "You think Grantz killed her?"

"Sure!" Cops found his sweater on the scene, didn't they?"

Sudden bland expression. "I wouldn't know, Mr. Dolan."

"Of course he did it!" A ferocious glee enlivened Dolan's blue eyes. "I'll bet Mona got under his skin again. She had the same effect on a lot of guys. Grantz couldn't handle it. When she walked out on him a second time, he went bananas." Whiteness receded from his knuckles. "Yeah, he killed her. But they'll never nail him for it, though."

"Why do you say that?" I asked, deeply impressed—to say nothing of *disturbed*—by Dolan's intimate knowledge of the events on Orcas Island.

"Come on! Jew lawyer like Grantz? I'll be surprised if it even comes to trial. He'll plea-bargain it down to manslaughter and then go away for a few years." The prospect delighted him, banishing all remaining traces of his anger.

"I'd sure like to see that Jewboy's face when he lands in the pen. He's going to have eight big jigaboos using him for a mattress." Gust of fierce laughter. "Man, I'd pay ten grand for a videotape of that!"

"You do seem to keep track, Mr. Dolan."

"Indeed I do ... of *all* my enemies." Dolan's icy smile sent a tremor racing up my backbone. "I've got this long, long memory. Somebody sticks it to me, and I don't ever forget it. Not ever! That's something to keep in mind, Anne Marie ..." His harsh smile broadened just a smidgen. "In case you're ever tempted to doublecross me."

"I'm very good at resisting temptation, Mr. Dolan."

"Very commendable." Dolan stood up at once. Deftly he buttoned his suit jacket. "Now, come with me. There's someone I want you to meet."

The *someone* turned out to be Rolf Lauridsen, the plant manager at Kulshan Paper. Lauridsen was a stalwart fellow in his middle fifties, lean and long-eared, with a high, smooth forehead, apple red cheeks, a blunt Scandinavian nose, deepset colbalt-colored eyes, and a neatly trimmed reddish brown moustache. His fine hair was a slightly darker shade of brown. That was only up top, though. Around the ears, it was as gray as his heather wool suit. He had an odd-looking smile, sort of friendly and aloof at the same time, and his handshake was fleeting, enthusiastic and faintly moist.

Dolan had introduced me as Anne Marie, and Lauridsen bade me welcome in a booming baritone. He had no need of an intercom to summon his secretary. Dolan thought it would be a fine idea if I had a V.I.P. tour of their pride and joy, the Kulshan Paper mill. Lauridsen reacted as if that was the most brilliant suggestion ever made.

Soon the two of us were heading west in his stylish new Crown Victoria. As we tooled down Shore Avenue, I gave some thought to my recent chat with Dolan. Oh, like Mr.

Lauridsen, perhaps I should say *Jack*. Hmmmmm . . . as in *Whiskey Jack*, maybe?

I saw a reflection of my fussbudget face in the Crown Vic's windshield. Nice try, princess, but perhaps that's a little too obvious. After all, why would the victim say "Whiskey Jack!" when it was just as easy to blurt out "Jack Dolan!"?

My frown deepened. What *were* you trying to say, Mona?

Still, I'd gleaned enough information back there to put Jack Dolan at the top of the suspect list. At least for now.

Chatting with the great man, I'd gotten the impression that he hated Mickey Grantz far more than he did Mona. He blamed Mick for Kulshan's courtroom defeat. Which leads to another intriguing question.

If Mick was the main target of Dolan's wrath, then what did he have to gain by killing Mona? Why take the risk?

Of course, I could be wrong. Perhaps Dolan despised Mona far more than Mick. Perhaps he was deliberately concealing that hatred because he truly was the murderer.

Hmmmmm—that's a possibility. Contrary to popular misconception, murderers don't kill innocent third parties in order to set in motion some arcane scheme of revenge against their real target. If they hate someone that much, they soon start measuring the intended victim for a pine box.

I sensed some strange shadowy linkages out there. Some weird triangle involving Jack Dolan and Mona Hanauer and their optometrist father. And I had to learn more about it if ever I was to make sense of the lady's murder.

Lauridsen's baritone voice boomed beside me. "Something wrong, Anne Marie?"

My sudden sidelong glance showed the manager behind the wheel, staring at me in mild concern. Touching my forehead, I murmured, "Oh, just my sinuses acting up." Friendly Angie smile. "Tell me about yourself. Are you from Port Wyoochee?"

Smiling, he shook his head. "Port Gamble. My wife Jan is a local girl, though."

With that, he proceeded to tell me about his charming wife, their heavily mortgaged home up there in Harbor Ridge, and his two lovely daughters. The older one was married and living in Vancouver. The younger one, Kelly, had just started high school, and Mr. Lauridsen wasn't too certain he'd survive the experience.

And then he became quite serious. Glancing at me once more, he remarked, "I saw you at the head table with Jack. You were with him for quite a while." Vibrant tone of eager curiosity. "What were you two talking about?"

I decided to test his reactions. "Mona Hanauer."

Surprise erupted on Lauridsen's lean face. And just as quickly it vanished. I watched his hands tremble on the steering wheel.

An interesting reaction, all right. And I wondered why Mona's name made him so jumpy.

Clearing his throat, Lauridsen added, "You knew Mona?"

"Just by reputation," I replied. "The word is, that group she started is mighty unfriendly to developers."

My answer seemed to put him at ease. So I knocked him off-balance again. "How about you? Did you know Mona Hanauer?"

Lauridsen took a long moment to answer. "We met a few times. When I was negotiating with the EPA. She and her husband had filed suit against Kulshan, alleging that we had deliberately dumped toxic wastewater into the river."

"Alleging?" I echoed.

Colbalt eyes narrowed in annoyance. "She made a number of accusations against the company. Accusations that were completely without foundation." He glanced at me. "Hanauer and Waterman have had their say, and now I'm going to have mine. The Kulshan Paper Company is not a conspiracy to wreck the ecosystem. I'm trying to run a business, dammit, not kill all the salmon in the Strait of Juan de Fuca!"

"Been a rough year, eh?"

"Could be better," he said candidly. "Our specialty has always been coated paper, but there's been a glut for the past few years. We've made the switch to supercalendered paper. The market's still pretty soft, though."

"Supercalendered paper?"

"You know, the glossy paper they use in catalogues and magazines." He slowed the Crown Vic as he approached the Gemini River bridge. "Sure looks like we're headed for another crunch. Pulpwood prices are on their way up. Damned union's going to want a pay increase." Dispirited sigh. "I sure wish Sales'd get off their ass and find some of those lucrative foreign markets I keep hearing about."

The Crown Vic's tires went *tub-thump* as we rolled across the bridge. The tinted windshield showed me a wide-angle view of the Kulshan Paper plant. Behind the tall chainlink fence stood several decades-old brick buildings with mansard roofs, Romanesque arched windows and jungly colonies of ivy. A massive spillway and canal, both made of chipped concrete, meandered down to the river. A surprisingly incongruous line of holly trees lined the canal.

"Oh, Christ!" he muttered.

As we turned left, heading for the main building, I saw the reason for that sudden expletive. Georgianna Waterman and about twenty protestors walked a circular picket line in front of the aluminum-trimmed entrance. Several Greenway people wore sandwich placards reading *Clean Up The Strait!* The others had invested their time and energy in more colorful hand-painted signs.

Hey, Kulshan! You're Pissing In Our Aquifer!
Salmon Have To Breathe, Too!
Your Wastewater Dissolved My Pantyhose!

Georgianna's denim-clad troops kept up a hoarse but resolute shout. "Don't fudge! Clean up the sludge!"

Lauridsen stared straight ahead, his thin features reddening in anger. He refused to acknowledge the protestors' presence. Someone recognized him, however, and the organized chant disintegrated into a medley of jeers and catcalls. A solid object thumped the car's left rear fender.

"Son of a bitch!" he exploded, snapping an infuriated glance at the rearview mirror. "If he scratched that finish, I'll kick his scrawny ass up around the moon!"

I managed to dissuade him from wheeling about and going after the malefactor. I hoped that Georgianna could keep her bunch under control. I should have known better!

As we emerged from the car, I heard the ominous drumroll of running feet. Instant upward glance. Greenway people were rapidly closing in. Long-legged college boys were out in front. Georgianna bustled along with a matronly dignity, escorted by a phalanx of grim-faced coeds.

Doing my best to defuse the confrontation, I showed Georgianna my cheeriest smile. "Hello, Ms. Waterman. Nice to see you again."

Well, she was damned surprised to see Angie there. But surprise just wasn't enough to deter that woman from her sacred mission. Gripping a protest placard, she turned to my host. "We want to talk to you, Mr. Lauridsen."

Fuming, he glanced at the crowd blocking the entrance, then faced Georgianna. "I don't seem to have a choice, do I, Ms. Waterman?"

I stepped between them. "Look, why don't we discuss this inside—?"

The jeers of the protestors cut me off. One began cavorting on top of the Crown Vic's trunk. Lauridsen shot him a baleful glare. In about two seconds, that kid was going to be the new Neil Armstrong!

The clamor drew two dozen faces to the windows. A platoon of highly pissed-off laborers gathered at the shipping bay. Then a pair of denim-clad collegians sidled up on either side of me. I flinched at their sudden proximity, wondering what they had in mind.

"When is your company going to comply with the EPA

directives?" Georgianna shouted. "When are you going to remove the sludge bed from Sahale Point?"

Trembling with suppressed fury, Lauridsen snapped, "May I remind you that you're on private property!?"

Their words sailed past each other. Georgianna kept right on shouting, as if he hadn't even spoken. "When are you going to take responsibility for your damage to the environment?"

He glared at all of them. "Get off this property! Or I'm calling the police!"

A baby-faced coed joined the shouting match. "If you have the right to pollute, then we have the right to trespass!"

Obviously a pre-law major, that one.

Rolf was losing it. "This is *private property!*"

Galvanized by his furious shout, the crowd came surging toward us. Baby Face swatted Lauridsen with her protest sign. Another youth grabbed the collar of his suit jacket.

Instantly I moved forward, hoping to break it up. Suddenly, a pair of masculine arms looped around me, lifting me right off the ground.

Chapter Seven

"Let go of me!" I hollered.

Male arms tightened their grip. A grinning collegian, one of the pair that had spooked me moments before, danced into my field of vision. Cackling with glee, he said, "He's a big boy, sweetie. Let him fight his own battles."

And he was fighting, all right. Eyes half-mad with fear, Rolf Lauridsen slugged and grappled with half a dozen youthful protestors. Georgianna's voice cut through the tumult like a fine-edged sword, pleading for nonviolence. Too late! The crowd had their hands on a real live polluter, and they were more than ready to exact penalties for past damage to the environment.

All at once, the Kulshan laborers came streaming out of the shipping bay, faces tense with fury, brandishing a variety of makeshift bludgeons. Lug wrenches and sawed-off broom handles. They hit the protest crowd like Marines storming a hostile beach. The point squad flailed and battered their way to Lauridsen's side, led by a big guy with close-cropped brownish blond hair.

I blinked in recognition. It was the man I'd seen peering into Mona's cabin—Mister Crewcut. But what was he doing here?

Squirming in my captor's grip, I shouted, "Help me! Please! Get him off me!"

To my astonishment, Mister Crewcut let out a hearty belly laugh. Brown eyes sizzled with frank hostility. I couldn't understand it. No way could he have recognized me from the cabin. Unless he had an owl's night vision, he couldn't have seen me crouched behind the sofa.

Deliberately ignoring my plight, he pulled a rolled-up newspaper out of his jacket pocket and returned to the fray.

Indignant Angie glare. Well, thank you very much, Prince Charming!

I had no time, however, to ponder the decline of chivalry. My captor was beginning to take liberties. My breath exploded in a gasp of outrage.

Just then, Mister Crewcut spotted a black youth struggling with a Kulshan mill worker. Holding his makeshift truncheon high, he bellowed, "Nigger! Get that nigger!"

Shoving his opponent away, the black kid turned to meet his new challenger. The rolled-up newspaper descended in a twinkling. Even over the background din, I still heard that dreadful *thunk!*

The kid went down like a gunshot deer.

Mister Crewcut scouted the melee for fresh prey. Spotting Georgianna, he shouted, "Get her! Get the Jewgirl! She's destroying your jobs!"

Fortunately, the mill workers ignored his harangue. The battle had splintered into a dozen individual brawls. Protestors versus Kulshan workers. Lots of pushing and shoving and punching and kicking. Not to mention sign-ripping, placard-stomping and language that would have had Sister Mary Katherine clapping her hands over her ears.

Georgianna the Valkyrie contributed to the stream of obscenities. The lady had a vile and vivid vocabulary. Wielding her tattered sign like a rolling pin, she hammered a Kulshan stevedore. She could really hit, too. Better than Aunt Della. It didn't take more than a dozen thumpings to teach him proper respect for women. Covering his head with both arms, he went stumbling away.

The whole thing reminded me of a riot in the Springfield laundry room. Only here there was no battalion of screws handy to break it up and send everybody to lockdown. The tide was turning against Georgianna. Kulshan people kept running out of the building, joining the battle by twos and threes.

The situation angered my two captors. Not enough to get in there and help their friends. But enough to take it out on little Angie.

Seizing my nyloned ankles, the first one showed me a lascivious smirk. "How many times have you spread these for Lauridsen?"

Twisting at the hip, I let him have it. Had I been two inches taller, that sidewinder kick would have won me an audition with the Rockettes. My high-heeled shoe smashed him squarely on the jaw. He reeled as if he'd been hit by Mike Tyson.

Before my captor could react, I whipped my head back—*hard!* Stars twinkled as my skull crunched his nose. Another little trick I learned at Springfield. Came in mighty handy against pushy lesbians.

Listening to his bellow of agonized surprise, I lifted one knee and drove my spike heel into his ankle. His bellow turned shrill, and his grip instantly loosened.

I slipped out from under, intent on making my getaway, but the first molester suddenly loomed in my path. A prominent bruise purpled his jaw. Snarling, he grabbed my wrist, and I reacted at once, taking a backward step, shifting my weight to my left foot, and letting fly with my right. Another grandstand Rockette kick that put my shoe's pointed toe where his trouser legs came together.

His bearded face lost all color. Both hands flew to his crotch. Sinking to his knees, he uttered a dismal groan and then keeled over like a sick elephant. Slowly I backed away, watching him shrivel into a fetal position. A firm male hand landed on my shoulder.

I spun about, ready to continue my Rockette routine, but the sight of that blue uniform and badge abruptly changed my mind. The Port Wyoochee cop waggled a warning finger. "None of that, now!"

I took a hasty glance around. Blue-and-white cruisers with flashing red lights lined the driveway. Uniformed officers herded the Kulshan people back toward the plant. A white van emblazoned with the legend KPWR-TV *Action News* was parked haphazardly on the lawn. Beside it, an attractive blonde in a jade linen suit tested a microphone while her hyperactive director screamed abuse at the languid cameraman.

Georgianna struck a pose. "We will not be moved!"

Then a trio of glum cops came over and slapped the handcuffs on her and three of her dishevelled compatriots.

"Shut it down!" Baby Face screamed. "Shut Kulshan down!"

A handful of bleeding and battered protestors took up the chant. This proved to be too much for one mill worker. Big, freckle-faced, slab-bellied guy in a greasy shirt. Joe Sixpack. He stood there and listened and seethed. And then, with a frighteningly silent and deadly haste, he tore into the nearest protestor. It took two cops and his best friend to pull him off.

"Come on, Harry, come on," the friend cajoled. "Jesus, Harry, don't—!"

"Get that asshole out of my face!" Harry bellowed, as the cops hustled him toward the cruisers. "Get him out of here! I won't be responsible!"

My old friend, Mister Crewcut, stayed safely behind the police line, contenting himself with a flurry of catcalls. I noticed that he'd ditched his lethal newspaper.

Glaring at Georgianna, he shouted, "Fucking Jew!"

An angry cop pointed right at him. "Give it a rest, fella!"

"What are you gonna do with 'em, huh?" he replied. "Put 'em in protective custody? Funny how you boys in blue always show up to save the Jew."

Another cop hooked his thumb in the direction of the cruisers. "Keep it up, Sargent. We'll let you ride downtown with your girlfriend."

Oblivious to their warnings, he went right on working the crowd. "Hey! Betcha that Jewgirl walks. What do you want to bet, eh? I say the Jewgirl's gonna walk." Then he shook his fist at the chanting protestors. "Those are your jobs they're talking about! You want to do something about it? Come to the Adamite church. Tomorrow night. Eight P.M. We're gonna do something about the big Jews once and for all!"

Adamite church, eh? Well, that explains what he was doing at Mona's cabin . . . maybe.

While Sargent ranted and raved, the fortyish cop who'd detained me rounded up both of my erstwhile playmates. Believe me, your Angie was a well-behaved little girl. Any resistance on my part, and I would soon be on my way to the police station with Harry and Georgianna. And that's one place I didn't want to go. One of those officers might have seen that FBI advisory.

So I stood around very patiently, arms folded, hoping the policeman would let me go. I thought I looked pretty disheveled with my slip hanging and my laddered pantyhose and my blazer sleeve torn at the shoulder. But that was before I got a good look at my captor. Blood seeped downward from his nostrils, matting his scraggly moustache.

The cop showed all three of us his riot baton. "Stand easy, people."

Three minutes later, we were joined by a tall, stalwart fellow with neatly combed chestnut hair, gimlet eyes and a lantern jaw. He could have been a distant cousin of Robert Redford's. A folded-over wallet, with the silvery badge displayed, dangled from the breast pocket of his crisp gray suit. "What have you got, Holloway?"

"Assault and battery." With a two-fingered jab, Officer

Holloway pointed out my attackers. "I saw them grab the young lady when we first arrived."

I wanted to kiss Officer Holloway, but I contented myself instead with a gleeful look at my two playmates.

"All right." The suit was all business. "Get her name and address. Cuff these two and take them downtown. Book them for A & B."

Holloway reached for his handcuffs. "Right, Chief."

Purple Jaw looked as if he needed a sudden underwear change. "Hey, man! We were just kidding around. You can't—"

"Save it for tomorrow morning," the police chief interrupted, turning away. "Judge Naughton is a real good listener."

Bloody Nose shot me an indignant glare. "Aren't you gonna arrest *her?*"

Forcing the man's wrists behind his spine, Holloway chuckled. "No law against a woman defending herself against assholes."

I hated to see those two walk, but I couldn't risk a visit to the police station—not even to swear out a formal complaint. As Holloway began his Miranda recital, I caught up with the police chief. "Uhm, wait a minute ... I-I've decided not to press charges."

Halting at once, the chief turned and stared. "Pardon?"

I detested the thought of making myself so gosh-darned memorable, but there was no other way. I had to talk him out of it.

"Look, they probably didn't mean any harm." Anxious Angie smile. "I'd rather not file a complaint. I just moved to town. I don't want any trouble."

He gave me a long, thoughtful look. I had the awful feeling he was memorizing my features for future reference.

"All right. Have it your way, then." Turning to Holloway, he added, "Turn them loose. Let's get this mess sorted out."

"Anne Marie!" Lauridsen's voice carried over the protest

chants. Flanked by two of Port Wyoochee's finest, he rushed to join us. His tie was gone, and his mud-spattered suit jacket lacked all its buttons. "Are you all right?" Frantically he grabbed my upper arms. "Did those people hurt you?"

"No, no . . . I'm all right." Touching my forehead, I smiled shyly. "I just got knocked around a bit."

"Who did it?" he shouted, outraged, and then turned to the police chief. "I want those people arrested. Miss Nahkeeta is my guest—"

"It's okay, Mr. Lauridsen," I added, tugging at his suit jacket. "I'm not pressing charges." Brave little smile. "I guess we'll have to do that tour another time."

"Come with me. You can use my office to clean up." Then his gaze met the chief's, and he fumed. "Well, Gallagher?"

"Well what, Mr. Lauridsen?"

"What does a man have to do to protect his property in this community? Hire a blasted SWAT team?"

"I wouldn't advise that, Mr. Lauridsen."

"Those people were trespassing!"

"That's right." Cool as a Lake Superior mist, Chief Gallagher summoned another officer with a wave of his hand. "The leaders have been arrested, and they will appear in court tomorrow morning. If you have any further complaints, sir, you're welcome to register them at the station."

"Damned right I'll be there!" the mill manager shouted, shepherding me toward the main entrance. "The mayor's going to hear about this, Gallagher. Just you wait and see."

Me, I was glad to be out of there. The KPWR anchorwoman was wrapping up her interview with the voluble Miss Baby Face. She'd be after us for a statement next. And the last thing I wanted was my lovely Anishinabe face showing up on TV screens all over the Pacific Northwest.

Once inside, I gratefully accepted a cup of coffee from Rolf Lauridsen, listened to his heartfelt apologies, declined an invitation to freshen up, promised to return for that tour another day, and consented to his offer of a taxi ride home.

Twenty minutes later, as the taxi ferried me back over the Gemini River bridge, I reflected on my recent unexpected reunion with Mister Crewcut, also known as Sargent, the pitchman for the Adamite church. One of Lemuel Thurber's boys. But what was he doing at the Kulshan plant?

Employee? That's possible. But I didn't see him follow the others back into the building.

Perhaps he was merely keeping tabs on the Greenway committee. I shuddered at the memory of the violence. Boy, he was really stirring up the crowd, wasn't he? Not that they'd needed much stirring up. The protestors' chant "Shut it down!" had been a red flag to poor Harry.

You can get pretty desperate, I guess, when you're on the high side of thirty and you have kids to feed and there's a recession and you're living in a one-industry town like Port Wyoochee.

I stirred restlessly in the taxi's backseat, unable to stop thinking about the riot. Three years in Springfield, including sixteen months in the custody of Miss Carlotta, and I'd seen more than my share of violent assaults. The sad fact is, I'd been an unwilling participant in a number of them. In case you're wondering where I learned to kick like the Rockettes.

I guess it was the crowd's visceral hatred that bothered me. I'd seen the same kind of hatred before, at the spearfishing protests at Lac du Flambeau, and it always left me with a distinct case of the shudders. Three years in Springfield, and I had never seen an inmate go after another fish the way Sargent attacked that black kid. The way he swung that homemade cosh—*wham!* Like he was trying to kill a spider or something.

What do you suppose Sargent had in that newspaper, princess? Short length of pipe, probably. Filling the pipe's interior with quick-drying cement turns it into a fairly lethal weapon. Remember the time Elena pulled that stunt at Miss

Carlotta's? She rolled her cosh in a copy of *Vogue*, then went looking for the dyke who'd pestered her pet. Ahhhhh, Elena! Crazier than a Mexican flea circus, but she certainly knew all the tricks.

I thought of Sargent peering through Mona's front window. Why did I get the feeling that wasn't exactly his first trip to the San Juan Islands?

Interesting linkages there. Mona was beaten to death by a bare-knuckled assailant. Mr. Sargent appears to get off on pummelling minorities. Sargent is one of Thurber's boys. Mona wanted to sue Thurber for libel. And then, following the murder, Sargent turns up at Mona's holiday cabin, looking for . . . *what?*

Fatigued sigh. Another task for us, Chief. We need some background on this guy Sargent. As of now, he's our key link between Mona Hanauer and Lemuel Thurber.

Friday night found me in a cozy cedar booth at Millicent's Pub, the prime watering hole for Port Wyoochee's swinging singles. Originally, I'd planned on making the trip all by my lonesome. But then I got a phone call from my new friend, Marcella Caputo. She suggested that we make it a combined trip—some early-evening shopping on Dollar Avenue, followed by a few drinks at her favorite "meat market."

By nine o'clock, we were calmly viewing the Beef Parade, commenting on the lean selections available, resting our weary legs, and sipping cold beer from frosty long-necked bottles. As always, I stuck with Lowenbrau. Marcella, looking very Felliniesque in her scoop-necked peasant blouse and dark woolen skirt, was a Coors woman—Silver Bullet all the way.

I was in a casual dress mood tonight, as well, wearing a cheery autumn outfit I'd picked up at the Tacoma Mall. Cotton denim jumper with the hem at mid-knee. Immaculate white blouse with cuffed half-sleeves. Plus a knitted tie and an oversized tam-o'-shanter in a bright tartan plaid.

Eyeing my tam, Marcella giggled. "I didn't know you were one of the Campbells, Anne Marie."

"I'm not." Puckish Angie smile. "It's just that we haven't yet designed a tartan for the Bear Clan."

Dark eyes brightened with interest. "Is that your people's clan?"

I nodded briskly. And, if you don't believe me, ask Chief. My mother's family name is Muckudaymakwah, meaning *black bear*.

"How about you?" I asked, lifting my Lowenbrau. "What part of Sicily are the Caputos from?"

"You've got me." She gave her slim, olive-tinted shoulders a hefty shrug. "Great-grandad got here a century ago. He took one look at Ellis Island and signed up aboard the first whaler bound for Seattle."

"He liked this coast a whole lot better, eh?"

"You could say that." Marcella put down her bottle. "How about you? What do you think of the shore?"

"I'm getting attached to the area pretty fast."

Curiosity gleamed in Marcella's dark eyes. "Did you leave any attachments behind in Spokane?"

My smile faded. No, Marce, not in Spokane, I thought. But not too long ago I met a man in Michigan's Upper Peninsula. The man who took my heart and holds it still. My darling heir apparent, Donald Winston Pierce. . . .

Frowning, I cast a glance out the window, staring at City Hall's square clock tower and its domed, wood-framed belfry. I wondered what Donny was doing, who he was with, and, most of all, if he ever thought of me.

Marcella took a sip of Coors. "He was married, right?"

I shook my head. "Afraid not. He was a warm, charming, single man." I caught her sudden grimace and added, "Most definitely heterosexual. And he didn't walk—I did."

Of course, I could walk right straight back to the U.P. any

time I wanted. If I did, however, I would immediately be booked, printed and jailed by the FBI. And maybe, after I finished my term of service at the federal women's prison in Alderson, West Virginia, Donald and I might be able to resume the relationship. Maybe. A *big* maybe!

"You let him get away!?" Marcella grimaced in disbelief. Then, one dainty hand on my shoulder, she added, "Anne Marie, you and I need to have a long, long talk." Sudden grin. "Later, though. We've got company. Look who just walked in."

Rising slightly in my seat, I spied Georgianna Waterman in the entryway. She seemed strangely at ease in the convivial atmosphere of the pub. She was wearing a navy cardigan jacket, a jade foulard blouse with a high-wrap neck, and a silken dirndl skirt. She exchanged merry greetings with the bartender, spotted the two of us, and weaved her way through the milling Friday night crowd. Ducking beneath a hanging drift net, she haltingly approached our booth. Timid as a doe.

Smiling in welcome, Marcella patted the tabletop. "Hi, Georgie! Care for a beer?"

"No thanks." Hesitantly she stepped forward, squeezing her vinyl handbag with nervous fingers. "I just wanted to thank you, Anne Marie. For not pressing charges, I mean."

"No need for thanks." My tone became cooler. "Just tell your boys to watch the horseplay, all right? Next time I might not be quite so understanding."

"I-I'll speak to them," Georgianna promised.

I didn't want her leaving on a chilly note. I still wanted to ask her about Jon and Mona. Warming my smile a bit, I asked, "How did you make out at the police station?"

Georgianna had the same one-shouldered shrug as her ex-husband. "They booked us for trespassing. We were released on our own recognizance. I have to appear in court tomorrow." Speculative frown. "I suppose I'll have to type up a press release."

Marcella's pretty face tensed in disapproval. "I'm not sure the committee accomplished anything today."

Georgianna did not take criticism graciously. Whirling at once, she snapped, "We might have accomplished *more* . . . had the *entire* membership been there!"

Seeing my companion's face redden, I beat her to the reply. "Such as?"

Striking a field marshal's pose, Georgianna said, "We confronted the structure of oppression on its own grounds. We served notice to the capitalist patriarchy that we will no longer tolerate their abuse of the environment. People will take us seriously now."

"The *judge* will certainly be taking it seriously," I predicted, then took another sip of Lowenbrau.

"I take it you don't approve of my tactics, Ms. Nahkeeta!"

"I'd behave myself if I were you, dear," I replied. "I hear it's pretty rough in the prison laundry."

Haughty glare. "I'm not afraid to go to prison for my beliefs!"

"Really?" I changed my mind about a conciliatory approach. That sanctimonious self-righteousness was rapidly shredding my goodwill. "Then I guess you won't mind scrubbing floors on your hands and knees."

Juvenile jeer. "You know all about it, I suppose!"

There was no talking sense to this one. She would have to experience Cedar Creek for herself. She needed to crouch on all fours, diligently pushing a scrub brush across a dingy lunchroom, listening to the nonstop catcalls of the guards. Only then would she ever wonder if those fleeting moments of television glory had been worth it.

I expected Georgianna to stalk off in a huff, but curiosity held her in check. She gave me a lengthy look of suspicion. "What were you doing at the plant today?"

"I met Mr. Lauridsen at the Rotary Club luncheon. He offered to show me around."

Look of astonishment. "And you agreed to go with him?"

"It's one way to meet new clients. And I need clients to stay in business." My firm gaze met and vanquished hers. "And maybe I was trying to accomplish with a quiet chat what you people failed to accomplish with your little parade."

Her astonishment grew. "You're in *favor* of the cleanup?"

"Of course. Does that surprise you?"

Taken aback, Georgianna sputtered, "Well, I'd hardly expect someone in your business to—"

"Georgianna," I interrupted, keeping my tone mellow. "Here's a newsflash. I am now and for many years have been a card-carrying member of the Sierra Club. And, yes, I would very much like to see Sahale Point cleaned up. That's why I asked you about joining the committee yesterday."

Her cheeks turned the same shade as raspberry lipstick. Moving her hands awkwardly, she stammered, "Oh! Well . . . uhm . . . I-I'm sorry, Anne Marie. I-I didn't mean to prejudge you. It's just that we don't attract many—" She groped for the right word.

"Rotarians?" I offered.

"Well, they aren't very friendly." Schoolgirl pout.

"Let's see if we can't change that, eh?" Smiling, I offered the woman my hand. She hesitated a second or two, then gave it a gentle squeeze.

"Would you still like to join the committee?" she asked, snapping open her handbag.

"Absolutely!"

"Drop by the library when you get the chance." She withdrew a small business card and handed it to me.

We said our goodbyes, and Georgianna mounted an empty stool at the far end of the bar. To her right hung a horizontal swordfish who had run afoul of the local taxidermist. Oblivious to the distraction, she rummaged in her handbag, then produced a ten-dollar bill and plunked it on the counter. The bartender arrived with an unnerving speed and placed a lime-colored drink in front of her. It had a tiny Chinese umbrella in it.

"Mai Tai," I murmured, glancing at Marcella. "Is she expecting somebody?"

"Jon Waterman, I guess, but he ain't coming back."

I watched Georgianna while my friend ordered another round. Then, fingering my sweating bottle, I remarked, "Difficult divorce?"

Sighing, Marcella nodded. "We keep hoping she'll get over it."

"The bartender knew just what to make," I observed.

"Georgie's a creature of habit." My companion felt ill at ease discussing their honcho with me. "She comes here every Friday night." She took another sip. "She's lived a fairly solitary life since the divorce."

"Maybe she'll meet the right man," I said, feigning a conviction I didn't truly feel.

"I sure hope so!" Pretty frown. "You know, if it'd been me, I'd have given Jon-boy the boot long ago."

"I ran into Waterman the other day." Quick sip of Lowenbrau. "He runs kind of a shoestring operation, doesn't he?"

Marcella let out a boozy giggle. "That's for sure! He has to scramble just to put fuel in the plane."

"Georgianna seems to be doing all right."

"Do I detect a catty note there, Miss Anne Marie Nahkeeta?"

Arch smile. "That's a very nice blouse she's wearing. I'm wondering how she can afford it on a librarian's salary."

Letting out a wry laugh, she replied, "Not much gets past you, does it?"

"I'm just curious, Marce, that's all. Waterman can't be contributing much in the way of alimony."

"Don't worry. He isn't." Marcella's tipsy smile was warm and knowledgeable. "Georgie's dad left her pretty well off. He was a colonel in the Canadian air force. That's how she met Jon, I think."

Fishing for leads, I remarked, "So she spends all her money on clothes?"

"Uh-huh! Clothes and antiques. You ought to see her collection of antique furniture."

The word *antique* rang a quiet alarm bell in my mind. I thought instantly of Mona's store. "Georgianna's interested in antiques?"

"Yeah. She buys old farm furniture, strips it down to the bare wood, and then slaps on varnish so it looks brand new." Quick glance at the librarian. Bare shoulders lifted in an insouciant Sicilian shrug. "Kind of an expensive hobby. But if you've got the money . . ."

She let the rest trail off. Hoping to keep up the flow of information, I asked, "Where does she keep all this furniture?"

"Well, some of it at the apartment. The rest at her cabin."

Heart pounding, I gave it a try. "In the San Juans?"

Marcella nodded. "Orcas Island. A lot of shore people have cabins over there."

"I've been over there. Where exactly is it?"

"Oh, just before you get to Olga. The old Taliaferro place. Right at the corner of Doe Bay Road."

An image sprang to mind. A gracefully aging, log-walled bungalow with a small overgrown lawn. I'd pedalled right past it Wednesday on my way to Mona's. It couldn't be more than a mile from the Hanauer cabin.

I swallowed the last of my beer. Funny how it no longer seemed to have a bite. My smile came without any conscious thought. It was just as bright as Marcella's. Giggling, she gave me a nudge.

"Think Georgie's going to get lucky tonight?"

We both collapsed in helpless laughter on the tabletop.

Saturday, October seventeenth, turned out to be another one of those gray-skies-over kind of days. Port Wyoochee was still smothered in mist when I woke up. And that's surprising . . . because I didn't crawl out of bed until after nine-thirty.

The vile weather matched my general health. My stomach felt as if it were competing in a jump rope contest. And my head! Judging from the clamor in there, somebody was dropping cast-iron bathtubs on an aluminum floor.

Another milestone in your life, princess. Your first Lowenbrau hangover. Hope you've learned your lesson.

Two hours later, I was parked down the street from Temple B'nai Emunath, lounging behind the steering wheel, gradually recuperating from that lively thunderstorm behind my forehead. The synagogue was an impressive sandstone building with a massive golden dome. It looked as if it had migrated to Port Wyoochee straight from Haifa.

The service broke up just before noontime. My eagle-eyed Anishinabe gaze scanned the departing assembly, then zeroed in on my target—Ruth Hanauer. She stood just outside the front door, chatting with the rabbi and an elderly man I vaguely recognized from Rotary. Then Ruth ambled over to a cranberry-colored Plymouth. I turned my own ignition key as she got in. And then followed her down the long, tree-lined boulevard through Klallam Park.

Mona's mom surprised me, however. Instead of heading for Alder Beach, she hung a left onto Wylie and then a right onto Cook, seeking the summit of the ridge. A street sign whizzed by my windshield. *Dungeness Circle.* Then I realized where she was headed.

Originally, I'd hoped to question Ruth about her daughter's association with Georgianna. But now, with the aid of an impromptu scam, I just might be able to get a peek at the inside of Mona's apartment.

The cranberry Plymouth pulled into the narrow driveway beside a large white stucco apartment complex. Across the building's face were stylized aluminum letters reading *Vista Del Mar.* I drove right on by, followed the circular drive back to Cook, and returned to the Parmenter House. It took me less than fifteen minutes to change clothes. Twenty minutes after that, I was parking the Topaz on Dungeness, seventy yards downslope from the apartment complex.

Show time, princess.

I ran uphill at a leisurely pace. Reebok soles slapped the asphalt. Running proved to be more effective than Tylenol. As my headache receded, I clenched my teeth and sprinted the rest of the way to the Vista gate. Enough exertion to really get my heart pumping. Perspiration beads sprouted above my eyebrows. My sweat-damp ponytail bounced vigorously. Making myself smile, I resumed my original speed and jogged up the driveway.

Rounding the building's corner, I found Ruth Hanauer loading a sizable cardboard box into the Plymouth's trunk. She wore a rumpled cable-knit sweater and a pair of khaki slacks. As I'd suspected, she was cleaning out her daughter's apartment. She turned my way, and I gave her a cheery wave. "Hi, Mrs. Hanauer!"

"Hello, Anne Marie." She dabbed quickly at tear-filled eyes. She really didn't feel like company right now, but she was determined to be pleasant, just the same. "What are you doing up here?"

Skidding to a halt, I took a deep breath. "Oh, just killing the calories with some old-fashioned roadwork." Quick glance at the overcast. "Trying to get back to town before it rains."

"I'll give you a ride, if you like." Ruth's gray hair quivered in the early-afternoon breeze.

"Thanks!" I smiled at my reflection in the Plymouth's rear window. The imagery was most convincing. Breathless brunette in her dark green leotard and white bike shorts. Straightening my terry headband, I added, "Are you visiting friends?"

"Not quite." Ruth's voice turned brittle. "I-I'm collecting a few of my daughter's things."

"Need some help?" Perky Angela.

146

"I wouldn't want to put you out."

"It's no trouble, Mrs. Hanauer."

"Well . . . there *are* a few big boxes."

"No problem," I said, taking the older woman's arm. "I always wanted to try weight-lifting."

Mona's place was on the third floor—a spacious, low-ceilinged garden apartment—one bedroom, one combination living and dining room, a cramped kitchenette, and a hideaway bathroom. The off-white walls were devoid of ornamentation. Large cardboard boxes stuffed with Mona's belongings littered the polished floor. Only the striped sofa remained.

Hearing the spattering sound of raindrops on glass, I wandered over to the shoreview balcony. On a clear day, you could see all the way to British Columbia. Not today, though. In that driving downpour, I could barely catch a glimpse of the lawn. Letting out a soft whistle, I remarked, "Boy, it's really coming down."

"That's what we call *Oregon mist.*" Ruth cast me a fond smile. "Because it missed Oregon and hit us."

Leaving the window, I grabbed a roll of masking tape. "All ready to tackle that bedroom?"

Wan smile. "I suppose so."

Actually, Ruth had already made quite a start, but those motherly memories kept getting in the way. I saw her facial muscles quiver with emotion as she approached the walk-in closet. So I steered her toward the Sedgefield bed, suggesting that she strip it down, and tackled the closet on my own.

In no time at all, I had Mona's clothes piled high on the bed's empty mattress. Old hatboxes lined the upper shelf. Peeping at the contents, I enjoyed a small chuckle. Like most coeds, Mona went through a brief Borsalino phase. And I should know. I spent my sophomore year at Utah State University looking like one of the Untouchables.

As I removed the final hatbox, I spied something dark and shiny against the closet wall. Obsidian eyes gleamed with interest. Rising on tiptoe, I hauled it out of there, then hefted it in both hands.

Hmmmmm—a telephone answering machine. Trade name *Phone-Mate*. The power cord circled the unit, pinning the receiver to its cradle.

Puzzled frown. What was it doing in the closet?

"Anne Marie, could you give me a hand here?"

Leaving the answering machine on the dresser, I helped Ruth fold and box the blankets. Afterward, as I turned to retrieve the Phone-Mate, I spied a framed photograph on the night table. It showed a thirtyish Ruth Hanauer with a handsome, distinguished, dark-haired man. He had one arm around Ruth, cuddling her close, his long chin at rest on her shoulder. And he was smiling as if he had just won the state lottery.

Ruth appeared at my elbow. Bittersweet smile. "We gave that to Mona when she was six. She'd just had her first school photo taken, you see, so we swapped."

"Your husband's idea?" I handed her the photo.

"Her father." Bitterness turned her voice crisp. "Leon and I divorced twenty-two years ago."

"Sorry." Humble Angie.

"No need to apologize, Anne Marie." She took the photo and lovingly tucked it away. Shoulders drooped as she sighed. "It was a long, long time ago."

"You divorced *him?*"

Ruth's sudden glance was swift and decisive. "Lee gave me ample reason." Seizing a wrinkled pillowcase, she smoothed linen with agitated hands. "A woman can only take so much humiliation, you know." With brutal efficiency, she slammed it into the box. "I-I thought I understood Lee. I thought we had something. How could he have put it all at risk?"

I gave her thin shoulders a comforting squeeze. "Nobody told you, did they?"

Muted sob. Slow shake of the head.

I guessed the rest of it. "Where did you catch him with her?"

"At-At his office." Swallowing hard, she groped for another pillowcase. "He-He'd been working extra hours. He told me he was taking up the slack for a vacationing colleague." Firm glance at Angie. "I almost *wish* someone had told me! Anything would have been better than finding him—"

A wrenching sob punctuated her words. Folding her into a sympathetic embrace, I made a soft shushing sound. "It's all right, Ruth. Go ahead and cry if you want."

But that wasn't what she wanted. Memories had stirred up that old anger and resentment. Taking a deep breath, she stepped away from me. Rapid blinking defeated her unshed tears.

Somehow Ruth fabricated an air of shaky dignity. "A woman doesn't like to think she's made a mistake. That the man she married has no sense of decency or restraint." Her teeth gritted. "You bet I divorced him! I refused to stay married to a man so blasted *stupid!*"

I helped her fold some more blankets. Gave her a good ten minutes to cool down. Then I shifted the focus of my inquiry.

"How old was Mona when you two divorced?"

Stuffing the folded blanket into an empty box, Ruth frowned. "She was ten. She-She practically worshipped her father. She sensed there was trouble, and I couldn't bring myself to tell her why." Blue eyes misted with regret. "If only she'd been a little older, then maybe I could have tried to explain . . ."

"You know, ten-year-old girls can be a lot more perceptive than you think."

Standing erect once more, she flashed me a rueful glance. "I know. Mona had a terrible time adjusting to . . . to the new situation. Lee was no help. First he moved in with that woman, and then—" Her eyes squeezed shut, reacting to

149

that ever-present remorse. "I-I couldn't make her understand. Nothing I said seemed to . . . she-she felt as if her father had abandoned her. And then, as she grew older, she blamed *me!*"

"No. She didn't blame you," I said softly, touching the woman's tear-stained face. "Haven't you heard? Mother turns into the enemy the minute you land in junior high. We all went through that phase."

"But . . . but, with Mona, it was *different*. She spent so much time away from home. She-She refused to talk to me."

"Uh-huh, and she spent a lot of time up in her room, listening to headphones. She was very secretive. She wore sunglasses a lot. Even at night."

Ruth gave me a strange look. "That's right! She—"

"Did everything I did when I was her age." I hoped my sympathetic Angie smile strengthened that necessary untruth. "In other words, you had yourself a typical teenage daughter. That's a memory you ought to cherish, Ruth."

Tears overwhelmed her. Lowering her face, she wept like an abandoned child. I plucked a box of tissues from the night table and put it in her grasp. Then I rose catlike from the bed and slipped away. The lady deserved and needed a bit of privacy.

On my way out, I picked up Mona's answering machine.

Go ahead and cry, Ruth. You had a daughter who grew up to become a remarkable woman. And some bastard took her away from you. So cherish those happy memories, please, and don't torture yourself with old guilts. Those memories are all you have left of Mona now.

As for you, Miss Angela Biwaban, remember what the kids used to sing at Park Point Elementary School? *"Liar, liar, pants on fire!"* To the woodshed with you, my girl.

I frowned at my reflection in the hall's dress mirror. Hey, what are you talking about? So I hid the ugly truth from a grieving mother. Big deal! What's wrong with making that nice lady in there feel better about her troubled relationship with the adolescent Mona?

That was a cheap trick, Miss Biwaban. Slipping that bit about the sunglasses into your speech. You know damned well you only wore sunglasses at Park Point Beach ... and *never* at night.

True enough, I mused. Of course, I knew more than a few kids at Central who wore sunglasses around the clock. They wore them to conceal their red-rimmed eyes—to hide the irritation brought on by chronic marijuana smoking.

I padded into the dining room. Okay, so maybe it was a cheap trick. I had just given Ruth Hanauer a description of all the behavior patterns of a chemically dependent teen. And she had unwittingly provided confirmation. Judging from the startled expression on her mother's face, Mona's drug use had begun a long time ago. Long before she married Mickey Grantz.

I began to wonder if Mona's murder had resulted from a dope deal gone sour. The pieces of that woman's sad, short life were beginning to fall into place.

A bright little girl becomes emotionally shattered as a result of her parents' divorce. Anxious to obtain peer approval, she starts smoking marijuana in high school. Fifteen years and one marriage later, she's still at it. Only she is very, very careful now. She has a lot of enemies—Jack Dolan, for one—who would dearly love to see her busted on a drug rap. So she conceals her smoking material in an extremely clever stash.

And buys from only one source?

Hmmmmm, could be. She wouldn't want word of her peccadillo to get around. Not with all those enemies in Port Wyoochee.

Okay, so Mona Hanauer had a single supplier. Who?

And did he or she make home deliveries, say, to the San Juan Islands?

I glanced at the Phone-Mate in my hands. You are truly

a lady of mystery, Mona Irene Hanauer. Why did you keep this thing hidden in the back of your closet?

Or did *somebody else* put it there?

My thumb struck the release button. Up popped the plastic hatch, revealing a small, rectangular plastic pit.

And what happened to the cassettes, Mona? If memory serves, the Phone-Mate comes equipped with two.

Padding softly along, I gave the living room a careful scrutiny. Ruth's muffled weeping stung my heart. This is the rough part of *nandobani*, you know. Lying to the good people. I don't mind sticking it to the John A. Dolans of this world. But conning the good ones . . . well, there's no pleasure in that. Not for me.

Ah, here we are. Mona's telephone jack. Small black widget set right inside the varnished pine baseboard. Kneeling on the rug, I ran the tip of my thumb around the tiny aperture. A fissure captured my thumbnail. Flattening out on the floor, I gave it a closer look. Well, well . . . look at all those cracks. Somebody gave the cord a good hard tug when he removed this machine.

Somehow I didn't think it was Mona.

Squatting on my ankles, I lifted the Phone-Mate in both hands and turned it toward the overhead light. Uh-huh. There's a little ding on the upper left side, right behind the receiver. The spot where this unit struck the floor. It must have hit pretty hard when he ripped that cord out of the wall.

Questions, questions. Who grabbed Mona's answering machine? And why? And who made off with the cassettes?

I didn't find any fingerprint powder on the receiver. So it was a safe bet that the Port Wyoochee P.D. had overlooked this little item. If they checked at all, they probably saw it on the closet shelf and assumed it was broken.

One thing was certain. Somebody didn't want the law listening to the taped messages on those cassettes. Which made me very much interested in finding them.

I left the Phone-Mate on the kitchenette counter, intent upon toting it along later. Then I dug a crystal tumbler out of a cardboard box, switched on the faucet, and ran a cold glass of water for Mona's grieving mother.

Chapter Eight

"Antique glass?" Mrs. McFadden echoed. Cornflower blue eyes blinked from behind a pair of gold-rimmed glasses.

"Uh-huh. Depression era glass." Putting my hands on my knees, I studied the porcelain bric-a-brac in the large oaken display case. "I was hoping to pick up one of those old glass rolling pins from the thirties." Standing upright again, I outlined a phantom cylinder with both hands. "My Aunt Della collects antique rolling pins, and that's one item missing from her collection."

The white-haired store owner nodded in understanding. "With the black screw-cap at one end, right?" She was an inch over my height, a sixtyish matron wearing a blue cardigan and white jeans. "Ooooooh, I'm not sure if we have any of those left in the inventory, Anne Marie. Depression glass is all the rage these days." Wry grimace. "When I think of all those jars Mother had in the attic . . ." Rounding the counter, she added, "Let me talk to the mister. I'll be right back."

"I'm not going anywhere, Mrs. M."

How true! Thus far, it had been a most unproductive afternoon. Ruth Hanauer had given me a ride back to the Parmenter House. There I'd traded in my jogging togs for a wine-colored turtleneck and a pair of white corduroy slacks.

Then, grabbing my rainproof anorak, I'd taken a cab back to Dungeness Circle to retrieve the Topaz.

My next stop was Keel Road. In particular, the cluster of gift shops bordering the town beach. Believe me, it was not a beach day. Energetic combers rolled ashore on deserted brown sands. An impenetrable mist concealed Sahale Point from view. Tendrils of fog swirled down from the overcast, tickling the whitecaps.

I struck out at the first two shops and then tried Bayside Antiques—Mr. and Mrs. R. McFadden, proprietors. The shop was a Cape Cod saltbox with a weathered clapboard exterior. Inside, every display case, shelf, carton and appliance was piled high with aging souvenirs. Prams from the First World War. Forty-five R.P.M. records. First-generation Barbie dolls. Souvenir glassware from the 1962 Seattle World's Fair.

"I'm sorry, Anne Marie." Mrs. McFadden came bustling out of the back room, her pudgy features showing sincere regret. "We had one of those around here for *years*. Bob sold it last July to a tourist couple from Rhode Island."

"Thanks for looking." Casual shrug. "You know, I'm having the hardest time finding one of those things. I called that place up on Dollar Avenue . . . you know, Heritage Antiques? The machine took my message, but nobody ever got back to me."

"Oh, my God!" Wide-eyed with horror, Mrs. McFadden touched her cheek. "I guess you haven't heard!"

"About what?"

"About the *murder!* Heritage's owner—Mona Hanauer—she was killed in the San Juans!"

With that, Mrs. McFadden launched into a detailed discussion of the slaying. Apparently, she had known Mona and Ruth quite well, expressing remorse over the mother/daughter estrangement. Turns out that Mona had come to the McFaddens for advice four years earlier, when she first opened Heritage. She and the McFaddens had often gone bargain-hunting in Seattle together.

"Decent people just aren't safe anymore," Mrs. McFadden said. "I told Mona time and again. 'You shouldn't stay over there all by yourself.'"

"She went to the islands quite often?"

"Once a week. She really looked forward to that trip." The store owner sighed. "Young girls! They simply don't realize how vulnerable they are. It's not like it was when Mona was a child. There are break-ins over there all the time now." Her sad, wistful gaze circled the store's cozy interior. "I'm just glad we live out here—away from the cities. All those junkies and trash! It's not so easy for them to get to Port Wyoochee."

Gently I steered our conversation back to the subject of Mona's answering machine. Puzzled Angie frown. "I wonder why Mona never got back to me." Quizzical glance. "The machine took my message. Maybe the playback was broken."

"I don't think so. I phoned Mona just before she left for the islands. I asked her if she wanted to go to the Queen of Angeles Bazaar next month. She returned my call that morning."

"One thing I don't understand, Mrs. M. Why did Mona route all her calls to her home?" I asked. "Wouldn't it have been easier to install a second phone in the store?"

Mrs. McFadden showed me an uncomfortable look. "Mona preferred to screen her calls."

"Why?"

"She was harassed quite a bit after she rejoined the Greenway committee." Blue eyes avoided my gaze. "There are people in this town . . . well, they used to phone her and call her names . . . hateful things . . . it was *terrible*, Anne Marie. Ruth was so upset. Then Mayor Woodward and Rabbi Rotenberg held that conference for Brotherhood Week. The harassment toned down a bit after that. But Mona was still getting an occasional hate call. That's why she installed an answering machine."

Sympathetic nod. The woman's story was perfectly consistent with what the Mick had told me. I was pretty sure it wasn't Mona who'd yanked the Phone-Mate out of the wall. Most likely it was the killer cleaning up a loose end.

I stuck around for another half-hour. Bob McFadden emerged from his backroom repair shop, and the missus introduced us, following right up with an invitation to tea. So I enjoyed a steaming cup of Lipton and discussed antiques with the couple. Their Victorian fainting couch was woefully underpriced, and I told them so. They thanked me for the tip and invited me to drop around some other time.

As I left the antique store, I spotted my grandfather leaning against the Topaz's fender. Chief resembled a beached fisherman in his navy blue woolen watch cap, Coast Guard peacoat and wrinkled gray Dockers.

I flashed a welcoming smile. "I see you got the message."

"Desk clerk gave it to me." Taking the index card from his pocket, he added, "I never realized my granddaughter was such an artist."

He showed me the card's face, and I grinned at my handiwork. Four Anishinabe pictographs in a row—princess, arrow, water sign, dollar sign. Translation—*Your granddaughter is at Chickamin Cove.*

"Any trouble figuring it out?"

"Well, it had me stumped at first," he admitted, tucking the card away. "Then I remembered . . . *Chickamin* is Klallam for *money.*" He waggled a blunt forefinger. "Let's you and me do some beachcombing, missy."

So we ambled along the windswept beach, Chief and I, heading for the rocks at the foot of Harbor Ridge. A squadron of grounded gulls lined the dunes, waiting for the fog to lift. Huddled in the sparse grass was a trio of bufflehead ducks. Damp sand clung to the laces of my Reeboks. We did a lot of talking—all of it in our people's language.

"So what do you think, *Noozis?*" he asked, warming his hands with his breath.

"It's beginning to look as if the killer lured Mona to the San Juans on purpose." I zipped my anorak a little higher. "I'm pretty sure he left a message on Mona's Phone-Mate. 'Meet you Wednesday night on Orcas.' Something like that. Mona kept the appointment, and our friend tried to kill her."

"Where does Mickey Grantz fit in?" asked Chief.

Thoughtful fussbudget face. "Mick was the wild card. The killer had no idea *he* was going to show up. He'd planned on Mona being alone, and there was Mick following her around like a lovesick teen. The problem resolved itself, though. The two of them quarrelled at the restaurant. Mona went home alone." A sleek gull skittered out of my path. "Way I see it, the killer began seeing Mick not as a threat but as an opportunity."

"What do you mean?"

"After he saw them quarrelling, the killer had a brainstorm," I added. "He decided to throw the police a ready-made patsy. He went straight to Mickey's motel, grabbed the sweater, and then headed for Mona's cabin. After he planted the sweater, he hightailed it back to Port Wyoochee to grab the incriminating phone tape."

"One question, *Noozis*. Why did he change his plans?"

"He had no choice, *Nimishoo*. The plan went wrong from the start. Our friend had to keep improvising."

"What do you think he originally had in mind?"

The wind tossed a wing of raven hair into my face. Peeling away strands, I said, "First time around, he probably planned to bludgeon Mona and deep-six her body in the sound. Simple, direct, no clues. But it all went wrong. First Mickey showed up unexpectedly. Later on, Mona got away from him."

Chief showed me a grim smile. "So now you know something about the killer."

"Like what?"

"One, he's a likely suspect. Someone who wanted Mona Hanauer dead. Therefore, he had compelling reasons to stay out of the police spotlight. That's why he needed a patsy." My grandfather counted off on his fingers. "Two, he's someone who knows a lot about Mona's background. He knew all about her acrimonious divorce. That's why he nominated Mickey Grantz for the role."

"Likely suspect!" I let out a fatigued sigh. "There's no shortage of those, *Nimishoo*. Looking at it from the romantic angle, there's the woman scorned—Georgianna. And the tossed-out boyfriend—Jon Waterman . . ."

Chief interrupted, "Not to mention the discarded husband."

I thought of the two teenaged eyewitnesses. Had they really seen Mickey at her cabin that night? Then I remembered the Phone-Mate, and my momentary doubts evaporated. "You can drop Mickey from the suspect list, *Nimishoo*. There's no way he could've gotten to Mona's apartment. He was arrested the minute he stepped off the ferry in Anacortes."

"Mona could have removed the cassette herself."

"Not likely, *Nimishoo!* You didn't see the Phone-Mate. I did. Somebody ripped that unit right out of the wall. And it wasn't Mickey Grantz. He was in jail."

Nodding, he conceded the point. "All right, so he was framed. How do we prove it?"

"By tracking down the real killer. Then fixing it so he tumbles into the outstretched arms of the law."

"Easier said than done. Who's left?"

"Well, in the political arena, there's Mona's archenemy on the left. Again, Georgianna. Over on the right, we have Lemuel Thurber and his merry men. Hassling outspoken Jewish women appears to be a longtime sport here in Yennis County. Then there's Jack Dolan and Rolf Lauridsen. They both stood to lose big if Mona had succeeded in forcing Kulshan Paper to comply with the EPA ruling."

"Bigger than you think, *Noozis.*"

"Oh?" I cast my grandfather a curious sidelong glance. "You heard something interesting?"

We halted beside a damp driftwood log. A few yards down the beach, a clam digger stalked his hard-shelled prey.

"I heard plenty, *Noozis.*" Obsidian eyes sparkled. "Talked to some Kulshan employees. Told them I was looking for part-time custodial work. The verdict was unanimous— forget about Kulshan."

"Reasons?"

"They've taken a bath four quarters running. Their over-all sales are down about fifteen million dollars from last year. There was one layoff in June, and another's planned for February." Aged features tensed in recollection. "Word is, they're pinning their hopes on cornering the market in some kind of special paper—"

"Supercalendered paper," I blurted, remembering my brief chat with Lauridsen.

"That's the stuff. Trouble is, those European mills are churning it out a whole lot faster than the Kulshan Paper Company."

"Which is driving down the wholesale price and killing Kulshan's earnings," I added, thinking aloud. "No wonder Dolan's so touchy. If he has to pay for that Sahale Point cleanup, it could put Kulshan in the toilet."

"That's what they're saying downtown. Dolan just might have bought himself a white elephant. A lot of people are updating their résumés. Some of them—the ones with long-time roots here—figure to collect unemployment for a while and see what happens. The rest are thinking seriously about the Alaska panhandle."

Facing the gentle surf, I shook my head. "It doesn't make sense, *Nimishoo.* Let's assume you're right. The Greenway lawsuit threatens Kulshan's continued existence. It'll put a great big dent in Dolan's wallet and finish Lauridsen's career. Still . . . what did they gain by killing Mona?"

"Maybe the EPA won't push so hard for compliance without Mona Hanauer around."

"Georgianna's still around," I pointed out.

Chief made a face. "Mona was the greater threat, *Noozis*. The other one is just a loudmouth."

No comment from Angie. How interesting, though, that my grandfather's assessment so closely matched Marcella Caputo's.

"Have we covered it all?" he asked.

"Not quite." Smoothing my hair back, I faced him once more. "There's still the matter of Mona's marijuana stash. I had a long talk with her mother earlier this afternoon. Apparently, Mona was a heavy user in high school and never dropped the habit."

Chief grimaced. "That is news. People had plenty to say about Mona. Mostly they called her a 'tree-hugging anarchist.' But nobody I talked to mentioned marijuana."

"Meaning Mona kept it a secret. She had to be buying from only one source."

My grandfather looked skeptical. "Word still would have gotten around. Dealers can be talkative."

Fussbudget face. Chief had me there. Why would a dope dealer keep silent about Mona's habit?

Chief's expression turned thoughtful. "You know, maybe that's why Mona visited the San Juans once a week."

"To make a buy," I murmured. "You're right, *Nimishoo*. That cabin provided all the privacy she needed."

"So who could have known she was a user?"

"Mickey, naturally, but we can rule him out." My sneaker dug a tiny trench in the sand. I watched the tall, lanky clammer wade into the sea. "Jon Waterman. He lived with Mona for better than three years." I licked my salt-tinged lips. "Jack Dolan. He told me he had Mona investigated out the kazoo. And whatever he knew, Lauridsen knew." I thought of Sargent's surreptitious visit to the cabin. "One of Lemuel Thurber's boys. Guy named Sargent. He kept tabs on Mona's place." Grimace of curiosity. "What are you getting at?"

"The killer's original plan, *Noozis*. Kill Mona and dump her in the sound. When she fails to turn up, the police search the premises and find evidence of her marijuana use. The murder's written off as a drug deal that went sour." He stuffed his hands in his peacoat pockets. "Anyone else?"

"Georgianna Waterman. She had a cabin on Orcas, too. The old Taliaferro place." Resuming our stroll, I headed for a sand flat overgrown with luxuriant green vegetation. "What do you want to bet they ran into each other on Orcas?"

"Makes sense. Georgianna saw Mona stoned one time and realized she was using. Could— ?"

He never finished the query. A sharp male voice rang out behind us. *"Wait!"*

Turning, I spied the tall clammer running our way. Knee-high Nokia boots kicked up a fine spray. He was in his thirties, a hawk-featured man with dark eyebrows, a broad handlebar moustache, and a noticeable five o'clock shadow. Clam shovel in one hand, aluminum pail in the other. Pine-colored ranch jacket, black jeans and a canvas cap emblazoned with a Mossberg patch. Sudden alarm filled his face. "You don't want to go that way, miss."

I halted. "What's the matter?"

Setting down his pail, he answered, "That's a tidal pool. It's like quicksand in there. You'll sink up to your neck."

"Looks solid enough to me," Chief remarked.

"Looks can be deceiving, mister." He leaned against the long handle of his clam shovel. "Where you folks from? Yakima?"

"He is." I lied, nodding to my grandfather. "I'm from Spokane."

"First time on the shore?"

Chief nodded. "What do you mean ... *tidal pool?*"

162

"There's no bedrock under that sand." He gestured at the grassy flat. "It's saturated clear through with water. That's why the eelgrass is so green. Got to watch your step along this shore."

Grateful Angie smile. "Thanks for the warning."

"You're welcome. Remember, if you see brown grass or some of that there rockweed . . ." He pointed out a garden of yellowish brown plants farther inland. "That means it's firm enough to walk on."

"Learn something new every day." Chief cracked a smile. "Thanks, Mister . . . ?"

"Nardinger. Ed Nardinger." Shaking hands with my grandfather, he shot me an inquisitive look.

"Anne Marie Nahkeeta." I offered my hand. The clammer's grip was firm but gentle.

"Oh, yeah! Girl who just moved to town."

My smile widened. "News travels fast in Port Wyoochee. How's the clamming?"

"Can't complain. This here beach is always pretty good for sand dollars and Jap littlenecks. Particularly at minus."

"Minus?" I echoed.

"Low tide," said Chief helpfully. I gather he picked up the shore jargon at Bremerton.

Nardinger's face reflected mild curiosity. "Pardon my askin', but . . . you folks lookin' for the old Taliaferro place?"

Playing along, I replied, "That's right."

The clammer's smile turned apologetic. "I was listenin' to you and him talkin' Indian. Recognized the name Taliaferro. Sorry—didn't mean to eavesdrop." Embarrassed shrug. "Man gets bored listenin' to the surf all day long."

Winsome Angie smile. "We came down here looking for it."

Deadpan, Chief added, "Heard all about it in town."

"I ain't surprised. Ol' Jack was quite a character."

"Jack Taliaferro?" I wondered if it was the same Taliaferro who'd built Georgianna's cabin on Orcas.

"That's him." Lifting a sinewy hand, Nardinger gestured at a rocky headland a mile up the beach. "The shack used to stand over there. Right at the edge of the cove. See? Tore it down in '61, '62 when they cut the top off the ridge and put in all them ranch houses."

"Didn't he have a cabin in the San Juans, too?"

"Sure did! Fact is, Jack had hideaway docks up and down the sound. He was a rumrunner back in the Prohibition days. Pretty successful at it, too. He got started right after the First World War. Ran the Scotch right across the strait. His boats used to leave Victoria at dusk, awash to the gunwales. They'd hole up in the San Juans during daylight. Then, the next night, they'd be making deliveries all along the shore—Sequim, Port Townsend, Bellingham, Anacortes." Rueful shake of the head. "I'm tellin' you, that Jack was one rich Eye-talian when he went back to Naples after Repeal. You thinkin' about goin' over to Friday Harbor? Ask about Jack Taliaferro. They'll show you some of the coves where his boats hid out." He grinned. "Next time you're over there, ask 'em about ol' Whiskey Jack."

Whiskey Jack!? I did an instant doubletake. My reaction startled Ed Nardinger, but fortunately my grandfather covered for me.

Tapping the shovel's handle, Chief said, "Don't see too many of these on my reservation, Ed. How does it work?"

"Well, here, mister, I'll show you." He took a few steps toward the sea, then knelt in the damp sand. "First you've got to find yourself a dimple."

"Dimple?" Chief echoed.

"Sure! Little hole in the sand about the size of a dime. See, when the tide's in, the clam sticks its neck all the way out to feed. When it pulls back into its shell, it leaves a tiny depression in the sand. That's what we call a *dimple.*"

Beaming with delight, Nardinger scanned the sand for dimples. People just love to talk about their work.

"You look for a whole bunch of 'em . . . like this spot over here. Then you dig your trench over to the side . . ."

For the next ten minutes, your Angie maintained a respectful silence while Ed Nardinger lectured us on the fine points of clam digging. Then we shook hands again, wished him luck, and made our retreat to Keel Road.

"Whiskey Jack," I muttered, as soon as we were out of earshot. "Last time I heard that phrase was twelve years ago. The Keeshigun powwow in Thunder Bay. Now it *haunts* me!"

"Whiskey Jack Taliaferro," Chief murmured.

"That might be our dying clue." Mist dampened my face as we strolled along. "Sister Mary Katherine distinctly heard Mona say 'Whiskey Jack.' "

My grandfather looked at me askance. "You can't be serious, Angie. Taliaferro was a grown man at the end of World War One. He's old enough to be my *father.*" Hoarse chuckle. "If he ain't dead, he's got to be pushing the century mark."

"Not him—Georgianna! She owns Taliaferro's cabin on Orcas."

"That's crazy!" Expression of distaste. "Mona was beaten to death. Could a woman do that?"

"This woman could." I fell into step at his side. "You should've seen Georgianna in action at the Kulshan protest. She went after a stevedore as rugged as Sylvester Stallone. Georgianna has an ugly temper. And she's no lady . . . especially when she gets riled."

Chief was in an argumentative mood. "Angie, the eyewitnesses both agree it was a man."

"Okay. Roll Georgianna's hair into a bun. Put her in an oversized camp shirt and baggy pants. Stick her out there in the middle of the night at least thirty yards from the witnesses. What have you got?"

"My granddaughter twisting the facts to suit her theories, as usual." Arch sidelong smile. "One question, Angie—why

165

did Mona say 'Whiskey Jack' when it would've been just as easy to say 'Georgianna'?"

"Mona was delirious," I replied. "Sister Mary Katherine told me so."

"And you're going to hang all that on the words of a delirious woman?"

"It's Mona's deathbed testimony, Chief. It has to mean something."

"Not necessarily." As we reached the Topaz, my grandfather opened the driver's door for me. "For all we know, Mona saw a Canada jay fly overhead."

Showing a fussbudget face, I got behind the steering wheel and opened the window. "Wellllll, there is *that* possibility."

He slammed the car door shut. "What now?"

Mischievous Angie smile. "I think I'll go to church."

Surprised blink from Chief. "Long time since you've been to Mass."

"I'm not talking about St. Luke's." Leaning to my right, I opened the passenger door for him. "I thought I'd catch Thurber's sermon tonight at the First Adamite Church."

Utter silence. And then, in a bellow that could be heard in Seattle, my grandfather thundered, *"Are you out of your mind!?"*

"Not at all, Chief," I replied, watching him climb into the car. "Thurber's going to be busy haranguing the faithful. Can you think of a better time to sneak a quick peek at his private files?"

Incensed mutter on my immediate right. "Lunatic! I've got a lunatic for a granddaughter!"

Chuckling, I put the key in the ignition.

And away we drove.

Dusk found us in the foothills of the Olympic range, heading uphill and south on Sadie Creek Road. The moist forest hemmed us in on both sides. Chest-high huckleberry bushes lined the shoulder. Behind them reared lofty Douglas firs, measuring four feet around the trunk, with moss-covered, corrugated bark.

Chief had the wheel. I occupied the passenger seat, pulling on my trusty moosehide moccasin boots. That was one damp forest out there, and my handmade Northland boots shed water a whole lot better than those spiffy Reeboks.

"Got to be the dumbest thing you've ever done!" Chief muttered, clutching the steering wheel.

"Dumber than showing up at Sunawavi's house?" I teased, tucking my pants leg into the left boot.

"Ten times dumber!" Chief jutted his chin at the car ahead of us. A green Ford Escort with Oregon plates. "Those seig-heilers ain't too fond of minorities, you know. If you get caught in there—!"

"I'll try not to get caught, then." Leaning leftward, I kissed my grandfather's leathery cheek. The Escort began to slow. "We're coming up on the entrance."

"I see it, Angie . . . *oh, shit!*"

He stomped down on the accelerator. Our Topaz zoomed past Thurber's access road. But not before I caught a glimpse of the guard shack, the leashed German shepherd, and the four grim-faced men in woodland camo toting scoped M-16s. Each of them wore a red-and-white swastika armband. To the right of the shack stood a large sign reading

National Headquarters
FIRST CHURCH OF JESUS CHRIST-ADAMITE
Camp Pelley, Wash.

My grandfather kept right on driving. "Face facts, young lady. No way are you getting through that gate."

Sigh of resignation. "Okay, then. On to Plan B. Another half-mile and you can drop me off at the side of the road."

Chief frowned in exasperation. "How do I keep getting talked into these damned foolish—!?"

"Hide the car. Then join me inside the compound." Fashioning a ponytail with a slender strand of rawhide, I added, "We'll need a recognition signal. Can you still do a Canada jay?"

Wheee-ah-chuck-chuck! Perfect imitation of the whiskey jack. Slowing the car, he muttered, "You know, I could be having dinner at the Northwoods Cafe right now—enjoying my retirement years back home!"

I levered the door open. "Come on, Chief. You don't really want to spend the rest of your days playing bingo at Fond du Lac."

"You live longer that way. It's a lot safer than running around Berchtesgaden making bird noises." As I eased the door shut, he became deadly serious. *"Baapiniziwaagan, Noozis!"*

"I'll be careful, *Nimishoo*, I promise."

The Topaz tooled away from the road's shoulder, its tires spitting sand. I melted into the roadside brush. Leaning against a lofty alder, I waited until I could no longer see the spires of the firs. Then, keeping an eye peeled for oncoming traffic, I sprinted across the asphalt, quick as a jackrabbit, and slipped into the rain forest on Thurber's property. I kept my head down, choosing each and every step with care. Commando Angie.

An electrified fence meandered through the forest. Tilted barbed wire crowned the top. Reminded me of the prison fence at Cedar Creek. No problem getting over it, though. Not with that bigleaf maple growing nearby. Tomboy Angie had a nickname when she was five years old. *Ausanawgo.* The Squirrel.

Dropping from a maple branch, I hit the mossy forest floor a bit louder than I would have liked. The sound spooked a big Roosevelt elk browsing nearby. Magnificent beast. Big as a horse, dark neck and tawny torso, with a full

168

rack of antlers. He wasn't used to princesses dropping out of trees. He bounded over a fallen spruce log, vanishing into the shadows like a buff-colored ghost.

Leisurely I made my way upslope, letting myself become one with the rhythm of the forest. My footfalls grew quieter. Night birds accepted my presence, resuming their trilling once more. A sensation of peace and well-being swam over me. As always, when walking alone in the forest, I felt as if I had somehow come home.

With the greenery cloaked in darkness, my nostrils took over the task of identification. Subtle scents touched my nose. The sweet smell of deerfoot vanilla leaf. Pungent odor of wild onions. Dull tang of spirea and Sitka columbine. As I padded along, prickly thistle spines snatched at my moosehide moccasin boots.

I saw the darkness at the foot of a red cedar and decided it would make a fine spot for a *dasanagun*. That's our word for *trap*. I made my very first one when I was five. It was one fine crisp sub-zero Minnesota December night. Tettegouche, of course. Daddy and Chief bundled me up, and we went grouse hunting. Snowshoeing along in that red oak forest at the foot of Papasay Ridge. I asked my father why he hadn't brought his gun. "Bullets are expensive," he told me, "so we're going to do it the traditional way."

You see, on those frostbitten Minnesota nights, ruffed grouse seek shelter from the cold by burrowing into snowdrifts. And my people were catching them long before Columbus introduced the firearm to the Tainos.

Chief scouted out some grouse tracks, and we trailed them to a sizable snowdrift. Imitating Chief and Daddy, I fashioned my loops with a twine made from basswood fibers. Then I watched breathlessly as my grandfather silently approached the drift's trackless side. Quiet as a ghost, that man. Expertly he set our snares, and then we all hiked back to his cabin and got some sleep.

Shortly before dawn, Daddy tenderly shook me awake,

handed me my winter clothes, and carried me on his shoulders back to the snowdrift. And there we stood when the first rays of dawn tinted the snow a roseate hue. With a heart-stopping suddenness, a grouse exploded out of the snow, a blur of brown against white. His beak soared right through the center of my *dasanagun* loop. Two seconds later, he was dangling at the end of the twine, wings beating madly, uttering a highly indignant *cluck-cluck*.

Now you know what Angie's family had for dinner that snowy Sunday afternoon.

As I neared the ridge, a frenzied canine howl reverberated through the rain forest. My skin turned to ice. Dropping into a crouch, I held my breath. Waited and listened. More excited barking. I fumed: Damn! The German shepherd at the gate. He'd sniffed me out.

Backing away from the skyline, I retreated downslope. The dog's barking subsided. I hoped the guards kept him on that leash.

Frowning, I composed a letter in my mind.

Dear Coco Chanel—Not only does your overpriced perfume make me irresistible to men, it also alerts every canine within a radius of three miles!

Well, princess, let's see what we can do about that.

I spied a flat rock at the foot of an alder tree. Groping about on the ground, I laid hands on a hefty round stone. After that, it was time for some forest grocery shopping. Let's see now. Wild onions. Butterweed. Star-shaped bell-flower blossoms. Last bunchberries of the season. Put the groceries on the flat rock. Pound and grind with the *mano*. Reduce them all to a sticky, pungent paste. And there we have it. Angie's camouflage perfume. *Joie de Bois Olympienne.*

I dabbed the concoction behind my ears. That ought to deaden the scent of Chanel Number Five. Then, for good measure, I smeared my forehead, cheeks and throat. Hopping onto the flat rock, I heartily rubbed the gunk into the soles of my moccasin boots. With that stuff tainting my footsteps, the German shepherd would have a hard time following my trail.

And then it was back to the skyline. I dropped to all fours. The dog remained silent. Crawling forward, I peered over a lichen-covered boulder.

The ridge circled off to the north, forming a box canyon about the size of a football field. At the foot of the slope stood the wooden Adamite church, quite small and distinctively rural, with whitewashed shingles, a gray tiled roof, and a small bell tower. Nearby were four lengthy one-story buildings vaguely reminiscent of army barracks. Beyond that, a spindly-legged guard tower, several feet higher than the church, kept watch over the compound. I spotted three riflemen moving about restlessly up there.

Slowly I worked my way downhill, slipping and sliding from spruce trunk to bunchberry bush. Like a gila monster, I slithered into the shadows of the parking lot. Awful lot of cars in there. Plenty of out-of-state license plates, too. I counted seven from Oregon, two from Idaho and one from faraway Wyoming. Keeping low, I flitted from car to car, always careful to stay out of the tower's line of sight. Anishinabe princess on the scout.

Tense minutes passed. At last I reached the cars closest to the church. Faint bluegrass music intruded on the chatter of the night birds. My mouth went dry. You know, maybe this wasn't such a smart idea, after all. *Four* buildings? Which one of them housed Thurber's files? This could take all night.

Ignoring the frantic beat of my heart, I cast a fleeting glance at the guard tower. Now or never, princess.

Instantly I shot up, then leaned against the car door, searching my pockets, acting as if I'd just come outside for a smoke. A guard's curious gaze struck me like a physical object, chilling my skin. I forced myself to look his way, pasted on an Angie smile, and lifted my hand in a jaunty wave. He waved right back. Slightly emboldened, I walked away from the car, making a beeline to the church door.

A stealthy two-toned whistle drifted down from the tower. Grinning to myself, I reached for the brass handles. Naughty boy!

Easing the door shut, I found myself in a deserted vestry. A second pair of doors barred my way into the main chapel. On the right stood a gilt-trimmed baptismal font. To the left, I spotted some folded chairs, a tall magazine rack, and a hand-painted sign reading *Tonight's Service—Live from Bentonville, Ohio—Kimmie Lee and her Aryan Defenders! Pastor's Sermon—"Will the Jews Succeed in Closing Our Paper Mill?"*

Shaking my head in amazement, I backed away from the sign. And got a better look at the magazine rack. A sense of unreality swept over me. Pamphlet City, gang. I mean, dozens of them. With such interesting titles as *Airwolf—Mossad's Secret Helicopter Police*, *The Vanishing White Man* and *Is Bigfoot a Lubavitcher?*

While Kimmie Lee's vibrant contralto belted out a Gospel ballad, your Angie did some hasty browsing in a booklet entitled *Our Savior's Escape*. According to the author, Adolf Hitler didn't really die in his Berlin bunker. Nope, the Moustached One made a clean getaway. In a UFO piloted by Judge Crater!

I replaced it in the rack. Yeah, right! And they're both wasting away in Margaritaville, the secret Nazi UFO base at the South Pole. Give me a break!

For school-age stormtroopers, there were comic books. Four-color bigotry and mayhem. Bruno the Barbarian, Action Team SS, Aryan Girl—all your favorite superheroes.

Shuddering in disgust, I backed away. Nothing like getting the kids started early. Right, Lem?

Suddenly, brass hinges squeaked. Reacting instantly, I melted into the shadows of the tower doorway. Breathlessly I watched a pair of solemn-eyed farmers push open the chapel doors. Applause cascaded into the vestry.

Craning my neck, I caught the end of the show. Behind the pastor's podium stood Kimmie Lee, the Adamites' answer to Tanya Tucker. She resembled a teenaged boy's fantasy of the girl next door. Angelic features, killer curves and bouncy blond hair. Like the cowpoke musicians in her backup group, she was wearing some kind of uniform. Light blue blouse, black wing tie, and a navy pleated skirt. As she turned to the left, I saw the swastika armband on her sleeve.

Oh, Kimmie gave them a delightful show. Superabundance of energy and poise. The way she went at it, you would have thought she was playing the Grand Ole Opry. Don't think the audience wasn't appreciative. Whistles and rebel yells. Lots of hand-clapping and foot-stomping. Shouts of "Jesus song, Kim!" and "We want Jesus Christ!"

Alas, it was not to be. A bow, a flourish, a Miss America smile, and the lady was out of the spotlight, as self-effacing as Patsy Cline. The crowd began to settle down. Then a tall man with a distinct military bearing took the podium. Clerical collar and a minister's black suit. Heroic square-jawed face and a Burt Reynolds nose. Thunderous baritone voice. "Let us pray!"

An ominous undertone welled upward from the congregation. My heart froze as I beheld the object of their devotions. A large oil painting of Jesus Christ and Adolf Hitler saluting a crowned broadsword.

How right you were, *Nimishoo!* This is definitely *not* the place for an Anishinabe.

"Amen!" Gripping the podium, the minister raked the audience with a ferocious gaze. "I never thought I'd see the day when the Jews, the liberals and the niggers would take over our paper mill and place it under the United Nations flag instead of Old Glory, the flag I fought for. I had three tours in Vietnam, getting my ass shot off, while the big Jewboy, Henry Kissinger, was selling us out to the Rothschilds. Same damn thing today! The big Jewboys are going to shut down Kulshan and ship your job down to Mexico. They're going to get some greaseball to make the paper. Pay him two dollars an hour. Average wage at

Kulshan is twelve. Now, where do you suppose that other ten dollars is going to go, eh? Straight to Jerusalem, that's where! Them old Elders of Zion are going to be filling their wallets while you folks sit around Port Wyoochee, waiting for the mill to open back up."

The crowd's undertone turned surly.

"You saw that Jewgirl Waterman on TV. Leading all them queers and liberals against the Kulshan plant." Impassioned crescendo. "If that mill closes down, what are you folks supposed to do for a living? How are you going to support your families?" Sudden switch to the folksy approach. "Now, I suppose one of them liberals is gonna say, 'Shame on you, Pastor Thurber. You're preaching hate. Ain't you ever heard of the Holocaust?' Yeah, I've heard about it. And so have all of you! Damned liberal media doesn't talk about much else. When's the last time you heard them cryin' about all the lost jobs here in the great state of Washington? Ain't heard about that, have you? When the TV ain't talking about the Holocaust, it's talking about some damned hoot-owl!"

Individual communicants stood and cheered. The viciousness of Thurber's monologue had my head spinning, but the crowd—two hundred strong—was eating it up. The jubilant atmosphere was part carnival, part revival meeting. And seething with hatred!

"That kike librarian is back on the street, I hear. So I guess you Kulshan folks will be entertainin' her again real soon. And if you don't know what to do when that heeb shows up again, you're too damned dumb to bother with." Thurber radiated a grin of sheer satisfaction. "Did you hear what happened to that Jewgirl Hanauer? Somebody went over to the San Juans and punched her face in!" Gleeful chuckle. "Ain't it wonderful to know there's at least one white man willing to stand up to the rabbis?"

Warpath scowl. You seem awfully certain it was a man, Thurber.

"Well, I heard a request for the Jesus song a while back,

so I'm going to shut up for a spell and turn it over to this lovely lady." He gestured at a beaming Kimmie Lee. "Let's have a few hymns. And then we'll talk some more turkey about the big Jewboys."

Sidling toward the exit, I decided that this would be the perfect time to take my leave.

Suddenly, a firm warm hand capped my mouth. Eyes goggling, I shivered all over. The restraining grip, however, remained gentle. My ear caught a familiar male whisper. "Don't worry—it's only me."

"Chief!" I whirled, hissing in alarm. "What are you doing—?"

"I came to get you." He tilted his head toward the door. "We've got to get out of here, Angie."

"Thurber's office—"

"Forget it," he whispered. "There's a couple of guys in the woods."

"Adamite security?"

"Not likely, girl. These two are in civvies. They're taking photos of every car here." My grandfather tugged at my wrist. "I spotted them while I was working my way past the guard tower."

Realization sent a cold surge through my stomach. "Oh, shit! The FBI! They staked out the meeting!"

"That's what I figured," Chief murmured. "It'd be worth another eagle feather to them if they could catch Pocahontas right along with Thurber's crew. Come on!"

By now, the din was deafening. The entire congregation was on its feet, clapping in unison, singing right along with Kimmie. A hymn of hate the like of which I'd never heard before.

"Do it for Jesus Christ.
Yeah, do it for Jesus Christ.
Grab your guns and
Tie your shoes.

175

Get out there and
Get the Jews!
And do it for Jesus Christ!"

As my hand reached for a brass handle, the door suddenly swung outward, revealing four big, beefy skinheads in denim and black leather. They stared in utter astonishment. Instantly I froze, my startled gaze riding up a *White Power* shirtfront to the face of the leader.

Sargent's harsh features tensed in sudden fury.

"Going somewhere, nigger?"

Chapter Nine

The skinheads charged through the doorway. Chief yanked me out of their path. With our backs to the baptismal font, we watched Sargent and his buddies close in. Shoving me behind him, my grandfather shouted, *"Noozis, maajiibatoon!"*

No way, Chief! Even if I could make it down the center aisle, I'm not leaving you to face them alone. Clutching my grandfather's arm, I trembled and watched Sargent double his fists.

The skinhead on his right blurted, "Hey! They ain't niggers—they're Injuns!"

"Mud people!" Sargent spat. "Three guesses what we do to redskins, old man."

"One guess is all I need, asshole!" Eyes narrowing in defiance, my grandfather levelled his fists. "So let me bend over—then *you* can give it a nice big wet one!"

Bellowing in rage, the skinhead leader swung. Sargent's punch skimmed my grandfather's head, knocking off his watch cap. Then they came together in deadly earnest, grunting and swinging. Blinding flurry of punches. My grandfather was willing, but Sargent had the height and the weight. And he was forty years younger than Chief. Breaking free, he uncorked a powerful overhand right. Chief's head snapped to one side, and down he went, hitting the vestry floor in a loose-limbed tumble.

"Nimishoo!" I screamed.

Victory yells from the skinheads. Kneeling beside my grandfather, I helped him sit upright. He was breathing heavily, and there was an angry swelling on his chin. Blood trickled from the corner of his mouth.

Blinking away the angry tears, I cried, "Big brave Aryan! Beating up a man in his seventies!" Then, switching to our language, I asked, "Are you going to be all right, *Nimishoo?*"

Grunting, Chief dabbed at the crimson stream with his wrist. "I'll live." Ragged sigh. "Should've stayed home and played bingo."

The fight quickly drew a crowd. Churchgoers poured into the vestry, jostling for a better look. Gasps and exclamations. Queries for the skinheads. Expressions of sheer hatred.

"Darkies! Boogies!"

"Mud people! In *our* church!"

"Lynch 'em!"

"I got a rope in my truck!"

Scanning the hostile faces in that crowd, I swallowed hard and hugged my grandfather more tightly. Just then, a tense black-clad figure eased his way into the mob's forefront. "Steve! What's going on here?"

Sargent snapped to attention. "We caught these two sneaking around, Pastor." His right arm shot upward. "Hail victory!"

"Hail!" Thurber's return salute was as casual as Goering's. He looked vaguely worried. "Don't harm them. Take them to my quarters. I'll question them there." Spreading his arms in a magnanimous gesture, he shepherded the onlookers back into the chapel. "Sit down, folks. There's nothing to worry about. Brother Guyot, please continue the service."

With two skinheads on either side of us, my grandfather and I were marched across the compound.

Glaring at Sargent, Chief fondled his swollen jaw. *"Ookwe!* Had I been your age, *Noozis,* I'd have kicked his pansy ass up around the moon!"

178

Holding his other hand, I murmured, "Once we're inside, *Nimishoo*, let me do the talking. Okay?"

Bark of laughter. "That's how we got into this mess!"

Scowling over his shoulder, Sargent snapped, "Quiet! I don't want to listen to any redskin jabbering."

"Then why don't you go back to Europe—where you *belong*?"

"You're just asking for it, you little—!"

"Newsflash, faggot! This land was known as Michimackinakong long before some Italian stuck his name on it." Enraged, Sargent took a menacing step in my direction. I lifted a warning finger. "Unh-unh-uh! Remember what Adolf Junior said."

The Adamites led us into one of their barracks. Inside was a large high-ceilinged assembly hall. Runic flags, scattered folding chairs and row upon row of empty card tables. Our footsteps echoed in the rafters. Dashing ahead of us, Sargent unlocked a cedar door.

Thurber's private office was panelled in knotty pine. The desk was Navy surplus, as were the two battered filing cabinets. A swaybacked couch braced one wall. An old-fashioned cast-iron safe squatted beside a color TV. My gaze slid from wall to wall. Thurber had turned his office into a virtual photo gallery. A pictorial history of the Adamite religion. Black-and-white photos of William Dudley Pelley and others I didn't know. A framed shot of a bright-smiling crewcut little boy with a middle-aged Theresa Noelle Thurber, circa 1955. Tessie's appearance startled me. She looked thirty years older than her 1938 photo. Years of hard drinking had wrinkled her face, deadened her once-bright eyes, and obliterated her chipmunk smile. Proof positive that nothing destroys a woman's looks faster than alcohol. Averting my gaze, I studied the other pictures. Cross burnings and skinhead rallies and, surprisingly, a photo from my father's war. Eight youthful warriors in combat camo, posing in front of a Blackhawk helicopter. Daddy called that kind of camouflage *tiger stripe,* I think.

Then the pastor himself sauntered in. This time I got a much better look at Thurber's face. In addition to the superhero jawline and the Reynolds nose, he had deep-set brown eyes, prickly eyebrows, and a small, thin-lipped, surly mouth. He seated himself behind the desk, gave his men an authoritative nod, and then gestured at two empty guest chairs.

"Please. You might as well be comfortable while we talk."

Chief and I accepted the offer, highly conscious of the skinheads' baleful presence.

"Now then, what are you people doing on my property?"

Chief flashed me a solemn-eyed look that said, *Your play, Angie.*

A new con game was rapidly taking shape in my mind. Believe me, there's nothing like imminent severe bodily harm to get those creative juices flowing.

Thurber's eyebrows lifted inquisitively. "Well?"

I took on the persona of my old prison nemesis, Elena Varo. Defiant stare and noticeable Mexican accent. "Ver-ry shoddy, Thurber." Tossing a bored look at the skinheads, I lounged in the chair, one leg over the armrest. "Back in Seattle, I heard you had a slick operation out here." Contemptuous smirk. "I'm still waiting for some evidence of that."

Thurber was not amused. "I asked you a question, girl. What were you doing out there?"

"Having a look at your operation," I replied, twining my fingers together. Insouciant shrug. "I thought maybe we could do some business." Sidelong glance at Sargent. "But if this is the quality of your muscle, forget it, *padre.*"

"Business?"

"*Claro que sí.* I know some *hombres* moving stuff through Seattle," I said, forcing myself to act completely casual. "It's a very valuable commodity. So maybe we're thinking about hiring some of your Aryan warriors. You know, provide a little protection against *los negritos.*"

"What kind of stuff?" Thurber asked.

By way of reply, I put my thumb against my right nostril, then sniffled loudly.

The heroic face turned skeptical. "Do you really expect me to believe that you two are coke dealers?"

"Thurber, I don't give a shit what you believe!" I channelled my growing anxiety into a reasonable facsimile of anger. "I came looking to do a little business. And Godzilla over there climbs all over my ass." Step up the Elena routine, princess! "By the way, *padre,* Ernesto and I aren't dealers. We're *compradores*—entrepreneurs." Ferocious glare at Sargent. "Next time you put your feelthy hands on me, *pachaco,* I make the phone call to Bogota, eh? Then some *matadores* come and stick your hands in the fish tank with the piranha!"

The intellectual skinhead snapped out a question. *"Cuando estuve usted en Bogota, mujer?"*

My prison Spanish was more than a match for his. *"Estuve en Bogota en el ano ochente nueve. Venga al Miami con madre mia."* Tart Angie smile. *"Muy bueno, compadre.* Tell me, as one woman to another, did your cellblock boyfriend teach you?"

The skinhead's face reddened in fury. Instantly Thurber extended a restraining hand. "No, Cotter! I'll handle this." Stern brown eyes pinned me to my seat. "You have me at a disadvantage, señorita. You known who I am, but I seem to have missed your name."

"Anne Marie Nahkeeta."

"How about the name you were born with?"

Taut smile. "I'd have to look it up."

"In Washington?" His tone deepened dangerously. "Or maybe your file is at the Bureau office in Miami."

"You think I'm an FBI plant?"

"Sweetheart, that's the only reason I haven't asked Mr. Sargent to take a blowtorch to your colored hide." Thurber's hate-filled glance gave me the shivers. "See, I'm not giving the rabbis an excuse to send the BATF in here. No way you'll find me violating some colored wench's civil rights." Humorous chuckle. "Got to admit, though. You two are a real change of pace from the usual FBI infiltrators. Blond boys fresh out of the Quantico academy yelling 'Nigger! Nigger!' It takes more than that to make an Adamite, my dear. It takes an absolute commitment to the preservation of God's special creation—the white race." Solemn-eyed stare. "Loyalty above all, señorita. To our cause, our race, and our savior—Lord Jesus Christ."

While Thurber raved, I thought of a way to shore up my cover. Slapping the chair's armrest, I cried, *"Gringo estupido!* You mean this place is under *surveillance?"*

"Sure." He turned in his chair. gesturing at one of the room's high windows. "There's probably a bunch of feds out there right now. How'd you like to meet them, Anne Marie?"

"No!" And I wasn't acting at that particular moment.

My reluctance amused him. Turning to the skinheads, he chuckled. "Boys, let's do our bit for a drug-free America. Turn these greasers over to the head fed out there."

My stomach turned over. I couldn't let him do it. Once I was in custody, the FBI would ferret out my true identity in no time at all. And then there'd be hell to pay back in South Dakota!

Sargent yanked me out of the chair. Struggling in his brutal grip, I glared at the pastor. "Thurber! Your life won't be worth *shit."*

His chuckle ceased. "You threatening me, little girl?"

Terrified, I watched two skinheads wrestle my grandfather to his feet. "Brother Guyot's going to like running this church . . . when you're *salmon food!"*

Thurber shot out of his chair. A curl of silvery hair spilled across his high forehead. "Young lady . . ." His clarion voice developed a deadly rasp. "Have you any idea what happens to people who threaten me?"

Go for broke, princess . . .

"Same thing that happened to Mona Hanauer?"

The pastor's rage-filled expression subsided, yielding to a taut grin. Then he let out a cascade of reverberant laughter. Gesturing at Sargent, he snapped, "Let her go." Then he turned my way. "Where'd you hear that, señorita?"

"Seattle." The Aryan goon squad released me and Chief. Touching my dishevelled hair, I added, "Word on the street is, you whacked that bitch over on Orcas."

"They don't know what they're talking about."

"They say Hanauer was planning to sue your ass. Sounds like a pretty good motive to me, *padre.*"

All at once, Thurber's face went deadpan. Slowly he rounded the corner of his desk, adding, "You're crazy! I had nothing to do with that heeb's death."

"Got an alibi, man?"

"As a matter of fact, I do." The pastor's forefinger selected Steve Sargent. "Him!"

"Yeah!" The skinhead laughed. "He was with me at a marshmallow roast."

Thurber's eyes turned livid. This time, though, it was Sargent who was the target of his wrath. Confronting his security honcho, Thurber snapped, "You've got a big mouth. Shut it."

"Shit, Pastor, I was only trying to—"

"Button it. If I want comedy, I'll watch Jay Leno."

The verbal assault turned Sargent's face the color of fresh cream. Thoroughly chastened, he stared at his paratrooper boots.

Thurber's reaction intrigued me. *Marshmallow roast?* I wondered where those two had *really* been. And if Thurber's alibi was as solid as he claimed.

Sensing my skepticism, the pastor turned to me and said, "The Jews would like nothing better than to pin that killing on me. It wouldn't surprise me if the Mossad did it. The bitch had probably outlived her usefulness."

This was too much for Chief. "Do you *really* believe that?"

"Absolutely." Cold superior smile. "I know they're trying to frame me. They're out to destroy me. The same way they destroyed Mother. But I have faith in the American system of justice."

Well, that put him one up on me. Tilting my head toward the family portrait, I remarked, "That's Mother?"

"It is." His tone became frostier. "And if you know what's good for you, chili bean, you'll show some respect."

Swallowing my anger, I let the jibe pass. *"Qué pasa?* Is she somebody famous or something?"

"She ought to be. If the rabbis weren't running this country, she would be." Pride flooded his face as he lovingly glanced at the portrait. "My mother was the foremost female patriot of her time. A twentieth century Molly Pitcher! She went to jail for this country!"

Chief couldn't resist it. "And they say treason isn't hereditary."

I blurted, *"Nimishoo—!"*

Thurber cut me off. "What do you know about it, Señor Green Card?" Confronting my grandfather, he gestured savagely in the direction of the helicopter photo. "I was fighting for this country while you were picking coffee beans for Juan Valdez! I left a gallon of my blood back there in the Nam! Three years as a boonie rat in the fucking Delta! Don't go calling me a goddamned traitor! If I didn't love this country, I wouldn't even be here!"

Pleading with my eyes, I advised Chief to cool it. But he stood right up to Thurber, refusing to give an inch. Family trait. Every time there's a war, you'll always find Blackbear men lined up in front of the Marine recruiting office.

Still showing his warpath scowl, Chief snapped, "You were a SEAL?"

The pastor made a strange sound. Like an Arkansas hog caller. *"Hoooooooooo-rawww!"*

My grandfather was not impressed. "What was the matter with the Marines?"

My heart stopped. Chief, don't you dare tell him you were a jarhead! You're supposed to be Colombian, dammit!

"My father was a Navy man," Thurber snapped.

"The Big One?" inquired Chief.

"That's right. He was a lieutenant commander. He was killed aboard the *Franklin*."

Obsidian eyes showed sympathy. "Okinawa."

Timbre of sadness in the pastor's voice. "He was killed a few months before I was born."

I jumped into the conversation, trying to divert attention from my grandfather. "What was his name, *padre?*"

"Weiler. Lieutenant Commander Harold Weiler."

All at once, an awkward silence enveloped us. Thurber stood erect suddenly, his expression wary and defensive. "I know what you're thinking, girl."

"Lo siento, que—?"

"You women are all alike." Chilly nod. "You like to do arithmetic. That's right. Mother and I share the same last name. Maybe my parents were never married in a fancy church wedding, but they were husband and wife in God's eyes. Mother worshipped that man. He was the greatest thing that ever happened to her. She told me so herself . . . right before she—" He cut himself off. Steilacoom was just too painful a memory. He didn't even like to think about her last years there, much less talk about them. With a shrug of brawny shoulders, he muttered, "Kindly keep your opinions to yourself."

Sassy Angela. "I didn't come here for no opinions, man. I came looking to do business."

Taut-lipped, he turned to his skinheads. "Get them out of here."

Sudden elation. "We're free to go?"

"That's right, señorita." He tugged at the lapels of his black suit jacket. "Contrary to what you may have read in

185

the newspapers, we're not a sect of assassins." He struck a noble pose. "We are servants of the Lord."

Chief cleared his throat suddenly. "Not down the main road. We don't want to run into the FBI."

Thurber's speculative gaze swallowed us both. "You really are scared of those feds, aren't you?"

"Ain't survived this long on the street, *hombre*, facing down the suits."

Thurber let out a mild sigh. He seemingly wished to be rid of us, and I was certain it had something to do with Mother. Perhaps he wanted to be alone with his memories. "All right. Burns, they pick the route." His pencil suddenly swivelled in my direction. "The next time you trespass on my property, bitch, I'm throwing that little ass in the brig. And maybe, if I'm in a good mood, I might even turn you over to Gallagher."

Jaunty Angie wave. *"Hasta la vista,* Pastor."

The Carnegie library's doors opened on Sunday at precisely twelve noon. And I was right there, eager to snoop about in Thurber's background. I couldn't shake the feeling that the Adamites had been involved somehow in the Hanauer murder. And I was more convinced than ever that it all went back to Tessie Thurber's internment fifty years ago. If Mona's mother or father had been involved, then that could be the motive.

I looked around for Georgianna, but apparently it was her day off. Better and better. I didn't want that woman coming up behind me while I was at the microfilm reader. It might be a little hard to explain Anne Marie's interest in a long-dead rightwinger.

Run the tape under the lens. Switch on the lamp. Screen lights up. Fire up the Wayback Machine, Sherman. Our destination is December 31, 1942. Let's have a look at the year's top stories in the *Seattle Post-Intelligencer.*

After much searching, I found the first story dealing with the Tessie Thurber case.

PORT WYOOCHEE WOMAN INDICTED FOR SEDITION

Seattle (AP)—The U.S. grand jury today handed down indictments against several outspoken Republican critics of the administration's war policy, including a former candidate for Congress here in Washington.

Theresa N. Thurber, 37, of Port Wyoochee was charged with six counts of conspiracy to destroy the morale of American armed forces. In 1940, Miss Thurber ran for Congress in Yennis County against longtime Rep. Thorvald Nilsson.

The Justice Department prosecuted Miss Thurber following the appearance of her new book, *Rosenfeld— The Hidden History of an Elder of Zion.*

Former state supreme court justice Arthur B. Littlefield denounced the Thurber book as "a scurrilous and hateful assault on our president" that "reads like a compendium of Dr. Goebbels's speeches."

"This country is at war," Judge Littlefield said. "We never had this kind of disunity when I was a lad. We supported our boys in the Civil War."

The judge added, "There's only one way to handle Copperheads like that Thurber woman and that's with a hangman's rope!"

Hitting the fast-forward button, I jumped into Tessie's future.

TESSIE IN THE CAN

Port Wyoochee, Wash. (AP)—Nazi sympathizer Theresa N. Thurber spent her first night behind bars following her arrest by a squad of FBI agents.

The G-men descended on the Thurber residence at 1472 Dollar Avenue, armed with submachine guns and hand grenades. They came upon Miss Thurber doing her housework and placed her under arrest.

The FBI also seized a quantity of fascist and Hitlerite literature, including Miss Thurber's subversive book.

Miss Thurber arrived at the Yennis County jail tastefully attired in a hunter green linen suit, a smart peaked Tyrolean hat, with open-toed pumps to match.

Doing her housework, I mused. Boy, nothing really changes, does it? No matter how prominent a woman becomes, no matter if she's an author and a candidate for Congress, she's still expected to go home and do the housework.

I shook my head ruefully. Poor Tess! Born a generation too early. Imagine if she'd come along at the same time as Friedan and Steinem. Think of the good she could have done.

In a strange way, Tessie was like the mirror-image of Mona Hanauer. Although separated by two generations, and the entire political spectrum, they seemed to have much in common—the same fire, the same passion for change.

It struck me that Port Wyoochee was not especially kind to its bright, outspoken daughters.

There was no further mention of Tessie in the 1942 papers. So I loaded the following year's tape onto the spool, cruised through the winter months, screamed with laughter at ads for an outfit called the *Victory Suit,* and found a short item buried in the Classifieds.

SEDITION DEFENDANT TO UNDERGO OBSERVATION

Bremerton, Wash. (AP)—The Navy has moved Theresa N. Thurber to the base hospital for psychiatric observation.

Miss Thurber, 38, of Port Wyoochee was indicted for sedition last year. A Justice Department spokesman said her case is presently "under review."

There are no plans for a trial, which cannot now take place until Miss Thurber's psychiatric evaluation has been completed.

Fuming, I scanned the microfilm tapes all the way to V-J Day. Damn! No mention of Mona's parents at all.

I did, however, find an item that brought a smile to my lips. It was a newspaper feature called *Today's Serviceman*. The photo showed a rugged, grinning black-haired man, smothered in bed linen, with his leg in a cast. Nearby stood two Navy doctors in hospital white. I laughed as I read the sidebar.

Today's serviceman is Lance Cpl. Charles J. Blackbear, USMC, son of Mr. and Mrs. Joseph Blackbear of Lax Lake, Minn. Chuck's recuperating at Bremerton following action on Okinawa. Get well soon, gyrene, and be sure to try one of our potlatches before you head back east.

I heard my grandfather's gruff voice behind me. "What are you laughing at?"

"Victory Suits."

"Your grandmother had one of those. She looked pretty sharp in it." One hand on my shoulder, he leaned forward and peered at the screen. Groan of embarrassment. "Oh, my God!"

"Look familiar?" I teased.

"Who is that good-looking guy?"

"You tell me, Chuck."

Lightly he swatted the back of my head. "Call me that again, young lady, and you're going to need a pillow for that chair."

"Did you know they took your picture?" I asked.

"Yeah." He smiled down at me. "Your great-grandmother cut it out of the *Duluth News-Tribune*. Don't know what ever happened to it, though. Guess it got lost in the shuffle." All at once, a strange, thoughtful expression washed over his aged features. "Of course . . . Bremerton."

"Chief?"

"That's where I heard his name before, Angie . . . *Bremerton*."

"Whose name?" I asked, peering up at him.

"Thurber's father." Slow smile of satisfaction. "Last night, remember? He told us his old man's name was Lieutenant Commander Harold Weiler. Name's been bugging me all morning. I *knew* I'd heard it somewhere before." Excited glance. "Weiler was at Bremerton, Angie, before I got there. He shipped out in . . . oh, March of '45, I think."

"Thurber was telling the truth?"

Chief nodded grimly. "You bet! Hospital staff told me all about it. A Japanese pilot put his Zero right through the *Franklin*'s flight deck. The bombs exploded in Sickbay. There were no survivors." He looked even grimmer. "They were all pretty shook up at Bremerton. Dr. Weiler was very popular with the staff. Pappy Weiler—they called him. On account of he was over forty. He was in the reserve, I think. An easterner. He had a private practice in Rhode Island."

"He was a doctor?"

Decisive nod. "Psychiatrist. Pappy Weiler was the head-shrinker at Bremerton for over two years."

Leaning back in my seat, I let out a hushed whistle. So that's how Thurber's parents met. Apparently, the patient had fallen hard for her Navy counselor.

"What was Weiler doing aboard the *Franklin*?" I asked.

"Angie, it's awful hard to remember after fifty years."

"Please try."

Closing his eyes, he was silent for several moments. And then . . . "Okay, maybe I did hear some scuttlebutt. Something about early treatment of combat fatigue. Pappy Weiler didn't want to sit out the war over here." Pensive glance. "Why are you so interested?"

I switched off the viewer. "Weiler's the shrink who counselled those American Nazis in the brig. That's how he met Tessie Thurber."

"You're kidding!"

"Not at all, Chief." Briefly I outlined the details of Tessie's internment.

With a thoughtful nod, my grandfather remarked, "That's all very interesting, Angie. But what does it have to do with Mona Hanauer?"

I dodged the question for the present. "Do me a favor?"

"Uh-oh! Sounds like I've got my work cut out for me."

"Would you see what you can dig up on the lieutenant commander?"

"No problem. I'll drop by the American Legion tonight." He watched me take the tape off the spool. "What am I looking for?"

"Some kind of connection between Weiler, Tessie Thurber and Mona's parents."

"You're reaching, girl. Mona's folks are too young. They were only kids during the war."

"If Thurber did it, Chief, he had to have a motive."

"Don't be too sure about that," my grandfather warned. "It doesn't take too much to set off them Nazis. What if it was a spur-of-the-moment thing? You know, a hate crime."

Shaking my head briskly, I replied, "I don't think so. Everything we've learned so far—the missing cassettes, Sargent skulking around Mona's cabin—suggests that her murder was planned in advance. Which means there had to be a motive." Scowling, I rose from the chair. "If Thurber did it—if we can learn what his motive was—we'll be able to turn it against him. Trip him up."

Chief put the microfilm tape back in its box. "And if we can't trip him up?"

"Then Thurber walks." I shouldered my bag, flashing him an apprehensive glance. "And Mickey spends the rest of his life in Cedar Creek."

Six o'clock on a quiet Sunday evening in Port Wyoochee. I had a booth all to myself at Millicent's Pub, taking occasional dainty sips from a frosty Beachcomber. Very slow sips. I'd learned my lesson two nights ago.

There I sat, ravishing Anishinabe princess in her fiery red multiyarn cable sweater and black crepe skirt. Thinking perhaps I shouldn't have stopped there. Six o'clock on Sunday is a time for the hardcore drinkers. Those grim, lonely, silent men and women, perched on their barstools, who stare at the flickering TV and their drinks and the bartender, never at each other. Quite a change from Marcella and the rowdy Friday night crowd.

I guess I needed a fleeting touch of Happy Hour. This town was beginning to depress me. Somehow I don't think this is what the Parmenters and the Alworths had in mind when they arrived here in 1905. This dreary moldering shore town with its dying river and its dying industry and its tense, frightened, angry people.

Even the fisheries were collapsing. Kokanee salmon were becoming as scarce as palm trees. Why was I not surprised?

In 1883, when Port Wyoochee was a rollicking lumber dock, jubilant white fishermen reported a gross catch of twenty-one thousand five hundred *tons* in Puget Sound. Last year, the annual catch was four hundred and eighty tons. For the statistically minded among you, that's a decrease of approximately 97.9 percent.

Only recently have scientists begun to understand the complex interaction between salmon and the streams in which they spawn. Salmon from a single river, like the Gemini, share common genetic traits that make them distinct from all others of their kind. Every river in the Northwest

192

that is dammed or diverted or polluted beyond repair results in the extinction of that particular salmon "family." The loss results in a further shrinkage of the gene pool, ultimately threatening the viability of the species.

For thousands of years, Klallam *tyhee* had stood on the Gemini's banks, arms upraised, intoning the sacred prayer song. *"Nika kwisha lolo salmon kopachuck!"* And the silver-finned multitude had come, leaping and splashing. Year after year. Century after century.

Today the Kulshan Paper Company pumps its toxic wastewater right into the Gemini, giving the stream the acid level of a glass of tomato juice. Meanwhile, that ninety-year-old sludge bed off Sahale Point sucks the very oxygen out of the water. And, if that's not enough, whenever the wind shifts, the river gets a nice shower of cadmium fallout from the smelters in Tacoma.

Next time you're preening for the TV camera, Georgianna, why don't you mention that?

All at once, a broad shadow fell across my tabletop. I glanced idly at the source—and froze. Depression vanished instantly, replaced by caution and alarm. I had a gentleman caller.

Steve Sargent!

He stood beside my booth, flaunting his skinhead colors. Army paratrooper boots, camo pants, brown leather jacket and a black shirt showing a white grinning skull. A black swastika marked the skull's forehead. "Been lookin' around town for you, tamale."

Forcing myself not to shiver, I reached for my glass. Feigned a look of casual unconcern. Slipped back into my Elena persona.

"Verdad? Wha's on your mind, *pachaco?"*

Sargent did not reply. Instead, he plunked down on the empty bench across from me, flashing a taut grin.

Bored Elena glance. "Why don't you have a seat, man?"

"I got one, thanks." All at once, he turned serious. "Hey, Mex, that offer on the level?"

I blinked in mild surprise. Hadn't realized I'd given such a command performance. *"Que—?"*

"You still want somebody to kick ass on them niggers?"

"Are you auditionin', man?"

"Fucking right!" Smile of sheer pleasure. "If your asshole buddies in Seattle want protection, I'm your boy. No monkey's gonna come near you. Not with ol' Sarge around."

"You seem pretty eager, *hombre.*"

"Why not?" Leather-clad shoulders shrugged. "Busting their kinky-haired skulls is the most fun a man can have. If I'm getting paid for it, so much the better."

Suspicious glance. "Did Thurber send you?"

"The pastor?" Sargent let out a guffaw. "No fucking way! He's a Boy Scout. He was really serious about rolling you two over."

"So what are you doing here?"

"I told you. Bash jigaboos and get paid for it." Spreading his arms in jovial anticipation, he added, "I might even be able to convince a couple of warriors to throw in with me. I'll pick some good stompers. Got a couple of guys in mind. There's some you can forget about, though. Like Cotter. He hates your guts, chili bean. You got under his skin with that crack about the boyfriend." Gust of wicked laughter. "I hear a couple of big jigs turned him out in the slam."

Fondling my glass, I plotted my interrogation strategy. Since Sargent was in a talkative mood, I might as well poke around the edges of Thurber's alibi. "Make me an offer, man."

Elbows on the tabletop, Sargent leaned toward me. "Here's the deal. No fucking time clocks. I'm on call, tamale. You need me to protect a deal when it goes down, get in touch. One deal, one payoff. Got it?"

"I can live with that. Quote me some numbers."

"Four hundred each for the boys. A grand for me."

"Pretty steep, *gringo*."

"You're gettin' the best, Mex." The harsh smile widened. " 'Sides, it costs more when the coons run off with the stash."

"*Padre* Thurber ain't gonna like it."

"The pastor ain't bothered by what he don't know. You let me worry about him, okay? You just come up with the cash."

"Sounds like you've got some job experience, man."

"Hey! The pay's good, and it beats gettin' up before dawn to work some trawler." Unpleasant memories soured his expression. "I had enough of that shit on my old man's boat."

"Suppose the work gets a little heavy?"

"Then the price goes up, bitch. Way, way up!"

"Got religion, *hombre?*"

"Look, Mex, you want some nigger shredded, it's gonna cost."

"How much did the Jewgirl cost?"

Sargent's face tensed instantly, casting jaw muscles into sharp relief. His porcine eyes flashed a silent warning. "Shouldn't believe everything you hear, bitch."

"The word is, you are one baaaaaad motherfucker, Stevie."

"Well . . . *that* you can believe." Fierce, pleased grin. "If you want to find out *how* bad, go ahead and call me *Stevie* again." His index finger jabbed twice at my nose. "For you, chili pepper, it's *Mister Sargent.*"

Lounging in my seat, I purred, "I suppose it was a real big surprise to you when that Hanauer bitch got killed."

"Hey! How was I supposed to know she was in the San Juans?" Aggrieved expression. "I figured she was down at the synagogue with the rest of the kosher."

"Why would you think that?"

"It was Yom Kippur, wasn't it? The rabbi toots his horn, and they all come running."

"I didn't know you were such an expert on Judaism."

195

"Hey, I seen it for myself." He jutted his chin eastward. "In Tacoma. Saw all'a them weird beards come out of the synagogue."

"What were you doing in Tacoma?"

"Ahhhhh, having some fun." Chuckles of reminiscence. "I heard the Tacoma skins were gonna play beanie snatch that night. So me and a couple of boys from Camp Pelley showed up, too."

"What happened?"

"Nothing! There were cops all around the synagogue. We couldn't get near the place." Sargent scratched his dirty neck. "When they came out, I saw one in a beanie and yelled, "Hey, rab! Where's your propellor?' That got things rolling. One of our guys was slugging it out with a kike, and I tried to get over there. Fucking cops arrested me for disorderly conduct."

Feigning a pout of sympathy, I murmured, *"Pobrecito!"*

"Yeah, it was *pobrecito*, all right. Yelling and screaming. Skins fighting with cops. Man, was I pissed off! I drove all the way out there, and I didn't even get to punch a rabbi. What a fucking waste of time!"

"So you spent the night in the tank."

"Nahhhhh, just the first half. Pastor Thurber came and bailed me out."

"What time?"

"Close to two, I guess." Fat lips puckered in thought. "He plunked down some green for me and Pettigrew. Then we had a news conference in front of the station house."

I frowned. If Sargent was telling the truth, there was no way Thurber could have been on Orcas Island at two-thirty. I made a mental note to phone the Tacoma TV stations.

Showing me a cold grin, Sargent growled, "You're okay, Mex . . . for a *tamale*. Want another drink?"

"Let me finish this first." I took a long, calming sip. "Mind answering a personal question?"

Relaxed shrug. "Depends on the question."

196

"Why do you hate the Jews?" I asked.

Sargent flinched at the word. It was as if someone had suddenly flicked a switch in his head. Deep-seated rage bubbled to the surface. "They're fucking up the country! The Pastor says—"

"*Caramba!* Don't give me that pastor shit, man!" Colombian Angie. "I'm asking *you.*"

"Why shouldn't I hate them?" He turned strangely defensive all of a sudden. "I ain't worked steady in a couple of years. They're giving all the jobs to your relatives below the Rio Grande—"

"Sargent . . ." Licking my lips, I struggled to keep my voice calm. "Do you really believe that? Do you really think there's this Orthodox rabbi shipping everybody's job to Guadalajara?"

"How come there's no jobs around here, then?"

My patience finally snapped. "What about that *Help Wanted* sign in the Safeway window?"

"Be a *stock clerk?* Are you out of your fucking mind?"

"What's wrong with being a stock clerk? You can get a lot of hours—"

"Yeah! Luggin' crates of canned goods around." He looked at me as if I'd just insulted his mother. "Mopping the floor every goddamned night! And they want you there on weekends, too. Fuck that! If I wanted to bust my hump, I'd have stayed on my old man's boat." Frustrated shake of the head. "I'm talking about the *good* jobs, Mex."

"Last time I checked, Mr. Sargent, there wasn't much call for *yarmulke* snatchers in the private sector."

Crimson flooded his meaty face. "You're a real comedian, aren't you?"

"If *you* don't want to stock shelves, Sargent, that's not the rabbi's fault."

Slamming his fist on the tabletop, he spat, "Laugh it up, chili pepper! I don't have to justify myself to you. Damned right I hate those kikes. They've got all the money. They

197

walk around town like King Shit. And their day is coming—
sooner than anybody thinks." Hateful snarl. "Then you'll be
the one down in Guadalajara, bitch. You and all the other
mud people!"

"I take it you're not buying me another drink?"

Incensed, he opened his mouth to say something; then his
gaze slid toward the entrance. And he stood abruptly.

As Sargent left the booth, I glimpsed the reason for his
sudden departure. Chief Gallagher was headed my way. The
skinhead's swagger did not impress him. The chief frowned
suddenly, and then Sargent gave him a respectfully wide
berth on the way out.

The chief nodded in greeting. "Anne Marie."

Pushing my glass away, I flashed a welcoming Angie
smile. "Good evening, Mr. Gallagher."

"My wife and I are having a drink over there." He
pointed out a booth occupied by a slender, smiling, fortyish
woman. "Would you care to join us?"

"Thanks, Mr. Gallagher, but I'm just about ready to
leave."

"Then I'll join you." Without waiting to be asked, he occupied Sargent's seat. Pulling out a pack of Camels, he tilted
his head toward the doorway. "That clown give you any
trouble?"

I shook my head. "We were just talking."

"Talking a little loud. I could hear you all the way over
there." Gallagher put the cigarette between his lips. Then,
forehead crinkling, he lit up. "You could file charges against
him, you know."

"I don't think there's any need for that."

Something about Gallagher's casual air put me on my
guard. I had too many vivid memories of the no-nonsense
police chief I'd met at the Kulshan protest.

Looking straight at me, he asked, "What were you two
talking about?"

"I really don't see where that's any of your business, Chief Gallagher."

"You're an awfully forgiving woman, Anne Marie." His speculative gaze never wavered. "You get manhandled at the paper mill, and you decline to press charges. That Nazi just shouted at you. *And* he made a threatening gesture, which constitutes assault. I offer to arrest him. And what do I get from you? Same thing as last time. No charges." Amusement flavored his stare. "I'm beginning to think you don't like me, Anne Marie."

"And I'm beginning to wonder why you're so interested in me, Chief Gallagher."

"Well, it's like this . . ." His steely gaze scanned me from my raven hair to my sweater hem. "You're young, bright and articulate, and, from what Bert Reisbeck tells me, you know your business. Seems to me, though, that a young lady with your talents would be on her way *to* Seattle—not trying to get away from it."

"There are a lot of bright young career women in Seattle," I replied, my mouth dry. So he'd had a talk with Bert, eh? But why? Why was he checking me out? "That makes for fewer opportunities. There's room for advancement here in Port Wyoochee."

He shook his head. "Not for an investments advisor."

Heartbeat quickening, I stiffened in indignation. "Just what are you getting at?"

"I used to be a cop in Seattle." Gallagher blew a thin stream of grayish white smoke. "I had twenty years in—the last seven packing a shield. Then I had the good sense to retire and take this job." Skepticism hardened his expression. "Sorry, I don't buy it. I can't see you ditching a good-paying job in Seattle to open a brokerage in a backwater burg like Port Wyoochee. Not in this economy. And that leads us to the big question, doesn't it? Just why are you here?"

My smile was brittle. "One has to take risks, Mr. Gallagher."

"That's right." He nodded in agreement. "What's your game?"

"Game?" I echoed, feeling my knees quiver beneath the table.

"You know what I'm talking about."

"I beg your pardon!"

"Good-looking girl like you . . . it's got to be some kind of scam."

I channelled my growing alarm into a virtuoso performance. Sudden indignant shudder. Angry pursing of the lips. Frosty glare. "You-you think I-I'm some sort of *con artist?*"

"I don't know what to think—yet! I do know one thing, though. A rich old man's liable to turn into a damned fool when a pretty girl smiles at him. He's liable to get careless with his money." He flicked a bit of ash from the smoldering tip of his cigarette. "I'd sure hate to pick up the *Port Angeles News* a few weeks from now and find out the money's gone . . . and so's Anne Marie." Relentless stare. "So if you're in the game, miss, this is your notice to leave town—pronto!"

In the game. I'd heard Toni Gee, my old mentor at Springfield, use that expression many times. Apparently, Chief Gallagher had spent a few of his Seattle years on the Bunco Squad.

Bewildered Angie expression. "I—I don't know wh-what you're talking about."

Gallagher gave me a long look, wary and uncertain. Then, grinding out his cigarette, he muttered, "Maybe you don't. In that case, please allow me to apologize. And you can chalk up what I just said to the paranoia of a former big-city cop." He stepped away from my booth. "We have a reasonably quiet town here, Anne Marie. I'd like to keep it that way."

I lifted my chin in indignation. "I'm not a criminal, Mr. Gallagher."

"Really? Then, you won't mind very much if I check you out."

"If you feel you must." I feigned a wounded look. "I'll send over my college transcript if you'd like."

"No thanks." His right palm rose in farewell. "There's some things I'd rather do on my own."

Watching him return to his wife, I grabbed my glass and emptied it in a hasty swallow. The rum's sudden bite did nothing to quiet my jangling nerves.

Oh, you made yourself memorable at the Kulshan protest, all right. Nice going, princess. You made yourself memorable enough to convince Chief Gallagher to go interview Bert Reisbeck and others all around town. And from the sound of things, he was just getting warmed up.

Bleak fussbudget face. A former Seattle bunco cop! My cover would never stand up to his detailed scrutiny. He'd start with the state licensing people in Olympia. Then he'd check every brokerage in Seattle. Everywhere he turned, it would be the exact same story. No one had ever heard of Anne Marie Nahkeeta.

Gallagher would realize that his initial hunch about me had been correct. He would have his officers haul me in for questioning. And that would be it—game over!

Unless I could pinpoint Mona's killer—and do it *fast!*— we'd both be languishing in prison cells. Mickey here in Washington. And me in South Dakota.

Chapter Ten

Monday morning's weather matched my mood—dour, gray and miserable. Here it was, October nineteenth, and I was no closer to a solution than the day I arrived. Even worse, my time was running out. The FBI was in town, keeping close watch on the Adamite church. How soon would it be before they began taking an interest in Anne Marie Nahkeeta, alleged dope dealer and sometime drinking companion of Steve Sargent? And what happens when one of the feds notices a striking resemblance between Anne Marie and the elusive Pocahontas?

Smothering a yawn, I strolled down Hiaqua Avenue. Weary princess in her belted raincoat and tailored taupe-and-black Vanderbilt suit. Stylish glen plaid it was, with a slim skirt and a double-breasted jacket with peaked lapels.

Forget about the Bureau, I told myself. First things first. You've got to lure the killer into the open and spring the Mick.

I had an idea or two along those lines, but first I had to wait for the downtown stores to open. So I sauntered into Pam's Coffee Shoppe, a cozy diner on the corner of Hiaqua and Third, and enjoyed a leisurely breakfast of rye toast and tomato juice. After that, it was east on Dollar Avenue. Destination—Radio Shack.

As I touched the door's aluminum bar, a familiar female voice called out. "Anne Marie, hi!"

I turned, and there was Lisa Rotenberg, the rabbi's wife. Tall, gangly lady in a sporty blue faille jumpsuit. Her rambunctious offspring, David, squirmed restlessly in her slender arms.

"Hi, Lisa." I held open the door for them. "What brings you out so early in the morning?"

"My son." She kissed the top of Davey's head. "He's learned a new trick—climbing out of the crib in the middle of the night. I found him in the living room this morning, playing havoc with our videotapes." Smiling wryly, she perched him on her hip. "Honestly, I think he's going to be the next Houdini! So I'm in the market for one of those nursery intercoms. That way, I'll hear him if he tries it again." She blinked in curiosity. "How about you?"

Well, I could hardly tell her I was purchasing surveillance equipment, so I smiled and said, "My brother's birthday is coming up. Paul's a real ham radio enthusiast."

As we strolled past the display tables, Lisa became quite serious. "I understand you were at the Kulshan demonstration."

"That's right." I wondered where she was going with this.

"Did one of Thurber's men really show up?"

Momentary hesitation. I didn't want to discuss Sargent with the rabbi's wife. She might be a little startled at my choice of drinking companions. "I couldn't say. A white guy jumped some kid. I don't know who he was with."

"He's with that *putz* Thurber!" Lisa's eyes sparkled in anger. "He put Lonnie Coleman in the hospital. The poor kid has a concussion." Holding Davey one-handed, she rummaged in her fringed leather bag. "Would you be interested in . . . oh, for—! Wait a minute."

"Here. Allow me." I scooped Davey out of her grasp, letting her search the interior of her purse.

Davey began looking at me as if I were Mount McKinley.

And began climbing. Hot, moist baby hands gleefully smacked my face. I grimaced as he grabbed a fistful of raven black hair.

"Ouch! Yes, David, it's attached." Fire tickled my scalp. "No, child, it isn't elastic. Don't yank on it! That's a good boy." Anishinabe teeth gritted. "Come on. Let go. Please?"

"Here!" Lisa handed me a mint green brochure. With a gasp of blessed relief, I relinquished her adventurous son.

"Sorry . . ." Wrestling with him, the harried young mother showed me an awkward smile. "He's so darned active."

Grooming my tangled hair, I replied, "No problem."

"We're having a human rights rally at City Hall next week," Lisa explained. "Avi's bringing a B'nai Brith speaker over from Seattle." She tenderly placed the bottle's nipple in her baby's mouth. "We're not taking sides in the Kulshan dispute, you understand. We simply feel that racial violence has no place in our community. What happened to that Coleman boy was unforgiveable."

"Can't argue with that," I replied, looking over the brochure.

Hopeful expression. "Then, you'll come?"

"If I'm in town, Lisa."

Seconds later, a salesman joined us, asking if he could be of service. Lisa explained her need for a bedroom intercom. While they chatted, I slipped away and busied myself with a careless examination of their pocket radios.

As soon as Lisa and her son were gone, I buttonholed the horse-faced salesman and told him what I was really after.

"They call it a VOX-Five," I said, tracing a small rectangle with my index fingers. "It's a voice-activated transmitter with a tiny condenser microphone. The frequency range is 92 to 112 megahertz."

I neglected to add that it was a favorite device of grifters working the Badger game.

The salesman's horsey face displayed uncertainty. "I'm not sure we have that item in stock, miss."

Noting the puzzled gleam in his eyes, I replied, "You're wondering why I need a miniature transmitter, aren't you?"

His jughandle ears turned bright pink. "Uh, sort of."

Tart Angie smile. "I'm keeping tabs on a footloose boyfriend."

He inched his way toward the stockroom. "Ah—let me go check in the back."

While I stood waiting at the counter, the door buzzer sounded, and a baritone voice remarked, "Well, well . . . Anne Marie Nahkeeta. What are you doing here?"

"Jon Waterman! What a pleasant surprise." Turning, I watched Mona's old boyfriend stride across the room. He was wearing the usual flight togs. Leather jacket, broadcloth shirt and knockabout jeans. The store's strobe lights reflected off the metallic rim of his glasses. Ontario's answer to the Flying Tigers. Polite Angie smile. "I'm afraid I have a little electronic emergency." Shift the subject. "What are you in the market for?"

"New Loran-C unit. The original finally pranged." He outlined an imaginary box. "I planned on picking up a Ross LCA 200. It'll fit right in with my existing antennae array." Mild concern wiped the pleasurable anticipation from his face. "I hear you landed in a bit of a spot at Kulshan."

"How'd you hear that?"

"It was in yesterday's newspaper." A small irritable frown tugged at his lips. "Those bloody fools."

"I thought they were your buddies."

"They're still a lot of bloody fools. They'll destroy the whole paper industry before they're through," Waterman said, eyeing me sharply. "How'd you know I was on the Greenway committee?"

I shrugged. "People like to talk."

"Well, it was Georgianna's idea, not mine." Sudden scowl of resentment. "Lord, that was the biggest mistake I ever made. Georgianna's a lot like her father, you know. Always barking out orders. A colonel in skirts!"

"You two were married a long time," I observed.

"And I could do without that reminder, thank you very much!" he replied, fuming. "I should have known what I was in for when I met the old man. I took enough orders up there at—" And then he cut himself short, as if realizing that he'd said too much. His scowl began to fade. "I'm my own boss now. And that's the way I like it."

I kept my personal opinion to myself. If Waterman was working for Dolan, then he was hardly his own boss. And speaking of Mick's nemesis, it wouldn't do for his aerial chauffeur to see Angie buying that miniature radio transmitter. Especially since Jack Dolan was the intended target.

Hastily I concocted some questions for the pilot. Either he'd answer them or else he'd storm out of Radio Shack in a huff. Either way, I'd be coming out ahead.

"I guess you really miss her, don't you?"

Doing a Monty Python doubletake, he blurted, *"Georgianna?* Good Lord, no!"

"Not her, dummy." Lightly I slapped his jacket sleeve. "Mona Hanauer. I hear you two were pretty close."

"Mmmmmm . . . a bit."

"How long were you two together?"

"Three years."

Sympathetic glance. "So what happened? Why didn't it work out?"

Flash of annoyance. "Look, I'd really rather not—"

I made a soothing sound. "Hey, we can talk about it. I mean, what are friends for?"

"Friends respect each other's privacy." Brown eyes sizzled angrily. "Do you really want to know? All right, then." He licked dry lips. "Mona became interested in another man. There . . . satisfied? Now, I'd really rather not discuss it, if you don't mind."

Chastened Angie expression. "Sorry."

"No need for apologies, Anne Marie. Let's just forget all about it, all right?"

206

Okay, so Mona was a sore point with him. But not prickly enough to drive him out of the store.

Pondering another tack, I became aware of his sudden hostile gaze.

"Why are you so interested in Mona?"

Uh-oh! Angie, what have you started? Running my fingertips across the back of his hand, I shaped my mouth into a coquettish smile. "I hear you and she liked to party."

Strange look. "What do you mean?"

If Mickey had known about his wife's fondness for marijuana, it was a safe bet Waterman also knew. Pursing my lips, I puffed on a make-believe cigarette.

Waterman's reaction wasn't what I'd expected. Drawing himself erect, he snapped, "Where'd you hear about that?"

"Does it matt—*owwwww!*"

Waterman's hand lashed out like an enraged rattler. A reptilian chill entered his gaze. Remorseless fingers squeezed my wrist. Flashing an icy smile, he crooned, "Anne Marieeeee . . ."

"Owww! You're *hurting* me!"

Still smiling, he maintained the pressure. "Now then, who's been telling tales out of school?"

My wrist felt like it was caught in a vise. Wincing at the surge of pain, I tossed out the first name that came to mind. "Georgianna."

Hooded gaze. "Damn! I might have known." With a snort of disgust, the pilot released my wrist.

Scowling, I tenderly massaged the bruised flesh. My doubts about Mona's judgment were on the ascendant. The floatplane pilot had enjoyed that just a little too much.

At least I'd learned one new fact, I mused. Georgianna was well aware of her ex-husband's smoking sessions with Mona.

He shot me a stern warning glance. "If you know what's good for you, Anne Marie, you won't go spreading that around."

Unrequited curiosity made me fidgety. Why was he so eager to keep their marijuana use a secret? Why, he was almost as paranoid as Mona.

Hoping to reassure him, I said, "Look, Waterman, I'm not going to turn you in. I'm just looking for a supplier, that's all."

Skeptical glance. "Why?"

"Why do you think?"

"I don't believe you. If you were using, you'd already have a dealer."

"I do." Exasperated Angie smile. "But it's kind of inconvenient driving all the way to Seattle."

That gave him pause. Relaxing a little, he adjusted his glasses. "I'm afraid I can't help you. I don't know who she bought from."

"Mona never mentioned any names?"

He shook his head. "Not to me."

"Did she ever mention where she was buying?"

"No." Frowning, he thrust both hands into his jeans pockets. "It was a sometime thing with Mona. Sometimes, if she was in the mood, we'd smoke a few joints and toddle off to bed." Sudden cold grin. "Sometimes we only made it as far as the bearskin rug."

Conceited ass! I thought. Ladies' man, indeed. He was about as attractive as Lem Thurber.

Waterman was still grinning when the salesman emerged from the stockroom. Clutching a small cardboard box, he said, "Miss? I've got your—"

"My CD modulator!" I interrupted, facing the counter. The salesman blinked in astonishment. Keeping my back to Waterman, I made a series of exaggerated facial gestures, all designed to convince the salesman that my companion was the footloose boyfriend. All at once, he beamed in understanding and said no more.

"How much do I owe you?" I asked.

"Base price is three twenty-five." The salesman reached for a photovoltaic calculator. "Let me ring up the sales tax."

Losing interest in the exchange, Waterman wandered over to the avionics display. I yielded to a mild shudder of relief.

Continuing the show for the salesman, I uttered a musical "Bye, Jon!" as I left the store. Then, tall heels tapping, I clutched my shopping bag and fled up Dollar Avenue.

Maybe I'd done a little better than expected, hitting Waterman cold that way. Most of his story sounded plausible, too. Like the rest of Mona Hanauer's lovers, he had thoroughly resented being shown the gate.

Yes, Waterman's reminiscences were readily believable. Indeed, I might have taken them at face value myself ... had I *not* visited Mona's cabin on Orcas Island.

I thought of Mona's clever undersea stash—the plastic-wrapped packets of marijuana concealed within that odd metal canister.

"It was a sometime thing with Mona," Waterman had said.

But that was an awful lot of grass for a *sometime thing*.

Then there's the troublesome fact of Mona's longtime usage, a fact inadvertently confirmed by her mother. Plus Mona's weekly jaunts to the island ... as a *passenger* aboard Waterman's floatplane!

And there was something else that bothered me— Waterman's final remark. *"Sometimes we only made it as far as the bearskin rug."*

Well, I'd been inside Mona's apartment, helping her mother pack, and—take it from Angie—there was no bearskin rug at 58 Dungeness Circle, Port Wyoochee, Washington. There was, however, a bearskin rug on the floor of Mona's cabin in the San Juans.

Meaning Waterman was very familiar with the inside of that cabin.

Which brings us to this morning's key question. Namely, if Jon Waterman was Mona's live-in lover and often smoked dope with her at the cabin, then how could he *not* know about the waterproof canister sunk just offshore?

You've been lying to me, Jon-boy.

I think you know all about that waterproof metal container. And you also know the identity of Mona's supplier. Chances are you do your buying from the same source. Only why are you keeping the name to yourself?

Who was Waterman afraid of? I wondered.

The Federal Aviation Administration, probably. If they ever found out he was using, they might yank his pilot's license.

Putting Mona's former live-in out of my mind momentarily, I strolled into the municipal parking lot. Too bad Waterman had come along when he had. I'd also been hoping to pick up a pocket-sized tape recorder at Radio Shack.

Oh, well, I thought, opening my car door. There's always Kit's Camera over on Crosshaul Avenue.

"Thanks for seeing me on such short notice, Mr. Dolan."

"No problem." Holding the door open, he tilted his head toward the plush leather guest chair. "Matter of fact, I've been hoping you'd show. Have a seat, Anne Marie."

Dolan's private office was lengthy, airy and spacious, with a recessed ceiling, cream-colored stucco walls and a shag carpet in cobalt blue. A mammoth mahogany desk dominated the far end of the room. Behind it stood tall French windows cloaked in gauzy drapery. Slate-colored file cabinets lined one wall. Like Lemuel Thurber, Dolan enjoyed hanging framed pictures on the wall. I spotted four reproductions of maritime maps and one color photo of a cocktail lounge. The curvature of the bar looked very familiar.

"That's Millicent's Pub, isn't it?" Smoothing the back of my skirt, I sat down.

"Nowadays it is." Dolan was all decked out in the Realtor's Special. Khaki wool blazer, gray dress slacks, light blue

210

Oxford shirt and a burgundy silk tie with a floral pattern. Flush with pride, he lingered beside the photo. "I sold it to Millie eighteen years ago. That pub was the first business I ever owned. Millie called it The Rock Cockle at first. I told her, 'Put your name on it. Gives the place a personal touch.' So she did, and the pub's been jumping ever since."

Facing the photo, Dolan straightened the frame. Me, I took immediate advantage of the diversion. While he had his back to me, I plucked the miniature VOX-Five transmitter out of my bag, flicked the on switch, and hurriedly tucked it into the small triangular space between the desk calendar and its backrest.

"A couple's out on the road," he added. "What do they say, huh? Let's go to Such-and-such? Nahhhhh! It's easier to remember the owner's name. It's the first thing that pops into a customer's mind. 'Let's go to Jack's place.' Listen, it worked for me!"

He started to turn. Sucking in my breath sharply, I dropped back into the guest chair. Showed a fragile Angie smile.

"What did you do before you bought that tavern?" I asked.

"Fished." He made his way around the big desk. "I spent a lot of youthful mornings on a barge, standing on a tower and looking out for the salmon." He shot me a humorless grin. "I gave that up when I found out the man on the dock was making a damned sight more than us guys hoisting the nets." Sudden inquisitive look. "So. What brings you around, Anne Marie?"

I sailed right into my cover story. "You'll be pleased to know my backers have decided to bid on the old torpedo plant."

"Have they now?" Porcelain blue eyes gleamed with wry amusement. Taking his seat, he reached into the upright file on his desk and selected a manila folder. "How high are you willing to bid?"

"We're prepared to offer the Alworth Trust a down payment of one-point-four million," I replied, crossing my legs demurely. Corporate Angie strikes again! "As for the remainder, we're willing to pay out over time. The funds will come from the profits of the condominium management corporation. At prevailing rates of interest, of course."

"Not bad, Anne Marie. That's twenty-five percent of the parcel's current market value."

"Personally, I think it's a highly attractive option for the trustees. Instead of an empty factory providing nothing but continued property taxes, Torpedo Junction will be a thriving condominium offering a long-term positive cash flow. A very productive asset for the trust."

Dolan's grin reminded me of a shark closing in on a salmon. "Before you call in your attorneys, though, you'd better have a look at this."

Taking the folder, I opened it and began reading. Hacking my way through the flowery legalese, I realized that this was a purchase agreement. An agreement between the property's owners, the Alworth Trust, and something called Whulge Development Associates, Inc.

I tossed the folder back on his desk. "Okay, Mr. Dolan, I'm game. What is this Whulge Development Associates, Inc.?"

"A brand-new corporation, Anne Marie." Still grinning, he smoothed his bristly iron gray hair. "The board consists of myself, my wife Elizabeth, my oldest boy Sean, and a couple of Foleys. That's Beth's family. And we're prepared to match your bid."

"You're buying Torpedo Junction out from under us?"

"Nothing of the sort, honey. Your crowd is making their bid, and we're making ours. The final decision will be made by the Alworth board of trustees."

"Right," I added, pretending to fume. "And with *you* as the executor of the Alworth Trust, three guesses which one they'll choose."

212

Dolan let out a steely chuckle. "I do enjoy dealing with an intelligent woman."

Sitting upright, I manufactured a scowl of defiance. "We're quite prepared to increase our bid, Mr. Dolan."

"So are we, honey."

"Can your firm come up with the money all at once?" I challenged.

"Anne Marie, you could pay for that factory with forty million *dimes!* You could haul the coins here in a fleet of armored trucks! It wouldn't change a damned thing." He laughed again. "You could buy that property, sure! Then you'd be the ones stuck with the white elephant. There's no way you're going to turn Torpedo Junction into profit-making condos."

Striking a formal pose, I added, "As soon as the first renovations are complete—"

"You still don't get it, do you?" Leaning back in his swivel chair, Dolan offered a predatory grin. "And here I thought you were all grown up. You need permits to renovate, Miss Nahkeeta. Zoning Board. Building Inspector. Construction permits. Plumbing permits. You could offer the Alworth Trust *ten* million in cold hard cash, and—I'm telling you right now—you'll never get a single permit for purposes of renovation."

I forced myself not to smile. My first impression of Jack Dolan at the Rotary luncheon had been right on target. Port Wyoochee had its very own Hibernian Caesar.

Feigning indignation, I snapped, "You're stealing my idea—is that it?"

"*Stealing?* That's a word they use in kindergarten, Anne Marie. You're a big girl now." Fingering his pen, he shot me a cold, pitying smile. "Didn't Mommy ever explain the facts of life?"

"I think maybe she overlooked this part."

Tapping the pen on the blotter, Dolan said, "Here it is, then. There's no way I'd ever let some bright young female

213

waltz into town and make a quick million off Torpedo Junction." His smile warmed just a smidgen. "Oh, we're very happy to have you around, honey. You've got some good ideas. First, though, you have to serve your apprenticeship."

"Apprenticeship?"

"That's right." Dolan dropped his pen. "It's like Bert Reisbeck always says. Port Wyoochee's a football team, and I'm the coach. And you don't get to play unless you clear it with me. *Capisce?*"

"So what position are you offering, coach?"

Dolan aimed a stern glance my way. "Are you in or out?"

Dispirited sigh. "Well, if this is the only way to renovate that factory, I guess I'm in."

"This is an all-or-nothing proposition, hon. Either you do it my way or forget the whole thing."

I had to play this scene very delicately. Too much resentment, and he might slam the door in my face. I'd lose all access to Dolan. But if my reaction didn't ring true, he'd know I was a fake.

"What kind of deal are you offering?" I asked quietly.

"We go into it together, Anne Marie. My new firm and your backers. We put together a new corporation."

"Which purchases title to the torpedo factory," I added.

"You catch on fast." Dolan showed me two upraised fingers. "We split the new corporation's common right down the middle. Each side gets half. Forty-nine percent to Whulge and the same to your crew."

"What happens to the remaining two percent?" I inquired.

"My personal share." Patting his breast pocket, he smiled again. "I'm counting on those dividends to provide me with a little extra pocket money come Christmas."

"It also gives you controlling interest in the new corporation," I pointed out. "Your cut plus the Whulge shares gives you fifty-one percent."

His grin widened. "What can I say? It's an imperfect

214

world." Sidelong glance at Angie. "Besides, your group will be raking in forty-nine cents of every dollar those condos net. That's nothing to cry about."

"Who's crying, Jack? I'm just stating a fact."

"A fact Mommy never taught you, eh?"

"She never got around to discussing the cost of doing business in Port Wyoochee."

Dolan laughed.

Now that he'd shown me that he held the upper hand, Jack Dolan became a jolly host indeed. He walked me back over the plans for my nonexistent project to renovate the old torpedo plant. He quizzed me about zoning variances, construction timetables, and—most importantly—the financing. A sharp and extremely cautious fellow, this Mr. Dolan.

"You're dreaming!" he told me. "You won't hit break-even point until you've marketed at least twenty of the two-bedroom units. To build them, you're going to need—*up front*—two-point-two million. Your backers got that kind of cash on hand?"

Careful, Angie, don't strain your credibility now.

"Well, no . . ." Rueful shrug. "We were counting on the banks."

He made a raucous sound. "Forget it."

"Come on, Jack. It's an extremely lucrative concept. You said so yourself. We'll have the site itself as collateral. With you putting in a good word for us—"

"Like I said . . . you're dreaming!" Dolan's tanned face tightened in frustration. "Money's too tight right now. They'd never go for it. My signature's on too many loans already. And you . . ." He shook his head in disappointment. "Sorry. They ain't in the habit of lending to schoolgirls."

"But—"

"You're going to have to change your approach, hon. Go in with a smaller amount. Figure on five hundred K, max, and start by building and marketing the first five units."

"That's the nickel-and-dime approach, Jack. It'll take *years* to complete the project that way."

"You've got a better idea?"

I showed him a broad Angie smile. And nodded. "There's always *the straw man.*"

His bronzed face registered bafflement. Resting both elbows on his desk, I leaned forward. "It's a common dodge back East. When a developer runs low and needs fresh financing. You line up four people. *Straw men,* they're called. They've never borrowed before. You send them to four different banks. That is, banks where *you* have influence. The bank loans the straw man six hundred thousand. He keeps twenty or thirty K for services rendered, then signs over the rest to you. When the smoke clears, everybody is happy. The straw men have their payoff. The banks have four shiny new loans on their books. And you have two million, three hundred twenty thousand dollars to finance the Torpedo Junction project."

Avarice gleamed in those blue eyes. Dolan was evidently considering other uses for this helpful scam.

"Cute. Very cute." He seemed to savor the idea. Then he shot me a wary glance. "And no questions from the bank?"

"Not as long as the boys keep up their monthly payments."

"What happens if they fall behind?"

"Well, they are *your* banks." Mischievous Angie smile. "You go before the board and ask them to give your boys a little more time. I'm sure you can be quite persuasive, Mr. Dolan . . . when necessary."

His sudden gale of deep-throated laughter made my skin freeze. But somehow I managed to keep my conspiratorial smile in place.

"You really earned your money today, Anne Marie." Rising slowly from his chair, Dolan offered me his outstretched hand. "I think it's going to be a lot of fun having you around."

"Let's hope so, Mr. Dolan."

All at once, he turned dead serious. "Go talk to your backer. Tell him you've got the money to build. If he wants in on the deal, I'm ready to talk incorporation. Lay it all out for him . . . and then get back to me."

Zipping my purse shut, I sneaked a fleeting glance at the tiny transmitter hidden behind his desk calendar, then swallowed hard. Mickey's future was depending on it.

Leaving my chair, I cast him a warm farewell smile. "I'll be in touch, Mr. Dolan."

"I'll be waiting, Anne Marie."

After leaving Dolan's office, I dropped by the Parmenter House and shed my business togs in favor of an Aztec print blouse, a pair of slim-cut burgundy Wrangler jeans and my trusty stadium jacket. For accessories, I had on a bright blue plastic baseball cap. It was a little novelty item I'd picked up at Kit's Camera, along with my brand-new, palm-sized General Electric AVR minicassette recorder.

Why the hat? Well, there was an AM/FM radio sewn right into the ball cap's right side, complete with a small earplug. The only clue to its presence was the slim telescoping antenna rising at a rakish angle from the brim. I fiddled with the cap for a while, seeking the proper tilt. Then I grinned at my mirror reflection and took off for Klallam Park.

By the time I arrived, the sun had found a few gaps in the overcast, and the park benches were well on their way to complete dryness. Seating myself, I put my shoulder bag on my lap, opened it, and withdrew my small, recently purchased tool kit. Then, biting the corner of my lip, I attempted to marry the ball cap's speaker to the recorder's tiny microphone.

This wasn't exactly my debut at this sort of thing. During my second year at Springfield, the Department of Corrections decided to "mainstream female prisoners into technically skilled occupations." So, instead of running washing machines, we spent about a month playing with soldering irons and needle-nosed tweezers.

Now we'd see if your Angie had mastered Electronics 101 as well as she had lockpicking.

The first time I switched on, a heterodyning whine struck my ears. Yeesh! Try again, princess. This time, string out some more wire and keep the recorder away from the cap radio.

When I tried it again, a faint static crackle came through, accompanied by a distant unintelligible mutter. My fingertips adjusted the volume and pitch. The mutter solidified into Jack Dolan's familiar baritone.

". . . and don't forget to tell Ginny she's showing that two-bedroom Cape at four o'clock."

Relaxing on the park bench, I listened in on life at the Luckutchee Real Estate office. Ooooooh, what an irascible boss. Temper, temper, Mr. Dolan. Mustn't shout.

So absorbed in eavesdropping was I that I failed to hear the muted crunch of male boots on autumn leaves. All at once, a hand grabbed the brim of my ball cap and tugged it down.

"Hey!" Peeling off the cap, I glared at the intruder. Wry fussbudget face. It was only my grandfather, the Eternal Tease.

"You know, I thought it was you." He sat on the bench at my side. "Last time I saw you, you were all dolled up. What's with the teenager outfit?"

"Change of clothes, Chief. Otherwise, I would have looked pretty silly with this on," I replied, showing him the plastic ball cap.

Baffled Anishinabe look. "What is it?"

Briefly I explained how I'd planted that bug in Dolan's office. The VOX-Five transmitted on an FM channel, a frequency easily picked up by my cap radio. Chief's expression lightened. He had a lot of fun pinging my antenna with his forefinger.

"I never could buy you enough toys." Hearty chuckle. "I don't know, girl. Every time I think you're going to make it past eighteen, you backslide right on down to eight again."

The telephone jangled in Dolan's office. Waggling my free hand, I whispered, "Sssssshhh—quiet, Chief!" Then I handed him the minicassette recorder's earphone. "Here, you can listen in on this."

I flicked the recorder's on-switch. Then, turning the ball cap's side button, I boosted the gain. Distant sound of factory noises. Dolan's voice sounded in the foreground. "Luckutchee Real Estate."

"Hi, Jack." The factory din nearly drowned out Rolf Lauridsen's voice. He must have been calling from the mill floor. "Those security people you wanted hired—they started work this morning."

"Great! How many did we get?"

"I contracted with Sound Security for the full dozen. I've got two apiece backing up our rent-a-cops at each of the mill's entrances. The second shift comes on at four."

Jovial chuckle from Dolan. "That'll keep those Greenway assholes off the property. Fax me over a copy of the contract, will you?"

"Sure." Lauridsen's voice sounded uncertain. "Uh, Jack, we've got a little problem down here."

"What kind of problem?"

"White liquor buildup in the vats." Despite the mill clamor, I could feel the anxiety in the manager's voice. "Normally, we'd drain into the clarifiers, but they're already at peak capacity. MacNeill recommends a shutdown—"

"Forget it!" Dolan snapped. "You have orders to fill. Advertisers are screaming for paper. Use the holding pits behind Building Two."

Plainly unhappy, Lauridsen protested, "We can't do that. The EPA advised against using those pits."

"Fuck the EPA! I'm not losing that United Advertisers account!"

I heard a man's voice in the background. "Let 'em roll!" And then the factory noise abated suddenly, overwhelmed by a mighty droning roar. It reminded me of a hundred diesel locomotives starting up simultaneously. Then I realized I was listening to Kulshan's gigantic rollers.

Closing my eyes, I strained to detect Lauridsen's voice amidst that stunning background rumble.

". . . those pits date back to the Twenties. I'm not certain they can hold all that wastewater."

"There's only one way to find out."

"This is raw effluent we're talking about. Sulfides! They could leach directly into the river."

"You're breaking my heart, Lauridsen."

"We are risking a major spill—"

"That's right!" Dolan's voice took on a dangerous edge. "That's what business is all about—*risk!* I want you to use those goddamned holding pits. Understand?" His tone turned vicious. "Or maybe you're getting a little tired of doing this kind of work?"

"No!" Anxiety gave the manager's voice a panicky lilt. "Of course not, Jack."

"It sure sounded like it a minute ago."

"I-I was merely concerned about the company, that's all. Another spill could be disastrous to Kulshan's public image."

"Look, you let me worry about the image." Dolan turned jovial once more. "You just concentrate on getting that United Advertisers order out of there by Friday. Okay?"

"Yes, Jack."

"Good man!" *Click!*

Holding the plug to his ear, Chief glanced at me. "Did you get all that?"

Patting my cassette recorder, I showed him a dazzling smile. My grandfather and I were both thinking along the

220

same lines. A copy of this tape would soon be on its way to the EPA office in Seattle.

It would be inadmissible in court, of course. But it would still provide the EPA investigators with a valuable starting point.

Suddenly, I heard the shrill piping of Dolan's telephone touch tabs. My friend was making an outgoing call. But to whom? Motioning for my grandfather to keep silent, I listened carefully.

Six rings, and then an automatic taped message came on. The words sent a sudden dreadful shiver through me.

"Hello, you have reached the First Church of Jesus Christ-Adamite. If you wish to learn the truth about our God, our nation and our race, please stay on the line. Hail victory!"

Chief and I exchanged surprised glances. Why was John A. Dolan, pillar of the community, putting through a call to Camp Pelley?

I had a really bad feeling about this. My stomach felt as if it were in freefall. I hoped my name—my alias, I mean—didn't pop up during the conversation. Both Dolan and Thurber knew Anne Marie Nahkeeta. However, Dolan knew her as the shrewd investments advisor. To the Adamite pastor, Anne Marie was a streetwise Colombian dope runner.

The pastor's vibrant speaking voice came on. "May I help you?"

"Yeah! But we'll get to that in a minute." Dolan let out a chuckle. "Did you watch TV this weekend, Thurber?"

"Afraid not. The church has been busy with preparations." I noticed the sudden timbre of sickly excitement in Thurber's voice. Faint chuckle. "We just might have a *marshmallow roast* coming up."

I made a fussbudget face. Odd . . . Sargent had used the exact same phrase. Wait a minute! I thought the Adamites had already *had* their marshmallow roast. . . .

221

Dolan gave me no time to ponder the matter. "Too bad! You missed a great documentary on the protest. I'm calling to compliment you. Your boy Sargent does good work."

"I'll be sure to pass on the message. Anything else?"

"Yeah. I've got some more work for him." Dolan's voice turned ugly. "I want him to teach Georgianna a little lesson."

"What kind of lesson?"

"That bitch needs to learn respect for private property. So here's what I want Sargent to do. Next Wednesday night, when Ms. Waterman heads for the San Juans, I want your boys to break into her apartment. Knock the hell out of it! I want all her precious antiques smashed to hell." He seemed to be savoring his vision of destruction. "Get a pencil."

I heard desk drawers slamming in the background. Thurber's laconic voice drawled, "Go ahead."

"Villa Klahtee Wapthee, 1200 Summit Avenue. The bitch lives in apartment number twenty-four."

"You're sure she'll be in the San Juans that night."

"Positive. Georgianna's a creature of habit. She takes the ferry over to Orcas every Wednesday." Dolan's tone hardened. "Two hundred for each guy. And, Thurber, limit it to five, eh? I ain't paying for the fucking Aryan army!"

"Two hundred's pretty thin for a rap like B and E."

"Don't try to hold me up, Pastor!"

"What happens if one of my guys gets caught and the FBI offers him a lighter sentence if he rolls me over?"

Harsh laughter from Dolan. "You know, Thurber, maybe you ought to think seriously about dropping this shit and becoming a Presbyterian."

"It isn't shit!" Thurber cried, thoroughly rattled. "We are engaged in a life-or-death struggle against the powers of darkness. We are fighting to ensure the survival of the white man. People like you are blind to the racial peril. The Elders of Zion—"

"Spare me the sermon! Just have your boys at that woman's place a week from Wednesday. Got it?"

Wariness from Thurber. "I don't like it. Gallagher's no fool. After that job we did for you on Hanauer's store—"

"You don't get paid to like it!" Dolan's acidic tone made me flinch. "And you don't have a choice, either, Pastor. I'm your umbrella, see? If I fold, you're standing out there in the cold, hard rain."

Thurber sounded surly. "Maybe I'm sick and tired of my men risking their necks for peanuts."

"Listen, Thurber, if not for me, you and your asshole followers would all be in Cedar Creek with that Jewboy Grantz. They'd all like a piece of you, Pastor—the FBI—Gallagher. Better you should think long and hard about keeping me happy."

"I don't need you, Dolan."

"You don't? What happened? Did some rich jigaboo-hating old lady drop dead and leave the church a bundle?"

Thurber rose to the taunting. "Maybe I've got a better offer."

My heart froze. Thurber was about to mention my offer. The earphone trembled in my nervous grip. Swallowing hard, I thought, No, Thurber, don't! Don't you *dare* mention Anne Marie!

Tense seconds passed. Utterly helpless, I waited for one of them to speak. My Anishinabe luck held. Dolan failed to inquire further about the pastor's new offer. Instead, he came on like a *Godfather* imitator.

"You know, Seattle's real nice this time of year. I'd think seriously about a trip, Thurber. Hang around here, and you just might wind up dog shit."

"Is this supposed to be scaring me, Dolan?"

"Boy, you really do take after your old lady, don't you? Crazy as a bedbug!"

Thurber's frenzied shout hurt my ears. "Fucker! Mention my mother again, and so help me, I'll—!"

"What do I have to do, asshole? Spell it out for you? If you don't do as I say—"

"What!?" Thurber exploded. "What's going to happen to me, Dolan!? Same thing that happened to the Jewgirl!?"

Dead silence. Holding my breath, I braced myself for Dolan's reaction. But when it came, it was as quiet and as deadly as a tarantula.

"You've got a big mouth, Thurber. Just like your old lady. That ain't something to aspire to, you know. Big mouths don't live very long. That's a statistical fact." His tone turned to ice. "A big mouth tends to get shut ... *permanently.*"

Click.

Chapter Eleven

Scowling, I switched off the recorder. "He hung up."

Chief removed the plug from his ear. "You sound disappointed."

"It was just getting good."

His glance turned inquisitive. "What do you make of all that?"

"Well, now we know why the authorities have been unwilling to evict Pastor Lem's little church. Dolan's running interference for them," I said, lifting the tiny cassette out of its cradle. "Very tidy arrangement, eh? Thurber uses Dolan as his umbrella, and Dolan occasionally uses the skinheads as his private enforcers."

My grandfather rolled the earphone wire onto its spool. "That's one hell of an umbrella, Angie. I was talking to some boys at the Legion Hall last night. One of 'em told me, 'Nothing—and you can take this to the bank—nothing moves in this town without Jack Dolan's okay.'"

"Lovely!" Trembling with pent-up anger, I stuffed my gear into my shoulder bag. "Pastor Lem can bash *mud people* all the livelong day. So long as he does an occasional job for Dolan, no one can lay a hand on him."

"Nothing new about that, missy." My grandfather rose slowly from the bench. "When I was a boy, there were a lot of millionaire Krauts who thought mighty highly of old

Adolf. They thought they could control him. They sure found out different."

"Let's get out of here," I snapped.

"You're taking this kind of personal, Angie."

Sidelong scowl. "You didn't see what Sargent did to that Coleman kid." With a sigh, I switched off the radio and put my ball cap back on. "What else did you learn at the Legion Hall?"

"I hate to sound like a broken record," he said, as we sauntered across the park lawn. "But you can forget about Mr. and Mrs. Hanauer. I must've talked to every War Two vet in town during the past couple of days. I bounced that name off every single one of 'em. Lieutenant Commander Harold Weiler. I drew a blank look every time. None of the vets I talked to were stationed at Bremerton."

"How about Mona's dad?"

"*Him* they did know," Chief replied. "I talked to this guy who bought his bifocals from Doc Hanauer. Says Doc moved here in 1956. He was born and raised in Terre Haute, Indiana."

I could see my Tessie theory exploding on the horizon, but I gave it one last valiant try. "Ruth Hanauer?"

"Oh, everybody knows Ruth. She was born in Port Wyoochee. Her maiden name is Vogel. Her father taught geometry at Denham High School for years. Oh, yeah . . . and in 1945, she was all of nine years old." Chief's gaze drifted across the park's broad, well-kept lawn. "Tell me, Angie, do you think Thurber was telling the truth?"

"About Mona? I don't know, Chief. If Dolan did it, and Thurber knows, then that could be his leverage against Dolan. The big man didn't enjoy being needled about that." Woeful grin. "On the other hand, it could've been a blind jab on Thurber's part. The pastor trying to taunt his protector."

My grandfather showed me a solemn-eyed glance. "I

don't think Thurber was bluffing, Angie. I think Dolan's the killer."

"Why are you so sure it's him?"

"Because of all those vets I talked to." He halted beside my parked Topaz. "You know that bar you and Marcella went to? Millicent's Pub?"

"What about it?"

"Jack Dolan used to own it."

"I know. He told me."

My grandfather did a doubletake. "He *did?* When?"

"This morning. At his office."

Sagacious smile. "He didn't tell you the pub's name, did he"

Mildly puzzled Angie glance. "No, he didn't. How did you know that?"

"Because you wouldn't be acting so nonchalant if he had." Reaching past me, Chief opened the car door. "When Dolan first opened the place, he called it *Whiskey Jack's.*"

Twenty minutes later, Chief and I were cruising east on Route 112. A mountain shower soaked our car as we meandered down from the heights. To our right loomed the snowy peaks of the Olympics. Four Goodyear tires grumbled as we crossed the Murdock Creek bridge. My grandfather lounged in the passenger seat, listening to some lively powwow music on the car radio.

I'm afraid your Angie was not very talkative. I was much too busy mulling over the circumstantial evidence against Dolan.

Whiskey Jack, I mused. Hmmmmm, perhaps Mona hadn't been that delirious, after all. She grew up in Port Wyoochee. She was a little girl when Dolan had first opened the pub. Perhaps Whiskey Jack was a longtime local nickname for the big man.

Holding the steering wheel, I grimaced. Dolan's record

had so many black marks on it, it was starting to resemble a leopard skin.

Motive Number One—Killing Mona Hanauer had frustrated the environmentalists' campaign against Dolan's company. With its rapidly declining earnings, Kulshan Paper would never have paid for an EPA-mandated cleanup. Had Mona lived, the paper mill might have been forced to close, and Dolan would have lost his shirt.

Motive Number Two—Vengeance! Mickey and Mona had already clipped his wallet once. During their initial courtroom clash five years ago, Dolan had threatened them both, vowing to get them no matter what.

Supportive Fact Number One—Dolan is the only one of the suspects with a plausible reason for framing Mickey Grantz.

A tiny dissenting voice piped up, informing me that I was overlooking Pastor Lem.

Perhaps, but my reading of the Adamite leader suggested otherwise. After all, Thurber had allowed me and my grandfather to leave his compound unharmed. He seemed unwilling to risk arrest. And I had a strong feeling Thurber was unaware of Mick's existence.

After all, had Thurber known that Mona's ex was a lawyer, would he have risked a damaging libel suit by printing that scurrilous flyer?

Mild frown. You realize, of course, that your argument is based upon the premise that Lemuel Thurber is a rational human being.

My frown deepened. Nope! Wouldn't want to bet the rent money on that!

On the other hand, Dolan was well aware of Mona Hanauer's former marriage. He was a frequent visitor to the San Juans. He had two compelling motives for killing the woman. And, for a man in his fifties, Jack Dolan is in remarkably good shape. Those fisherman's hands could have easily pummelled Mona to death on that lonely beach.

228

But was Dolan on Orcas that night? That's the big question.

All at once, I became aware of the absence of powwow drums. Turning my head, I saw my grandfather switch off the radio. He showed me a curious smile. "Coming around to my way of thinking, are you?"

"Okay, maybe you're right." Impatiently I drummed my fingers on the steering wheel. "Dolan does make a more plausible *Whiskey Jack* than Georgianna."

"She had one last breath, Angie, and she made it count."

"Did she?" Leery expression. "I just don't know. It's the same old problem, Chief. Why did Mona say 'Whiskey Jack' when she could have just as easily said 'Jack Dolan'?"

"Mona was delirious. That's what your nun said."

"I know! And that's what's so maddening about it." I shook my head in frustration. "Exactly how delirious was she? Did she know what she was saying? If she knew Jack Dolan had tried to kill her, then why didn't she come right out and say so? And, if she was that delirious, then how can we be certain the phrase means anything?"

My grandfather chuckled. "It's your clue, missy."

"Some clue!" I muttered, slowing the car as we approached the town limits. "It could mean everything . . . or *nothing!*"

Okoke was the easternmost town in Yennis County and the only one flat enough for an airstrip. Washington 112 doubled as the main street. Come to think of it, that was the only paved street. Six buildings comprised the downtown area—a Victorian general store, a Blue Seal feed store, a Chevron gas station, a yellow-brick WPA schoolhouse, and two charming bungalows with madrona trees out front. A dirt road angled away from the highway, shooting off toward the airport and the strait.

Slowing to a crawl, I nudged the Topaz off the asphalt and down the embankment onto the dirt road. A pair of rusting Navy hangars appeared in my windshield. Four single-engine planes sat on the tarmac. Cessna 180s, also known as *the Alaska state bird*.

Cocking an inquisitive eyebrow, Chief asked, "Have we got a reason for stopping here?"

"Best reason of all. We know who the suspects are. Now we start checking alibis," I replied, halting in front of the brick airport tower.

"Watch yourself in there."

"I'll be the soul of caution. Girl Scout's promise."

Once inside, I veered immediately to my left and entered the ladies' room. Perching my shoulder bag on the sink, I gave my reflection a hasty scan, then reached for my brush, comb and compact.

With the grooming completed, I ruffled through the business cards Chief had packed up for me in Tacoma. Found a likely entree. The face showed a silhouette of three mountains and a legend reading

Anne Marie Nahkeeta
Claims Investigator
Cascades Insurance Corp.

It was a little risky, adding yet another occupation to the versatile Anne Marie's résumé. But I had no choice. If the air traffic control people asked to see an I.D., all I had on me was my Anne Marie Washington driver's license.

Card in hand, I stepped into the lobby. Vacant vinyl seats filled the center of the room, all of them facing a wall-mounted TV. A varnished knotty pine counter separated the passenger waiting area from the inner office and baggage carousel. Standing at the counter was a serious-faced woman with brown eyes, wavy cinnamon hair and a mouth coated with strawberry lipstick. She was in company uniform. Gemini Airlines. Long-sleeved white blouse, trim green slacks and a nametag reading *Patrice*.

230

Seeing me, she put her pen aside, tilted her head curiously, and asked, "May I help you, miss?"

My winning smile unfolded like the dawn. "Hi, I'm Anne Marie Nakheeta." Handing her the business card, I added, "I'm investigating a personal injury claim for my employer, Cascades Insurance. Could I please have a moment of your time?"

"Oh, of course."

I rested my bag on the counter. "Two weeks ago, one of our policyholders . . ." Frantic tickle of the imagination. "Ah, Mrs. Emma Stoneberger of Klallam Bay . . . broke her ankle—"

Patrice blanched in sudden horror. "Here at the *airport?*"

Reassuring Angie smile. "No, no, she was at home. You see, this floatplane dropped out of the clouds, and Mrs. Stoneberger thought it was going to crash into her house. She took a step backward and fell off the cedar deck."

"That's terrible!" My tale piqued Patrice's curiosity. "Are you saying the plane deliberately buzzed her house?"

"Well, that's what Mrs. Stoneberger says."

"Did she get a look at the wing number?"

"Uh-huh." I took my notebook out of my purse, flipped it open, and grimaced thoughtfully at the sight of a blank page. "She gave us a pretty good description, too. A white floatplane with bronze and yellow trim. The wing number was N5973WJ."

"Have you been in touch with the FAA?" she asked.

"My boss, Mr. Langston, is handling that end of it," I explained. "He asked me to touch base here—try to determine the plane's flight path. I figure you people tracked it on radar."

She nodded. "It's possible. We cover the entire shore."

"Could I have a look at the radar records for that day?"

All at once, Patrice went bureaucratic on me. Uncle Sam was paying her to run the counter, not make the decisions.

"I'm sorry Ms. Nahkeeta. I'm afraid you'll have to speak to Mr. Lussier about that."

And so, up the stairs we went—right into the heart of Yennis County air traffic control. The tower reminded me of the video arcade at the Tacoma Mall. Lots of hooting and beeping and lime-colored alphanumerics suddenly appearing on glossy screens.

The airport manager's name was Gary Lussier. He was in his early thirties, a short, ferret-faced guy with a Zapata moustache, protruding ears, and red-rimmed, world-weary eyes. He cheered right up when he caught a glimpse at your Angie. The dull eyes suddenly brightened, and he stood erect, casting me a longer, more appreciative glance. Tucking in his rather large managerial belly, he raised his thick cowboy belt to hold it in, then hurried my way.

I would have happily settled for confirmation of Jon Waterman's flight to Nitinat, B.C., on Wednesday, October seventh. Instead, I was treated to a grand tour of the tower. See the great big transceiver console, Anne Marie. Over here, we have the all-weather radar the FAA installed just last month. Oh, and by the way, have you made any plans for Friday night?

Gary seemed a bit disappointed when I told him I was already booked into a weekend training session down in Portland. But that didn't stop him from showing off his pride and joy, the tower's mammoth green radar screen, and explaining how it functioned.

"You see, Anne Marie, every airplane carries a transponder. That's a small radio beacon that makes the plane show up on this screen as a numbered slash of light. The aircraft's abbreviated call sign appears right next to the blip—"

Slightly confused Angie smile. "Abbreviated?"

"We never use the whole registration number in a pilot/controller dialogue," Gary explained. "We always shorten it to the final three or four digits. The flight you're after, that'd be listed as seven-three-whi—"

"Gary!" one of the controllers interrupted, touching his headphone. "Sea-Tac's on line. They're vectoring traffic out this way. We're to clear Flight Level One-Seven-Zero."

"Send it. Get 'em out of there." Shaking his head, he led me over to his desk. "Nothing spoils our day faster than a Piper Apache wandering into the flight path of Boeing 767." He picked up a flimsy manila folder. "What time did that woman have her accident?"

Thinking back to the logbook on Dinah's counter, I mentally converted from military time to civilian. "Four o'clock in the afternoon."

Gary showed me a grimy photostat. I spied the thumb-sized blip and its accompanying numerals just above the Washington shoreline. The logbook's information was accurate. According to the FAA photostat, Jon Waterman had just taken off from Sahale Point.

The manager peered over my shoulder. "Looks like your client has a case."

Warm Angie smile. "Could you tell me his final destination?"

"No problem!"

After shuffling the folder's photostats, Gary laid them faceup on his desk. Together we traced the flight of Waterman's plane on its northwesterly course across the Strait of Juan de Fuca. Then he led me over to a large wall map.

"He landed at Nitinat." Gary Lussier pointed out a small resort town at the northern end of long and narrow Cowichan Lake. The lake was about twenty miles long, I guessed, a miniature Baikal nestled away in the snow-capped mountains of Vancouver Island.

I could have phoned Nitinat for confirmation, but I decided to let Gary carry the ball for me. "I wonder what time he arrived . . ."

"Let's find out." He smiled, eager to please.

Stepping up to the console, Lussier took the microphone from the controller, uttered the tower's call sign, and asked to speak to Nitinat air traffic control. Three times he repeated the request. Each time we were rewarded with a burst of static from the overhead loudspeaker. Then . . .

"Yennis Tower, this is Charlie Victor Seven-Three-Five-Zulu, Kamiakin Lodge, Nitinat. How may we help you? Over."

"Three-Five-Zulu, did you have an arrival the evening of October seventh? A floatplane. Yellow and bronze livery—"

The Canadian never gave him a chance to finish. "Oh, yes! Jon Waterman. He was here that night."

"Ask what time he arrived," I whispered.

Lussier repeated my query. Our Canadian friend became downright talkative. It must get kind of lonely manning a fishing lodge up there at Nitinat.

"Waterman flew in about half past six. Then he had dinner at the Blue Goose Cafe. He told me he was scheduled to meet a fishing party in the morning. He was planning to fly them to Nanaimo."

That was consistent with the information in Waterman's logbook. My gaze rocketed to the wall map. Nanaimo . . . ah, there we are. East side of the island. Sudden fussbudget frown. Waterman's flight path was zigzagging north—*away* from the San Juans.

I motioned for Gary to give me the mike. Then, pressing its transmit button, I asked, "What time did he take off the following day?"

"Oh, just after eight o'clock."

"Did you see him take off?"

Good-natured chuckle. "To tell you the truth, miss, I didn't see too much of anything. There was a very thick fog that night. Waterman just beat it into Nitinat. It was even worse the next morning. I couldn't even see the tourist cabins from my front porch. Waterman rang me up promptly at eight, asking for permission to take off. I told him to wait, but he was eager to get cracking. Of course, he was no stranger to that sort of takeoff. He flew out of Cambridge

234

Bay when he was in the air force. Nothing but bloody fog up there. He doubled back once he was airborne. I heard him pass right overhead."

"You're sure it was him?" I prodded.

"Positive, lass. I'd know the sound of a Beaver motor anywhere. He was here the night of October seventh, miss. I'll swear to that." Sudden hearty chuckle. "Of course, I couldn't say who he was *with.*"

So Waterman's ladykiller reputation extended above the border, eh? The lodgekeeper must have thought I was one of his girlfriends checking up on him!

Thanking the Canadian for his help, Gary Lussier signed off. Then he escorted me downstairs. He wanted to know if there was anything else he could do for me. Showing a mildly flirtatious smile, I said no.

As I stepped outside, my grandfather pushed open the driver's door for me. "How'd you make out?"

Sliding onto the seat, I replied, "Looks like Waterman is in the clear. He was on Vancouver Island the night Mona was killed. The lodgekeeper at Nitinat said he took off again at eight the following morning."

"Sister Mary Katherine found Mona an hour earlier—at seven." Thoughtful nod from Chief. "One down—four suspects to go. What next, missy?"

Switching on the ignition, I said, "It's high time I made that long-distance call to Tacoma."

Chief tilted his head toward the tower. "Why didn't you use their phone?"

"Because the pay phone's in the lobby, and I couldn't very well perform right in front of Patrice."

"Patrice?" he echoed.

"Long story! Listen, I'm going to need your help . . ."

Ten minutes later, my Topaz was parked in front of the Okoke General Store. The store's interior was right out of

235

an old episode of *Bonanza*. Old-fashioned brass-trimmed counter hewn from a single block of redwood. Shadowed ceiling and narrow rows and a cedar plank floor. The pungent scents of overripe fruit and fresh-baked bread tickled my nostrils. My peripheral gaze found the pay phone hanging on the wall right next to the magazine rack.

The owner's name was Tim Sullivan, and he greeted my grandfather and I like visiting royalty. Which we were! When Chief asked him about the best spots for steelhead, the store owner's eyes lit up. The two of them plunged into a lively discussion of the performance characteristics of the cork-handled, pistol-grip, graphite spincasting rod. Neither one noticed as I sidled over to the telephone.

Three shrill ringings, and a high contralto voice came on the line. "Afternoon. Kay-Tee-Pee-Ehm Television."

Pinching my nose, I gave myself a nasal voice. "Would you hold for a call from New York, please?"

Definite surprise. "Oh! Of course."

Resuming my normal voice, I sailed right into my breathless spiel. "Hi! I'm Lorraine Krieger, and I'm a producer here at CBS. We're putting together a segment on hate crimes for 'Sixty Minutes.' I understand you people have footage of the skinhead arrests that took place on Yom Kippur."

"Yeah, we covered that." The receptionist didn't know quite how to handle me. "Uhm, Ms. Krieger, would you like to speak to our station manager?"

"Actually, I'd like to talk to whoever covered the arrests."

"That'd be Delilah Dawes. Let me connect you. Hold on."

Take your time, hon. Deep breath. I had four whole seconds to concoct the script for my telephone con. Then the canned Mozart gave way to a throaty alto voice.

"Delilah Dawes speaking."

"Dee, hi! This is Lorraine Krieger in New York." Rat-a-tat-tat! Angie the hyper Manhattanite. "I heard about your

236

story. Good job! Listen, how much footage of those skinheads do you have?"

Delilah wasn't quite as dazzled by the phrase *New York*. "Excuse me, who ... Lorraine? ... how did *you* hear about that?"

"I read about it yesterday in the *New York Times*. I thought it would make an excellent lead-in for an upcoming show. So I talked it over with Morley—"

"Morley Safer?"

That got her! Nothing like a little name-dropping to firm up the con. Adroitly dodging her query, I made my pitch. "We're doing a twenty-minute segment on hate crimes nationwide, with me producing, and I want to lead with your Tacoma synagogue incident. I'm willing to use your footage and your voice-over. So talk to me, Dee. What have you got?"

"We were right there when the fighting began." Excitement charged the anchorwoman's lovely voice. No doubt visions of a transfer to network headquarters danced through her head. "One of the skinheads shouted an insult at a rabbi. Then a handful of scuffles broke out."

"You have film of this?"

"Absolutely. Vin Murphy's camera was running from beginning to end."

I thought back to Sargent's boasting at Millicent's Pub. Thus far, the stories meshed. I already knew the answer to my next query, but I went ahead and asked. "Any arrests?"

"Four men. All of them skinheads. Only one was a local man. The rest were from Port Wyoochee—Warren Pettigrew, George Cowan and Stephen Sargent. It was Sargent who started the altercation."

"Is that the same Sargent who attacked the demonstrators at the Kalshan paper mill?"

"The same!" Delilah's voice turned tart. "He's a real troublemaker. He's been arrested for disorderly conduct up and down the sound."

"The *Times* said he was some kind of Aryan leader."

"I wouldn't call him a leader, Lorraine, but he is a member of the Adamite church. It's an Aryan group based in Port Wyoochee. Their leader is a man named Lemuel Thurber."

Giving Delilah a nudge in the right direction, I asked, "You've met Thurber?"

"Oh, yes! On many occasions. He's a real media hound. When we heard the Adamites were responsible, Vin and I hung around the police station. Sure enough, Thurber came marching in at two A.M. He brought a bail bondsman with him. Once his men were released, he held a news conference on the station house steps."

"Did you interview him?"

"Uh-huh!" Cynical tone. "We're Kay-Tee-Pee-Ehm, the station that brings you complete coverage of all the nuts."

I pressed on. "How long did the interview last?"

"Fifty-five minutes!"

"You have footage of that interview?"

"Uh-huh. In the vault. Were you planning on using it in your segment?"

"Definitely! Plus any historical footage of this group you may have." Shifting gears, I added, "How about Thurber's men? Were they with him all that time?"

"You bet! From the way they were huddled around him, you would've thought they were the Secret Service."

"Was Sargent with them?"

"Are you kidding? He was at Thurber's elbow the whole time." Disgust hardened her voice. "He kept mugging the camera. Muttering, 'You're next, Rabbi!' " Weary sigh. "Believe me, it was *quite* an interview."

I shot a quick glance at my grandfather and Mr. Sullivan. They were still busily pantomiming spincasting techniques.

"Dee, what time did Thurber's news conference end?"

"Let's see . . ." She made a quiet humming sound. "We signed in back at the station at three-thirty. Twenty minutes

238

to get here . . . I'd say it broke up at ten past three. The Adamites left with Thurber."

I grimaced. So Thurber *and* Sargent were both standing on the steps of the Tacoma police station at precisely three A.M. The approximate time Mona Hanauer was being beaten. There's no way those two could have been on Orcas Island at that same moment.

Congratulations, Lem. Videotaped at the Tacoma police station. You couldn't have a better alibi if you handcuffed yourself to the president.

And then I remembered Sargent's quip in Thurber's office. That crack about a *marshmallow roast*. What was that all about? And why had Thurber been angered by it?

Jumping right back into character, I chattered, "Sounds like you have plenty of interesting footage, Dee. Listen, I'm flying out to the coast in a few days. Mind if I screen it at your station?"

"Not at all!" Her tone brightened. "In fact, I'll meet you at Sea-Tac, and we—"

"I haven't yet made the flight reservation," I interrupted, trying to head her off. "Look, I'll call you the minute I arrive in Seattle. We'll do lunch. Oh, and please tell your station manager our Contracts Division will be in touch with him."

"I will! Nice talking to you, Lorraine."

"Same here, Dee. And *thanks!*"

I hung up. A long and soothing breath calmed my jittery nerves. Another command performance, princess. If there's one thing you excel in, it's *ikwekazo odaminowin*. Which is what our people call *woman's make-believe*. Well, I hoped Delilah Dawes wouldn't be too disappointed.

Our suspect list was rapidly thinning out. I could now name three who had been nowhere near Orcas Island the night of Mona's murder. Jon Waterman had spent the night way up there in Nitinat, B.C. And a TV station videotape showed Pastor Lem and his sidekick, Skinhead Steve, on the steps of the Tacoma police station at the time of the murder.

That left three suspects who could have been on Orcas that night. The teenaged eyewitnesses claimed to have seen a man approaching Mona's cabin. That could have been either Jack Dolan or Rolf Lauridsen.

Or Georgianna *disguised* as a man.

Oh, well, I thought, rejoining the two fishing enthusiasts. I certainly had plenty to discuss with my grandfather.

"You've got nothing," Chief said.

We were westbound on Washington 112, headed back to Port Wyoochee. I shot him a heated glance. "What do you mean—*nothing?* You heard Smilin' Jack put out a contract on Georgianna. Maybe he took care of Mona Hanauer personally. Or maybe Lauridsen—"

"That's a whole lot of maybes, Angela," he said adamantly. "And none of them is going to break the case against Mickey Grantz. While you're fooling around with maybes, the D.A. has hard evidence—"

"*Planted* evidence!" I yelped.

"But still admissible evidence," Chief said sternly. "Then there are all those eyewitnesses who saw Mickey scrapping with his ex-wife just prior to her murder."

"They can't convict him on the basis of that!"

"No, but it goes a long way toward strengthening the prosecutor's case. And if he puts Ruth Hanauer on the stand—"

"Don't say it!" I had a horrifying mental image of Ruth reminiscing out loud about her son-in-law's dire threats. "Ohhhhh! Tell me something I don't know."

"If you insist . . .," Chief added amiably. "Paul Holbrook's going to be back in Pierre tomorrow. What happens if he drops by the Dunning House and you're not there?"

A cluster headache took shape behind my brow. "Thanks, Chief . . . you always know how to cheer me up!"

"We're going to have to cut our losses and run, Angie."

Scowling, he raised the brim of his ball cap. "It's all up to Mickey's lawyer now. We can tell him about Mona's Phone-Mate. And what we've learned about Kulshan. Whoever grabbed that answering machine is the killer, and that can't be Mickey. He was in police custody when it happened. His lawyer ought to be able to build a good reasonable doubt defense out of that."

"Not good enough." My warpath scowl deepened. "That leaves too much to chance. Mick's trial could go either way. Even worse, it means Mona's killer makes a clean getaway."

"So do we, Angie. So do we."

"Damn! There has to be a trail," I said, fuming. "I don't care which one it was—Dolan, Lauridsen or Georgianna—the killer had to have made a slip-up."

"Sure! Only how do we find it?" my grandfather argued. "We don't have the time or the manpower to backtrack all three of them. And you can hardly walk into the FBI office asking for help. The minute they realize who you are—"

Sudden inspiration! My lips shaped themselves into a subtle Angie smile.

"Uh-oh!" Chief said. "You've got that look in your eye."

Instantly I checked the rearview mirror. "What look?"

"The *Angie's-about-to-do-something-cute* look."

"Relax." My smile turned impish. "I just thought of a way to get the FBI to do our work for us." My smile showed flawless teeth. *"Miss Murphy."*

His eyes narrowed in curiosity. "Who?"

"Not who, what." I slowed the Topaz, letting a logging truck pass us on the left. *"Miss Murphy* is a scam, Chief. I learned it from Toni."

My grandfather did a very poor imitation of W.C. Fields. "The old con game, eh?"

"You've got it." I nodded. "The Bureau is keeping a close watch on Thurber's church, right? I'm going to swing the federal spotlight over to Jack Dolan."

"I'm not sure I follow, Angie."

241

"Look, you and I know about the clandestine relationship between Dolan and Thurber. Right? Well, imagine what would happen if that relationship suddenly went public in a big way."

Stroking his chin thoughtfully, he murmured, "I get it. If the FBI suddenly found out Dolan was running interference for the Adamites." His obsidian eyes met mine. "Well, first thing they'd do is open a file on Dolan. They'd trace him all the way back to his mother's womb—try to find out if he's connected to any other neo-Nazi groups."

"Exactly!" Shifting my gaze forward, I scanned for any oncoming traffic. "If Dolan killed Mona, the FBI will find out. There's no way Jack can stand up to that kind of scrutiny."

"That's assuming Dolan's guilty," he replied. "But what if he isn't? What if he didn't kill Mona?"

"Does it really matter?" I lifted my chin decisively. "Dolan's as dirty as they come, Chief. His clout has enabled those neo-Nazis to thrive. One way or another, that bastard's going down. Pastor Lem's about to lose his umbrella."

My grandfather sighed. "I thought you weren't going to play Robin Hood this time around."

"Can't be helped. You said it yourself. There's no way we can backtrack all three of them. Not in the time we have left. So I'm turning the Bureau loose on the Kulshan twins. That frees us up to move in on Georgianna."

Seeing his proud face in profile, I detected an air of misgiving. My hand patted his. And I murmured in Anishinabemowin.

"What happens the next time Thurber's men encounter a person of color on the streets of Port Wyoochee? We cannot turn our backs on this evil, *Nimishoo*. We have to stop them."

"You're right, of course, *Noozis*." His fond gaze met mine, and he gave my hand a tender squeeze. "You'll make it go public in a big way?"

I chuckled, reverting to English. "I'll be on the front page of every newspaper in the great state of Washington."

"What do you need from me?"

"I need you to go to Tacoma. Remember that novelty store where I bought my Joanne Larue disguise? Well, I want you to take some of our war fund and invest it in play money. Say, fifty thousand in bogus tens and twenties."

"Play money?" He looked at me askance.

"Cheese for the rat trap." And then I explained my plan.

Chapter Twelve

"Are you about finished with that?" Chief asked, looking nervously down the darkened alleyway.

"Just about," I replied, kneeling before the rear door of Heritage Antiques. With painstaking care, I diddled the door's tumbler lock with a hardened steel pick. My grandfather was doing sentry duty. Together we huddled on the store's back stairs, taking care to keep well within the night shadows.

Whisper of astonishment. "Where'd you learn to do that?"

"Springfield." Keeping my voice down, I dug the pick in deeper, then gave it a gentle twist. "Tingo Maria ran a B and E class for us new fish. She had an old padlock and made us practice with bobby pins."

"You got quite the education in there, didn't you?"

"You don't know the half of it!" Vile memories erased my smile. I gave my tension wrench a slow turn to the left. *Click!* Hastily I extracted my burglar tools, stood upright, and clutched the doorknob, holding the bolt back.

And now, Maria, we'll see how well your Anishinabe student mastered the art of unlawful entry.

Sticking my steel pick between the door and jamb, I ran it up and down that narrow aperture. No resistance. That meant no deadbolt or chain. Bad sign, princess! There must be a burglar alarm.

Crouching, I held the doorknob with my left hand and dipped into the shoulder bag with my right. Chief and I had done a bit of shopping before coming to Mona's store. Dahlberg's Hardware contained all the items needed for a successful break-in. Pix-Quik lockbreaking kit, complete with two tension wrenches, five steel picks and a broken key extractor. A tube of rubber cement. And a surplus U.S. Army anglehead flashlight.

Pulling out the flashlight, I gave it to my grandfather and asked him to install the blue filter. He accomplished the task with remarkable speed.

Whispery whistle. "That was quick."

"Angie, I was a Marine Raider long before you were born." Grinning, he handed me the flashlight.

My thumb flicked the on switch. A dull blue beam illuminated the door. Rising on tiptoes, I slowly moved the beam toward the top crossbeam. A metallic gleam winked back at me.

"Damn!" I hissed.

"What is it?"

"It's a contact burglar alarm," I explained, pointing out the metallic gleam. "There are two electrodes built into the jamb, with the third on the door itself. When the door is closed, all three touch, and an electric current flows through them. When the door opens, contact is broken, and the alarm goes off."

"There must be a shutoff switch," Chief muttered.

"There is . . . but we'd never find it in time," I whispered, reaching into my bag once more. "Fortunately, we're prepared."

While Chief kept hold of the doorknob, I took out a two-inch strip of aluminum foil, then folded it over and over and over, squashing it each time with my thumb. Within a minute, I had a flattened silvery square ready to serve as a replacement electrode. Then I withdrew a small roll of masking tape from my bag, peeled off two sticky chunks, and installed them at either end of my aluminum connector. Taking a deep breath, I stilled my quaking hand and carefully slid the connector between the doorjamb's two contact points.

I nodded to Chief. He eased the door open. We both tensed, waiting for the shrill alarm bell.

Silence! The only sound came from passing nighttime traffic over on Dollar Avenue.

Once indoors, I made Chief put out his hands. Talk about role reversal, eh? I deposited a dollop of rubber cement on each one of his fingertips. Repeated the procedure for myself. He shot me a questioning glance.

Waggling all ten digits, I whispered, "If you must burgle, it's always best not to leave fingerprints."

I took some other precautions, as well. Such as wiping the doorknob—inside and out—with my jacket sleeve. Then I tucked all my burglar tools into their handsome leather carrying case and hurried to the bathroom. No, it wasn't the call of Mother Nature. I lifted the toilet's porcelain lid and dropped my tool set into the five-gallon water tank. *Ker-plunk!*

That was twenty dollars down the shitter, but it was a whole lot better than getting caught with a set of burglar tools in my back pocket.

Yes, indeed, your Angie got quite the education at the Big Dollhouse.

Rejoining my grandfather, I saw him masking the flashlight lens with his broad palm. His gaze circled the darkened room, sweeping over Mona's shadow-cloaked antique furniture. "Where do we start?"

"Let's find out where her office was."

It took us less than three minutes to find the narrow alcove Mona had been using as her business office. It had once been a kitchenette, with a high ceiling and varnished elm baseboards. Now it was crammed with wall-to-wall office furniture. Olive green filing cabinets, IBM personal computer and accessories, and an old-fashioned rolltop oakwood desk. Apparently, Mickey's ex had never suffered from claustrophobia.

Perching our flashlight on top of the printer, Chief and I gave that desk a thorough search. Sitting cross-legged on the floor, I rummaged through the bottom drawer, occasionally lifting sheets of paper into the path of that blue beam. Frustrated Angie sigh. Bills, bills and more bills! Nothing of interest from either Jack Dolan or Georgianna Waterman.

Just then, I heard my grandfather's startled exhalation overhead.

"Angie!"

I reached my feet in one fluid motion. Chief pointed out the black Phone-Mate beside Mona's desk telephone. Gnarled hand shaking, he fumbled with the release. Suddenly, the lid sprang open, revealing a small white tape cassette.

"All right!" I breathed, then plucked it out of its cradle. "This may tell us who was in touch with Mona just before her murder."

"How?" he asked.

"My AVR recorder," I whispered, patting my shoulder bag.

Two minutes later, I had the cassette firmly in place within my own recorder. Chief quietly closed the office door. I hit the rewind button, flinched at the tape's sudden squeal, and immediately lowered the volume. Then the playback began. Fine hairs bristled on the back of my neck as I heard Mona's soft and sexy contralto voice for the very first time.

"Hello, this is Heritage Antiques, your best stop for bargain collectables on the shore. We're very busy right now, so please leave a message when you hear the beep."

Beeeeep! Male voice, breathless and hate-filled. "Quit destroying our jobs, you fucking commie!"

Beeeeep! Another unfamiliar male voice. "You're dead, Jew!"

Chief's eyebrows lifted slightly. "Prophetic, wasn't he?"

247

And then a change of pace from Mona's rightwing fan club.

Beeeeep! "Mona, this is your mother. Will you be home for Yom Kippur or not? Lisa's giving me a ride to the synagogue, and she wants to know if you're coming, too. Please, Mona, give me a call as soon as you get home."

Beeeeep! "Mona?" The familiar tenor clutched my heart. Mick's voice! "Look, if you don't want to take my advice about Thurber, I understand. It's just . . . hell, we can't let it end this way, Mona. Not like this. Look . . . all right, I apologize. Can't we get together one more time? Just once more, Mona, that's all I'm asking. I'm sorry . . . I just . . . I-I have to see you again. Okay? You've been part of my life for ten years now. And in all that time, Mona, there wasn't a day that went by when I wasn't thinking of you . . . okay, okay, I'm begging. I realize that. I-I have to see you. Please? One more time, that's all I'm asking. One—" *Beeeeeeeep!*

My throat muscles tightened in sorrow. Poor Mick, I thought. He still loves her.

Beeeeep! Another man's voice. I could barely make it out against that rumbling drone in the background. I hit the rewind, then the pause, raised the volume a bit, and let her roll.

A deep-throated rumble assaulted my ears. Straining to tune it out, I detected a faint male baritone. "Listen, Ms. Hanauer, we have to talk. Can we get together Wednesday night? You pick the spot."

Then Mona's voice came through. A ghostly echo. "Wednesday? Yom Kippur? Is he kidding?"

Chief and I exchanged meaningful glances. Mona must have been in her office when the man called. She hadn't bothered to pick up. Still, the Phone-Mate had recorded her sardonic comment.

"There's our boy," Chief murmured. "He called Mona here, hoping to set up the meet. Then he called her at her

248

apartment later on. That tape has his invitation to the San Juans."

I was thinking along those exact same lines. But who had made the call? Who was that guy? And why did his baritone voice seem vaguely familiar? Frowning, I hit the stop button.

Chief whispered, "What is it, Angie?"

"That last guy," I said, rewinding the tape again. "I've heard him on the telephone before. Here in Port Wyoochee, too. But I can't seem to remember where."

Again I tapped the playback button. We both listened carefully to that droning rumble in the background. Then the man's voice came on. Recognition danced tantalizingly beyond my reach.

All at once, my grandfather uttered a hushed laugh. Grinning, he teased, "Don't you recognize that sound?"

Scowling, I shook my head.

"The mill, Angie! That's the sound of those big rollers at the Kulshan paper mill."

And that gave me the name of Mona's mysterious caller. I'd heard his voice earlier that day while eavesdropping on Dolan's office. A voice that had nearly been smothered by the rumbling of those giant rollers. *Rolf Lauridsen!*

Tuesday found me up before dawn, grooming myself for the day's upcoming business meetings. Torrential rains hammered the tiled roof of the Parmenter House. I turned up in the dining room at precisely six-fifteen, dressed for success in my navy wool blazer, power blue tuxedo shirt with lace-embellished collar, gray flannel slim skirt and white hand-embroidered wool cardigan.

After availing myself of their delicious Continental breakfast, I paid the tab, asked the front desk clerk to convert three dollars into quarters, and strolled over to the public telephone in the oak-trimmed lobby.

Lifting the receiver, I popped in my quarters one by one.

It was already nine A.M. in Pierre, and I had to catch my quarry before he set out for the Dunning House.

Seconds later, that familiar calm baritone said, "Department of Corrections. Holbrook speaking."

"Welcome back, Kemo Sabe!" That's my nickname for Paul. He thinks it means *trusted friend*. I haven't got the heart to tell him it's Paiute for *horse's ass*. "How was Wonderland on the Potomac?"

"Angie!" Paul's voice brightened. "Thanks for calling. Listen, it was a great trip, but I think I'm meetinged-out for the rest of the month." His tone turned curious. "Steffie tells me you're out on a job development leave. What's going on?"

"Uh—that's right." Anxiety rendered me slightly hoarse. Pursing my lips, I asked, "Have you, uhm, talked to Mr. Langston yet?"

"No." I slumped in relief. Thank goodness he hadn't seen that phony letter! "He left for Rapid City just yesterday. I have a memo from him, though. He wants to meet with us. Any idea what for?"

To discuss my job development efforts, no doubt. But I didn't dare tell Paul that. Sheepish tone. "We sort of got our wires crossed, I guess. Mr. Langston asked me to call in last Friday, and I forgot."

"An-ge-la!"

"Hey! Couldn't be helped, Kemo Sabe. The company switched the interview site from Belle Fourche to Watertown."

"Whoa! Back up a minute, princess. What is this job?"

"Oh! It's a clerk-typist job with Pacific Lumber. They're opening a number of warehouse stores here in South Dakota."

"How did you hear about it?" he asked.

Improvisation time! "Uhm, at powwow. You know, Columbus Day weekend? Mary Anne Medicine Horse said they were still hiring, so I decided to give them a try."

"Well! That is encouraging." Pride filled his pleasant baritone voice. "I guess all those chats we had finally did some good."

"I couldn't agree more," I added, tongue in cheek.

"Angela, you have no idea how delighted I am to see you taking the initiative this way." Uncertain tone. "You did mention you were a parolee . . . didn't you?"

"Of course! I'd *never* lie to a prospective employer, Paul." Putting one hand behind my back, I gingerly crossed two fingers. "I was completely open and upfront about my time in prison. And I told them how I went right into Work Experience as soon as I made parole. I did everything you told me, Paul, and *guess what?* They're calling me back for *another* interview!"

"Good girl! Say, where are you calling from?"

"Watertown," I replied cheerfully. I mean, it wasn't *really* a lie. Port Wyoochee is a town on the water. And, peering through the front door's oval window, I could see Luckutchee Bay. "I should be back in Pierre in a few days."

"All right. I'll pencil you in for Friday," he replied, his tone turning thoughtful. "Hmmmmm . . . listen, Angie, why don't you give me their number? I'll put in a good word with their personnel manager—"

"*No!*" I panicked, looking anxiously around the vacant lobby. "I mean . . . thanks, Paul, that's very sweet. But I'd really like to do this on my own."

"I understand." Amiable chuckle. "Oh, and one other thing, Miss Biwaban . . . whether you get the job or not, I'm going to need documentation for your client file. Be sure to ask their personnel manager for a formal letter of notification, eh?"

"Will do, Kemo Sabe. Have a nice day!"

"You, too, princess. So long."

Giggling to myself, I put the receiver back on its hook. And thank *you*, Mr. Holbrook, for a truly helpful suggestion. A trio of turn-down letters from large Seattle lumber firms would certainly look convincing in my Work Experience file.

To say nothing of allaying the suspicions of that devious soul, Mr. Randolph T. Langston.

I made a mental note to stop at the library later on. Using the resource room's typewriter, it shouldn't take too long to concoct a few query letters and Angie résumés. I'd list my prison service right at the top. That would be sure to guarantee an instant rejection.

I had another hour to kill before Luckutchee Real Estate opened, so I breezed back into the small, cozy dining room and put in an order for tea. Then I found a linen-covered table beside a tall arched Victorian window. Peering through the glass, I watched the raindrops dance on the century-old sidewalk and gave some thought to my upcoming *Miss Murphy* scam.

It's one of the oldest con games around, and I'm pretty sure a woman invented it. It definitely wasn't one of Toni Gee's favorites. She called it a pimp's game. She only played it once—that time she was flat-busted broke in Fitchburg, Massachusetts.

As to how *Miss Murphy* goes, we start with one very attractive woman, who usually has absolutely nothing to do with the scam. She sashays down the street in her spring finery, and, naturally, all the male heads swivel for a prolonged second glance. And that's when our con artist moves in, buttonholing one or two of the watchers. "That's Miss Murphy," he says. "She's a real looker, eh? How'd you like me to fix you up with her?"

Now, if the mark is Beetle Bailey's pal, Zero, by now he's jumping up and down and pleading for her address. On the other hand, if he's a little more worldly wise, he asks what the angle is.

And then . . . ah, hell, let's let a certain actor from Philadelphia tell the traditional con man's tale.

"My boy, Miss Murphy is just one of a stable of bee-yoo-tiful girls, and I have the unique privilege of being their—ahem—business manager. Unfortunately, your chief of police takes a very dim view of our rather unique profession, and he has given us the proverbial twenty-four hours to get out of town. His loss is your gain, my boy. Yaaaaas, indeed! For a mere fifty dollars, I shall arrange for you to spend an hour consoling Miss Murphy upon her imminent departure. You give me twenty-five dollars right now, my boy, and then convey yourself to 321 Courtesan Lane at precisely six P.M. Miss Murphy will collect the remainder of the fee, and she will be most delighted to have your company. Just knock on the door and tell her Mr. Fields sent you, yaaaaas. A pleasure doing business with you, my boy. A distinct pleasure."

Of course, Miss Murphy's address always turns out to be the local supermarket or something. And, his dream of romance shattered, our mark shuffles away, less affluent, perhaps, but certainly wiser in the ways of the world.

I would be doing a variation of the Miss Murphy game. Money would serve as the lure. To be specific, that play money Chief was buying in Tacoma. I'd use that phony cash to manuever John A. Dolan into a particular time and place. Then I'd turn him against his cat's paw, Thurber, triggering a confrontation so explosive that the FBI would have to take notice. Once the feds were after Dolan, I could concentrate on Georgianna.

Mild fussbudget frown. And Lauridsen?

Quietly I sipped my tea. There was no denying the facts. Lauridsen had phoned Mona and specifically asked for a meeting on Wednesday night, October seventh, Yom Kippur. And Mona had left her Orcas Island cabin that night to meet someone. Rolf Lauridsen, perhaps?

Thoughtful Anishinabe scowl. If Lauridsen did kill her, then what's his motive? To prevent the collapse of the Kulshan Paper Company, thereby saving his own career?

You know, had I never eavesdropped on Dolan's office, I probably would have accepted that motive at face value. But listening to his conversation with Dolan, I couldn't quite see

253

Lauridsen as the murderer. He had been extremely reluctant to divert the wastewater into those aging holding pits. Could a man so scrupulous about preventing environmental damage be capable of murder?

But if he wasn't trying to lure Mona to the murder scene, then why had he phoned her? What was the reason for that Wednesday night get-together?

The saucer rattled as I put down my cup. Easy, princess. Let's not get carried away here. You don't know for certain that Lauridsen was the man who visited her cabin at midnight. You don't even know if he was on the island.

And then I thought of a clever way to find out.

I aimed a swift glance at the corner grandfather clock. It was five past nine. Dolan must be at his office by now, I thought. After tucking a dollar bill beneath the saucer, I grabbed my leather bag and headed for the lobby once again.

Dolan answered on the third ring. "Luckutchee Real Estate."

Leaning against the wall, I held the receiver and absentmindedly ground one spike heel into the carpet. "Hi, Mr. Dolan. Got a minute?"

"Anne Marie . . ." Chuckle of pleasure. "I was just thinking about you, hon."

"I talked to my backer over the weekend. He's willing to play it your way . . . and so am I." No need to fake a tone of breathless urgency. "I thought we might get together and discuss a memorandum of agreement."

"Sounds good to me. Can you be here in half an hour?"

"Ah . . . no offense, Mr. Dolan, but I hate to be seen going in and out of your office. That might raise a few of the wrong eyebrows. We do want to keep this deal private."

"I couldn't agree more, Anne Marie." Shrewd tone. "What do you have in mind?"

"Why don't we meet at the paper mill?" I suggested. "Rolf Lauridsen's office."

"Why there?"

"It's private. It's out of the way. And if we arrive in separate cars and at separate times, nobody will ever suspect there was a meeting."

Silence enveloped the other end. Dolan was thinking it over.

"What's with all the secrecy, honey?"

Heart thumping, I replied, "My backer is willing to assist you with your straw man problem."

"Yeah?" Dolan's voice betrayed keen interest. "What kind of assistance are we talking about?"

"The green kind."

Anticipatory chuckle. "Give me the magic number."

"Fifty, Mr. Dolan . . . as in fifty *large!*"

"Well, now! I guess we had better keep this meeting private," he replied, sotto voce. "Be there at noon. I'll phone Lauridsen and let him know you're coming. I'll be there at one."

"Good enough. Thanks again, Mr. Dolan."

"Thank you, Anne Marie. Believe me, I'm looking forward to this meeting."

The phone clicked in my ear. Smiling to myself, I replaced the receiver. My quarry had taken the bait. And, in three short hours, he'd be making the acquaintance of Miss Murphy.

By the time I left the Parmenter House, the morning downpour had subsided to a chilly drizzle. Snug and dry in my London Fog and evergreen hood wrap, I dropped by the public library, typed up my résumés and job query letters, and, after browsing through the Seattle Yellow Pages, selected the names of three large lumber companies. After all, large firms tend to use a standard rejection letter. Something along the lines of . . . *Dear Angela—Thank you for your letter of application. I regret to inform you that we are unable to offer you em-*

ployment at this time. We wish you every success in your current job search blah-blah-blah.

With any luck, my rejection letters would be arriving at my Pierre post office box during the next few days.

I went looking for Georgianna only to learn that she had the afternoon shift that day. The desk librarian advised me to return at four o'clock. I showed the lady a look of sincere regret, bummed a handful of blank business envelopes off her, and then returned to the resource room to finish my correspondence.

After mailing my bogus job queries at the post office, I headed for Bay Vision Associates. Figured to bounce a few questions off Mona's dad. Another strikeout! Doc Hanauer's partner, Dr. Pamela Welbes, informed me that he was honeymooning in Honolulu with his brand-new twenty-five-year-old bride. He was expected back November first. Judging from the lady optometrist's tart tone, I had a feeling she didn't exactly approve of the new missus. I think Dr. Pam was hoping to become the second Mrs. Hanauer. Or was it the third?

I sure hoped Chief was having better luck in Tacoma.

Promptly at eleven-forty-five, I sauntered into the Kulshan plant, turned right at the soft drink machine, and headed for Rolf Lauridsen's office. I found his secretary busily keyboarding in front of an imposing IBM office computer. She was thirty and blond, with an oval face, deep-set gray-green eyes, low eyebrows, a slender nose, a cleft chin and a rigid Katie Gibbs posture. Her hair was silky and impeccably styled, parted on the left and curling inward just beneath her golden disk earrings. Impeccable wardrobe, too. I cast a covetous glance at her smart tailored pinstripe linen suit, pale pink with cream-colored striping, with its double-breasted jacket and matching slim skirt.

Standing before the heavily cluttered desk, I uttered a polite cough. Her well-scrubbed face peered over the jacket's padded shoulder.

Pleasant Angie smile. "Hello, I'm Anne Marie Nahkeeta. I have an appointment with Mr. Lauridsen at noon."

"Of course, Miss Nahkeeta." She was out of that chair in an instant, standing behind her desk, peering down at the pages of her appointment book. "Mr. Lauridsen's on the mill floor right now. He'll be back shortly." Her delicate hand fluttered in the direction of a naugahyde bench. "Please have a seat."

"Thanks." I did a crabwise step into my investigation. "I'm sure glad Mr. Lauridsen was able to see me *this time.*"

Flashing an uncertain smile, the secretary responded, "You had a *previous* appointment?"

"Yes. October seventh. Mr. Lauridsen didn't show. I guess he was out of town or something."

"I don't think so." Features troubled, she leaned over the appointment book and flipped back several pages. "No . . . Mr. Lauridsen was here all that day."

"Are you certain of that?"

"Absolutely!" She ran her index finger down the page. "He met with Mr. Sheninger of Finance from nine until eleven-thirty. Then he was down in the factory until noon. After that, he and I had lunch in the managers' lounge and reviewed the payroll. He had two more meetings that afternoon. Mr. Cauley from one till three. And Mrs. Baird from three till five."

"He left the plant at five?"

"Five-thirty, actually. He had a few letters for me to type." Mild smile of fatigue. "It was one of our busier days around here."

"I guess! You left the plant together?"

She nodded. "Uh-huh. At exactly five-thirty." Puzzled glance. "What time did you get here?"

"Twelve-twenty." Innocuous Angela. "There was nobody here at the desk. I hung around for fifteen minutes and then left."

"Oh, dear! Mr. Lauridsen and I were just down the hall." Apologetic smile. "Did you phone for an appointment first?"

"Sure! A week earlier."

"Well, who did you talk to?"

"I don't know." I gave my own padded shoulders a quick shrug. "She said her name was Mary. She took my name and gave me that twelve-twenty appointment."

Frosty tone. *"I'm* the one who handles Mr. Lauridsen's appointments!"

"I, uh, take it your name isn't Mary."

"Uh-uh! Sharon Bateman." Her pale lipsticked mouth tightened in aggravation. "Somebody in the mill was having a little fun."

Giving the woman a cheerful smile, I said, "Oh, don't worry about it, Sharon. There's no harm done. At least now I know who to ask for whenever I call Kulshan."

Just then, I heard male footsteps behind me. A familiar baritone called out. "Anne Marie! This is a pleasure."

Pivoting, I beamed. "Hello, Mr. Lauridsen."

The manager stood in the middle of the hallway, tie loosened, trousers wrinkled, shirtsleeves rolled back. He draped his suit jacket casually over one shoulder. Black oil stains speckled his knuckles. Definitely a hands-on supervisor.

"Have you had lunch?" he asked.

I shook my head no.

"Well, let me get cleaned up, and we'll try today's special in the cafeteria." Then he turned to Sharon. "Mr. Dolan's coming in just before one. He'll want to have a look at those purchase orders. Mind taking a late lunch today?"

"Not at all, sir," said Sharon, her smile professional. Katie Gibbs would have certainly been proud.

So we had lunch in the main Kulshan cafeteria, Mr. Lauridsen and I, occupying a two-person table beneath the large frosted-glass window. He was putting on a show for me—the boss having lunch with his loyal employees. The effect was ruined, however, by the four empty tables all

258

around us. Beyond the cordon sanitaire, mill workers ate, drank, burped, swore, laughed and gossiped, mildly resentful of our presence. It was, after all, their lunchroom.

No sooner had I finished my overdone veal, French fries, coleslaw and lukewarm coffee than Lauridsen whisked me away on that long-promised tour of the paper mill. He showed me the pumphouse and the oil bunkers, those gigantic pressure cookers called *digesters,* where the wood chunks are boiled down into fibers, and the huge bleaching vats. We finished the tour at the rollers, just in time to watch them go into full spin. *Thrumm-thrumm-thrumm!* The awesome drone numbed my ears. The rumbling enveloped us like a hurricane wind. I could feel the oil-stained factory floor vibrating beneath my feet.

Returning to his office, we found Jack Dolan relaxing on the couch, idly reviewing a sheaf of salmon-pink purchase orders. He was wearing a crisp three-piece suit in gray flannel and oxblood wingtipped shoes. A pair of glasses rested halfway down his nose. His alert gaze swivelled in our direction as we came in. Taut welcoming smile. "It's about time you people got here."

I extended my hand in greeting. "Rolf was showing me the plant."

Dolan declined the offer to shake hands. Behind me, Lauridsen suddenly cleared his throat. "Uh, Jack . . ." The manager had quickly resumed his obsequious tone. "You want me to sit in on this?"

"No need. This won't take too long."

"I'll be down in Shipping, then." And I heard the office door snap shut behind me.

Tossing the purchase orders on the coffee table, Dolan gestured at an empty chair. "Have a seat, Anne Marie." Then he took a thin legal document out of his briefcase. "I've got something for you."

Smoothing the back of my skirt, I seated myself, then accepted the proffered document. "What is it?"

"Draft memorandum of agreement." Leaning forward, Dolan rested his elbows on his knees. "Look it over, make any changes you want, then bounce it back to me ASAP. That is, if you're still interested in teaming up."

"Very much so, Mr. Dolan." Casually I perused the typed pages. "So much so that I'm willing to put money on it."

"Please . . . call me Jack." He had the toothy smile of a well-fed tiger shark. "You mentioned money on the phone. Fifty thousand."

"That's right." I put the draft memo aside.

"What's the deal, eh?"

"Simply this, Jack . . ." I tugged at my blazer cuffs. "You've got a few people in mind for the role of straw man. Right?"

He nodded. "I've talked to three or four guys."

"So I say we give them a little incentive to approach the bank."

Dolan was certainly a quick study. "Pay them up front, you mean."

Curt Angie nod. "And here's how we work it. We develop a joint fund. Each of us kicks in some money. The straw men are paid out of that account. They secure the loans and turn that money over to us. Then we're off and running on the rehab project."

Thinking it over, Dolan murmured, "And you've already got some upfront money on hand?"

"Fifty thousand," I said, scratching my nyloned knee. "If you want in, you have to match that amount. Those are my backer's terms."

He let out a muted whistle. "That's a lot of cash. Where are we supposed to keep it?"

I shrugged. "Safety deposit box?"

His feral grin broadened. "I suppose you already have one in mind, eh?"

"Wrong guess, Jack." I gave my tone a mild edge of indignation. "I only thought of it just now."

Fingering his chin thoughtfully, he added, "You'll let me pick the bank?"

"Sure! On one condition."

"What's that?"

"That we meet downtown tomorrow at nine A.M. I pick a copy of the Yellow Pages and open it at random. You close your eyes and put your finger on a bank."

Hearty gust of baritone laughter. "What's the matter, Anne Marie? Don't you trust me?"

"Not with fifty grand in cash, Mr. Dolan."

"Smart girl!" Cracking his knuckles, he added, "Okay. You've got yourself a deal. Nine tomorrow morning. We each bring cash. It goes into the safety deposit box. Then we sign the memorandum of agreement."

"And neither of us touches the cash until your four straw borrowers are ready to make their move."

"I can live with that. Where do we meet?"

"Public library." I caught his curious expression and added, "I'll feel a lot less nervous with a whole lot of people around."

"All right. I'll meet you there at nine." Only then did he offer to shake my hand. "I'm looking forward to tomorrow, Anne Marie."

Folding my draft memorandum, I rose gracefully from the chair. Removing his glasses, Dolan shifted his imperious gaze to the door. "Go fetch Lauridsen for me. I want to talk to him."

Expression of surprise. "Me?"

Another icy Dolan grin. "You're the junior partner, kid."

I got out of there before he asked me to make a fresh pot of coffee.

By five o'clock, I was back in my room at the Parmenter House, sitting on the rose-striped comforter, rereading Jack Dolan's draft memo. My navy blazer was draped over the

261

vanity chair, and my ouch shoes were hiding beneath the canopied bed. The Princess phone sounded a muted jangle. Swiftly I scooped up the receiver. "Hello?"

"Anne Marie?" The husky soprano voice belonged to Mrs. Talbot, my landlady. "There's a gentleman here to see you."

Gentleman callers! I thought. No doubt about it—my sorry love life was definitely on the upswing. "Who is it, Mrs. Talbot?"

"Mr. John Nuquispum. Want me to send him upstairs?"

The name threw me for a few moments. Then I remembered that *nuquispum* is Chinook for *blue lake*. A rather apt description of Lake Superior. And that, of course, told me who my visitor was.

"Sure, Mrs. T. Send him up."

Three minutes later, knuckles tap-tapped on my bedroom door. Slipping on my white doeskin moccasins, I sang, "Come innnnn!"

My grandfather stepped through the doorway, dressed like a shore dockworker and holding a black leather briefcase. *"Machiya, Noozis!"* He closed the door behind him. "Here's that money you wanted."

"Mügwetch, Nimishoo," I said, thanking him. And stuck to our native language. "Any problems up in Tacoma?"

Shaking his head, Chief slung the briefcase onto my bed. "None! The store manager got curious, though." Brown hands snapped open the brass latches. "I told her we're planning a retirement party for my brother."

"You were gone all day, *Nimishoo,*" I observed, standing by his side.

His obsidian eyes danced in excitement. "I was very lucky."

"What do you mean?"

"I visited the American Legion hall," he explained, unable to suppress a grin. "I was in the city, so I figured, 'What the hell—might as well ask about Weiler.' And I got lucky." His tone tingled with triumph. "I met a World War Two vet named George Marchant. He was in the army. He served in one of those Graves Registration units. Lives in Fircrest now. He helped ship Weiler's body back to the States after the war."

"Back to Bremerton?" I asked.

"No, no . . ." Chief waved an impatient hand. "Weiler was from the East, remember? They buried him in his hometown—Newport, Rhode Island. George said his unit got the request for disinterment in '47."

Fussbudget face. "It took all day to find *this* out?"

"No. *Noozis,* it took all day for George to get me a copy of that disinterment order." Slowly my grandfather withdrew a folded paper from his inside pocket. "George went to work for the Veterans Administration back in 1950. He retired a few years ago, but he still has quite a few friends at the VA office. Good thing, too. Otherwise, it would've taken weeks for us to pry this off of Uncle Sam."

Curious, I peeled the photocopy open. The glossy print showed me an antique typeface.

NAVY DEPARTMENT
Washington, D.C.

13 March, 1947

TO: Director, National Cemetery of the Pacific
　　Puowaina, Hawaii Territory
FROM: Commandant, Tenth Naval District
　　Bremerton, Washington
REQUEST FOR ACTION: On 10 April, 1947, you will disinter the remains of WEILER, Harold Frederick, Lieutenant Commander USNR, 004-2219-5683, said remains to be shipped to the Zone of the Interior aboard USS *YORKTOWN*. Arrangements for burial

have been made with the Hebrew cemetery in Newport, Rhode Island.

This action is being taken in compliance with the request of the deceased's common-law wife, Theresa N.
Thurber.

I gasped. My startled gaze flew to Chief's grim face.

"That's right." He nodded slowly. "Weiler's buried in
Newport's Jewish cemetery."

My hand trembling, I lowered the photocopy. I couldn't
quite believe what I had just read.

Thurber's father was a Jew.

Chapter Thirteen

On Wednesday morning, October twenty-first, I saw the sun for the first time in days. At least I *think* it was the sun. Actually, it was a bright patch in the roiling overcast, somewhere over there in the direction of Port Townsend.

When I spotted it, I was mired in morning rush hour traffic on Hiaqua Avenue, heading for my rendezvous with Jack Dolan.

Even with the black briefcase on the seat beside me, I had a hard time keeping my mind on the scam. I couldn't stop thinking about Theresa Noelle Thurber, also known as T.N.T., ardent Silver Shirt, fiery anti-Semitic editor and outspoken foe of President Franklin Delano Roosevelt. Yet she had made the arrangements to return Harold Weiler's body to the United States.

I thought of the notation on that old Navy document. *Common-law wife.* And remembered what Pastor Lem had told me about his father.

How wrong you are, Pastor! It wasn't the nefarious Elders of Zion who had blocked your mother's return to politics. Tessie had taken herself out of that hateful movement. By 1947, she was no longer the same woman who'd been interned at Bremerton. Love had changed her. At some point she had stopped seeing Harold Weiler as her jailer and had come to see him as a man—as a rather likable, divorced, fortyish Rhode Island doctor serving his country during a long and terrible war. As for Weiler, he had probably been first fascinated and then enchanted with the strong-minded and articulate woman who was his patient. Mutual attraction had blossomed into a full-fledged wartime romance.

I remembered what Chief had told me the previous night. *"It was a strange time, Angie. The war permeated every aspect of life. When you woke up in the morning, you didn't know if you were still going to be alive at sunset. There was a tendency to—what do you kids say?—go for it. To squeeze every precious second you could out of a relationship. Because you just never knew. Tessie and Weiler? Nahhhhh, that doesn't surprise me. The war threw together stranger couples than that. Your grandmother and I knew a lot of 'em. Most headed for Reno right after V-J Day. But there's quite a few coming up on their fiftieth anniversary."*

However, there were to be no anniversaries in Tessie's future. Just those long years of single motherhood and official disgrace in her hometown of Port Wyoochee. Bittersweet memories of what she had lost at Okinawa. And finally, when her son entered school, the endless stream of cocktails that helped to dim the memories.

I couldn't help thinking how different Lemuel Thurber's life would have been, had his father survived the war. Tessie would have probably married her naval officer and returned with him to Rhode Island. Lem Thurber would have grown up on the shores of another ocean, basking in the warmth of a loving home. Never would he have become the tense and angry adolescent, keenly conscious of his outcast status, unable to comprehend the profound loneliness engulfing his alcoholic mother. Maybe then he wouldn't have joined the Navy SEALS in order to prove himself. And maybe the carnage of Vietnam wouldn't have roused a taste for racial Armageddon.

Thurber doesn't know the truth about his father, I thought. He couldn't possibly know and still hate his father's people the way he does.

266

Oh, Tessie, you should have told him. Better yet, you never should have gone home to Port Wyoochee. You should have moved to Los Angeles with the rest of the rootless ones—destroyed every memento of your Silver Shirt career—anything but allow your son to become seduced by the same madness.

But she hadn't, of course, and I think I understood why. What do you do when you're thirty-nine and pregnant and the man you love won't be coming back from the Pacific? You seek sanctuary in the only home you've ever known, and, for Tessie Thurber, that was Port Wyoochee. It probably seemed easier to face the disapproval of the shore people than to risk the larger, more frightening world outside.

I remembered Pastor Lem haranguing the faithful at the Adamite church and wondered who was to blame for this mess. Thurber himself, for following in Mother's footsteps? Tessie, for getting swept off her feet by that suave and elegant Nazi, William Dudley Pelley? Perhaps we ought to blame old man Cook and his sawmill. After all, it was his bandsaw that broke and killed Dan Thurber. Grim Angie smile. A bandsaw snaps, and eighty years later the victim's grandson is stirring up a pogrom in good old Port Wyoochee. Cause and effect.

I was beginning to feel like a character in an old myth. No, not one of the Greek tales—one of ours. *Naniboujou and the Four Thunders*. Thanks to my grandfather's persistence, I had been given the magical arrow needed to slay the Nazi beast—the secret of Thurber's parentage. Only one problem remained. How to determine the best way to use it.

Well, whatever you do, Miss Biwaban, you'd better keep a low profile. The FBI is still beating the bushes for Pocahontas, remember? You can't stay in the Pacific Northwest much longer.

The FBI . . . now *there's* an idea! On my way out of Seattle, I could mail my photocopy to the local Bureau office.

Wouldn't that make for interesting reading in the Domestic Terrorism Division?

A few minutes later, I put my rental Topaz in an empty spot in the municipal parking lot. Then, briefcase in hand, I crossed Second Street and headed for the Carnegie library.

Into the well-lit lobby strolled Angela Biwaban, stylish as ever in her new crepe de Chine blouse and raspberry print bow, a tailored tea-rose double-breasted jacket and matching slim skirt, and white leather pumps with snakeskin trimming. My wandering gaze located half a dozen browsers, the librarian behind the counter, a matron at the New Books stack, and a quartet of retired fishermen scanning newspapers in the Resource Room. There was no sign of Jack Dolan.

I cast a sharp gaze at the library's grandfather clock. Three minutes past nine. Turning toward the counter again, I spied Georgianna Waterman checking in. She was wearing a silk jacquard tunic dress patterned with roses and a pair of noticeable mother-of-pearl earrings. Her stiff scowl and opaque sunglasses spoiled the feminine image, however, giving her the frostily aloof appearance of a Secret Service agent.

Mild fussbudget face. Maybe the flourescent lights do make it a bit bright in here. But certainly not bright enough for sunglasses. What gives?

Had it been anyone else, I would have shrugged it off and waited for Dolan. But this was Georgianna Waterman, Mona's rival and one of the two prime suspects in her murder. If some new factor had intruded into La Waterman's life, I wanted to know about it.

Georgianna made a sudden dash to the ladies' room. I took my time getting there. Waiting outside the door, I listened to the symphony of furtive sounds. Georgianna's spike heels on the bathroom tiles. Her purse unsnapping. Whisper of brush bristles through dark hair. Faint hiss of the hairspray can. Then, smiling to myself, I pushed open the door.

The woman's idle gaze found my reflection in the wall-length mirror. Shuddering in recognition, she hastily scooped up brush, compact and hairspray and dropped them in her purse. With her gaze deliberately averted, she tried to rush past me.

Intrigued by her panicky reaction, I entered her path. "Morning, Georgianna."

No reply. The mouth beneath the opaque sunglasses quivered with suppressed emotion.

"I was hoping you had a minute to talk," I added.

Her fists clenched, then trembled. "I'm not supposed to talk to you, Anne Marie."

My obsidian eyes narrowed. *Not supposed to . . . ?* Then I added plenty of warmth to my friendly smile. "Really? Who gave that order, Georgianna?"

"You know who," she responded bitterly.

"I'm afraid I don't."

"Then, pardon me if I *don't* explain it to you."

With that, Georgianna tried to shove me aside. I did a graceful sidestep to the left, darted forward again, and plucked the sunglasses from her face. Her sudden shame-faced gasp pinched my heart.

Holding the glasses, I studied the moist bluish-purple bruise underlining her left eye. Putting out a shaking hand, she whispered, "Please . . . ?"

"Who did that?" I inquired, handing back the sunglasses.

"A man. I-I don't remember his name." Her tone tearful, the librarian fumbled with the eyepieces.

"A man you met at Millicent's Pub?"

She jumped right on it. "Yes! I-I was there . . . ah . . . *Sunday.*" Frightened eyes met mine. "He-He got rough. I told him no. And he hit me!"

At that moment, Georgianna reminded me of a small

trapped animal. Folding my arms, I asked, "What are you afraid of?"

"N-N-Nothing . . ." The response was automatic, as it is with so many battered women. Any second now, she'd be telling me she'd had an accident. All at once, I remembered Dolan's telephone chat with the Adamite pastor—his plans for the Kulshan protestors.

"Did Sargent hit you?" I asked.

Georgianna shot me a startled stare.

"Steve Sargent," I added. "Is he the man who hit you?"

Slipping on her sunglasses, she murmured, "Yes, yes."

"Why did he hit you?"

"He . . . he, uh, said we were giving the town a b-bad n-name." Falsehood did not come easily to Georgianna Waterman. She had trouble making things up on the spur of the moment.

I'd known all along she was lying. After all, Steve Sargent had been with me Sunday evening, discussing the drug racket at Millicent's Pub. We even had two eyewitnesses to our conversation—Chief Gallagher and his wife.

Georgianna had seized Sargent's name as a plausible alternative the moment I'd mentioned it. It made sense, too. Sargent had threatened her at the Kulshan protest. But I knew she was lying, just as I knew she was taking her cues from me—using them to build a believable cover story in order to hide the true identity of her assailant.

Questions crowded my mind. Who had really done the hitting? Why was Georgianna protecting him this way? And why was she so visibly scared?

Continuing the game, I fed her a false lead. "Did Sargent mention Orcas?"

Gray-green eyes blossomed wide. "What?"

"Did he tell you to keep quiet about Orcas Island?"

Georgianna merely blinked.

I touched her shoulders. "You were there, weren't you?"

"W-When?"

"October seventh. You must have seen Sargent."

She nodded stiffly. "S-Sure! I saw him in Eastsound. Uhm, a little after eight."

"And that's the real reason he hit you, isn't it?"

"I-I guess. He told me to forget all about seeing him there."

Goodness gracious, dear! Whatever happened to that story about you getting hit because you were disgracing the town?

Of course, Georgianna had realized the significance of the date October seventh. And she was not averse to diverting the spotlight of suspicion onto avowed neo-Nazi Steve Sargent. No matter. I'd gotten her to admit to being on the island that night. And I also noticed that she had neglected to mention either Mona or Mick, both of whom were dining in Eastsound around eight P.M.

"Come on," I muttered.

Georgianna flashed me a perplexed look.

"You've got a phone call to make," I told her, pushing the bathroom door open. "You can't let Sargent get away with it. You have to file a complaint."

Genuine alarm filled her voice. "No!"

"But he assaulted you. You have to tell the police."

"The police!" Bitter memories twisted Georgianna's soft mouth. "They never do anything—they just write up the report! They're scum—all of them! Part and parcel of the same rotten capitalist white male patriarchy. If a woman gets hit, it's always *her* fault!"

My frown deepened. Sounds as if you've been hit before, Georgianna.

Shying away from me, she shook her head. "Forget it! No police! I-I shouldn't have told you." Waving me off, she muttered, "Don't mention this to anyone, Anne Marie, please! I-I just want to forget the whole thing."

I watched her hurry back to the central desk. So Georgianna didn't want to share the story with Chief

271

Gallagher, eh? That was one very frightened lady. I had a feeling she was more afraid of the man who had battered her than she was of Mr. Sargent.

And I was certain of one thing, too. No way could Georgianna have seen Steve Sargent on Orcas Island. At eight that night, he had been hanging around the Tacoma synagogue with the rest of the skinheads, itching to start a riot.

I spent another five minutes in the ladies' room, touching up my eyeshadow and lipstick. And then it was back to the lobby, black briefcase in hand, to begin the next phase of my Miss Murphy game.

Dolan waited by the door, wearing a tweed topcoat and woolen gray slacks. A tuft of hair tickled his left eyebrow. His blue eyes gleamed in annoyance when he spotted me.

"Hello, Mr. Dolan." Broad Angie smile. "I trust I'm fashionably late."

His tanned hand gestured at the grandfather clock. "I've been standing here for the past seven damned minutes."

"Sorry, I was just getting spruced up." Smile widening, I lifted my briefcase. Dolan had one just like it in oxblood leather. "Shall we get started?"

Twenty minutes later, Dolan and I were at the Lumbermen's Bank, the institution his stabbing forefinger had picked out of the Yellow Pages. It was one block north on Second Street, standing right across from City Hall, a two-story red brick structure in the Georgian style with shingled arches, roof brackets and an interior lushly furnished in varnished elm.

An old-fashioned barred door sealed the entrance to the safety deposit vault. Dolan and I, gripping our respective briefcases, watched as the elderly bank president fiddled with the lock. The president's name was F. Theodore Woodbridge, and he was at least as old as the bank's huge time-lock vault. Tall and slender, with a well-oiled head of fine white hair and a Sherlockian nose, wearing a banker's standard uniform—a three-piece suit in navy blue pinstripe.

His key rattled noisily; then a latch clanged open. Gripping an upright bar, Woodbridge rolled the weighty door back on its set of gimbals. Then, with a courtly bow, he ushered us inside.

I glanced at the rows of sealed drawers and the pastel green walls and the large Formica-topped table in the center of the room. Woodbridge slammed the barred door shut. As the clanging sound dissipated, he turned to us and smiled. "What size box would you like to rent, Jack?"

Dolan tilted his chin toward the lower rows. "The deep kind."

Making a sound of assent, the bank president stooped and turned the key of a large box in the bottom row. Once he had it open, he examined the key, memorized its number, put it in his vest pocket, and said, "Yours will be Box Six-Seven-Four. Rent is payable the first day of the month. When we return to my office, I'll give each one of you your own key."

"Good enough." Taking that as my cue, I slung my briefcase onto the table, then snapped it open. Then, turning the case around, I lifted the lid and gave Jack Dolan a real eyeful. Fifteen one hundred dollar bills floated at the summit of the piles, concealing the play money underneath.

Dolan's sapphire eyes gleamed with avarice. Looking down, I located the single stack with the slight tear in its brown paper binding. That was Chief's signal that this stack was genuine. Twenty portraits of Ben Franklin and twenty portraits of Grant. This gambit had just about exhausted our war fund. I'd be on a strict diet of cheese and crackers all the way back to South Dakota.

Wiggling the legit stack out of the briefcase, I tossed it to Dolan. "Here. We held up our end."

With the sure swiftness of a casino croupier, he ruffled through the stack of bills.

Heart thumping, I murmured, "Want to see another one?"

My right hand rested on the neighboring stack. On top was a portrait of Franklin. The remaining bills all bore the amiable features of Alfred E. Neuman.

"No need." Dolan's predatory smile flashed suddenly. He tossed me the first stack, then placed his own briefcase on the table. My ears flinched at the snapping sound of the latches. As the lid came open, the faint grimy smell of worn currency filled the small room. My mouth dry, I gaped at Dolan's fifty thousand dollars.

"Aren't you going to count it?" he asked.

I shook my head. Turning the corners of six bills at random had told me that it was all genuine. Glorious Angie smile. "I think we can trust each other, Jack."

And so, into the box went Angie's boodle, followed by that of Lem Thurber's favorite sugar daddy. We closed our respective briefcases, then watched as Mr. Woodbridge slid the drawer shut and locked it.

Turning to Woodbridge, my partner said, "Let's make sure we're clear on this. There are only two keys. I get one—Anne Marie gets the other. Only the two of us have access to that box. Understand?"

Clearing his throat, Woodbridge sputtered, "Of-Of course."

"The two of us . . . or our *designated surrogates*," I amended.

Dolan glanced at me in disbelief. "You'd let *employees* near that box?"

"No, I'm merely suggesting that Mr. Woodbridge, here, control subordinates' access."

Puzzlement filled the banker's narrow face. "I'm not sure I follow you, Miss Nahkeeta."

"There may come a time when either myself or Mr. Dolan is out of town," I explained. "In that event, we might have to dispatch an employee to cover some unforeseen *loan business.*" Dolan's blue eyes showed sudden comprehension. "I'm proposing that we leave the access decision in the hands of Mr. Woodbridge. Sir, Mr. Dolan and I will each give you a copy of our handwriting. In order for one of our designated surrogates to be admitted to this room, he or she must first present you, Mr. Woodbridge, with our brass key. In addition, this employee will present you with a handwritten letter, signed by either myself or Mr. Dolan, specifically naming him or her as our designated surrogate. Again, Mr. Woodbridge, the final decision to admit will be left to you."

He looked to Dolan for approval. "Well, it is rather irregular . . . but it appears to be a sound security procedure."

Dolan scowled. "Let's tighten it up a bit. What's your mother's maiden name, Ted?"

"Seeber," the banker replied.

Turning to me, Dolan added, "Okay, we'll use your procedure, Anne Marie, but with one addition. A code phrase. One known only to the three of us. When you write that admission note, be sure to add this . . . *Please check on the Seeber account.*" Swift glance at the banker. "If it doesn't have that phrase, Ted, you'll know it's a fake." Another stern glare at me. "And keep that phrase to yourself, Anne Marie!"

"I will," I promised, following the men to the door. "Don't you trust your employees, Jack?"

"Not with that much cash lying around. Come on. Let's get those keys."

Woodbridge's office had almost as many plants as the Hoh Rain Forest. With the banker looking fondly on, Dolan and I signed the lease for the safety deposit box. Then, smiling like a mall Santa Claus, Woodbridge handed each of us a small brass key.

Holding my breath, I watched the bank president drop the lease agreement into a long brown envelope. He hadn't

275

even given it a second glance. Good thing, too. Because I had written *Lemuel Thurber* on my signature line!

On our way out, Dolan asked, "Are you free for a meeting tomorrow?"

"Sure, Jack."

"Fine." He opened the bank's glass door for me. "Drop by my office around two o'clock. I want you to meet the people who'll be doing the borrowing."

"So you've already got them picked, eh?"

He let the door swing shut. "I didn't waste any time."

"Is Lauridsen one of your straw men?"

Glance of suspicion. "Yeah. Why do you ask?"

"Is that wise? Everybody in town knows he's tied in with you."

"Don't worry about it, Anne Marie." Comforting pat on the shoulder. "Rolf's a good man. Reliable. We can count on him to sign the money over." He paused on the sidewalk. "Just be sure you're there."

"I'll try to make it."

"Don't try, kid. *Be* there!"

Ten minutes later, I was strolling briskly through the Port Wyoochee City Hall, searching diligently for the public telephones. I had a couple of hours to kill before beginning the next phase of my Miss Murphy game, so I decided to test Lauridsen's alibi.

Very quiet in there. My heels raised a noticeable clatter on the polished marble floor. I passed the imposing statuary honoring Chief Ahtchakud and his wife, Eeloolth, who'd been foolish enough to sell their waterfront property to the disreputable McGrath brothers, turned the corner, and found a trio of phone booths right next to the Weights and Measures Office.

Once inside, I mentally rehearsed my pitch, inserted my quarters, and put through a long-distance call to Sea-Tac airport.

A cheerful lady responded. "Good morning ... Horizon Air."

"Hi, my name is Sharon Bateman, and I'm the administrative assistant here at Kulshan Paper in Port Wyoochee." Crisp professional tone. "We put through a travel invoice for our general manager, Mr. Rolf Lauridsen, for a round-trip flight on October seventh. The bill hasn't come through yet."

"Can you give me the flight number, Miss Bateman?"

Tone of regret. "Oh, I'm afraid it's slipped my mind. It would have been an afternoon flight, though. Port Wyoochee to Eastsound."

The receptionist sounded confused. "Miss Bateman, I'm afraid we don't have direct service to Eastsound. We do have a daily flight to Friday Harbor. Let me check." Clacketyclack of a computer keyboard. "What was that name again?"

"Lauridsen. Rolf Lauridsen." And I spelled it for her.

Thankfully, I was spared the ordeal of elevator music. Within seconds, she was back on line again.

"Miss Bateman, I'm afraid there's no one by that name on our passenger list for October seventh."

"Are you certain of that?"

"I have the list right on the screen," she added. "There's something else you ought to know, too. There was no afternoon flight that day. There was only one flight from Port Wyoochee to Friday Harbor, and it left at ten-thirty-five that morning."

So he didn't fly with Horizon, I thought. Immediately I set about terminating the conversation.

"I just don't understand it." Frustrated Angie sigh. "I ... oh, dear! I misread the voucher. It's *Heartland* Air, not Horizon. Oh, gosh, I'm sorry I bothered you. You must think I'm an idiot."

"Not at all." The receptionist was a true diplomat. "I'm glad we could be of service. Thank you for calling Horizon Air."

After hanging up, I hustled the Yellow Pages onto the phone booth's wooden podium and flipped pages until I reached the display ads for private air charters. I found four serving the San Juan Islands. Three were based in Friday Harbor.

I struck out with all three. There was no record of Rolf Lauridsen or anyone else from Port Wyoochee booking passage on a floatplane the afternoon of October seventh.

My fourth and final call went out to that general store at the tip of Sahale Point. I deepened my contralto voice a bit, praying that Dinah wouldn't recognize it.

Someone picked up at the other end. Hearty female voice. "Yeah? Whattaya want?"

Obviously, Dinah could use another cup of her own coffee. Mellifluous Angie greeting. "Hello, this is Ms. Bateman at Kulshan Paper. I understand you handle the bookings for Jon Waterman."

"Yeah, sure. You want to make a reservation?"

"No, I'm just checking on a recent flight. One of our people submitted a mileage reimbursement request which included a flight to the San Juan Islands October seventh. I simply called to confirm before we processed the check."

Dinah sounded thoughtful. "Come to think of it, Jon did have a flight that day. What's the name, honey?"

"Rolf Lauridsen."

"Lauridsen . . ." She tasted the name. "Hey, ain't he some big shot over there at Kulshan?"

"Very big!" I added, my tone anxious. "That's why I have to process this check right away."

"Okay, okay—give me a minute, huh?" I heard the flutter of turning logbook pages. "October seventh . . . yeah, here we are. Jon had one flight that day. Took off at four P.M. No passengers."

"You're positive?"

"Damned right! I fixed him a snack just before takeoff."

"No last-minute boarders?"

"Not a one. He took off alone. I saw him myself." The more time Dinah spent on the phone, the friendlier she became. "He said he was meeting a fishing party up north. He wanted to get into Nitinat ahead of the weather."

That fits with what the Nitinat lodgekeeper told me, I thought. Time for the blowoff. "Oh, dear! Mr. Lauridsen must have given me the wrong date. I'd better go talk to him. Thanks for your help, ma'am."

Dinah let out a chuckle. "Good luck!"

Hanging up, I made a fussbudget face. According to Sharon, her boss had left the plant at five-thirty. So there's no way he could have been aboard the Horizon flight or Waterman's floatplane.

Think, Angela! How else could Lauridsen have reached the San Juans that day?

Speedboat? Unlikely. It's too far to the San Juans. On the other hand, Lauridsen could have zipped right across the strait to Victoria and tried to reach Orcas from there. And there was yet another possibility—the state ferry!

I had no need to look up the number. It was splashed across the colorful poster on the bulletin board, right across the hall from my phone booth. Lifting the receiver, I popped in a fresh quarter. My forefinger played hopscotch on the touch tabs. Four-six-four-six-four-zero-zero.

"Good afternoon. You have reached the Washington State Ferries. All of our operators are busy right now. Please stay on the line until the first available operator can reach you."

I listened to an old show tune from *South Pacific*. Midway through the chorus, a brash soprano intruded. "Hello, I'm Brianna. Thank you for calling the Washington State Ferry System. How can I help you?"

"Hi, Brianna." I didn't bother to identify myself. "I'm staying in Port Wyoochee for a few days . . ."

Truly an eager beaver, Brianna cut right in. "Yes, ma'am, we have one daily sailing from Port Wyoochee."

"Direct to the San Juans?" I asked.

"No, ma'am. I'm sorry. To go to the San Juans, you'll have to leave from Port Angeles."

"What time is the last ferry for the San Juans?"

"Five-thirty P.M."

Twisting the telephone cord, I scowled in frustration. The last ferry had sailed out of Port Angeles the same moment Rolf Lauridsen and Sharon Bateman were leaving the mill. Even if Sharon was wrong about the exact time, there was still no way Lauridsen could have reached Port Angeles in time.

I decided to explore the Canadian option. "What if I crossed the strait and left from Victoria, B.C.?"

"I'm sorry, ma'am. We have no direct service from Victoria to the San Juans. You'd have to leave from Sidney the next morning."

"Ah, how far is Sidney from Victoria?"

"Eighteen miles on Route 17, ma'am. Bus service is available—"

"Thanks, Brianna!" I interrupted. "You've been a great help."

Replacing the receiver, I thought, *Scratch the Canadian option, Angie!* Even if he made it to Sidney, Lauridsen couldn't have left for the San Juans until the following morning, October eighth.

All of which means Rolf Lauridsen couldn't possibly have been on Orcas the night Mona was murdered.

Yet, with my own ears, I'd heard him extending an invitation to a Yom Kippur rendezvous. Puzzled frown. But if he had no intention of being on the island, then why did he call Mona?"

I snapped my fingers in sudden comprehension. *Dolan!* The plant manager had made that call on Dolan's behalf. Distinct possibility, that. After all, I'd heard the big man bullying Lauridsen myself. In addition, Jack struck me as too cagey to go around leaving his voice on answering machines.

Hmmmmm—could be onto something here, princess.

Lauridsen called Mona and didn't get through. He reported that to Dolan, who tried Mona's apartment later on. After the murder, mindful of Mona's answering machine at the store, Dolan checked out her apartment and discovered the Phone-Mate. Then he grabbed the cassette and stuck the unit in the back of the closet.

Okay, so that narrows it down to two—Dolan and Georgianna.

My frown deepened suddenly. *Georgianna . . .*

There was still so much I didn't understand about that woman. Who had given her the black eye? And why did *he* frighten her more than Steve Sargent? And, if Georgianna had indeed murdered her rival, then how had she known Mona would be on the island that night?

Grabbing my shoulder bag, I made a graceful and unobtrusive exit from City Hall. Georgianna Waterman dominated my thoughts all the way to the parking lot.

Just what do you know about Georgianna, Miss Biwaban? Well, she's Canadian. She's lived in Port Wyoochee for several years. She works at the public library and has been involved for some time with the Greenway committee. And she has a decidedly nasty disposition.

I went deeper into what little I knew of her background. Georgianna came from a military family. Her father was a colonel in the Canadian air force. According to ex-husband Jon, Georgianna took after her father. The colonel was a bit of a martinet. Hmmmmm, maybe he was the prototype for Georgianna's much-despised male patriarchy.

After opening the Topaz's door, I slid behind the steering wheel. The rearview mirror showed me a pronounced fussbudget face. I concentrated on the colonel. He had been Waterman's base commander, right? At some place in the far north—Cambridge Bay. Could be he didn't approve of Jon Waterman. Perhaps that's why Georgianna married him. You should have listened to your father, dear.

All at once, I remembered that strange olive green canister I'd found behind Mona's island hideaway. A tingle of excitement danced along my nerves. *Olive green!* That canister could have been some kind of military item, right? Perhaps an item used by the Canadian air force.

I thought instantly of Jon Waterman. Could he have given it to Mona? Then I grimaced and thought, No way, Angie! It can't be Waterman. You know he spent the night on Vancouver Island, fogged in at Nitinat.

Which leaves *Georgianna* as the only other person with a military background.

Instant fussbudget face. Now that didn't make sense. Why would Georgianna have given her enemy—Mona Hanauer—a present? A gift as unusual as that?

Turning on the engine, I backed out of the parking space, pulled back the shift lever, and nudged the Topaz out into Second Street.

Still doesn't make sense, I thought. If Georgianna had given Mona that canister, then that meant Georgianna knew about the woman's dope habit. And if Georgianna had known that, then why hadn't she tipped off the San Juans police to the location of Mona's stash?

Had the police found Mona's undersea cache, they would have written off her murder as a random drug killing. And Georgianna would have been home free!

But then there would have been no need for such an elaborate frame of Mickey Grantz—no need to risk that break-in at Mick's motel.

I didn't understand it. With one phone call, Georgianna could have put herself beyond the realm of suspicion. But she hadn't done it. If she was the killer, then why was that?

A cold chill meandered up my backbone. I had the oddest feeling there were only three people who knew about that olive-colored canister. The late Mona Hanauer, her secretive and anonymous dope dealer, and little Angie.

Figure it out later, I told myself. Right now, I had to round up my grandfather. We'd grab a late lunch and prepare to ring down the curtain on Jack Dolan and Pastor Lemuel Thurber.

Prepare to meet Miss Murphy, guys!

Heading west on Ahtalah Avenue, I tried not to think about the Mick, locked away in Cedar Creek, facing yet another night laden with the threat of violence. Hang in there, Mr. Grantz. Our trap is ready to spring.

If Dolan killed her, the feds will nail him.

If not ... well, hopefully I had enough with Mona's Phone-Mate to spring the Mick out of Cedar Creek.

Chapter Fourteen

"Better give it to me one more time, *Noozis,*" my grandfather mumbled, sawing away at his fried fish fillet.

Sighing, I put my elbows on the bright red checkerboard tablecloth. We were having lunch at the Drift Net, he and I, occupying a two-person table beside the front window.

"As soon as Dolan takes the bait, we're out of here," I said. "We split up, head for Seattle by different routes, and grab the first flights east. Separate flights, of course."

"How will I know you made it?"

"I'll give you a call from Pierre."

Chief took another mouthful and chewed it quietly. A pensive expression covered his weathered face. "What if he doesn't go for it?"

"Oh, Dolan will go for it, all right." I cleaned my lips with a thick linen napkin. "I'm not so sure about Thurber."

"Speak of the devil . . ." He fired a glance at the old-fashioned maritime wall clock. "Shouldn't you be giving him a call? We're rapidly running out of workday."

Dropping my napkin on the empty plate, I whispered, "Wish me luck." And then switched to English. "Enjoy the meal, Mr. Nuquispum."

Reaching the pay phone, I lifted the receiver, let out a deep and soulful exhalation, and gave myself a few seconds to get into character. Then in went my quarter. A muted tinkle, followed by a persistent dial tone. Receiver in hand, I leaned lazily against the cigarette machine and did a perfect imitation of Elena Varo. Too bad I didn't have any gum to snap.

Thurber's canned greeting came on. I let it pass, then chattered brightly, *"Buenas tardes, padre. Esta su amiga colombiana.* Hey, I know you're listening, man, so how about picking up? Come on, Thurber. Don't be a shit, man."

For a few dreadful seconds, there was utter silence. Panic clawed at my mind. *Oh shit! He isn't going for it!* All at once, I heard a dull click, punctuated by the pastor's vibrant voice.

"What can I do for you, Anne Marie?"

I smiled in sudden relief. "I got a real problem, *hombre.*"

Thurber let out a hateful chuckle. "You called the wrong church, chili pepper. Why don't you try the Catholics?"

I let his jibe pass, hoping that the Pope and Sister Mary Katherine would forgive me. Tone of desperation. "Come on! I'm in deep shit, man. The shipment's ready to move, and I've gotta hold up my end. You want to reconsider?"

Interest colored his speaking tone. Apparently, that scrap with Dolan had made him much more amenable to the idea. "Let's talk about it, Anne Marie. But not on the phone. Face-to-face."

"Sounds good, *padre.* Pick a spot."

"You know the old Coast Artillery emplacement on Sahale Point?"

"I think so." I had a mental image of sandswept concrete bunkers. "Just before the general store, *verdad?*"

"That's it. Be there in thirty." *Click!*

Stepping away from the cigarette machine, I hung up the phone. So far, so good. Now all I had to do was persuaded that Nazi bastard to accept my little brass key.

As I headed back to Chief's table, a cheery voice cut through the hubbub of dinner conversations. "Anne Marie!"

Stopping at once, I spied Lisa Rotenberg beside the cashier's counter, casual as ever in a Windbreaker jacket and cranberry stirrup pants. I almost didn't recognize her without baby David. Then I saw the man she was with, and my stomach promptly turned over in dismay.

Tayaa! Just the fellow I need to see after chumming it up with Thurber—Lisa's husband—*the rabbi!*

At any second, I expected a lightning bolt to come crashing through the Drift Net's skylight.

"I thought it was you. Here, I want you to meet my husband." Lisa ushered her curly-haired spouse forward. "Avi, this is the woman I was telling you about—Anne Marie Nahkeeta."

Showing a serene smile, Rabbi Rotenberg extended his long-fingered hand. He was a slender, somber man with a scholarly expression and a short, well-trimmed auburn beard. Conservative navy suit and black yarmulke. "How do you do, Anne Marie? Welcome to Port Wyoochee."

"Fine . . . uh, thanks!"

We shook hands. The rabbi's bright brown eyes, instantly reminiscent of Davey's, gave me a mildly quizzical stare. No doubt he was puzzled by my skittish expression.

"Did you just get here?" Lisa asked, unzipping her jacket. "Why don't you join us for an early supper?"

"Sorry, Lisa. I'd join you for coffee, but I have to meet a client in thirty minutes." I kept a wary eye out for lightning bolts. "What's with the early supper?"

"We're on our way to Tacoma." She hugged her husband's arm. "There's a big Hadassah meeting, and Avi's the guest speaker."

"We'd better make it a quick supper. You still have to change." The rabbi's gaze flitted my way. "Lisa tells me you were born here. Are you back to stay?"

No way out! It had to be a direct fib. "Sure looks that way, Rabbi." Quick worried glance at the skylight.

"Well, you'd better watch out for this one," he added, patting his wife's forearm. "She'll have you signed up for a committee in no time."

A look of mock outrage from Lisa. "Avi Rotenberg!"

He gave her cheek a playful kiss. "You'd make a top-notch recruiting sergeant, my dear."

"Listen, somebody has to get this town off its ass."

Casual Angie smile. "Where's Davey?"

"Home," Avi said. "This is his first time with a babysitter. Lisa's ready to start climbing walls."

"I am not!" She bumped him with her hip. "This is my first night out since delivery, and I'm kicking up my heels!"

The rabbi laughed. "At a Hadassah meeting?"

"We have a highly recommended babysitter, and we'll be home before midnight," she added, smiling. "This is my evening away from the diaper pail, and I fully intend to enjoy it."

Still beaming, I sidled past the happy couple. "Have fun, you two. Nice meeting you, Rabbi."

I paused momentarily, watching the two of them select a table. My last view of the Rotenbergs. You could tell that their marriage was one of the good ones, brimming with mutual tenderness and respect. And maybe—just maybe—I was a teensy bit jealous.

Come what may, I wished the both of them well.

I'd seen the Coast Artillery bunkers before, of course, on my trip out to Sahale Point to see Waterman. They were just as I remembered. Four huge circular cement pillboxes swimming on a ridge of sand dunes. As I took the Topaz down that long, narrow, winding dirt road, the fortifications grew larger in my windshield, revealing pebbly cracks around the gun ports and tall weeds poking up through the concrete apron. They reminded me of an old movie I'd seen on TBS—*The Guns of Navarone*.

Nobody was ever going to confuse that beach with the sunny Aegean shore. Gunmetal waves rolled ashore on the sands, chasing the quick-striding gulls. Twenty yards out, a

287

long-necked black cormorant buzzed the wave tops in search of prey. Fast-moving clouds, pregnant with impending rain, veiled the setting sun.

Chief called my attention to a navy blue Taurus parked at the foot of the slope. A Washington license plate with the numerals AG7-483. The left rear tire was wearing badly on the outside.

I pulled up right behind the Taurus. Its two front doors popped open. Steve Sargent emerged from the driver's side, clad in skinhead leather and sporting spiked gloves. Cotter came out the other side, toting a Winchester Model 42 pump-action shotgun cut at least six inches under legal. They glared menacingly at my grandfather and I, did some perfunctory scouting around, and then gave the Taurus the high sign. Only then did Thurber emerge from the rear seat. Folding his arms, he leaned against the fender, looking very ministerial in his white collar, black sweater vest and houndstooth gray suit.

Nervous glance at my grandfather. "Show time!"

"I just hope we live through the matinee," he muttered, pushing the passenger door open.

Approaching the Adamites, I spotted a Boston whaler about a half-mile out. A lone fisherman dropping nets. Cotter kept a constant watch on him, the sawed-off shotgun cradled lovingly in his arms. Sargent showed us his White Pride sneer. Thurber's face bore a cool, lofty smile.

"Buenos dias!" Smart-alecky Angie smile. "Deserted spot you picked, *padre.*"

"Yeah." Sargent's hateful laugh gave me a shiver. "Good place for a marshmallow roast."

"Can it!" Thurber snapped, then turned my way again. "What's the deal, Anne Marie?"

"Same as before, *hombre.* I got stuff moving through Seattle in three days, and I need a posse. You interested?"

"Maybe." He drew himself erect. "Who's after it?"

I manufactured a disdainful expression. *"Los negritos."*

"That's what you said last time." Skeptical glance from the pastor. "You sounded a little more anxious today. What's up?"

Faking a frustrated scowl, I kicked the sand. "Fucking DEA! There's this suit sniffling around Pioneer Square. He knows my face, man. *Comprende?* I got to set this up, *padre*, and I can't be seen in Seattle."

Thurber nodded. "So you need out-of-town talent. That it?"

"And I'm willing to pay for it, Thurber," I said, hands on my hips. Sassy Angela. "Cash up front. Ten big ones. That's for you. You take the rest of my hundred large to Seattle and give it to the man. What do you say, *hombre?*"

Disbelief hardened his expression. "I don't believe you have a hundred K."

By way of reply, I dug the brass key out of my purse, then tossed it to him. Thurber's quick hand plucked it out of the air. He gave it a bewildered glance.

"Go see for yourself, *padre.*" Then I pulled out the access authorization letter I had written at lunch. "I rented a safety deposit box at the Lumbermen's Bank. *El dinero's* in there. One hundred grand—cash! It's in Box Number Six-Seven-Four. The number's right on the key, see?" I handed him the letter. "Just show this to *Señor* Woodbridge, the bank president, and he'll let you into the vault."

Thurber studied the letter, his lips curling in a speculative frown. "What if I'm not interested?"

"No hay problema, amigo." I let my own natural apprehension rush to my face. "That shipment don't go through, you won't be seeing *me* no more!"

"And if I am interested . . . ?" The pastor folded the letter and tucked it away in his jacket's inner pocket. "What's the deal?"

"Hey! Like I tol' you before, *gringo*, it's easy! You go to the bank and count out ten grand. That's yours to keep, *padre*. I call you Thursday with the time and place. You take the rest of *el dinero,* give it to five of your boys, and send them to Seattle." Yielding to a naughty impulse, I added, "Your contact's name is Langston."

"Langston, eh? That's some name for a coffee bean." Idly he flipped the brass key. Then, all at once, his fist snapped shut. "What happens if I help myself to *more* than ten grand?"

Cracking a savage grin, I gestured at Sargent. "Then I don't have to be nice to you no more, *pachaco.* I'll be making all my deals with *him!*"

Thurber's cold smile vanished. Veins bulged at his temples, and those bright mad eyes glittered in fury. For a tense second there, I thought he was going to hit me. Then he made himself relax, and his vibrant voice cut loose with a burst of hearty laughter.

"Little lady, you've got yourself a deal."

Turning his back on me, Thurber snapped his fingers. Both skinheads returned to the car. Pocketing the key, the pastor waited for Cotter to open his door. He smiled at me over his broad shoulder. "I'll be waiting to hear from you, Anne Marie."

My hand lifted in a casual wave. *"Hasta la vista, padre."*

The Taurus's engine rumbled to life. With Chief at my side, I watched Sargent do a three-point turn in the eelgrass. Then the car lumbered past, its rear tires tossing sand.

My grandfather's hand landed lightly on my shoulder. "That was the dumbest-ass thing you ever said, missy!"

"Chief! I had to stay in character, you know."

"Yeah! And it would've been our curtain call if he'd told that baldy to use the scattergun."

"He didn't, Chief. So stop worrying. We've *got* him!"

"You really think so?"

"Absolutely," I replied, running for our car. "Come on, Chief. We've got to stay on them."

Minutes later, our Topaz was speeding down Sahale Point

Road. Traffic was pretty sparse, so I was careful to keep at least two cars between us and Sargent's Taurus.

"Now . . . ," I murmured, watching the Taurus round a long bend. "If we've done this right, he'll be heading straight for the Lumbermen's Bank."

"You sound pretty sure of yourself."

"The bank closes in twenty minutes, Chief." I turned the steering wheel to the left. "We've tweaked Thurber's curiosity. He's wondering if there really is a hundred grand in that box. He doesn't want to lie awake all night thinking about it. So he'll check it out before the bank locks up for the night."

My grandfather chuckled. "That's why you waited until after three to call him."

"Can you imagine the look on Thurber's face when he opens that drawer and sees all those hundred-dollar bills?"

"Christmas in October!" Chief aimed a warning glance at me. "He'll try to take it all, you know."

"Hey, I'm hoping he *does!*" I replied. "I want Thurber busily emptying that safety deposit box when Jack Dolan arrives at the bank!"

Ahead, Sargent's Taurus halted at the stop sign, then turned left onto Ahtalah Avenue. I followed at a discreet distance. As I hung a right on Second, my heartbeat quickened with excitement. The Taurus was pulling into the bank's parking lot.

"Damn!" Chief muttered. "You're right! They're going for it!"

I drove right on by, aiming the Topaz uphill. I turned right once more, joining the stream of traffic on Dollar Avenue. Then I snaked my car into the first available parking space. Three doors up the street was a venerable Ben Franklin store. I left the engine running, grabbed my shoulder bag, and told my grandfather to watch the car.

Ninety seconds later, I was at the store's pay telephone, thumbing through the Yellow Pages. Instantly I memorized the proper number, then dropped the book and rummaged in my bag. Frantic fingers knocked aside the compact and the AVR miniature cassette recorder, seeking my deerskin wallet. Then a quarter tinkled down a mechanical gullet. Feverishly I tapped out seven digits.

"Good afternoon. KPWR Action News."

"Listen!" I had no need to fake the excitement in my voice. "This is Cindy at the Lumbermen's Bank. That guy—that Nazi—whatzisname—Lem Thurber—he just came in here and grabbed Mr. Woodbridge. I saw one of them with a shotgun. I-I think they're *robbing the bank!*"

"What? Slow down, miss. Give us your full name—"

"I-I can't talk . . . oh, no, here he comes!"

With that, I promptly hung up, creating a suitable dramatic effect.

So much for the matinee. And now, the main performance.

Taking deep breaths, I made myself remember the Rotenbergs at the restaurant. How happy the two of them had seemed. Then my memory conjured up a host of old heartaches. Old boyfriends at USU. Rory McDaniel up there in Bozeman, Montana. And the biggest heartache of all—the man I'd been forced to leave behind in upper Michigan. The bittersweet memory of Donald Winston Pierce filled my throat with warm cement. The sudden surge of tears blinded me. Sobbing quietly, I tapped out Dolan's office number.

"Luckutchee Real Estate."

"J-Jack?" Sorrow twisted my lovely contralto voice. "I-I'm sorry. I c-couldn't stop h-him . . ."

"Anne Marie?" Curiosity put a hard edge on Dolan's baritone. "What happened? What's wrong?"

"It-It's Thurber."

"Thurber!" he echoed.

"I-I tried to stop him, Jack. Honest! B-But he had these two guys with him—these skinheads—"

292

"What *about* Thurber!?" he interrupted.

"He-He jumped me, Jack. Him and his skinheads." I made the tale very plausible indeed. "They said they didn't want redskins in town. And . . . and they hurt me, Jack."

I could hear Dolan's angry breathing at the other end. He was buying it, all right. It was just the sort of stunt the Adamites might pull.

"I-I threatened to tell you. Thurber just laughed. H-He kept right on hitting me! Then-then he . . . he made me tell." Breathless sobbing. "He made me tell all about our deal."

"Jesus H. Christ!" Dolan exploded. "What the hell did you tell him?"

"Ev-Everything!" I sobbed. "H-He hurt me! And . . . Jack, I-I couldn't stop him. He . . . he took my *key!*"

"WHAT!?"

"M-My key to the safety deposit box, Jack. Thurber has it!"

"You stupid little—!"

"Jack, I tried to stop him! I-I did! He was too strong—"

"Shut up!" he bellowed. "Just go home. All right? Stay out of sight for a while. I'll send a doctor over later. And keep your goddamned mouth shut about this, Anne Marie! You hear me?"

Click!

Rubbing my ear one-handed, I replaced the receiver. On my way out, I took a fresh tissue from my purse, blew my nose softly, and rejoined my grandfather.

"Want to watch the fun?" I asked.

Chief was definitely game. He shut off the engine, locked the car, and followed me downhill. We entered City Hall through the side door, hastened up the marble stairs, and took up position in the lobby. The glass front doors offered a panoramic view of the Lumbermen's Bank across the street.

Peering through the glass, I watched the KPWR Action

293

News van roll into the bank's parking lot. No sooner had it stopped than Sargent's Taurus farted some exhaust and, like an overgrown metallic rat, crept into the street and darted away.

"Look at that! Running out on their fuehrer." Chief clucked his tongue. "What would old Adolf say?"

"*Auf wiedersehen,* probably." I gave my grandfather a soft nudge. "Here comes our pigeon."

Tires screaming like scalded cats, Dolan's dark green Lincoln skidded to a halt in front of the bank. Leaving the car in the middle of the street, Dolan scrambled out and dashed up the front walk. Judging from the desperate expression on his face, reaching the safety deposit box ahead of Thurber was the only thing on his mind.

A crowd of pedestrians gathered, watching the KPWR crew set up their equipment. I held my breath, waiting. . . .

Suddenly, a torrent of frightened and angry voices erupted from the bank, followed by a clanging alarm. The crowd reacted at once, closing in around the entrance, craning their necks to get a better look. I listened to the approaching crescendo of a police siren. Then chuckled merrily as a Port Wyoochee cruiser screeched to a wobbly halt, grille-to-grille with Dolan's Lincoln.

In went the grim-faced officers. A few seconds later, a pair of backup cruisers arrived.

Sporting identical Anishinabe grins, my grandfather and I watched as the police escorted Dolan and Thurber out of the bank. The rugged realtor was suitably dishevelled, and Thurber had a pulped eye far worse than Georgianna Waterman's. Three cops struggled to keep the maniacal Dolan away from the pastor.

"What do you mean *your* box!? It's *hers!*"

"Ripping *me* off!? You're dead, you fucker!"

"You're crazy! She *gave* me that key!"

"You lying—! You stole it, Thurber!"

"I did not!" He looked helplessly at the arresting officers. "This man's out of his mind."

"Dead!" Dolan screamed, as they hustled him into a cruiser's rear seat. "You're dead, Thurber! Fucking whale food in the strait! You hear me?"

Turning away from the lobby, my grandfather and I headed back down the basement stairs.

"Satisfied?" asked Chief.

Laughing, I danced down the steps. "Definitely one of those Kodak moments!"

Heading for the side entrance, he remarked, "You realize we just lost twelve hundred dollars."

"A small price to pay to spring Mick out of the slammer." I pushed open the glass door. "Too bad we can't stick around for the rest. You know, the Bureau's chat with Mr. Dolan. Wouldn't you just love to hear ol' Jack explaining why there's a safety deposit box rented out to him *and* Thurber?"

"And what it's doing with all that cash money in it. The IRS is gonna be damned interested in that." My grandfather chuckled. "Afraid you're going to have to spare yourself the pleasure, girl. Paul Holbrook's going to be looking for you."

"I know." I reached into my shoulder bag and withdrew a stamped envelope. "Do me a favor, would you? When you pass through Tacoma, drop this in the nearest handy mailbox."

Chief studied the salutation. "Who do you know at the *News-Tribune?*"

"Bob Hanlon. I promised him an exclusive, and that's it. The truth about Lemuel Thurber's father. Let's see how well the Adamite congregation holds together when that story breaks." Together we sauntered down the driveway. "Time to saddle up and ride, Chief. Say hi to everybody in Duluth for me."

"I will. You just worry about getting yourself back to South Dakota in one piece."

After dropping off my grandfather at the Surf 'n' Sand Motel, I zipped right back to the Parmenter House. There I set the world's speed record for getting packed. By five-thirty, my suitcases were securely locked away in the Topaz's trunk, and I'd settled my bill at the front desk. Crossing the *bon-bon's* lobby for the final time, I spotted the pay phone and wondered if the boys had made bail yet.

Oh, well ... might as well satisfy my curiosity before heading for Seattle.

Camp Pelley's canned message had been disconnected. Instead, I made contact with a nervous female who asked me for my name, rank and Social Security number. The camp was on a war footing, she informed me. The Zionist enemy had captured their pastor. I asked for Steve Sargent, but he wasn't there. So I settled for Cotter.

"Nahkeeta!" The skinhead's bellow raised static in the receiver. "You set us up! You're dead, bitch!"

"Que—? Caramba! What you talkin' about, man?" Colombian Angie.

"The bank!" he shouted. "Me and Sarge heard it on the scanner. Even the TV people showed. It was a fucking trap!"

"Hey, Cotter! Wasn't me, *hombre!*" I bleated. "Oh, shit, man! The rowboat!"

"Rowboat!?" he echoed.

"Claro que sí!" I chattered. "The beach, man! Remember that *pescadero* in the rowboat? He must've been DEA, man."

"DEA! Ahhhhh—*shit!*"

"That dude must've followed me from Seattle, man. Bet he had one of them electronic things, uhm ..."

Cotter's paranoia supplied the answer. "Shotgun mike!"

"Yeah! He was probably listenin' in, man. Listen, I'm

outta here. Where do I find the Sarge, *hombre?* Gotta tell him where to find Langston in Seattle."

"Hey, I don't know where he is, bitch. He took off twenty minutes ago. He went apeshit when he heard the pastor got busted."

I frowned uneasily. "Took off . . ."

"Yeah! Grabbed his piece and a can of gas, then split. Pastor's gonna be ripshit. We're supposed to hole up here during a Mossad offensive."

"You hole up if you wanna. I'm gone, *gringo.*"

I hung up. So Sargent had hightailed it, eh? Without Thurber's firm hand, Camp Pelley was beginning to fray at the edges. I wished it a swift and complete dissolution.

Then I dialed the Luckutchee office.

A soft feminine voice answered. "Luckutchee Real Estate. Mrs. Seyfried speaking."

"Hi, this is Anne Marie Nahkeeta," I said, shedding my Elena accent. "Is Mr. Dolan back yet?"

"Oh, dear! He's still at the police station, Miss Nahkeeta."

Hand over my mouth, I stifled my burgeoning laughter.

"Police station!?" Award-winning impression of utter surprise.

"Yes. Mr. Dolan rushed out of here a while ago . . ." All at once, Mrs. Seyfried remembered proper office decorum. Clearing her throat, she added, "Ahem! Well, I'm sure he'll fill you in himself, Miss Nahkeeta. He called fifteen minutes ago and asked me to get in touch with his attorney." Tone of mild awe. "Goodness! We haven't seen this kind of excitement around here since that meeting with Mr. Lauridsen."

"What meeting was that, ma'am?"

"Oh, he was in earlier this month to discuss the court case."

Court case! Those two words kindled a sudden preternatural chill. For once, I paid attention to a premonition and fed the nice lady some bait. "You mean, the meeting on *October seventh?*"

"That's right. How did you know about that, dear?"

"Oh, uhm, I was supposed to attend, but I couldn't make it. What happened?"

"That's the day the EPA ruling came down," Mrs. Seyfried explained. "Mr. Lauridsen told the newspaper that he was thinking about complying with the cleanup order. Mr. Dolan phoned him and told him to come in for a meeting right after work. They met that evening for nearly two hours. Mr. Dolan was quite adamant. Under no circumstances were Kulshan funds to be budgeted for a cleanup."

"I wasn't aware of that, Mrs. Seyfried." Somehow I managed to roll with the shock. Forcing a pleasant chuckle, I added, "Thanks for telling me. Oh, and be sure to tell Mr. Dolan I'll be in touch."

"I will, dear. Bye!"

Five minutes later, I was behind the wheel of the Topaz, speeding east on Washington 112. Once again, my rearview mirror displayed a tense fussbudget face.

I had completely misjudged Rolf Lauridsen. He had been in favor of the Sahale Point cleanup. At least until he'd been countermanded by the company's majority shareholder, Jack Dolan. That must be the reason why Lauridsen phoned Mona. He had wanted to discuss a joint cleanup effort.

I glared at my scowling reflection. You guessed wrong, princess. Both you and the Mick. Dolan didn't kill her. He has the same alibi as Lauridsen. There's no way Dolan could have gotten from Port Wyoochee to Orcas Island in time to commit the murder.

Which leaves Georgianna Waterman as the last remaining suspect. And, with Angie on the dodge, there was no way I could guide the lady's wayward steps into the arms of the law.

Gripping the steering wheel, I peered ahead at the damp forest. The headlights painted twin light pools on the wet asphalt. Phosphorescent red numerals gave me the car's current speed. Double nickel. With luck, I'd be at Sea-Tac by eight o'clock. Plenty of time to catch the red-eye east.

My warpath scowl deepened. Damn! It *would* have to be Georgianna, the one suspect I'd never really gotten a handle on. There were still so many questions about that woman remaining to be answered.

For instance, who had busted her in the eye? And why? And why was she so frightened of him? Why had she been so willing to frame Steve Sargent for the assault?

Georgianna's tale about the island also bothered me. Had she really been there? Or had she lied about that, too?

If Georgianna had been on the island, and she'd seen Mick with Mona, then how had she known he was staying at the Crestwood Inn?

And if she hadn't known Mick was at the Crestwood, then why had she gone there to steal his black cable-knit sweater?

How could Georgianna have known where to go? Mick hadn't announced his trip to Orcas. He'd turned up on Mona's doorstep quite unexpectedly.

I realized that I'd been going about this all wrong. I'd let Mick's suspicions of Dolan lure me away from the facts. Later on, I'd become distracted by the Adamite threat. I'd lost sight of the two key questions. Namely, who had wanted to kill Mona Hanauer? And why?

At that moment, I felt as if the answer had been sitting in front of me all along. Mona's marijuana stash. The reason for her weekly trips to the San Juan Islands.

Groaning softly, I pushed the matter out of my mind. There was nothing more I could do about it. My role in l'affaire Thurber was about to go public. Chief Gallagher would soon be after me, warrant in hand. If I got busted in the Evergreen State, there'd be merry hell to pay. Sargent has the right idea, princess. Take it on the lam.

Funny thing about the human mind. Once those big wheels start turning, the machinery isn't so easily halted.

The more I thought about Steve Sargent, the more vivid and disturbing the imagery that came to mind.

Gas can? Why would Sargent grab his firearm and some gasoline before making a break for it? Why gasoline? Surely there was no shortage of filling stations along Route 112.

My mind drifted back to the Coast Artillery site. Sargent's voice echoed in my memory. *"Good place for a marshmallow roast."*

The remark triggered another echo. Sargent backing up his pastor. *". . . he was with me at a marshmallow roast."*

Can full of gasoline . . . marshmallow roast.

Steve Sargent in a frenzy because of Thurber's arrest.

Oooooooh, I don't like this, princess. I don't like this one little bit!

A Chevron station loomed just ahead. The attendant was filling a black pickup's gas tank. Slowing the Topaz, I wheeled into the lot and parked beside the air pump. As I emerged from the car, I scolded myself for jumping at shadows. Sargent was probably halfway to Portland by now. (But what if he *isn't?*)

I told myself I was seriously endangering my own getaway. (But your clever sting is what set him off, Angela.)

Well, it couldn't hurt just to check. (Let's just hope Chief Gallagher hasn't put out a BOLO on Anne Marie Nahkeeta yet.)

Once inside, I rifled through the pages of the local telephone directory. Ran my finger down the R page, seeking Sargent's potential target. And there it was . . .

ROTENBERG, Rabbi Avi—42 Wyammah
Circle—555-0849

Just then, the gas jockey reentered the station. He was a rugged seventeen-year-old, unruly blond hair, greasy coveralls and a ball cap worn backward.

"Excuse me," I said, putting down the phone book. "Where do I find Wyammah Circle?"

"That way," he replied, pointing back toward town. "It's in Alder Beach. Go back a half mile or so. There's only one road in there. Harbor Ridge Road. It'll be on your right."

"Thanks!"

The Chevron lot was deserted as I drove away. Within minutes, I was tooling down Washington 112, heading west. Rain forest gradually gave way to isolated ranch houses. My peripheral gaze caught a gleam in the rearview mirror. I looked closer. A pair of headlights cruised half a hundred yards behind me. I made out the vague outline of a cab and grille.

The pickup? I thought. Sudden shiver of apprehension. Is he following me? Then I took a deep calming breath. Don't get paranoid, girl. He's probably headed back to town, same as you.

The Harbor Ridge Road sign suddenly appeared in my low beams. Tapping my signal lever, I spun the wheel to the right. Tires squealed as I lurched onto the side road. It wouldn't hurt to take a quick swing by the Rotenberg house. I had a mental image of baby David playing with a laughing teenaged sitter. Knuckles paled as I clutched the steering wheel. Check it out, Biwaban. Just to make sure.

I fired another glance at my rearview. The tailing beams were gone. The pickup truck hadn't followed me into Alder Beach. Mild shiver of relief. That was one less problem to worry about.

I spurred the Topaz into Wyammah Circle. Slowly I rolled down the winding street. Nice neighborhood. Upper middle class homes and artfully placed madrona trees. I found the Rotenberg mailbox, half-hidden by a salal hedge. My mind began a frantic mantra. *Oh, let me be wrong. Oh, please, let me be wrong!*

Well behind the mailbox, atop a small well-kept knoll, stood the Rotenberg house—a two-story, steep-roofed country home with three gables, a large front porch and a brick-and-stucco exterior. Light poured from the first floor and one upstairs window.

Creeping past the shrubbery, I swivelled my head to the left and let out a gasp of alarm. There was a car in the driveway. Sudden recognition nearly stopped my heart. Navy Taurus. Washington license plate AG7-483. *Sargent's car!*

Immediately I swerved against the curbstone and killed the car's engine. No time for the police, I thought. I've got to take him down myself!

But how? He was twice my size, and he was armed. Even if I could lure him away from the house, how could I ever hope to subdue him?

Then my gaze discovered the slender vine maple saplings just to the left of the Taurus, and I had the glimmer of an idea. Too bad I didn't have a rope with me, I thought. Using those trees, I could whip up a pretty handy *dasanagun*. That would ensure Sargent's presence here at the scene when the police arrived.

And then I glanced at my nyloned legs. *Inspiration!* Rolling up the hem of my tea-rose skirt, I jammed both thumbs into the waistband of my pantyhose, gasped and tugged, then slid the diaphanous fabric down my legs. Hurriedly I peeled off my ouch shoes, replacing them with the comfy moccasins I carried in my shoulder bag. Stealth was needed for a successful stalk, and I couldn't very well sneak up on Sargent in heels.

Moccasin soles made no sound as I ran up the driveway. I pulled sharply on each pantyhose leg, stretching the nylon fibers to their limit. Squatting beside the Taurus, I snapped three branches off the salal bush. Stripped away the twigs and leaves. Fashioned a trio of crude Y-shaped stakes. Then, selecting the tallest and springiest vine maple, I began climbing.

For the *dasanagun* to work properly, I'd have to bend the

302

sapling nearly in half. I wasn't all that sure this would work. Sargent weighed a whole lot more than your average Minnesota ruffed grouse. Still, it was the only weapon at my disposal.

As I reached the top branches, the vine maple swayed alarmingly. Gripping the slender trunk with both hands, I let my dainty hundred and five pounds pull it toward the ground. Damp maple leaves caressed my face. Dangling, I watched the driveway slowly rise to meet my moccasin soles.

Touchdown! Grunting softly, I wrestled the springy trunk beneath my armpit. Agile Anishinabe fingers quickly lashed one nylon ankle to the trunk. I gave it a sharp tug, making certain the knot was secure. Then, with remarkable dexterity, I fashioned a second stout knot near the crotch. Now for the stakes. Throwing my weight against the treetop, I draped my pantyhose across the ground, then drove the first Y-shaped stake right in front of the crotch knot.

Speedy anxious glance toward the house. Still no sound or movement up there. But that didn't mean anything. Little Davey and his babysitter might be lying on the floor at this very second, watching in abject terror as that neo-Nazi psychopath takes aim with his pistol.

I purged the horrendous image from my mind. Don't even think about it, Angie! Keep your mind on the *dasanagun*. It's their only hope.

Concern for that baby's safety lent speed to my efforts. I transformed the other slack nylon leg into a noose, then stuck the other two stakes in the damp turf and carefully draped my loop over them. And then I released the maple sapling.

Taut nylon hummed like a sleepy bee. My first stake kept its grip on the ground. Wouldn't take much to dislodge it, though. The nylon loop resembled a smoke ring. The other stakes held it aloft like a lei, eagerly awaiting the quarry's appearance.

My plan was simple. Angie as Little Miss Target. Sneak

up on Sargent, get him to chase me, and then lead him straight back to the *dasanagun*.

Suddenly, I heard the jarring sound of shattering glass, punctuated by a young girl's terrified scream. Forget the fancy plans, princess. Get up there—*now!*

I reached the Rotenberg porch in ten seconds, gaping at the smashed bay window. Instantly I sought a lower profile, crouching on the porch, and peered over the glass-strewn windowsill.

Steve Sargent had the petite babysitter by her long ash-blond ponytail. He lifted his free hand as if to take the oath of office. My eyes blossomed wide at the sight of the squat, ugly firearm tucked carelessly in his belt. A SIG-Sauer P226 nine-millimeter automatic. Extremely lethal at close range. The babysitter sobbed hysterically. A surplus U.S. Army jerrican stood near the coffee table, a mute witness to the ongoing drama.

Smack! Sargent's wallop sent the teen cartwheeling into the couch. She bounced off the cushions and landed facedown on the carpet. Gripping her by the back of her sweater, he yanked her upright. Then he shoved her back onto the sofa.

"I ain't asking twice, bitch!" Sargent bellowed, raising his palm again. "Where's the rab?"

"H-H-Hadassah meeting!" Fourteen and terrified, she extended a quaking hand in a futile plea for mercy. "Please! D-Don't hurt me, mister!"

"Goddamned race-traitor! I'm gonna ask you one more time. Where are those fucking Jews!?"

All at once, my ears detected a faint infantile wailing somewhere overhead. Easing my way off the porch, I rounded the corner of the house. Light spilled out of a corner window. The wailing was coming from up there.

A vine-covered trellis reached from the ground to the gutters. Grabbing the wooden slats, I started my climb. I hated to leave the sitter alone with that lunatic, but Davey needed my help. If Sargent found him alone up there. . . .

Leaves tickled my bare legs. Damn these pencil-thin skirts! Hand over hand I went, my moccasined feet probing for solid footholds. *Stall him!* I thought, sending the babysitter a telepathic message. Keep him occupied long enough for me to reach the baby.

The trellis vibrated under my weight. Fortunately, it remained securely anchored to the house. A splintered twig raked my hand. I choked down my gasp of pain. My heart chilled as I heard a crash down in the parlor. Sargent's swearing pursued me up the vines.

Reaching the bedroom window, I braced myself with one foot on the trellis, then put both elbows on the sill. Quick visual scan of the nursery. White wallpaper emblazoned with Disney cartoon characters. Beige chest of drawers and matching toy chest with a circus motif. In the old-fashioned crib sat Davey, dark hair mussed, wearing a wrinkled white undershirt and diaper, and shedding frightened tears.

I put the heel of my hand against the window. Prayed that Lisa hadn't locked it. Grimacing, I gave it a firm and steady push. Weathered wood creaked softly as it slid upward.

Sniffling, Davey watched me climb over his windowsill. He was sitting upright, lifting his undershirt as babies so often do.

"What's the matter, punkin?" I whispered, padding across the nursery. "Don't cry. It's me—Angie."

Unimpressed, Davey let out another wail. Brown eyes flickered in recognition, though. He made no resistance as I plucked him out of the crib.

"Are you hungry?" I cuddled him close. His warm little face nuzzled my collarbone. "Must be time for bot-bot." My anxious gaze scoured the crib's interior. A pacifier nestled behind the tiny foam pillow. "Here—try the hors d'oeuvres." Gently I placed the rubber nipple in his mouth. "Now, let's get the hell out of here."

Holding Davey close, I made a catfooted dash into the darkened upstairs hallway. Happily slurping on his pacifier,

Davey stopped crying and began playing with my long raven hair. Ouch! Gritting my teeth, I padded down the hall and ducked into the master bedroom. And grinned thankfully. A telephone's shadowy shape topped the bedside night table.

My grin wilted as I raised the receiver. No dial tone. Shit! That motherfucker Sargent must have cut the wires before breaking into the house.

To make matters worse, Davey began fussing again. "Sssssssh! Quiet, hon!" Flustered, I rocked him in both arms, unable to figure out what was wrong. Ohhhhh, Aunt Della, I could sure use some maternal advice right now. And then my right hand discovered the moist mass in the seat of his Pampers. I dipped my chin, taking a long sniff. A dull stale odor masked the scent of talcum.

"Look, I know you've got a poopie," I whispered. "And I'll take care of it—Girl Scout's promise." Swiftly I carried him back down the shadowy corridor. "Right now, though, there's a big two-legged poopie downstairs, and we have to get past him without making any noise. So be a good boy for Angie, okay?"

You know, for a moment there, I actually thought we were going to make it. Reaching the end of the hall, I glanced down the darkened stairwell. My heart lifted at the sight of that front door at the bottom of the stairs.

And then the stairway lights winked on!

I froze instantly, my horrified gaze tumbling down the stairwell.

And there he was—Steve Sargent, the skinhead avenger. He had one paratroop boot on the first step, and he was lugging that big olive green jerrican. Liquid dribbled down from the cap. The raw stench of gasoline overwhelmed the smell of Davey's diaper.

Sargent's aquamarine eyes goggled wide. "You!"

Hugging the baby tighter, I cried, "Oh, shit!"

Chapter Fifteen

"Redskin bitch!" Putting down the jerrican, Sargent reached for his deadly Swiss automatic.

By then, however, I was already retreating back down the corridor, clutching Davey for dear life. Sargent was far more surprised to see me than I was to see him. And I took full advantage of those first few seconds of stunned recognition.

Frantic footsteps pounded the stairs, followed by a gunshot. It sounded like thunder in the narrow confines of the hallway. Davey let out a horrified wail. Ducking into the bathroom, I slammed the door and punched the lock button. Then I spied the polished brass turnbolt two inches above the doorknob. Giving it a savage twist, I thought, *Bless you, Lisa!*

Sargent's footsteps drew closer.

Comforting Lisa's baby son, I stepped into the empty tub and hunkered down beside the stainless steel faucet. The molded shower and tiled wall offered adequate if not ideal cover. Your Angie was taking no chances—not with a raging lunatic who considered minorities a lower form of life.

Blam-blam-blam-blam! Steel-jacketed slugs tore through the plywood. His fusillade put two in the tiles beside the toilet. Another bored through the medicine cabinet, creating havoc within. The final shot pinged angrily off the porcelain washbowl.

Heart pounding, I held Davey closer and huddled and sobbed and crouched behind the rim of the tub. Fear rose in my gorge like bile. Swallowing hard, I thought, you play rough, fella! But even an ingenue like me knows better than to stand in front of a door.

Yowling in terror, the baby trembled like a frostbitten kitten. I kissed his ear and murmured an Anishinabe lullaby, willing my own thundering heart to slow its supercharged beat.

The doorknob rattled impatiently. *Blam-blam!* The unexpected shot nearly had me in need of a diaper. Sargent's bullets mangled the brass. He gave it another try. The knob came loose, but that security turnbolt held firm.

Okay, I was breathless and faint and terror-striken. And there was an excellent chance that he was going to boot down that door and shoot us both where we lay. But it's not the way of an Anishinabe to die meekly. So I struck at him the only way I could—with words.

"You couldn't hit the john pissing, Steverino!"

"Shut up, bitch!" A gunshot punctuated his inspired repartee.

"Maybe you ought to get a bigger caliber!"

Blam! The bullet struck the medicine cabinet, shattering the mirror, then ricocheted into the shower molding. Hugging the wailing babe, I shot a horrified glance at the nine-millimeter crater several inches above my head. Uncontrollable shudder. If I'd been standing. . . .

I heard the clacking sound of a gun hammer falling repeatedly on an empty chamber, followed by Sargent's bellow of frustrated rage.

"Son of a bitch—!"

"Where's the other clip, Stevie?" I needled, rising shakily to my feet. "In the glove compartment?" Decided to shake him up a bit. "It was until I found it . . . asshole!"

Sargent's boot hammered the door. Holding the terrified child, I sent a silent prayer heavenward. Must have been somebody listening up there. Both the bolt and the hinges held.

Breathing hard, Sargent muttered, "Look, my fight isn't with you. Give me that rugrat, and I'll let you walk."

"Right, Stevie, and I still believe in Santa Claus, too."

"You can't stay in there forever, Nahkeeta."

"I don't plan to, asshole. Just till the cops get here."

The notion that we might escape infuriated him. Giving the door one last frenzied kick, he shouted, "Think it's a Mexican standoff, huh? Well, think again, bitch!"

"Go suck a doorknob, Sargent!"

No answer. Scowling, I stepped out of the tub. Where was he? I wondered. Beating a retreat before the police arrived? Or lurking down the hall in the master bedroom, just waiting for me to unlock this door?

Just then, I heard slow-motion footfalls on the carpet along with Sargent's labored breathing. Strange sounds immediately followed. Loud splashing sounds. Liquid splattered up and down the hallway.

Sargent let out a gleeful chuckle.

The fearful stink of gasoline touched my nose.

Keeping a one-armed hold on Davey, I clambered onto the toilet seat and shoved the small bathroom window open. The screen resisted my flailing fist.

Then I spied Davey's stunned and weeping babysitter tottering across the front yard. Shrill Anishinabe whistle. She looked up immediately. "Next door!" I hollered. "Go get help—*hurry!*"

The blond girl gaped in astonishment, no doubt wondering what I was doing upstairs. Then she began running toward the big Tudor house next door.

"Cops'll never get here in time to save *you*, redskin!" Sargent sounded as if he were backing away from the bathroom. "You like that Jewcub so much? Then you can fry with it!"

A hideous *whoomph* smothered Sargent's retreating laughter. Flames crackled hungrily just beyond the door. I trembled all over at that fiery roar. It sounded like a blast furnace out there.

Wisps of gray smoke curled inward through the narrow space at the top of the door. Struggling against a surge of blind panic, I snatched a pair of coral towels off the rack and stuffed them into the aperture.

Okay, so that had bought us a precious few minutes of safety. With the towels keeping the lethal gases out, and the open window offering a direct pipeline to fresh air, the bathroom had become a temporary sanctuary. But not for long. The fire was already climbing the corridor walls. Soon it would fan out into the large attic space between the ceiling and the roof.

Holding Davey close, I stood rooted to the spot. My desperate gaze circled the bathroom. Gasping and weeping, I thought, *We're going to die here!*

And then my rangerette training automatically kicked in. My mind leaped back to those training lectures at North Cascades.

Step One: Don't panic. Easy for you to say, Mr. Head Ranger, sir. You're not the one trapped with a baby in an upstairs bathroom in a three-alarm fire.

Step Two: Don't open the door. Right! Flames need oxygen to breathe, just like us, and they always flow toward a source of ventilation.

Step Three: Test all doors until you find one leading to safety.

Well, there's only one door, Mr. Head Ranger, sir. But I'm going to test it anyway. It's only ten feet to the stairwell. If it's not too hot out there, I just might be able to wrap Davey in a wet towel and make a break for it.

My palm touched the door, then shot away instantly. Shrill pained gasp! The wood felt like the surface of Grandma Biwaban's pancake griddle. Oh, I might be able to reach the stairs, all right. *If* I had an asbestos suit.

Which I didn't!

My gaze returned to the door. Droplets of moist varnish oozed out of the wood, running down the door like so many tears. That door wouldn't last much longer.

Pulling open the linen closet door, I let out a yowl of dismay. There were towels in there, all right, but not enough to cover my petite Anishinabe form. And there were no terrycloth robes on the closet hooks.

Then my gaze found the Rotenbergs' teal shower curtain. *Cloth!* I thought, whirling at once. Let it be cloth. Please! Because if it's plastic or vinyl it'll melt like beeswax. My hand clutched a fold of the material . . . Yes!

After setting Davey on the bathroom floor, I threw myself at the polycotton curtain, grabbed two big handfuls of fabric, and tore it off the stainless steel rod. Davey's wailing ceased. He watched my antics with big, curious eyes. See the funny Anishinabe lady destroying Mommy's bathroom.

Dumping the shower curtain in the tub, I bunched it beneath the faucet, then gave the cold water lever an enthusiastic push. Water cascaded into the tub. Clusters of fabric, plump with trapped air, floated to the surface. Hopping into the tub, I mashed them underfoot. The chilled water set my teeth on edge. Ignoring the discomfort, I did a merry Irish jig, stomping and stamping and kicking, until both my moccasins and the curtain were thoroughly soaked.

Snatching a big bath towel from the rack, I doused it under the faucet. You're next, Master Rotenberg. Stop that screaming. I know it's wet. Listen, you want to grow up and quarterback for the Port Wyoochee Mariners, right? Then quit kicking and do as Angie says.

Once I had Davey bundled up, I cradled him in my left arm and used my right to haul that waterlogged shower curtain over my head. Sopping fabric smothered my backbone. Pulling and tugging, I swaddled myself in drenched material. A mirror fragment showed me a crazily lopsided image—Angie of Arabia.

I reached for the turnbolt lever. *Tayaa!* My hand couldn't

even touch it. Heat waves emanated from the brass. Reaching overhead, I snatched one of the smoking towels out of the doorjamb, then wrapped it round and round my right hand. This time, the lever turned easily. Then I rested my hand on the mangled doorknob.

Moment of hesitation. The second I cracked that seal, those flames would come pouring in. Shaking with apprehension, I made certain Davey was completely covered. Then, averting my face, I yanked open the door.

Wooooosh! I put my spine to the fiery surge. Hot winds clutched greedily at my wet makeshift burnoose. Holding my breath, I willed myself to remain motionless, waiting for the flaming wind to subside.

And we're off! Left turn in an upstairs corridor boiling with thick, acrid smoke. Flames appeared as bright yellow flickers in a fog of stinking gray. I couldn't even see the opposite wall. I heard a familiar echo in my memory. The head ranger at North Cascades telling us how easy it is to become disoriented in a fire.

Come on, princess. Just like the drill, remember? Move quickly but don't panic—don't rush! Long strides now—one, two, three. Ignore the maddening smoke itch around your eyes. And whatever you do, *don't breathe!* You're Davey's one and only ticket out of here.

Flaming rings nibbled at the carpet. I sidestepped them carefully, blinking rapidly to ease the smoke itch, seeking the dark stairwell. Bits of fiery debris dribbled down from the ceiling, smacking my shoulders. The rapidly drying curtain rendered me as sweaty as a Northland sauna. Davey's crying barely carried over the roar of the flames.

Where is that goddamned stairwell? I wondered, pawing my way through the swirling smoke. A tightening invisible pressure band squeezed my lungs. I resisted the overwhelming impulse to suck in a breath of air. One good whiff of that noxious smoke would knock me to the floor, wheezing and choking.

My drying moccasin soles found the corridor's precipice. Just in time, too! The shower curtain was bone dry. Wisps of white smoke fluttered away from it. I felt the heat of the first flames eating into the polycotton.

With a cry of relief, I tossed off the smoking curtain and dashed downstairs into that blessed cool air. Reaching the front hallway, I spied Davey's baby carrier on the walnut side table. Hastily I peeled away the damp bath towel, rubbed him dry with the soft baby blanket, and set him in the carrier's reclining seat. I found another pacifier in the side pouch and let him chew on that. And sincerely hoped he would grow to manhood with no memories of this nightmare.

Grabbing the carrier by its movable handles, I galloped out the front door into the damp chilly night.

Outraged masculine shouts serenaded me down the lawn. Looking around, I saw a pair of open-mouthed neighbors on the Tudor doorstep and an equally astonished elderly couple farther down the street. And then I spotted Sargent. He was doing a leisurely pendulum routine—upside down—dangling from Angie's pantyhose. Back and forth, back and forth. His right leg shot skyward, caught in the taut loop of my *dasanagun*.

I set Davey down on the lawn, where Sargent could get a good look at him, and made my approach. The jerrican lay on its side near the pistol. Amber fluid drained steadily from the nozzle. Swinging forward, Sargent made a frantic grab for the automatic. Straining fingers clawed empty air. Taking no chances, I crouched, swept my moccasined foot under there, and kicked it well out of reach.

Only then did I permit myself the luxury of a cold Angie smile. "I'm surprised you're still hanging around, asshole."

"Bitch!" The skinhead's face had turned the color of an autumn maple leaf. Beefy arms waving helplessly, he gave his fisherman's vocabulary a strenuous workout.

Ignoring him, I watched the flames consume the second

floor of the Rotenberg house. The sight triggered a sudden eerie lightheaded feeling, as if I were viewing all this from far away. I thought for a second I was going to faint, and then that hideous smorgasbord of burning smells yanked me back to full consciousness. The acrid stench of scorched wood. The sour cloying smell of melting vinyl. An uncontrollable shaking took hold of my knees. Touching my forehead, I let out a long shaky exhalation. Close call, there! A few seconds more, and Davey and I would have never made it out.

Sargent was still raving. "The racial struggle will go on, bitch! Our war is just beginning. Hail victory!"

"It'll go on without you, Stevie. Arson's good for fifteen-to-twenty in this state."

His spittle struck the ground just short of my moccasin.

"They won't hold me forever. I'll get out someday, and then I'm coming looking for you, redskin. You and the little Jewboy!"

That did it! Features frozen with anger, I picked up the jerrican. I doubted that this murderous psycho would even get to Cedar Creek. He'd probably spend a few years in Steilacoom, cutting out paper dolls, while some headshrinker spent hours trying to soothe his ravaged psyche. I thought of how he'd beaten my grandfather and how he'd tried to murder that baby. Four brisk twists had the nozzle off. Gasoline swirled at the bottom as I lifted the can.

My warpath scowl took the smirk right off Sargent's face.

"Wha . . . What are you doing?"

"My grandfather told me all about you Nazis," I said, hefting the jerrican. "But there's one story that's always stuck with me. You probably know it by heart, Stevie. The SS rounds up Russian Jews, herds them into a synagogue, and then sets the building on fire. Is that what you had in mind when you came here tonight?" Contemptuous glance at the dangling arsonist. "Marshmallow roast? That's what you call major-league psychosis."

Stepping forward, I sloshed the gasoline around. There

was less than a gallon left in the can. More than enough for my purposes. I showed him a big wicked Angie smile.

"Hey! What—? Jesus, no! Don't!"

I splashed Sargent's dangling body with gasoline, drenching him from crotch to chin. Walking a slow circle, I doused him twice more and then made a great show of pouring gas on the ground. The pungent stink numbed my nose.

"Hey! You crazy bitch!" he screamed, wiping the fuel from his face. "What do you think you're doing!?"

"Three guesses."

Backing away up the driveway, I poured out a thin trickle of gasoline.

"No!" Sargent's eyes bulged in sheer terror. "Nooooo! Are you crazy!? Don't do it!"

"Why, Stevie, I thought you enjoyed playing with fire."

The jerrican suddenly went dry. Putting my back to him, I kept right on pouring in pantomime. I mimicked the sound of gurgling liquid.

"Jesus, no! Don't!" Sargent was going apeshit at the thought of being charbroiled on his own flaming petard. "No! Somebody stop her! Help me! Help!"

I halted the Angie sound effects. Sargent was too far gone to even notice. He struggled like a hooked bass, writhing and screaming, straining to reach the *dasanagun* knot. "Don't let her do it! Stop her—please! I-I don't want to burn!"

I set the gas can on the asphalt, then used my blazer sleeve to obliterate my fingerprints. Klaxons warbled in the direction of downtown. Facing the skinhead for the last time, I said, "Sargent, you'd better hope the Fire Department gets here *before* that can explodes."

"Nooooo!"

His terrified howling nearly drowned out the Klaxons. Racing across the lawn, I scooped up Davey's baby carrier and dashed downslope to my car.

Sargent was in no real danger, of course. The jerrican was

315

empty. And even if it had been full, it was too far away from the burning house for the heat to touch off the fumes.

Right now, though, the only image running through the sick mind of my arsonist friend was the gas can exploding like a bomb, followed by a trail of flame snaking its way down the driveway, heading straight for him.

Sargent would be caught at the scene, reeking of gasoline, a sure candidate for conviction if ever there was one. And he would experience the torments of the damned during the agonizing moments before the firefighters' arrival.

A small price to pay for trying to murder Lisa's child.

And what of Angie? I mused, as I drove away from there. Reaching to my right, I gave Davey's tummy a comforting pat. Suppose I'd had a cigarette lighter handy. Knowing what he'd done to Chief and to the Rotenbergs, would I have flicked my Bic? Made Sargent's worst nightmare a gruesome reality?

Honest answer? Well, let's just say I would have been tempted. But I wouldn't have gone through with it. Not your Angie. You see, I'm a princess and not a savage. Like Columbus!

Ten minutes later, I pulled into a convenience store at the corner of Keel Road and Shore Avenue. Davey let out a hissing sneeze. I wiped his little nose with a tissue. I had to get him out of that damp undershirt before pneumonia set in.

Inside, I purchased a box of Pampers, a blue fleece baby-sized pajama top, three bottles of Veryfine juice, rubber baby nipples, a package of Handi-Wipes, baby powder, safety pins, a memo pad and a felt pen.

Yes, I'm fully aware of the fact that Pampers do not require pins. I needed them for another purpose, though.

First things first, princess. That diaper is getting mighty ripe.

There was a picnic table right outside the store. Mist had dampened the wood, so I put down Davey's baby blanket and set him on top of it. Off with the old diaper. Somehow I resisted the temptation to mail it—fully loaded—to the Adamite church. Lift the infant ankles. Quick scrub with the Handi-Wipe. Aunt Della, you should see me now!

After putting him back in the carrier, I gave Davey a choice of three drinks. He responded most enthusiastically to the orange juice. I replaced the Veryfine cap with a rubber nipple and let him have at it. Then, getting behind the steering wheel, I picked up my felt pen, flipped open the memo pad, and began to write.

Hello, my name is David Rotenberg, and I live at 42 Wyammah Circle, Port Wyoochee. A Nazi named Steve Sargent just tried to kill me. But a nice lady rescued me and brought me here. Please contact my parents immediately.

Taking a safety pin, I fastened the note to the front of Davey's pajama top. He squirmed in the carrier seat, kicking with both feet, gurgling with pleasure. Tiny bubbles formed at the corners of his satisfied smile.

"Ooooooh, aren't you silly?" I crooned, my hand tickling his plump little stomach. Then, hoisting him onto my shoulder, I tenderly patted his spine. An orangey burp moistened my hair. I put him back in the carrier, covered the note with his blanket, and glanced at the carrier's white plastic side.

Moment of temptation. Should I? Oh, hell, why not? The FBI's going to know who it is the minute they finish interrogating Dolan. Might as well take full credit for this one.

I plucked the lipstick tube from my bag, flashed a scintillating Angie smile, and then carefully drew a stylized tomahawk on the side of Davey's baby carrier.

Pocahontas, indeed! That, gang, is the sign of Angie Biwaban!

Soon we were heading west on Shore Avenue, speeding through the darkened, dilapidated neighborhoods of Sawdust Flats. Original spawning ground of the hatred that had levelled the Rotenberg house this evening. A sickness that seems to be growing in our fair land of Michimackinakong. Genocide . . . ethnic cleansing . . . does it really matter what you call it? It's one European export we could do without.

This continent was far from empty when your ancestors arrived, people. There were ten million of us here. Klallam, Nuche, Shoshoni, Lakota, Anishinabe. Different people. Different customs and languages. To be perfectly honest, we didn't always get along in perfect harmony. Far from it! We all did our share of fighting. But we never attacked people merely because of what they were. The black bear is my clan totem. To the Nuche, he's a god. To the Anishinabe, he's Uncle Bear, a spirit and a source of food. That difference was not the signal for an all-out race war between us.

If you people are going to live in Michimackinakong, please be good enough to send your ancient European prejudices back home.

Relaxing behind the wheel, I showed the rearview mirror a sardonic smile. Who was I to lecture anyone? Angie Biwaban, girl outlaw! Not exactly the career path I had in mind when I graduated from Central.

True, your Angie is an outlaw. But occasionally she does something right. Such as following tonight's hunch. And perhaps saving this darling baby from a fiery death makes up for some of the less-than-noble things I've done.

I sure hope so.

Minutes later, I pulled into the well-lit parking lot of Yennis County Memorial Hospital. I found an empty spot in the third row and deposited the Topaz there. Then, with the baby carrier dangling from my right arm, I strolled nonchalantly into the Emergency Room.

Families crammed the antiseptic chamber. Mothers and children, mostly. Runny noses and hacking coughs and

'Mommy, my tummy hurts!" There were more black people n the Emergency Room than I'd seen thus far in all of Yennis County. But that's no surprise. Hospital emergency rooms are often the sole source of medical care for low-income people. Three white workmen in coveralls and yellow hardhats occupied one naugahyde sofa. One of them had a makeshift bandage, wet with blood, tied around his left thigh.

The E/R duty nurse was a sharp-featured, frosted brunette in her early forties. She summoned me over to the counter, handed me a plastic number, and informed me that Dr. Heroux would be available in an hour or three. In the meantime, I could peruse their well-thumbed collection of *Today's Health* and *National Geographic* magazines. I opted for the TV, keeping Davey well away from the ailing children.

"Hey!" said one of the workmen. "Look! They got *Dolan!*"

My gaze swivelled instantly to the wide screen. News footage showed the infuriated Jack Dolan being pushed into a police cruiser.

"You're shitting me!" the bandaged one cried. Then, leaning forward, he stared at the screen and cackled, "Well, whattaya know? There *is* a God!"

I toted Davey back to the counter. Kissed his forehead as I put down the carrier. Time to go, little one. The nurse busily scribbled on a clipboard. I cleared my throat, and she looked up impatiently.

"Excuse me." I tilted my head in the direction of the pay phone. "I have to call my husband and let him know where we are. Would you watch Davey for a moment, please?"

"Of course, dear." Her angular face softened all at once. Nothing like the sight of a baby to mellow even the sternest R.N. She gave his cheek a teasing tweak. "Ooooooh, are you Mummy's good boy? Yes, you *are!*" Soft-hearted maternal smile. "He looks just like you, dear."

He *does?* Shaking my head, I walked away from the

counter. Hmmmmm, maybe there is something to this Ten Lost Tribes business, after all.

Lifting the receiver off the hook, I had an imaginative conversation with the dial tone. Every so often, I shot a fleeting glance at the duty nurse, to see if she was still watching me.

She wasn't. Patient reports had reclaimed her immediate attention. Davey's pudgy hands patted the sides of the carrier. Hanging up, I sauntered down the hospital corridor and ducked into the laundry room.

Within minutes, I was jogging across the parking lot, highly pleased with my successful fade. No need to worry about Davey. When I failed to return, the nurse would become alarmed and notify hospital security. They'd soon find the note I'd pinned to his pajama top. With luck, he'd be back with his parents by midnight.

And I'd be on the dodge in Seattle.

Halting beside the Topaz, I reached for the door handle. And my gaze picked out a familiar shape blocking the access driveway. A black pickup truck. . . .

Suddenly, I sensed a blur of motion to my right. A large manlike shape burst out of the shadows. His right hand clutched what looked like a sodden handkerchief. My mouth opened to scream, and he jumped me, pinning me to the hood. The damp cloth smothered my nose and mouth.

A pungent scent spiralled up my nostrils. My stomach churned at the onset of nausea. The queer odor stunned my senses, dragging my consciousness down into a lightless and bottomless void.

"Whiskey Jack!"

Mona Hanauer's lovely voice penetrated the stygian blackness, stirring the embers of my comatose mind. I began clawing my way out of oblivion, creeping ever so slowly toward that faint, distant, insistent voice.

"Whiskey Jack!"

With painstaking slowness, my consciousness crystallized into a series of coherent thoughts.

All right. Don't rub it in, Mona. I admit it, I never understood your dying clue. What *were* you trying to tell us, lying there on that stony beach, dying of exposure, putting your rapidly fading strength into one last desperate shout?

Eyes glazing over with delirium, you belted it out. Those two maddening words. *Whiskey Jack!* Spit it out like a radio announcer. That's what Sister Mary Katherine said.

"Whiskey Jack!"

Yeah, just like that! Like a radio announcer—crisp, sharp and punctuated by the muted crackle of static . . .

Static?

Sudden realization sharpened my mental focus. My other senses began to rouse. I marshalled my powers of concentration, sent them plunging down my auditory nerves. My hearing became as sensitive as a bobcat's.

And there it was—the faint spattering of radio static. Somewhere beyond it, in the impenetrable blackness, I heard a vaguely familiar low-pitched monotone droning.

Then the woman's voice returned. It was a soft contralto, close enough to Mona's to fool me, with a mild British Columbian accent. "Seven-Three-Whiskey-Jack, do you copy? Over."

That sound banished the last traces of drugged slumber. Comfortable cushions supported my spine and derriere. A broad nylon strap ran diagonally from my left shoulder to my right hip. My stomach informed me that I was in motion. Sort of a mild rocking motion. Up and down mostly, with an occasional fishtailing sweep.

"Seven-Three-Whiskey-Jack, you are twenty degrees off course. What is your new heading? Over."

Up came my weighty eyelids, slower than a first grader on his way to school. A flashing red UFO hovered in the night sky an indeterminate distance from me. My chin sagged in disbelief. Impossible! Then I blinked my eyes—once, twice—and that dreamlike vista congealed into a sharper reality. My crimson UFO was an airplane's running light, a rotating red beacon on the leading edge of a silvery wing. Scarlet flashes illuminated the huge numerals on the wing's underside—N5973WJ.

"Seven-Three-Whiskey-Jack, do you read? Over."

In my mind, I was back in the Yennis County tower, listening to Gary Lussier explain all about controller's shorthand—how they use the last three or four digits of an airplane's registration number over the radio. Air traffic controllers have an alphabet of their very own. Too many letters in English sound alike. Did he say *B, C, D* or *E?* So, to avoid confusion, *A* becomes Adam, *B* Baker, *C* Charlie, and so on. WJ . . . Whiskey Jack, as in *Seven-Three-Whiskey-Jack*.

Mona had heard that phrase countless times over the radio, and she'd repeated it in her dying delirium. As a matter of fact, she heard it every Wednesday, whenever her killer flew her over to the San Juan Islands.

Isn't it amazing how quickly the puzzle pieces fall into place once you have the key?

Eliminate Mickey's paranoid suspicion of Dolan and the Adamites' harassment of Mona, and what do we have left in terms of motive?

Why, we're right back to the original triangle—Mona Hanauer, Jon Waterman and Georgianna.

Marcella believed that Georgianna gave her husband the boot after she found out about him and Mona. But my friend had the story ass-backward. It was Waterman who dumped the long-suffering Georgianna.

Which puts a whole new spin on everything, right? Such as Georgianna's black eye. Now I understood why she was so bitter about men. And why she was so afraid of her assailant. Waterman must have thumped her plenty while they were married.

And don't forget the painful way he squeezed your wrist,

Angela. The pilot seems to get off on hurting women, doesn't he?

I wondered why he had hit her, and the answer came in a twinkling. Uh-oh! That was your doing, princess. You inadvertently sicced him on Georgianna when you mentioned that she'd told you about Mona's dependency.

And why should the floatplane pilot be so concerned about that? Well, Princess Slow-on-the-Uptake, let's gather all the known facts and see if we can flesh out his motive.

Once upon a time there was an RCAF pilot named Jon Waterman, stationed in the Arctic, who met and married the base commander's daughter, Georgianna. When his enlistment was up, Waterman took his bride below the border and set himself up in the air taxi business. Shortly thereafter, he became involved in the lucrative drug trade. Or perhaps that was his intention all along. After all, there are hundreds of small wilderness lakes in British Columbia. And it's no trouble at all setting down to pick up the dope, then flying it into the United States.

Waterman walked out on his Canadian wife and moved in with the divorced Mona Hanauer. The couple lived together for three years. And that's why nobody knows the identity of Mona's supplier. Waterman was feeding her marijuana himself, keeping her well-supplied with a kilo or two out of the main shipment. He's the one who gave Mona that waterproof military canister and showed her how to safely cache her private stash.

Ah, but now the bloom is off the romance. Perhaps Waterman has slapped Mona around just once too often. She gives him the boot, and her insider knowledge of his dope running is the perfect blackmail threat to keep him at bay.

Blackmailing a killer like Waterman is a risky game, though. Extremely unhappy with the situation, Waterman began considering ways to permanently resolve the Mona problem. Then Mona's ex-husband enters the picture, and Jon-boy sees his chance.

So Waterman lures Mona to that lonely Orcas beach. For a fellow who gets his jollies out of hurting women, the prospect of what he's about to do must have him creaming his jeans. I wonder, did he give Mona's lovely face one last fingertip caress before the first wallop?

A mild sickish shudder ran through me. No thanks! I'd really rather not know.

Yeah, Waterman needed a patsy. As Mona's longtime lover, he knew who Mickey Grantz was. He must have seen Mick on the island. Indeed, he and Mona might have even quarrelled over her decision to contact her ex.

Had I never become entangled with the Adamites, I might have figured this out earlier. Waterman really threw me for a loop with that cagey alibi of his. How did he work that, anyway? How did he convince the Nitinat lodgekeeper he was still on the island?

I cast a peripheral glance at the plane's dashboard. Luminescent dials and indicators glowed a soft green. I caught Waterman's faint verdant reflection in the windshield. Grim-faced pilot holding the yoke. Tension lines on either side of the harsh mouth. Pitiless eyes lurked behind his steel-rimmed glasses.

"Seven-Three-Whiskey-Jack, this is Vancouver Control. You are losing altitude. Is there a problem? Over."

Scowling, Waterman lifted the microphone off the hook. Pressing the transmit button, he said, "Vancouver Control, this is Seven-Three-Whiskey-Jack. My oil pressure's dropping. The power plant's beginning to overheat. I'm putting down in the islands. Over."

A quick peek at the oil pressure gauge told me what a facile liar Jon Waterman was. The needle hovered well above the red line.

"We copy, Whiskey Jack. Can you make it to Rosario?"

"Negative!" Waterman snapped. "I'm going to try to land in the West Sound. Over."

"Copied and understood, Whiskey Jack. We'll alert the Coast Guard. Keep us informed."

"Roger. Out!"

Still playing possum, I did some frantic thinking. Obviously, Waterman had bushwacked me in the hospital parking lot. But why? Why had he come after the woman he knew as Anne Marie?

Kind of a big surprise for the FBI, too. They'd be wondering for years how Pocahontas could have pulled off such a complete disappearance. They'd probably never know that she'd been shanghaied by Mona's real killer and spirited out of Port Wyoochee aboard his bronze-and-yellow floatplane.

I could easily guess the reason for Waterman's unscheduled landing. According to the dashboard clock, he still had six hours of darkness left. More than enough time to dispose of your Angie in some lonely corner of the San Juans.

I had one slim chance at retaliation. Preoccupied with the plane's descent, Waterman was still unaware that I was awake. Perhaps I could put those precious few moments to good use.

Even if Waterman finishes you, princess, you still want to make certain he goes down for the Hanauer killing.

Through slitted eyes, I studied the darkened floor of the cockpit, seeking my shoulder bag. Surreptitiously I moved my bare legs apart. Something smooth and bulky bumped my right calf. Ah, there we are! I knew he was too careful to leave any trace of Anne Marie behind. Now, let's just hope he didn't scour the inside of my bag.

Sinking slightly in the passenger seat, I pushed my right hand through the darkness and pinched the zipper tab. The engine's monotone drone masked the sound of the zipper sliding open.

Waterman kept his gaze riveted onto the flight instruments.

Shoulder muscles shrieked as I reached all the way into the bag. I forced my facial features to remain smooth and

325

placid. The strain nearly tore a gasp from my lips. Then my wandering fingers closed around my AVR cassette recorder. My thumb tapped the rewind tab. I held my breath at the sudden whispery squeal, firing a panicky sidelong glance at Waterman.

If he heard that, I was finished!

Waterman lifted his hand suddenly. I tensed all over. And then, to my utter relief, he reached for the compass and adjusted the setting. His gaze never wavered from the dash.

Stepping on the left pedal, Waterman eased the yoke in the same direction, then reduced the throttle. The Beaver banked leisurely to the left. Opaque mists swirled past our windshield. We were going down.

Click! The unit stopped rewinding. Clutching it tightly, I eased it out of my bag, then put that hand behind my seat. I gave the record tab a discreet push. As we reached the apogee of our turn, I let it go. The minirecorder tumbled into the shadowy framework beneath the pilot's seat.

Let's see you explain that tape recorder, Jon-boy, the next time U.S. Customs boards your plane for a spot check.

The curtain rises on a new performance. Feigning a groan, I stirred in my seat. My head swung feebly from side to side. Grabbing my blazer collar, Waterman gave me a most ungentlemanly shaking. Masculine fingers whapped my cheek. "Wake up!" Another stinging slap. "Damn you! Wake up, Nahkeeta!"

"Ohhhhh!" I had enough of a headache to make my grimace absolutely convincing. "W-Waterman? Wha—? That smell . . ."

"Chloroform. You'll live. But maybe not for long, eh?" Flashing me a hate-filled glance, he put both hands on the yoke. "Talk to me, lovey. What do you know about Mona? And who have you told?"

Breathing in frightened gasps, I murmured, "I don't know what you're talking about."

The pilot's gaze turned murderous. "Either you answer

326

my questions, Nahkeeta, or you're leaving this aircraft—*right now!*"

My throat tightening in terror, I huddled in the far corner of my molded passenger seat.

Savoring my fright, he jutted his chin toward the altimeter. "That's the President Channel down there. Ten thousand feet is a long way to fall. Hitting the water from this height . . . why, it'd be just like hitting the sidewalk."

Instantly I glanced out the side window. Impenetrable fog met my gaze. President Channel, I mused. *North* of Orcas! Which means he has no intention of landing in the West Sound. He's headed for one of the small outer islands, all of which are generally deserted after Labor Day. Ooooooh, not good, princess!

"If you want to finish this flight," he threatened, "you had better answer my questions. Who are you working for? The DEA?"

I kept mum. Maybe the FBI would take my silence for affirmation and stop looking for me.

"What have you told your superiors!?"

I did my celebrated impression of actress Debra Winger. "I haven't told them about Mona, if that's what you're worried about."

Hissing in fury, the pilot snapped, "Why not?"

"It's standard agency policy," I replied, trying to sound fearless. Federal Angie strikes again. "We never turn suspects over to local authorities until we have an ironclad case for the prosecution." I added some more trimming for the Bureau. "We've had you under surveillance for quite a while, Waterman. Oh, we know you killed her. We just don't have the smoking gun—*yet!*"

His panicky gaze flitted from the instrument panel to me. The word *we* seemed to rattle him. "How did you know? How!?"

"We found Mona's dope stash." Might as well tell the Bureau where to look for corroborating evidence. "It was wrapped in plastic, sealed away in your RCAF container. She'd sunk the canister just offshore. Did you teach her that trick, Waterman?"

"Bloody right! By the way, it's an ammo can, not a *canister.*" Derisive glance. "I picked it up at a military surplus store in Vancouver. It's perfect for underwater concealment."

Realizing I had to keep him talking, I took a guess. "Is that how you transported the dope?"

"Smart girl!" Self-satisfied chuckle. "I did some customizing when I first purchased this aircraft. I welded steel brackets onto the inside of the floats. It was all quite simple, really. Stuff the ammo cans with bricks of marijuana. Snap them into the brackets. Then flood both the floats, covering them with water." Another chuckle. "Your Customs people have been all over this plane. But they never thought to check the floats."

"Don't be too sure about that, Waterman."

Narrow features tensed in anger. "That's right. You've been watching us, haven't you?" He turned to me again. "Why did you DEA bastards go after Mona?"

I did some hasty improvising. The more I sold him on my DEA tale, the less likely he was to go after Chief and the Mick. Licking dry lips, I stammered, "Sh-She had a couple of dope busts in Seattle. We knew she was a heavy user." I spit out the tale as quickly as it took shape in my imagination. "One of our informants above the border got word of a smuggler. A lone wolf operating out of this area. We did some on-site snooping and—surprise, surprise—there was Mona Hanauer. Bigger surprise—heavy user Mona hadn't made a buy in three years. We began wondering if she'd latched on to her own personal sugar daddy. And then we found out she was shacking up with a floatplane pilot—"

Waterman's fist thumped the dashboard. The microphone clattered out of its mount. Eyes blazing, he shot a graveyard stare my way.

"You put two and two together, eh?" He switched off the radio. "You've really messed me up, lovey. I'd figured on milking this scheme another year or two. Looks like I'll be heading for Rio a little ahead of schedule."

I could see him pulling it off, too. A quick stop in the San Juans to bury Angie. Reclaim the drug money from those Vancouver banks. Fly back into the States, pick up a phony U.S. passport, and go. A clean getaway for Ontario's answer to Indiana Jones.

I steered us back onto the topic of murder. "Nice frame job, Waterman. But the agency never bought that crap about Mona's ex-husband."

"Too bad! I thought I lucked out when I saw Grantz with Mona at the restaurant. The two of them were quarrelling, and there were plenty of witnesses. I went to a public phone and rang up every motel on Orcas. It didn't take me ten minutes to find the one where the bastard was staying." Slowly he eased the flap lever back. "Grantz made it so bloody easy. I opened his sliding glass door with a credit card. His sweater fit me like a glove. I waited until after midnight, then I went to see Mona. At first she refused to let me in. So I told her I had a shipment aboard the plane. Told her I needed a safe place to stash it for a week. She invited me in, and we talked. I left Grantz's sweater on the couch. Mona wanted a look at the dope. She was running low, and she was thinking about buying some for herself. So I walked her down to Obstruction Pass."

I gave him another prod toward full confession. And hoped the minirecorder was getting all this. "I'm not sure I follow you."

He shrugged. "I killed her." Bluish gray eyes turned strangely pensive. "You know . . . I wasn't quite sure I could do it. Oh, I wanted her dead, of course. I'd wanted that since the moment the bitch threw me out. You don't know how many times I've daydreamed about it. About meeting Mona on some lonely fogbound beach and giving her a sly little smile and doubling my fist and letting her have it! Wham! Hard enough to make those lovely eyes spin!" Facial muscles went slack, as if he were having an orgasm. "But that was nothing—*nothing!*—compared to the real thing. Seeing her there, on that moonless beach . . . seeing her turn toward me, her face tensing in confusion because the plane wasn't there . . . looking so lovely, so vulnerable. I wasn't certain I could go through with it. I stepped forward. Then I put my hands on her face. And it was as if we were about to make love. And then I remembered. Remembered her laughter as she walked into the restaurant with Grantz. Thought of them alone in that cabin together. I thought of all the times *we'd* made love in that cabin. And I remembered how it hurt when she threw me out. She threatened me—*me!*—the arrogant cunt. Told me she'd turn me in if I didn't keep my distance. I don't take that kind of shit from *any* woman! So I made a fist, and I showed her that tight little smile. I hit her in the stomach—hard! As if Mona were a man. It felt so damned good. A-A sort of release, you know? I smashed her on the chin. I hit her again and again. It was much better than I ever could have dreamed. Ten times better than belting that whining bitch, Georgianna. It was as if there was an electric current surging through me. I wanted to hammer that beautiful, lying, treacherous face right down into the stones. I-I loved her, you see." He gave me an abrupt look of embarrassment, as if he'd dropped a fork at dinner. "I-I couldn't let Mona walk out on me. I just couldn't let that happen. I *knew* I was going to lose her, so it was better if I lost her *this* way. Better that my hands were the last to fondle that soft, sweet flesh . . . fondle and squeeze and smash it . . . smash that unfaithful bitch . . . smash her right down into the ground!"

Waterman lapsed into a lunatic silence. I sat trembling in my seat. Once he found a likely beach, there was little doubt what he intended to do to Angie. Then, showing a small triumphant grin, he added, "Guess you're wondering how I found you out, eh?"

I swallowed hard. "A bit."

"I was in Nitinat yesterday." He flicked on the plane's landing lights. "The lodgekeeper told me some woman had been asking about me. Said the call had come from Yennis County airport. So I stopped there on the way home. Lussier's secretary told me all about a certain lady insurance investigator named Anne Marie Nahkeeta."

Sour Angie grimace. I should have used another name at the airport!

"You got a little nervous when I began nosing around the edges of your alibi."

"You might say that." Waterman nodded. "I wondered why a stockbroker was so bloody interested in Mona. When I heard you'd been snooping about the airport, I knew for certain you were DEA."

All my questions about Mona's dependency had given him the wrong idea. But I didn't bother to enlighten him.

"I'm curious, Waterman. How did you con the Nitinat lodgekeeper the next morning?"

Leaning back in the pilot's seat, he let out a burst of good-humored laughter. "I let him have a good look at me the evening of October seventh; then I told him I was on my way to the cafe for dinner. Right after leaving the lodge, I rowed back out to my plane. Cowichan's a long lake. I taxied a couple of miles out, until I was well out of earshot, then I gave her full throttle and took off. It was a bit dicey, but I got out of the mountains before the fog closed in. I rounded Cadboro Point and scooted straight across to the San Juans. I stayed ten feet above the water, well below the radar net." Wry chuckle. "I was on Orcas by six-thirty."

"And camped out at your ex-wife's place?"

"Good guess. There's a dock out back. I tied up there for the night." Waterman's voice softened in reminiscence. "That was the hard part. Sitting on that dock and waiting

331

for sunrise. After I killed Mona, I was too charged-up to sleep. I had the weirdest feeling that the police knew what I had done. That they were sneaking up on my plane." He eased the yoke gently forward, and the Beaver's nose dipped. "Once it was light enough to see, I took off again and headed back to Vancouver Island."

"That's right," I added, my voice hoarse with emotion. "The lodgekeeper never really *saw* you take off that morning, did he? He couldn't see anything in that fog. He told me he recognized your motor as you flew overhead." Sharp glance at the killer. "You were already airborne when you made that eight o'clock call. You put on a little radio show for his benefit."

"Actually, I was at fourteen thousand feet at the time."

"Kind of risky, wasn't it? Buzzing the lodge in that pea soup fog?"

"Piece of cake!"

"Sure! For an RCAF pilot who's flown hundreds of missions in the fogbound Arctic."

Waterman did a doubletake. His grin turned icy. "You DEA people are thorough, aren't you?" Reaching over, he gave my safety strap a tug. "Hold on tight. It'll be a rough landing."

I slapped his hand away. "Your concern is touching!"

"Don't even think about bailing out that hatch the moment we touch down." He flicked several overhead switches. "We'll be travelling at better than a hundred miles an hour. The impact will break your bones."

That warning necessitated a slight change of Angie plans. I'd wait until the plane had nearly finished its splashdown, then out the side hatch. I'd be halfway to shore before he could bring the Beaver's nose around.

"Anne Marie . . . ?"

I lifted my gaze, just in time to see Waterman's clenched fist speeding toward me. Something black and leathery

332

twirled in his taut grasp. I had a split-second close-up glimpse of the sap. Then it collided with my forehead.

An eye-searing white light exploded behind my brow. Agonizing pain! Felt as if he'd split my skull with an axe. Then my seat seemingly vanished out from under me, and I was falling—whirling—spinning downward to meet the lightless sea of oblivion.

Chapter Sixteen

Frigid water smacked me in the face, tumbling me instantly out of unconsciousness. Salt stung as my eyelids shot open. Seawater clogged my nostrils. I writhed on the soft ground, hacking and gagging, then spitting up a pint of the Pacific Ocean. Sodden clothes weighed me down. I shivered as the night breeze swept across my soaked face.

Sand gritted my left cheek. Excruciating headache pain kept me conscious. I was lying on my side on a damp beach. A lump the size of Mount Baker throbbed agonizingly at the top of my forehead. Stirring feebly, I fell onto my back and emitted a soft anguished moan.

Mushrooming surge of pain! This time from my hands. I was lying on top of them, and I couldn't pull them out from under me. Instantly I became aware of the taut manila rope grinding against my wrists. Groaning, I flopped onto my front side.

As soon as the fire in my wrists subsided, I glanced over my shoulder and saw a rope trailing away from the middle of my back. Its far end was securely lashed to a whitish gray deadwood log. Waterman was taking no chances. Tethering me to that weighty, half-buried tree trunk would ensure that I stayed put.

My chilled, puffy fingers plucked impotently at Waterman's knots. Biting back a piteous moan, I forced myself to study my surroundings. I was lying on the gentle slope of a sand beach. A stony headland marked one end of this horseshoe-shaped cove. Low boulders and a spread of wind-warped alders obscured the other. Several feet upslope, the sand gave way to a tangled forest of lichen-encrusted trees. Grunting, I raised my head and looked out to sea. Water-man's Beaver floatplane rode at anchor a dozen yards off-shore. Heading for the beach was the assailant himself, paddling a small inflatable dinghy.

Playing possum, I pressed my cheek to the cold, wet sand. Waterman beached the dinghy and picked up a long-handled spade. Cowboy boots kicking up plumes of fine sand, he headed upslope for a look at me. I lay perfectly still, observing him through slitted eyelids.

Leaning against the spade's long handle, Waterman gave a soft grunt of satisfaction. The victim, he thought, was still out cold. Chin up, he looked around carefully. The incoming tide washed his boots. Hefting the spade, he strolled away to my left.

So he'd made two trips, I figured. The first with Angie, the second with the tool needed for her burial. I had no idea where I was, but my best guess made it a distant and little-visited cove on one of the smaller islands. A placid final resting place for the pilot's latest victim.

Chuff-sigh, chuff-sigh. The spade bit deeply into damp sand. Cool skin prickled at the back of my neck. It is a very disconcerting thing to hear your own grave being dug. That sound conjured up even more disturbing imagery. Waterman lifting his spade high. The metal blade crashing down hard on my Anishinabe skull. The pilot dragging me by the ankles across the beach. Dead princess rolling into the crumbling grave. And finally, the swift cascade of all-concealing sand.

A muted high-pitched sound drifted through the night, sending a dreadful shiver through me. Waterman was whis-tling. I even recognized the macabre tune. "Roll Me Over in the Clover." Roll me over, lay me down, and do it again.

Just like you did with Mona. Wham-bam! You're dead, ma'am. I caught the flavor of delighted anticipation in his cheery whistling. Truly a man who enjoyed his work.

Killing Mona Hanauer with his fists had provided Waterman with a unique erotic thrill. Smashing Angie's skull with that spade would provide an amusing variation of the same theme. And, once I'd been taken care of, no doubt Waterman would continue to explore the sexual aspects of woman slaying. That's the thing about murder. It definitely can be habit-forming.

Just then, a rampart of sea foam rushed up the beach. I held my breath, averting my face, but I still got a soaking. I stifled my instinctive cry of dismay, reminding myself to be thankful that we'd gotten here at high tide. Otherwise, I might still be lying unconscious beside that big driftwood log, heedless of the killer lifting his spade for that final, fatal blow.

My shivering intensified. Grimacing with strain, I twisted my wrists in a futile attempt to loosen those knots.

Then, sobbing in frustration, I fell back helplessly on the sand. No use! The seawater had already shrunken the fibers. There was no way I could pull those knots apart. I needed a knife.

I cast a desperate glance at the floatplane. Undoubtedly there was a blade in Waterman's tool kit. For all the good *that* did me!

Raising my head, I peered over the log. Waterman was about thirty yards away, his back to me, shovelling with brisk, energetic sweeps. He was already up to his ankles. A small white mound grew rapidly on his right.

I sent my frantic gaze scurrying around the beach. I needed something to cut these ropes. A knife . . . a shard of glass . . . a sharp stone . . . *anything!*

Darkened sands mocked me. The nearest stone lay a dozen yards away, scattered among the alders.

Furious tears stung my eyelashes. Gritting my teeth, I

struggled against the rope's relentless grip. In no time at all, Waterman would have my grave finished, and then he'd be back for me.

Suddenly, something prodded my bare leg. I flinched immediately, letting out a whispery gasp. A crab scuttled beneath the arch of my leg, heading for the sea. Then a second crab skittered past my face.

Of course, I realized. It's high tide. The crabs are coming out to forage.

High tide! Inspiration sent a surge of adrenaline pulsing through my chilled and weary limbs. I remembered my Saturday chat with clammer Ed Nardinger on Sahale Point. Lowering my chin, I aimed my desperate gaze at those moist glistening sands.

And there they were—sand dimples!

Nardinger had told me that clams burrow to the surface at high tide to feed. Sand dimples mark the spot where they lay. With the tide coming in, there might be one or two clams within easy reach.

Shakily I rose to my knees. Grit-clogged hair swung into my face. Spitting, I shook it aside, then crossed the sand on my chafed kneecaps. Wobbly step after wobbly step, my knees sinking into the gritty mush. Seawater soaked my tea-rose skirt. Then the rope pulled tight, triggering a fireburst of pain at my wrists. End of the line, princess.

With a hushed gasp, I plopped onto my side. Tidal foam tickled my face. Rolling onto my spine, I put my weight on my shoulder blades. Kept it off my trussed wrists. Limbo Angie. Ignoring my throbbing headache, I dug my moccasin heel into the wet sand, then pushed with all my strength.

Again! My foot plowed a furrow through the muck. Calf muscles trembled at the strain. Again! My moccasin went deeper this time. Something hard and ribbed scraped my bare ankle.

Clam! I gave it one last push, snowplowing my way through the sodden sand. Then, rolling onto my side, I wig-

337

gled through the soft moist sand and thrust my swollen fingers into the muddy trench.

My fingernails sideswept a rigid shell. The clam was withdrawing into the sand, trying to escape the intruder. Oh, no, you don't! I thought, driving my right hand into the trench wall. A clam as big as a bar of soap wriggled away from my palm. Huffing and puffing, I thrust deeper and got my fingers around him. And then, with a savage gasp of triumph, I rolled away from the collapsing ditch.

I shot a hasty glance at Waterman. He was still digging away, only now he was visible from the knees up. My heart thudded frantically against my rib cage. I had to move fast. He would be reaching the waterline in just a few minutes, and he wouldn't bother digging any deeper than that.

Keeping a firm grip on my shelled prize, I crawled back to the log. This task would have been a whole lot easier with a hammer or a nutcracker, but all I had to work with was that weathered wood. Sitting upright, I threw the clam against the driftwood log. And hoped my moccasined feet could break it open.

Roll you over in the sand, princess. Roll you over, lift both legs, and strike that shellfish just as hard as you can. Strike it again and again. Gritting my teeth, I gave it another two-footed smash. Dammit, why did I change shoes? A Bandolino heel would have cracked that shell on the third stomp. But all I had were my own heels, sheathed in doeskin, and they were beginning to blister and swell.

Success! Jaws agape, the clam bounced off the iron-hard deadwood. Rotating on my fanny. I worked my thumbs between the halves and broke them apart. The shell's keen edge bit into soft flesh. Yeeeesh! No wonder they call them *razor clams!* The stinging pain took my mind off my sore heels.

Leaning forward, I took one clamshell and slid its razor-sharp edge across the restraining rope. Back and forth, back and forth. Tufts of manila fiber caressed my fingertips. As silent as those roving crabs, I sawed away at my tether, listening with deep satisfaction to the whisper of parting strands.

Let's give it a try, shall we?

Bunching my shoulders, I lunged forward, and the rope parted with a dismayingly audible snap.

Ohhhhh, I hope he didn't hear that! I thought, struggling to my feet.

A glance at the pit, however, told me how forlorn that hope really was. Waterman stood knee-deep in the grave, hefting the spade like a rifle, his face swivelling my way. Stark fury glittered behind those steel-rimmed glasses. "How the blazes—!?"

Up the beach I ran, lightheaded and swaying, still clutching the clamshell behind my back. The wrist bonds could wait. First order of business was putting some distance between myself and that lunatic. I scooted past the wind-twisted alders, hopped a dwarf cedar, and dashed into the gloomy rain forest. My night vision showed me a muddy trail meandering uphill into a stand of cedars. Exactly where I *didn't* want to go! So I ran twenty feet up the trail, made a bounding leap into a patch of knee-high ferns, and, still gripping the shell, dropped behind a moss-covered boulder.

"Anne Marie!" Waterman's shouts spooked the cormorants. Wings fluttered in the treetops. "You can't get away, you know."

Ignoring him, I squatted on my haunches, one shoulder at rest against the damp moss, and falteringly placed the clamshell's sharp edge against my wrist knots. My fingers felt like numb sausages. Clenching my teeth, I shakily moved the shell back and forth.

Brandishing the spade, Waterman tiptoed up the trail. "Do you really think you can hide from me?"

Frantically I sliced away at the sodden ropes. I'm going to give it one hell of a try, Jon-boy.

"You little fool!" Waterman's enraged face swivelled left and right. Knuckles whitened as he firmed up his grip on the handle. "This island's no bigger than a football field. You can't hide for very long."

Are you kidding? I thought. There's enough cover in this forest to keep me safely hidden until I'm Chief's age.

"Show yourself!" They probably heard that bellow in Seattle. Waterman's merciless gaze zigzagged through the forest. "I'll make it quick, Anne Marie." The promise sounded sincere, but that feral grin of his hinted otherwise. "One blow . . ." He swung like Babe Ruth. Steel hummed as it split the air. "Then it's all over. Come on, lovey. Make it easy on yourself."

All at once, the rope's grip slackened. Wriggling my hands free, I dropped the clamshell, then peered around the side of the boulder.

Waterman hustled up the trail, looking around in frustration. His boots made squishy noises in the thick mud. "Goddamn you!" He stirred up the cormorants again. I could barely hear him over their frenzied squawking. "Where the hell are you?"

Rubbing my chafed wrists, I watched him enter the cedar grove. Decision time! Sure, I could elude him for a few weeks. The Caucasian hasn't been born who's a match for this Anishinabe princess in the woods. But that wasn't exactly advisable. Not in these wet clothes. People have been known to die of hypothermia in sodden clothes at a nighttime temperature of only fifty degrees.

If I truly intended to survive, I needed to find some shelter—*fast!*—and to dry my soaked garments. That meant I had to find some way to either escape the island or else overcome Waterman.

First things first, princess. Reduce the danger of hypothermia. Get some of the moisture out of these clothes.

So I did an impromptu striptease in the lee of that boulder, taking care to stay out of the night breeze. Couldn't afford to let the windchill factor steal any more of my precious bodily warmth. Off with the jacket, the blouse and the skirt. Shivering uncontrollably, I sat back on my chafed heels, took my jacket in hand, and savagely twisted it round and round, squeezing out the water. A hearty stream dribbled from its upside-down collar.

Then I repeated the procedure with my blouse and skirt. The persistent shivering was starting to drain my strength. Squeezing worsened the pins-and-needles sensation in my puffed hands, but I gritted my teeth and kept at it. I had to squeeze as much moisture out of those clothes as possible.

As I went about my prehistoric washday chores, I mulled over a number of plans to bushwack and disable Waterman. All seemed foolishly risky. Without a weapon of my own, I had little chance of disabling a taller, heavier, physically fit pilot.

One plan, however, appealed to me. Double back to the beach, grab the dinghy, and row out to the plane. I could taxi out into the sound, use the cockpit heater to dry off, and radio the Coast Guard. As I donned my slightly damp clothes once more, that scheme began to look more and more attractive.

Sure! I thought, stealing away into the underbrush. I'd leave Waterman stranded on the island. Then I'd radio the Coast Guard and tell them were to pick him up. After that, I'd take the dinghy and row over to one of the other islands. Pleased Angie smile. Hmmmmm, maybe I wouldn't have to surrender to the FBI, after all.

The hushed sound of incoming surf lured me to the beach. I stepped boldly onto the sand, thoroughly enchanted with my clever plan. Twenty yards ahead stood the rocky headland, partially obscuring my view of the anchored floatplane. I set off with a leisurely swagger.

So delighted was I was my clever plan that I nearly didn't hear the sound of ragged male breathing forty yards behind me. The instant the sound registered, I whirled. And there he was—Jon Waterman, with his spade held high, charging down the beach like an enraged buffalo.

"Oh, shit!" I yelped, and I was off—Jackrabbit Angie—running at top speed for that rocky headland. And kicking myself for my presumed cleverness, which somehow failed to take into consideration the fact that Waterman undoubtedly knew this island a whole lot better than I did. That he was well aware that his dinghy was the only means of escape. And that when he failed to find me in the cedar grove, he just naturally picked out the best observation spot on the island, secure in the knowledge that Angie would eventually appear on the beach. Gasping for breath, I quickened my step. Damn! Your cleverness will be the death of you yet, Miss Biwaban!

Loose sand tugged at my moccasins. I felt myself sinking with every step. Waterman's angry breathing seemed ominously close.

To hell with this! I thought, veering toward the sea. The damp packed sand at the water's edge offered a better, more solid running surface. I ran like a frightened deer. Waterman's furious bellow rang out twenty yards astern. I put everything I had into it, my knees churning high, sprinting on the balls of my feet.

Gasping and sobbing, I scrambled up the sandstone face of the headland. Loose stones clattered away beneath my churning moccasins. The spongy moss offered fitful handholds. Gripping some skyline weeds, I grunted and hauled myself onto the summit. And then let out a shrill cry of despair!

On the floatplane side, the headland fell away abruptly, leaving a sheer fifteen-foot wall. At its foot lay a broad sandy hollow overgrown with lush eelgrass. Instantly the sight kindled a twinge of alarm. Ed Nardinger's warning reverberated in my mind. *Tidal pool!*

High tide had saturated those sands, turning the entire hollow into a deceptively deadly quicksand bog. I didn't dare jump for it. Even with a running start, I'd never reach the high, dry sand on the far side.

I shot a hasty fearful glance back up the beach. Waterman was coming up fast, clutching his spade like a spear. He loped along like a Klallam warrior stalking an elk. His narrow features split in a murderous grin.

Trapped!

Okay, I couldn't jump, but maybe—just maybe—I could climb. Sliding my legs over the brink, I felt with my toes for a sandstone ledge. The first pebble-strewn shelf I touched snapped noisily, but the second held my weight. Gripping the turf with all ten fingers, I eased myself over the edge.

Careful, Angie, careful. Lose your grip now, and you'll land smack dab in the middle of that tidal pool. Come on, girl. You did a little mountaineering at North Cascades. And how many times have you climbed those cliffs at Shovel Point? Keep your face pressed to the rocky wall—that's it. Feel for firm footing with your moccasined toes. Slowwwwwly . . .

Now down the cliff we go. Hand over hand. Just like descending a ladder, right? Cheek jammed against the gritty sandstone, I saw that the headland extended well behind the tidal pool. With luck I could work my way over there—get close enough to dry sand to safely make the jump.

I inched downward. Eelgrass fronds waved languidly several feet below. Aching fingers dug their way into a stony crevice. Again I extended my trembling leg to the left. Probing toes found another firm ledge. Sudden hysterical chuckle. Suddenly I was very, very glad that I'd worn my moccasins. No way could I have ever done this in Bandolino heels.

A merciless baritone laugh erupted overhead. Looking up, I saw Waterman kneeling at the headland's brink. The spade wavered threateningly. "What's the matter?" he teased. "Afraid of heights?"

Instantly I understood his intention and scrambled farther down the cliff's face. Hearing the sudden rush of displaced air, I ducked my head.

343

Clang! The spade splintered the sandstone shelf above me. Grit and pebbles cascaded onto my back.

Clang! I'd plucked my hand off that ledge just in time. Waterman was determined to dislodge my grip. And I couldn't let him do that. If I fell now, I'd land right in the middle of that quicksand.

Clang! Clang! He took wildass swings at my head and hands, but I managed to stay out of range. An avalanche of rock chips pelted my spine. I climbed still lower, my cheek rasping the rough stone. Quicksand remained deceptively motionless three feet below my moccasin heels.

Sobbing aloud, I ducked as the spade whizzed above my head.

"Son of a bitch!" Waterman swore. Frustration was getting to him. He was lying prone on the summit, swinging the spade with both hands. And my every downward motion took me farther beyond his reach. The spade wigwagged back and forth, but he couldn't dislodge me. He needed leverage to maneuver that long-handled shovel effectively, and he couldn't do it lying there on his stomach.

Clang! The spade rebounded off a small protuberance. Waterman let out a howl of fury. The impact had dislodged his grip. Hugging the cliffside, I screamed as the spade cartwheeled past. One very frightened Anishinabe princess perched a precarious thirty-five inches above the tidal pool. Shoulder muscles pulsed in agony. My feet wobbled on a crumbling ledge. I wasn't sure how much longer I could hold on.

"Bloody hell!" Impatience got the better of him. Rising to his knees, he hollered, "Damn you! You won't escape!" Then he scrambled to his feet. "I'll pull you off that bloody wall!"

Waterman took a single backward step, readying himself. Insane fury glittered in his bluish gray eyes.

Open-mouthed, I gaped in absolute horror.

And down he plummeted, his jacket fluttering in the slipstream, both feet poised to land like a paratrooper. I averted my gaze.

Sploosh! Sandy muck spattered my skirt. Waterman's plunge submerged him all the way to the collarbone. An animalistic howl tore the tissues of his throat.

"No! No!" he screeched, flailing both arms in blind panic. Glasses askew on his face, he looked around in horror. Clawing hands ripped the floating eelgrass. The ooze lapped hungrily at his neck.

"Relax!" I shouted. Probing with hand and foot, I struggled to reach the small bluff at the rear of the tidal pool. "Waterman, listen to me. It's quicksand. You have to relax." If I could find a long enough branch, I might be able to help him. "Stop kicking! You're digging yourself in deeper!"

"Help meeeee!" Eyes bulging, he fought to keep his fear-filled face above the surface.

"Relax! Get on your back and float." Aghast, I watched the quicksand creep up the sides of his face. And I knew I'd never make it to dry land in time. "Relax and float!"

"I can't!" he shrieked, his head tossing maniacally. His steel-rimmed glasses twirled through the air, shattered against the cliff, and then vanished with a muted *ker-plunk!* Spitting damp sand out of his mouth, he wailed, "Aaaagh . . . I-I can't swim!"

Sickened, I put my forehead to the sandstone. Finally I understood how Mona had escaped him that night. Former lifeguard Mona had taken refuge in the sea, knowing that her ex-lover could not possibly follow.

Squeezing my eyes shut, I listened to the dreadful cacophony of screams and gasps and gurgles. Then a profound silence encompassed the tidal pool. Somewhere in the distance, a lone cormorant squawked. I forced myself to look, and my stomach did a complete flipflop.

Only a single motionless hand jutted from the fluid sands.

By the time I reached the bluff, even that had disappeared.

For the rest of the night, I sat on a dune overlooking the tidal pool, sobbing and shivering and trying my best to forget the horror I'd just witnessed. Trembling with profound relief at my own razor-thin escape. And knowing full well that Waterman's death had just taken up residence in the compartment of most fearsome memories.

One hideous image I'll never forget—a freeze-frame of horror that will stay with me all the days of my life. That stunned expression on Waterman's face the instant his boots penetrated what he believed to be solid ground.

Never had I seen anyone look quite so *surprised*.

Saturday, twenty-fourth day of October. A crisp morning free of fog. Standing at the kitchen window of my temporary new home, I studied the patchwork blue sky and wondered if I ought to risk a daylight cruise over to Orcas.

My new residence was a beachfront holiday cabin on Lummi Island. Judging from the postcards tucked into the bedroom mirror frame, the place belonged to a family named Rozinka. Strictly summer occupancy, though. The TV and radio were gone. The water and the electricity had been disconnected. The Rozinkas had secured their thick windowless storm door with a shiny new padlock.

But the lock had yielded to the jackknife I'd found in the Beaver's toolbox. Fortunately, the Rozinka kids had left some food on the shelf—a box of Cheerios, two cans of carrots, a box of Bisquick and a can of tuna. And there was an Ardennes wood stove, plus a goodly supply of weathered wood in the bin beneath the house. All the comforts of home.

I'd gotten to Lummi Thursday morning about an hour after sunrise. With a few minor variations, my escape plan had worked rather well. As soon as I felt strong enough to walk, I'd stumbled back to the beach, loaded up the dinghy, and then paddled out to Waterman's anchored floatplane. After

I got the engine started, it took me the better part of an hour to safely taxi away from Clark Island.

I didn't know it was Clark, of course. Not at first. Not until I studied the fading color map of the San Juans pinned to the wall of the Rozinka parlor.

Sunrise found me adrift in the Strait of Georgia. Minus tide gently rocked the floatplane. I retrieved the tool kit, survival kit, canteen and life jacket from the Beaver's equipment bay. Then I filched some cash from my own wallet, leaving it and my shoulder bag carelessly strewn about the cockpit floor. I wiped away any telltale fingerprints, then made certain that the AVR cassette recorder with Waterman's confession was still beneath the pilot's seat.

And then it was . . . *abandon ship!*

As I paddled the dinghy toward Lummi's forested shore, I wondered what the Coast Guard would make of the derelict Beaver. To say nothing of those tantalizing hints of foul play. A headline blazed in my mind. WHERE IS ANNE MARIE NAHKEETA?

Another mystery of the sea.

By Friday morning, I knew the floatplane had been found. Judging from the frequency of the overflights, I'd say the authorities were mighty anxious to lay their hands on me and Jon Waterman.

That night, a county mountie came down the shore road and aimed his spotlight at the Rozinka cabin. Fortunately, my ears had detected the laboring rumble of that big Chrysler engine before he reached the bend. I had plenty of time to retreat to my hideyhole in the cedar forest.

First thing Saturday morning, I fired up the old wood stove, heated a few gallons of well water, tossed my tea-rose suit in the bathtub, grabbed a bar of soap, and did my laundry the pioneer way. Afterward, dwarfed in Mr. Rozinka's castaway vacation clothes, I hung the wash out on the line.

Believe me, I never would have made the cover of *Vogue* in that outfit. Sturdy mackinaw shirt with rolled-up sleeves.

Baggy corduroy pants buttoned just beneath my bosom. And a pair of light gray slipper socks. All I needed was a white plastic belt, and I would have been all ready for the next Barry Manilow concert.

Placing one hand against the window frame, I glanced at the rapidly clearing sky. With no radio and no TV, I had no idea what was going on in the outside world. Had they called off the search yet? Had Mick been released? Questions, questions.

At that moment, I heard a shrill four-toned bird song in the cabin's backyard. *Wheee-ah-chuck-chuck!*

Recognition triggered a fussbudget face. The song of the whiskey jack!

The bird trilled again. *Wheee-ah-chuck-chuck!*

All at once, in my mind, I was back on Clark Island, groping for that razor clam, hiding in the rain-soaked forest, running down that stretch of darkened beach with an enraged Waterman in hot pursuit.

Whiskey Jack! I shuddered. If I *never* hear that name again, it'll be too damned soon!

For several minutes, the bird kept up that four-toned serenade. Finally, I could stand no more. Showing a warpath scowl, I descended the back steps and strolled into the backyard.

And there he was—a plump gray Canada jay. Perched on an alder branch, he rotated his head in every direction. Jet black eyes stared in utter confusion.

I clapped my hands. "Whiskey Jack!"

Plunging from the branch like a dive-bomber, my little friend veered away from the cabin and, wings blurring, rocketed toward the other San Juans.

Three seconds later, the birdcall sounded right behind me. I stopped dead in my tracks, letting out a groan, as I realized who it was.

Salal bushes rustled. His gravelly voice held an affectionate teasing tone. "I was wondering when you were going to figure it out."

"Chiiieeef!"

He was wearing a denim jacket, brushpopper jeans, and a dark green slouch hat. A day pack dangled from his firm shoulders. We flashed each other identical welcoming smiles and then embraced beside the clothesline.

Holding me at arm's length, he chuckled. "Right about now, I wish I had my camera."

"Don't even think it!" Expression of complete embarrassment. "How'd you find me?"

"Wasn't too hard. They found Waterman's plane off Waldron Thursday afternoon. I figured, if you were still alive, you'd have to be on one of the out islands." His gaze took in the surrounding trees. "Lummi was my first choice. I saw the smoke from your chimney at dawn. Seeing as how vacation cabins are closed this time of year, that definitely stirred my interest." Aged features turned somber. "What happened, anyway? Last time I saw you in Port Wyoochee, you were on your way out of town."

"Long story, Chief," I said, putting my arm across his shoulders. "I'll explain it all over sassafras tea. Come on."

And I did. He listened avidly to it all, asking questions here and there, then he told me how he'd made up his mind to stick around Seattle when I failed to show.

Chief unzipped his day pack and withdrew a folded newspaper. Handing it to me, he muttered, "Yesterday was Port Wyoochee day in the *Post-Intelligencer*. See for yourself. You really stirred up a hornet's nest this time, missy."

While my grandfather sipped his tea, I scanned the relevant articles. There was a big photo of Waterman's plane on page one, accompanied by a banner headline. MANHUNT IN THE SAN JUANS! Just beneath was a smaller headline—HANAUER MURDER REOPENED—PILOT SOUGHT FOR SLAYING.

Further on in the lengthy article, I encountered myself.

Still missing and presumed dead is another alleged victim of Waterman's, Anne Marie Nahkeeta of Port Wyoochee.

Witnesses identified the woman's voice on the Waterman tape as Nahkeeta's.

Police believe Waterman murdered Nahkeeta and dropped her body in the sound after the tape was made.

However, FBI agent Walter Channing said the search for Nahkeeta would continue.

"This woman has been the subject of an ongoing Bureau investigation," Channing said. "We believe the suspect Waterman assisted this woman in leaving town. We have many questions for Waterman once he has been safely apprehended."

Fussbudget frown. So the hunt for Pocahontas continues, eh? Well, maybe if I behave myself for the next seven years, the FBI will finally accept the theory that Anne Marie Nahkeeta perished in Puget Sound.

Happier news filled the inside pages. A photo of Davey Rotenberg's reunion with his frantic and relieved parents. An in-depth interview with Lisa entitled *My Night of Terror*. A short piece of Mick's release from jail.

All at once, Lemuel Thurber's name caught my eye. Peering over the newspaper, I scowled at my grandfather. "Suicide attempt?"

"His second one." Chief put down his teacup. "Tacoma paper broke the story about his dad. After he read it, Thurber put his pistol in his mouth. Aides talked him out of it. Then there was a helluva rumpus at the Adamite church. His own people threw him out on his ass. Kept callin' him a Mossad infiltrator. Fella just couldn't take it. He called a news conference yesterday morning and tried to eat his gun again. He got sent to Steilacoom for observation. Heard that on the radio this morning."

Shaking my head, I folded the paper and put it aside. Steilacoom. Like mother, like son. Tessie's boy had followed in her tragic footsteps all the way.

I told myself I wasn't going to feel sorry for him. After all, Steve Sargent wasn't the only one I'd heard talking about a marshmallow roast.

Still, Thurber had a life, and perhaps some day, with the doctors' help, he could make something worthwhile of it. There were no second chances for the lady Mona.

Or at the bottom of that tidal pool.

"You given some thought to getting off this here island?" my grandfather asked. "Or are you planning to take up permanent residence?"

Carrying our stained cups to the sink, I replied, "Well, it's Saturday. There's bound to be a few coeds biking over on Orcas. I thought I might row over there. Blend in and ride home on the ferry."

"Wouldn't advise it." He came over and handed me his teaspoon. "There's some Bureau boys watchin' the dock in Anacortes. You'd never get past them."

Putting the kettle on the wood stove, I asked, "How'd you get over here?"

"Sea kayak." He pantomimed a rowing motion as he sat down again. "Big enough for two. I've got it tucked away on the other side of the island." Knowledgeable Anishinabe smile. "Soon as it gets dark, we can cross over to Bellingham."

"Kind of risky, wasn't it? Renting that kayak?" I asked, turning away from the stove. "The dealer's liable to remember you."

"I didn't rent it, child. I bought it. He helped me load it on my car. Thinks I took it home to Port Angeles."

Delighted Angie grin. "Smart!"

"I'm glad you think so, Angela. You can pay me back as soon as we reach South Dakota."

"*What?*"

"You heard me. Re-im-burse-ment." Chief tasted each and every syllable, then shook his head wryly. "You really burned up the bucks this time, didn't you? No one is ever going to believe you used to be a business major."

"Chief!"

"Not only that ..." His obsidian eyes flashed fire. "But you are going to row, too!"

I glared in frustration. "What has gotten into you, anyway?"

"Consider it your punishment, young lady, for what I've gone through these past forty-eight hours." Haunted gaze. "How do you think I felt, Angie, turning on the radio and hearing that my granddaughter was *missing and presumed dead?*"

Maybe a half-dozen flippant remarks entered my mind at that moment. Seeing my grandfather's troubled expression, though, I squelched them all, came up behind his chair, and gave him a warm, loving hug.

"You know, I haven't really thanked you for coming back for me." Kissing the top of his snowy head, I murmured, *"Mügwetch, Nimishoo."*

Chief smiled, his broad hand patting my wrist.

I hugged tighter. "Still mad?"

And then, in a low-pitched voice, he began to sing. "Row, row, row the boat swiftly across the strait!"

Giggling, I swatted his shoulder. "That's *not* how it goes."

He grinned up at me. "You used to love that song when you were a papoose."

Crooked Angie smile. "I like to think my taste in music has improved."

"Would you like to hear a contrary opinion?"

Bursting into laughter, I gave him one more Anishinabe-sized bear hug. "Let's go home, Chief."

If you liked *Whiskey Jack,* watch for Angela Biwaban's next adventure, *Corona Blue,* coming to bookstores in October.

Corona Blue

"How do you pronounce this?" the honey-haired deputy asked.

Sprawled in an aged oak chair, I let out a weary sigh. "Biwaban. *Bih-wah-bahn.*" I cast an anxious look at the big wall-mounted Western Electric clock. Twelve minutes past six. I wondered what time they fed the prisoners here at the Davison County sheriff's office.

Carefully she looked over my intake forms. I'd spent the last eighty minutes filling them out. Detailed questionnaires about my personal and medical histories, my involvement with the criminal justice system, and my term of service at the South Dakota Correctional Facility for Women at Springfield.

The deputy was in her middle twenties. She had the posture and queenly bearing of a high school gymnast. Pretty Slavic features, slightly cleft chin, stern and businesslike emerald-tinted eyes. Her hair was pulled back in a taut, nononsense bun. A generous bosom disturbed the fabric of her khaki uniform shirt. She'd probably heard more than her share of tiresome jokes in the squadroom. The mammary swell aimed her shirt pockets at the ceiling. Pinned above the left pocket was a nameplate reading *Lambanek.*

"This one here?" She tapped her pencil against the page. That high forehead wrinkled in confusion. The small lipsticked mouth tried to shape the word. "Ay-ah-ah-nih—"

"Ah-nish-ih-nah-bay," I said. "It means *original people.* It's what we call ourselves."

Deputy Lambanek pursed her lips. "Is-is that some kind of Sioux?"

I grinned. Better not let my ancestor, Kichiwaubishashe, hear that. He led the Noka, the Black Bear clan, against the Lakotas three hundred years ago, during the war for control of the Oshkebuge-zibi. The River of the New Leaves. These days, it's known as the Minnesota River.

"Not quite," I replied. I hated to use the C-word, but I had no choice. "It's Chippewa."

Putting down the form, she said, "Well, why didn't you just write *Chippewa?"*

Somber Angie glance. "Tell me, what kind of name is Lambanek?"

She flashed me a guarded look. "It's Czech."

"Would you like it if I called you a *hunkie?"*

"Of course not!"

"Right. Because it's insulting," I added, crossing my legs. "Like calling Italian people wops. That's how *we* feel about the word *Chippewa."*

Unwilling to discuss the issue any further, the deputy returned to her paperwork. Judging from the highly annoyed look on her face, this wasn't the moment to ask about supper. So I laced my fingers together, settled back in the roomy chair and glanced around the sheriff's office.

It was about the size of a ranch house kitchen. Oaken furniture dating from the McKinley administration. Ten-year-old desktop computers. Plastered walls painted a sallow light green. Someone had put up a pair of colorful posters touting the Corn Palace. Most of the desks were empty. One youthful deputy manned the dispatch console. Across the room, my nemesis, Deputy Kramer, tentatively tapped out his arrest report with two uncertain index fingers.

I had already been through one round of indignities—booking, fingerprinting, strip-search and breathalyzer test.

There were two charges against me, malicious mischief and operating a farm vehicle under the influence of alcohol.

It would be interesting to see the results of that breathalyzer test.

"Sign here." Deputy Lambanek rolled a pen across her surprisingly tidy desk-top, then followed up with a thick pile of intake documents. "One signature on each form." Lacquered red fingernails tap-tapped her telephone. "Soon as you're done, you can make your phone call."

So I began signing, pondering the greatest of all mysteries. Namely, how did the new people ever get *Chippewa* out of *Anishinabe?*

One case of writer's cramp later, I dropped the pen and reached for the telephone receiver. My first impulse was to call my grandfather in Minnesota. Then I hesitated. My anxious gaze flitted toward the deputy's desk calendar.

Damn! I would have to get arrested this week. Right now Chief's closing up our cabin at Tettegouche. He might still be there. Then again, he might've already moved back to the Fond du Lac reservation. Fifty-fifty shot either way. If I guess wrong, there goes my one and only phone call.

If it was up to Chief, he'd live at Tettegouche all year round. But the family gets a little nervous about a seventy-five-year-old man living out there all by himself. One good Lake Superior blizzard, and he'd be snowbound for days.

Briefly I considered my parole officer. However, it was too late in the day to reach Paul. The Department of Corrections office closed at five.

That left me with one other option.

Disarming Angie smile. "Can I make a long-distance call?"

The deputy lifted her chin. "Where to?"

"Pine Ridge."

"Go ahead. But make it short."

My fingers tapped out the number. The speech center of my brain changed gears, shifting from English to Lakotiya.

357

I had plenty to say, and I didn't want Kramer or Lambanek listening in. Two rings, and a vaguely familiar female voice came on line. "Hello?"

"Hau, Ina Echam'namapeya!" I said, *"Jill tokiyaya he?"*

"Angie!" Mrs. Stormcloud's voice was a blend of surprise and regret. "You just missed her. Her date picked her up fifteen minutes ago. Where are you calling from?"

"Mitchell. The sheriff's office. I'm in trouble, Mother Stormcloud. Real trouble!"

"What's wrong, *winchinyona?*"

"There's this deputy, He's a real *oonzeh odoka.*" I sneaked a glance at Kramer. Oblivious to the insult, he kept right on typing. "I think he's related to Custer. He pulled me in on some bullshit charge. It's a roust, Mother Stormcloud, pure and simple. Grab a pencil and pad, would you?"

Paper rustled at the other end of the line. "Go ahead, Angie."

"Have Jill get in touch with my grandfather. If he's not at Tettegouche, try the Fond du Lac reservation in Minnesota." I rattled off the area code and number. "And get me a lawyer! I'm due to appear in district court first thing tomorrow morning. If I don't have counsel, that deputy's going to ship my ass straight back to Springfield."

"Understood, *hokshayopa.* Do you want Jill to get in touch with your parole officer?"

"Don't bother, Mother Stormcloud. He'll get the word." Doleful frown. No doubt there'd be a teletype from the Sheriff's Department sitting on Paul's blotter first thing in the morning.

"I'm calling Jill at the Cineplex right now. Don't you worry, Angie. We'll get you out of there." I could feel the concern in her voice. "Take care of yourself."

Grinning, I replied, *"Lila pilamaya, Ina Echam'namapeya. Wakan Tanka nici un."*

After I hung up, Deputy Lambanek ordered me out of the chair, seized my upper arm, and conducted me downstairs to the Depression-era cellblock. Stale odors buffeted my face as we marched down the well-lit corridor. The stiff scent of ammonia predominated, but I could still detect traces of dried urine and alcoholic vomit.

"Here we are." Deputy Lambanek introduced me to my accommodations. The cell was five-by-five, with steel bars on three sides and a peeling cinderblock wall at the rear. Two fold-down steel-frame beds were chained to either side. Rolled-up mattress pads were tucked between the chain and the frame. There was a distinct lack of blankets. Even less inviting was the leaking porcelain toilet bowl in the right rear corner.

Jangling of keys. Creaking of tired hinges. Tart feminine command of "Inside!" And the door clanged shut with a dreadful finality. The cell was slightly roomier than my old *personal space* at Springfield but nowhere near as pleasant as the Thunderbird Lodge.

Turning, I eyed the grim-faced deputy through the intervening bars. "Any chance of supper?"

Deep frown. The kind deputies reserve for people with prison records. "We don't offer room service, Miss Biwaban."

I was hungry enough, so I swallowed my pride. "I haven't had a bite to eat since five this morning."

Sympathy softened her features. Rehanging the keys on her belt, she murmured, "I'll see what I can do."

"Thank you." I wasn't being sarcastic. I already had one enemy in that sheriff's office. I didn't need to lock horns with the entire department. One thing I learned in the Big Dollhouse—you don't survive without friends among the guards.

I unrolled the mattress, patted it down, and then stretched out, using my forearm as a pillow. Long sigh of dismay. No telling how long I'd be a houseguest of Sheriff Fischer's, I thought, so I might as well get comfortable.

Staring at the ceiling, I thought about my good friend and

former cellmate, Jill Stormcloud. We spent many an evening in hushed, lengthy conversation. Discussing what women in prison usually talk about—their men and their mothers. When we finally exhausted those topics, we made a game of teaching each other our respective languages. Thanks to Jill, I could speak Lakotiya as fluently as anyone at Pine Ridge.

Sorry to ruin your evening, *amiga*. But I'm going to need your help if I'm to avoid a return engagement at the prison laundry.

Then I thought of Deputy Kramer. Sudden warpath scowl. Son of a bitch! I wonder how many ex-cons that bastard's put behind bars. Kind of a sloppy job at the crime scene, too. He didn't even try to search the area. He made a snap judgment and slapped the handcuffs on. Bet he's a political appointee. Probably has a relative on the county board.

Well, I was grateful to the deputy for one thing. My arrest had whisked me out of the danger zone. For the time being, I was safely out of the killer's gunsights. He wouldn't be able to reach me. Not in here.

Wry Angie smile. You've really done it this time, princess. You're the only witness to a murder in which the corpse has disappeared. The killer saw you at the scene. He knows that you know. Worse than that, he knows what you look like! And you didn't even get a glimpse of him.

Frosty paranoid shiver. Mister Beach Tan's killer could conceivably be anyone in Mitchell. Male, female . . .

Hmmmmm, maybe we can scratch female. Mister Beach Tan tipped the scales at close to two hundred. I didn't know very many women who could lift that much weight on their own. Unless the killer was Rachel McLish. Which I doubted!

My forehead tensed in bewilderment. How did he do it? I wondered. How did he pull that vanishing act with the corpse?

Forcefully I redirected my thoughts. Pondering that would keep me awake all night. Crossing my legs at the ankle, I gazed ruefully at the ceiling and wondered what Paul would say about all this.

Good old Holbrook. If anybody could get Sheriff Fischer to take me seriously, my stalwart parole office could.

Just then, I heard a clamor in the outer hallway. Swinging my legs off the bunk, I sat up straight. Into the cellblock came a parade of civilians, men and women in raingear and heavyweight jackets. Puzzled frown. Surely the sheriff didn't permit guided tours of the county jail!

Then I noticed the trio of somber deputies moving the column along. The lawmen segregated the group by gender and marched the men farther down the hall. Into my cell-block streamed the ladies—some of them alarmed, some of them angry, most of them highly excited—chattering at each other. The lead deputy had to holler to make himself heard. "Awright! Pair off! Two to a cell. Let's not take all night, ladies."

A couple of minutes later, the stern-featured deputy led one of the women to my cell. She was in her middle twenties, two or three inches taller than me, with short ash-blond hair that looked as if it had been styled by Mr. Christophe, a pert nose, a slight overbite, elegantly trimmed eyelashes and maybe a shade too much mascara. Large silvery loop earrings dangled from her small delicate ears. Navy peacoat, snug indigo jeans and a cream knit turtleneck that tickled her chin like a surgical neck brace.

"Hey, Biwaban!" The deputy's key rattled in the lock. "Got a roommate for you. Fresh fish!" The barred door swung open. "Better listen good, Sievert. She'll tell you what to expect when you get to Springfield."

As the woman stepped over the threshold, I heard a faint sharp smack. My roommate's mouth dropped open. Bluish gray eyes sparkled in rage. "Owww! Son of a—!"

Clang! The lock snapped shut. Gingerly touching the seat of her jeans, Ms. Sievert glared at the chuckling deputy.

"Friend of yours?" I asked, rising from my bunk.

361

She gave me a look. "Hardly!" Turning away from the door, she added, "His name's Linton. He comes into the bank all the time. Until tonight, he's been content to stare." Uncertain smile. Tentative extension of her long-fingered hand. "Uh, hi! I'm Julie Sievert."

Flashing a warm, reassuring smile, I gave her hand a gentle shake. "You're a banker?"

"Teller, actually. At the Commercial Bank over on North Lawler." Rueful grimace. "That may change, though. Especially if Mr. Dillard sees the eleven o'clock news. And you?"

"Angie Biwaban. Apprentice farmer."

"Excuse me?"

"It's a long story." I was mightily intrigued by the campaign button on Julie's peacoat. Big white button with the letters SPSD. I tilted my head toward the other prisoners. "What's all this about?"

"We were holding a protest rally over in Mount Vernon," Julie explained, folding her arms. "Protesting that new transmission line Sam Covington wants to run through the county. About fifty of us showed up."

"You were arrested for trespassing?"

Julie nodded. "The sheriff busted us right after we put our group's stickers on the tower. He said that was vandalism."

"What was on the sticker?"

"Here, I'll show you."

Julie reached into her coat pocket and withdrew a bright orange plastic sticker. The face showed a transmission tower and the legend *Warning: This tower is hazardous to your health.*

"What does SPSD stand for?" I asked.

"Safe Power for South Dakota," she replied. "My boyfriend Scott started the group. He's a physics professor at Dakota Wesleyan." Curious look. "I don't think I've seen you around town. Where are you from?"

"Duluth, Minnesota, originally. I was living in Pierre. Just moved to Yorktown last week."

The women in the adjoining cell came over to the bars.

One of them gave me a long, searching look. She was a farm wife, aged thirty-five or thereabouts, with a round, sun-weathered face, curly dark brown hair and a slightly protruding lower lip. Recognition gleamed in her acorn brown eyes. "Hey, ain't you Josh Elderkin's hired girl?"

"That's right." Winsome Angie smile.

Julie formally introduced us. "Angie, this here's Brenda Traudt. Brenda, Angie Biwaban."

I recognized the last name. The Traudts owned a dairy farm just north of the Elderkin place. Brenda was delighted to encounter a neighbor in these dismal surroundings. She fired a flurry of questions at me, inquiring about the health of Josh and Trudy and the kids and old Miss Edna, Trudy's widowed aunt.

". . . course, that pacemaker sure slowed Miss Edna down some," Brenda said. Reminiscence softened her blunt features. "She's had it ten years now, and she's still complainin'. She told me it was a damned inconvenience, havin' to change the setting every time she wanted to climb the stairs. Poor Miss Edna. She don't get around half as much as she used to. Sure is a damned shame. Well, at lest she's got Trudy to look after her now." Sudden look of intense curiosity. "What are you doin' in here, Angie?"

"I'm sort of wondering the same thing myself, Mrs. Traudt."

"What's the charge?"

"Operating a combine under the influence of alcohol."

Brown-eyed look of keen appraisal. "Don't look drunk to me. And I know drunk. My daddy came home often enough smellin' of White Mule. Made it hisself. Had him a still in the cottonwoods down along the Jim."

"Who made the arrest?" asked Julie.

"Dan Kramer," I replied.

Brenda nodded as if that explained everything. "He's snake-mean, that Danny. Couple years behind me in school. Picked a fight one time with Joe Spotted Horse. Joe whipped his ass good. Hated Indians ever since. That's one ol' boy you'd better stay away from, Angie."

"Will do!" Still curious, I led us back to the original topic of conversation. "Why were you guys out planting stickers on transmission towers?"

Julie exhaled deeply. "You're new around here. So I guess you haven't heard about the project."

"Project?" I echoed.

"The Southeast Hydroelectric Initiative Project. Otherwise known as SHIP."

Sour smile from Brenda. "Ought to stick a T on the end instead!"

"It's the brainchild of Owechahay Power," Julie added. "You've heard of them."

I had. Owechahay Power, OP for short, touted in numerous television commercials as "your energy friend," was one of the three largest electric companies in South Dakota. If ever you're in Sioux Falls, look for their lofty glassine skyscraper on Sixth Street. Can't miss it—there's a great big OP on the penthouse.

"Five years ago, the Corps of Engineers finished that new dam on the Missouri River. The Charles H. Burke Dam. OP won the contract for the hydroelectric station." Julie seated herself on the corner of my bunk. "Originally, the station was supposed to serve the Chamberlain/Oacoma area. There was supposed to be a lot of new development down there. An Indian casino, two new malls, large housing developments. Then the recession came along and ... well, that was that. OP was stuck with plenty of leftover kilowatts, so they came up with SHIP." She made a long sweeping motion with her right hand. "They want to run a brand-new transmission line due east through Brule and Aurora counties, cut through the southwest corner of Davison County, and link up with the main line in Bridgewater."

"What for?" I asked. "There can't be more than eight hundred people in Bridgewater."

"Actually, there are less. Six hundred and fifty-three, according to the last census." Julie's mouth formed a distasteful moue. "It's the usual power company scam. They promise all kinds of pie-in-the-sky benefits. Give us right-of-way, and we'll run distribution lines off the main. Industry will be knocking on your door. There'll be hundreds of new construction jobs. Best of all, your rates will be coming down."

"Bullshit!" Derisive snort from Brenda. "Hens'll be layin' six-sided eggs the day electric rates come down!"

"If OP really wanted to lower their rates, they could do it in Oacoma. There's already a power surplus." Thoroughly agitated, Julie rose from the bunk. "But no . . . to maintain their all-important fee structure, they've petitioned the Department of Public Utilities to let them ship the surplus power across three counties!"

"Gonna run that damned high-power line across some of the most productive farmland in America!" Brenda's soft chin quivered in indignation.

"How far has the project gone?" I asked.

"Brule and Aurora approved the project last year. Owechahay Power's going all out to lay the transmission line. They've already reached the northern end of Yorktown." Frowning, Julie paced our cell. "Our county board hasn't voted yet. But we hear Sam Covington's been doing a lot of politicking behind the scenes."

"Who's Covington?"

"He's chairman of the Industrial Development Commission," Julie replied. "Owns the Middle Border Savings Bank right here in town."

Brenda grinned. "No shit on that man's shoes."

One hand on a vertical bar, Julie added, "Not only is the project unnecessary, Angie, it's a direct threat to Yorktown and every township in the south county."

I thought immediately of the Elderkins. "How so?"

Features tense with concern, Julie outlined an imaginary tower with her hands. "The project is building a 900-kilovolt

365

transmission line. That's almost double the voltage carried by most power lines." She bit a corner of her lower lip. "Oh, I wish Scott were here to explain it. He's the physicist. You see, Angie, every power line generates an electromagnetic field. What we call an EMF. The hotter the power line, the larger the EMF. The plain fact is, any electrical device you plug in and use creates an EMF force field. Low-frequency fields are considered harmless. But high-frequency EMFs, such as microwaves, can severely damage animal cells."

"What's the safety limit, Julie?"

"The EMFs occurring in nature are a very weak 0.5 milligauss. The safety limit set by the EPA is 2 milligauss."

I leaned against the door frame. "And beneath a high-voltage power line?"

Julie gave me a sickish look. "That's where the real hazard lies. Standing directly beneath a 500-kilovolt line, you're exposed to 100 to 600 milligauss. The field weakens the farther away from the line you move. That's why those high-tension towers all have a right-of-way measuring 100 yards. Beyond that point, EMF exposure falls to 20 milligauss." Tart look. "Which, by the way, is *still* ten times greater than the national safety limit. But OP won't talk about that!"

Just then, the matronly woman sharing Brenda's cell stepped up to the bars. "Don't you believe a word that company says, girl. Ben and I farmed twenty-five years up in Esmond. Had us a prize herd of black Angus." Her head tilted to the left. "There was one of them big high-voltage lines back of the north forty. Year after year, our calf losses were double our neighbor's. Cows kept miscarryin'. We had a man come out from Pierre to test the water. Said it was just fine. Then we sent a letter to them Owechahay folks. Asked 'em to come out and have a look at our herd. They sent us this glossy color magazine tellin' how great they were!"

Unquenchable hurt filled the woman's thin face. Gripping the bars, she murmured, "B-Ben talked about goin' to see a lawyer. Never quite got around to it, though. Too much to do on a farm, I guess." Muffled sniffle. "Then one day he was carryin' a sack of feed into the barn, and he keeled right over. Just like that. He was dead by the time I reached him. He was five months shy of fifty. Doctor said he had a growth inside his brain. Little thing 'bout the size of a crabapple. Cancer. No tellin' how long it'd been in there." Her dark eyes turned savage. "I don't believe a word they say—that damned lyin' power company! I don't, girl, and neither should you!"

Bursting into tears, she turned away suddenly. Brenda put a comforting arm around the distraught woman, steering her toward a quiet corner of their cell. "Gonna be all right, Esther . . ."

I sensed Julie's gaze on me. Faced the younger woman once more. Her face was somber. "She lost him only last summer."

"And their farm?"

"Sold at auction. There was no way she could run it by herself. She's living with her daughter here in town now." Julie lowered her voice to a whisper. "There are a lot of scientists who'd agree with her. I know Scott would. He says health effects have been documented in EMF exposures greater than 5 milligauss. High-frequency fields hamper the body's immune system, allowing cancers to flourish. Swedish researchers have found a direct link between high-frequency EMFs and leukemia in children." Her knuckles whitened as she clutched the bars. "There are 350,000 miles of transmission lines in this country, Angie. Too damned many of them run right past schools!"

As I opened my mouth to comment, Deputy Lambanek stepped up to our cell door. "Biwaban? I'm going off duty in a few minutes. I can pick you up something at Burger King."

"And something for Ms. Sievert, too?" I caught the leery

expression in the deputy's eyes. Flashed my brightest Angie smile. "I'll pay you back first thing tomorrow morning."

She thought it over momentarily. "All right." Out came her back-pocket notebook. "What are you ladies having?"

As things turned out, I had the whole cellblock to myself that night. Shortly after Julie and I consumed our Whoppers and medium Cokes, her boyfriend, Scott Hasner, arrived with the bail bondsman and freed all fifty-three jailed members of Safe Power for South Dakota. My new acquaintances trooped out in single file, squeezing my hands, wishing me luck, and promising to see me at our arraignments in the morning.

Promptly at ten, the overhead lights dimmed. I unzipped my parka, unbuttoned my blouse and, facing away from the door, dipped my fingers into the left cup of my brassiere. Retrieved the fifty-dollar bill I always keep hidden there. Emergency money. One President Grant in each cup. And, no, I didn't learn that trick at Springfield. I learned it from Aunt Della!

When the trusty made his rounds, I flashed the fifty and traded it for a pair of cream-colored woolen Navy blankets. Removing my parka, I folded it twice, pressed it into a reasonably puffy pillow, then went to bed.

Snug and warm beneath my surplus Navy blankets, I stared at the darkened ceiling and wondered what kind of an EMF reading a 900-kilovolt power line threw out.

Rough night! I remember only fragments of the nightmares. Miss Carlotta raising her meaty arm to slap. Elena's lascivious grin as she jabs with her razor-sharp shank. Lunatic whistling of the insane pilot, mingled with the muted *chuff-sigh* of shovelled sand.

The final nightmare stayed vivid in my memory. Angie frantically climbing an impossibly tall transmission tower. Down there, in the darkness, the killer's feet pounded steel crossties in grim pursuit. *Tank-tank-tank!* And then, from above, the rush of displaced air. Looking up, I saw a man's limp body plunging toward me. I hugged the beams as he plummeted past, catching a fleeting glimpse of his placid face. It was Mister Beach Tan.

I awoke with a shudder, my mouth hot and dry. The sight of those jailhouse bars triggered a panic-stricken reaction. *Elena!* Blinking heavy-lidded eyes, I looked every which way, ready to ward off that woman's assault. Then I realized that this wasn't the Disciplinary Unit in Billsburg. Took me another twenty seconds before I realized that I wasn't back in Springfield. Shaking all over, I sat upright in bed. Shudder of relief. *County jail!*

Ten minutes later, a woman deputy came to fetch me. She let me wash up in the ladies' room, loaned me a plastic hairbrush, and then marched me into the squadroom. Breakfast was on the county. Scrambled eggs, two overdone sausages, a slice of rye toast and a glass of tepid orange juice. And then, flanked by a husky male deputy, I was marched upstairs to the courtroom.

The corridor was rapidly filling with SPSD defendants. I spied Kramer, with his Stetson tucked under his arm, talking to a wire-haired man in a dark gray suit. All at once, I heard a familiar alto shout. "Angie!"

I turned, and there was Julie Sievert, dressed to the nines, weaving her way through the crowd. Just behind her was a tall, ruddy, sandy-haired man with brittle eyebrows the same shade as his thick hair, deep-set sky blue eyes, a blunt nose and a broad, friendly smile with just a hint of overbite. Tweed sportcoat with leather patches at the elbows, dress slacks, button-down shirt with light blue stripes and a navy blue tie. At first glance, he reminded me of a coach in Pop Warner football. Then I noticed the SPSD button on his lapel.

"Angie, I want you to meet Scott." One look at the lovelight in Julie's eyes, and I really didn't need her introduction. "Scott, this is the woman I was telling you about. Angie Biwaban."

"Hi!" He had a firm, masculine handshake. "Julie tells me we might be able to interest you in a membership."

"You can skip the sales pitch, Scott." Oooooh, love that sexy smile! "I'm a longtime member of the Sierra Club."

"So how long will you be in the area?" Scott asked. "We can always use another environmentally aware volunteer—"

"Mr. Hasner?" A heavyset fortyish man, armed with a pen and a bent notebook, barged into our conversational circle. "My name's Tate. *Sioux Falls Argus-Leader.* How do your people intend to plead during this morning's proceedings?"

Facing the reporter, Scott said, "Innocent, of course."

"Are you still pursuing an injunction against Owechahay Power?"

"We have our court date, Mr. Tate. January eighth."

Scribbling away, Tate tossed his journalistic bomb. "Mr. Hasner, how do you justify taking construction jobs away from a rural county mired in recession?"

"For one thing, Mr. Tate, those are *temporary* jobs. They won't survive the construction of the power line." Scott's baritone voice tingled with suppressed anger. "Let's get something straight right now. Our group is not opposed to economic development. Our name says it all—Safe Power for South Dakota. If OP wants to run that transmission line through Yorktown, let them put it underground. Burying power lines eliminates the danger of EMF exposure."

Other reporters joined us. I spotted a TV crew setting up on the fringes of the crowd and quietly slipped away. Thanks to my surprise appearance on "America's Most Wanted," I'd become extremely camera shy.

Leaning against the bulletin board, I watched the impromptu press conference. Scott made a very articulate spokesman. And then I heard a woman clear her throat behind me.

I turned. The newcomer was an elegant and slender lady

370

whose age I pegged at thirty. She was a queenly five-feet-six, with a pert nose, a delicate chin, deep-set eyes like sparkling emeralds and firm, full lips. Her hair glistened like cornsilk, curling inward at the collar. Styled sheepdog bangs, parted in the center, concealed her high, intelligent forehead.

What really impressed me, though, was her outfit. I don't know where that woman did her clothes shopping, but it certainly wasn't South Dakota. She wore a tailored woolen suit in a smart shade of raspberry. Trim one-button blazer and hip-hugging slim skirt. Lace-trimmed white blouse with a big soft satin wing-tie. Taupe pantyhose and Dutch chocolate *peau de soie* pumps with stiletto heels.

"Excuse me, young lady . . ." Smoky contralto voice. "Have you seen a Native woman around here? She's a few years older than you. Her name's Angela Biwaban."

Crooked Angie smile. No makeup and my farmer togs made me look more adolescent than usual. Believe me, it's a mixed blessing. You don't know how many times I've been carded in Pierre.

I stood up straight. "Look no further. Jill sent you?"

Emerald eyes widened in mild surprise. "Yes. I'm Sarah Sutton." Quick presentation of her business card. "From Jill's description, I expected someone . . . er, a little older."

"Don't worry—I am." Glancing at the card, I let out a hushed whistle. Hipple, Tanner, Page and Sutton. Whoa! That is one high-powered law firm. They ought to have their own show. *Pierre Law.* And the lady was a full partner, too. I sure had plenty of questions for my friend Jill.

Snapping open her briefcase, Sarah shot me a no-nonsense look. "All right. Let's have it, Angela. What are you doing here?"

So I told Sarah Sutton all about the combine and the stray shot and finding Mister Beach Tan in that neighboring field, concluding with my arrest at the hands of Deputy Kramer. Sarah kept interrupting me with questions. She had many, many questions.

"The body was gone when you returned to the field?"

Curt nod from Angie.

"Are you certain he was dead? Did you actually touch the body?"

I clammed up at once. After all, I'd only met this woman five minutes ago. I didn't really trust her yet. Meaning that I wasn't about to admit to having tampered with a crime scene. That could put a quick, decisive end to my parole.

"Welllll . . . he *looked* dead."

Sarah's mouth tensed in an arch smile. "I think the locals were having a little fun with you, Angela." Shuffling some legal-sized papers, she added, "Did that deputy share the results of the breathalyzer test with you?"

"No, ma'am."

"Hmmmmm, interesting . . ."

While she studied the papers, a balding, heavyset man with a face like a fussy baby ambled through the crowd. Pudgy features lit up as he spotted my companion. "Sarah!"

Sarah flashed a truly dazzling smile. "Hello, Gabe."

"What brings you all the way out here?" he asked, tenderly squeezing her proffered hand. "This time of day, I'd figure you to be at the statehouse."

"Oh, just a favor for a former client." She tucked away the legal papers. "When are you and Emma coming up to Pierre? We've missed you at the club."

"Well, we've had the grandchildren at the farm every weekend. You know how it is."

She let out a muted chuckle. "Not quite." Looping her arm around his, she walked him into the vacant courtroom. "Listen, could I see you in your chambers for a moment? A situation has come up, and I really think we ought to talk about it."

And away they went, leaving me stranded in that crowded corridor. I shook my head slowly. That settles it, Jill Stormcloud. You and I definitely have to talk!

The courtroom was a spacious chamber with an arched

ceiling, a pair of sunburst windows behind the gallery, and a high tooled oak judge's bench. Flanking it on either side were upright aluminum poles displaying Old Glory and the South Dakota state flag. A panelled door on the right led to the judge's chambers.

I picked out a seat in the packed gallery. As I was making myself comfortable, the wire-haired man I'd seen earlier appeared at the judge's doorway. Pointing at me, he said something. His words vanished into the gallery's conversational hubbub. Frowning, he made a gesture of invitation with his hand.

Entering the cozy oak-trimmed judge's chamber, I saw Gabe behind the desk, resplendent in judicial black, with a shaken, white-faced Deputy Kramer at his side. Standing demurely in front of the desk, holding her briefcase like an oversized purse, stood Sarah Sutton.

"Angela, you'll be pleased to know that Deputy Kramer has offered to drop both charges." Dimples enhanced her smile. "We just had a little chat about proper police procedure, and everything's been settled."

Judging from the snarl on Kramer's face, I sincerely doubted that. He stood at attention, still holding the Stetson at his side, tight-lipped and fuming. I watched the ruddy color rise from his khaki shirt collar.

Just then, the wire-haired man appeared at the doorway. "Mrs. Sutton? You've got a phone call. Your office in Pierre."

"Thanks, Oscar." Turning to me, she smiled. "Don't go away, kiddo. I want to talk to you." Ladylike smile at the judge. "Back in a minute, Gabe."

The moment the door closed, Kramer let out a gasp of fury, slamming his hat on the desk. "God damn it all to hell, Judge! Are you gonna sit there and let that fancy-assed blonde wipe her shoes on me!?"

"Sure looks that way, Danny." Leaning back in his swivel

chair, the judge shook his head ruefully. "I've seen trips to the woodshed before, but yours was surely a classic."

Kramer's face turned the color of the Elderkin combine. "You're gonna let that gal come into *my* county and—!"

"Danny," Judge Carlson interrupted, "I'm going to explain this so even a dumb shitkicker like you can understand it. That there is Mrs. Sarah Sutton. When she isn't shaking hands at the statehouse, she represents Fairmont Foods. Name ring a bell? It should. That name's on an awful lot of grain elevators between here and Aberdeen. Company owns supermarkets from Columbus, Ohio, to Casper, Wyoming. Plus a whole bunch of corporate farms here in South Dakota. Why, if you set those Fairmont farms side by side, you'd have a spread as big as New Jersey. And that big ranch out in the West River—the Bar-F-Bar—that's a Fairmont operation, too. Makes the old Diamond A look like a feed pen." His grin broadened. "So if Mrs. Sutton comes down here and says she's of a mind to tear the hide off one of my deputies, I'm going to let her. I'm too damned old to hunt up a new job."

"I don't have to take her shit!"

"No, you don't." The judge nodded slowly. "Fact is, you can put that badge on my desk right now, go on home and start packing a suitcase. See if they're hiring in Nebraska." He cast a solemn-eyed glance at the deputy. "Come on, Danny. You knew you were in the wrong. You had no call to go slapping the cuffs on this well-mannered young Indian lady. Cal's warned you about that sort of thing, boy." He leaned forward, levelling a blunt forefinger. "And now I'm going to give you some free advice. You'd better hope Sarah walks out of here today and forgets all about you. Next time you lock horns with that lady, you'd better start reading bus schedules. Because you're all through working in the state of South Dakota!"

Kramer's gritted teeth barely contained his shout of inarticulate rage. Grabbing the Stetson, he tore out of the office.

I winced at the door slam. Judge Carlson rose majestically from his chair, then aimed a meaningful scowl at me.

"You going to behave yourself in my county, young lady?"

Solemn Angie smile. "Absolutely, Your Honor."

"See that you do." He shepherded me to the door. "And you'd better get that smirk off your face. Your turn in the woodshed's coming right up. Sarah wasn't exactly impressed with your record."

My smile wilted. "Well, you see, Your Honor, since my release, I've been having these adjustment problems—"

"You picked the right lawyer then, Miss Angie. Believe me, Sarah thrives on attitude adjustment."

There's just one problem, Judge, I thought, leaving the crowded courtroom. I didn't pick her! Oh, Jill, what have you gotten me into?

The last thing I needed right now was representation by some pushy lady lawyer. La Sutton was one of those take-charge women. She wouldn't rest until she'd poked her pert nose into every intimate corner of my life. And that could be extremely hazardous to my continued freedom. Under assumed names, I was wanted for sundry felonies in three states. How could I be sure Sarah wouldn't turn me in?

The lady in question strolled out of the Clerk of Courts office, leather briefcase in the crook of her arm. Mild tilt of her soft chin. "Let's take a walk, Angela."

We ambled away from the courtroom, then halted beside the water cooler. After setting her briefcase on the old-time wooden bench, Sarah faced me and planted her right hand on my shoulder.

"Jill didn't tell me you were a *Bobbi Jo.*"

I blinked. The lady was awfully familiar with Springfield slang. A *Bobbi Jo* is an inmate of the Disciplinary Unit in Billsburg. That's where you go when you misbehave at Springfield. The slang is derived from one of our nicknames for the place—*Petticoat Junction*. Me, I always called it *Miss Carlotta's School for Girls.*

"Judge Carlson told me." Sarah's features tensed in annoyance. "That was a surprise. I don't like surprises when I represent a client. How long were you in Mrs. Calder's custody?"

Fussbudget face. "Too long!"

"Angela!"

"Sixteen months."

"You had a very unsatisfactory record at Springfield."

Smiling, I raised my forefinger. "But excellent S.A.T.s!"

Mascaraed eyelids closed in frustration. "Now, look! I don't take many criminal clients. But those I do take I expect a lot from. Ask Jill. When a girl signs on with me, the first thing she does is straighten up and fly right. And if she thinks she can waltz *me* around the ballroom floor . . . well, she'll find herself back in the Springfield laundry so fast, her foolish little head will spin!" Lips turning upward in a superior smile, she added, "Now that we understand each other, Miss Biwaban, let's hear your story, eh? The embezzlement—did you do it?"

"Hold on, lady! I haven't signed on for anything." I pushed her hand off my shoulder. "Thanks for springing me. I'll mail you the fee. In the meantime, why don't you go chase an ambulance back to Pierre?"

Sarah's lips parted in indignation. But before she could properly vent her feelings, I heard male footsteps on the courthouse stairs, followed by a familiar baritone voice.

"So there you are!"

I whirled at once. *"Kemo Sabe!"*

Standing at the edge of the stairs was my parole officer and part-time oversized hemorrhoid—Paul Holbrook.

As parole officers go, he's not that bad-looking. He's quite tall, well over the six-foot mark, with curly, wheat-colored hair, low, thick eyebrows and a pair of warm, friendly chestnut-colored eyes. His face is a tad on the lengthy side, with a strong jawline—the kind associated with the RCMP. Sergeant Preston, that is, not Yukon King.

"Hi, Angie . . ." All at once, Paul's gaze drifted past me, and those humorous brown eyes gleamed suddenly. "Sarah!"

"Hello, Paul."

Gone was Take-Charge Sutton. In her place stood this soft-voiced blonde flashing a butter-wouldn't-melt-in-my-mouth expression. She spread her arms in invitation. Rooted to the spot, I watched my parole officer scoot right past and gather that woman into a sedate bear hug. Clenched my teeth as she playfully kissed the corner of Paul's mouth.

Pleasant memories stirred his laughter. Holding her at arm's length, Paul said, "Been a while, hasn't it? I didn't know you were back in criminal practice."

"I'm not. I took this case at the behest of a former client." Her arms remained draped around Paul's neck. "Tell me, are you still with the department?"

He nodded. "Uh-huh. Langston took over for old man Robb."

Tightening the knot of his tie, she smiled coyly. "You should've gotten that job, Paul."

"You know me, Sarah. I'm no administrator. I'm a field man. Always have been, always will be."

"Same old Paul. You're looking remarkably fit."

His grin found me. "Angie keeps me hopping."

Emerald eyes zeroed in on me. Her subtle smile hinted at retribution for past Angie impertinence. "Your client, eh?" Her hand smoothed the lapel of his herringbone blazer. "You know, Paul, we really ought to get together sometime. We have so much to talk about. Why don't you call me when you get back to Pierre?" Catlike glance at me. "Now that we're both working with young Angela, we really ought to sit down and think through a positive program of rehabilitation."

Young Angela!? Obsidian eyes glittered furiously.

"That's not a bad idea, Sarah."

She knew just when to release her grip. "Then call. You can leave a message with our receptionist."

With that, she stalked off, briefcase wedged beneath her arm, tall heels rapping the oakwood floor. Paul's trailing gaze never wavered. Male lips pursed in thoughtful reminiscence.

Coming up beside him, I gave Paul's hip a vigorous nudge. Instantly he glanced my way.

"Hanes," I muttered.

"What!?"

"Silk Reflections." Innocent Angie look. "The way you were staring at her pantyhose, I just figured you wanted to know."

Pink colored the tips of his ears. "I was *not* staring."

"Yes, you were, Holbrook. Don't deny it." Frosty glower. "Let's face it . . . she is an attractive woman. For her *age!* Those Swiss plastic surgeons did a marvelous job on her facelift, don't you think? To say nothing of the liposuction on her rear end—"

"An-ge-la!"

"Of course, she still needs that girdle—"

"Enough, princess."

"More than enough!" I snapped. "You ought to see yourself, Kemo Sabe, standing there with steam coming out of your ears! Dis-grace-ful!"

He tried hard not to smile. "You said it yourself. She's a very attractive woman."

"Well, don't get too hot and bothered, Holbrook. I hear there's a *Mister* Sutton."

"Past tense, Angie. There used to be."

My head swivelled instantly. "You know quite a bit about that woman, don't you?"

Ignoring the jibe, Paul gently grabbed my upper arm and led me down the hallway. "Don't you have a court appearance this morning, Miss Biwaban?"

"Not anymore, Holbrook."

Curious gaze. "What do you mean?"

"Slinky-dink La Sutton got the charges dropped." Seeing

his look of unbelief, I added, "I kid you not, guy. Don't believe me? Well, ask Judge Carlson. You can't miss him." Reaching up, I tweaked Paul's chin. "He's got a lipstick smudge just like yours!"

Paul's ears turned redder. His thumbtip scoured the point of impact. "All right. We'll try the clerk's office."

"No wonder she's such a successful lawyer. So long as she keeps her lipstick loaded—!"

"Angieeeee!" Stopping short, he fired an exasperated glance at me. "Are we going to listen to this all the way back to the farm?"

"No. Just until you tell me where you know that peroxide blonde from!"

Exhaling in exasperation, Paul counted off on his long, sinewy fingers. "One, that is none of your business. Two, Sarah is *not* a peroxide blonde."

Outraged gasp. "How do *you* know?"